THE DAWN AND THE PRINCE

THE DAWN AND THE PRINCE

KINGDOM OF CURSES AND SHADOWS III

DAY LEITAO

SPARKLY WAVE, MONTREAL 2021

The Dawn and the Prince

Copyright © 2021 by Day Leitao

All rights reserved.

Cover illustration by Natalia Sorokina (Jwitless)

Map by Sekcer

CONTENTS

SUMMARY OF BOOK 2

THE CURSE AND THE PRINCE

At the end of book 1, Zora is running away from Gravel City with Griffin, to whom she had given a potion to slow his reflexes, thinking that he would battle her in the final of the Royal Games. Instead, his brother, king Kiran made him face a lion. He did this for revenge because Griffin was having an affair with his betrothed, princess Alegra (actually Riadne pretending to be her, but Kiran doesn't know it). Zora jumped in front of Griffin and saved him, but then his brother ordered him to be killed by his soldiers. Griffin was unconscious because of the potion and Zora was heavily outnumbered and was hit by an arrow. They were saved by Riadne, still pretending to be princess Alegra. She sang and enchanted the soldiers and the audience in the arena, giving Zora and Griffin a chance to escape. Hurt and not knowing where to go, Zora decided to go to the Dark Valley. On the way, she stopped to check on Griffin, he awoke, realized she had saved him, and they kissed, but she didn't trust him and pushed him away. He noticed that it was a night with a new moon, told her there would be a monster, and that it was him.

Book 2 starts with Zora surprised at Griffin's revelation.

He tells her he usually shackles himself in nights with no moon, but that he doesn't know what he looks like. Zora tells him that it will be different tonight because she'll light a fire and she'll be with him. She ties him to a tree and holds his hands, but it doesn't work and he transforms anyway.

The following morning, Zora tells him that his eyes glowed but that he didn't change his appearance much, and that she crossed a stream and climbed a tree. He tells her that the blood cup, which she won, might be his cure, but that he doesn't know where it is, and only the winner of the royal contest can find it. They ride to the Dark Valley, but she's very hurt and loses consciousness. Griffin carries her to her parents' house and they treat her. He feels guilty that Zora got hurt because of his mistakes, but doesn't explain what happened to her parents. Still, her parents notice that he cares for her and admires her.

Zora wakes up feeling better the next day and Griffin tells her they have to leave soon, before his brother, Kiran, looks for him in the valley. She agrees, but goes to visit her sister before leaving. On the way back, she's threatened by Seth, her ex boyfriend who she replaced in the Royal Games. Griffin saves her, but he's transformed. He runs after her and transforms back. When he learns what happens he gets worried that he could have killed her and that he might be transforming for good. She says it's just the magic of the Dark Valley. When they go back to her house, they find out that there are Gravel soldiers after Griffin, but they manage to escape.

Griffin and Zora get along well as they escape, but when night falls they find out there's only one hammock for them. It's a special hammock to be hung high in the trees, where they sleep. The next morning, Griffin catches fish for them, they eat, but end up arguing when Zora confesses she wasn't chosen as the Dark Valley champion. He gets angry because he knew she wasn't a champion and he was right and she gets angry because she thinks the only reason he suspected she wasn't a champion was because she is a girl. In a moment of anger, she confesses she was the one who gave him the potion that incapacitated and made him almost killed by the lion. Angry, Griffin walks away to have some time alone and calm down.

Zora is captured by Stavos, the blond assistant to the crown, and some soldiers, obeying King Kiran's orders. Irene, a female commander loyal to Griffin, is there and tells Zora there will be help for her. Zora's taken to the castle and placed in a room by Kiran.

Meanwhile, Riadne receives her brother, Lukas, and the real princess Alegra, who goes by Tris and was kidnapped by Lukas while Riadne was pretending to be her. Lukas and Riadne are Solanas, magical people from the mountains, and Riadne was in Gravel to get the royal brothers to kill each other because she believes it will help her people. That said, she saved Griffin from being killed by Kiran, so her dedication to her plan was questionable. Tris, the Linaria princess, hates her parents and brother because they tortured and killed a young man she loved. She wants Riadne to convince Kiran to invade her kingdom Riadne doesn't like the plan, but promises to think about it.

Larzen was hidden in her room and heard everything, including Riadne's plans to get him and his brothers killed. Riadne tries to sing and enchant him but her magic doesn't work on him. He imprisons Riadne and then also imprisons Lukas and Tris. Larzen believes Kiran has been acting crazy and tried to kill Griffin because of something Riadne did.

Riadne explains that his overreaction is not her fault and that she can't do anything about it, but Larzen tells her she has to "fix" Kiran or else he might hurt her brother or at least keep him imprisoned. Larzen releases Riadne so that she'll try to find a solution for Kiran. But Riadne can't really control the oldest brother. In Fact, Kiran threatens her and decides to advance the wedding. She's scared and her magic works poorly on him, but she needs to find a way to do something in order to free her brother.

Zora is locked in a room by Kiran and has no way to come out. To her surprise, Griffin comes to her rescue. They hug, no longer angry at each other. But Kiran shows up with soldiers, and orders them to kill Griffin and Zora. Griffin fights his way out of the room, with some help from Zora, but in the hallway they are ambushed by more soldiers and are definitely outnumbered. Larzen shows up and tries to intervene but has no success, then Riadne shows up, enchants the soldiers, and lets Zora and Griffin escape. Kiran then tries to choke Riadne, who turns Kiran's soldiers against him and escapes. Larzen sees this and realizes that perhaps Riadne can't really control Kiran, but he also realizes that she's quite powerful and could have gotten them killed if she wanted.

Griffin takes Zora to his basement, where he has some magical artifacts and some books. He shows her some writings saying that the red cup might undo his curse, and a book about flying witches, claiming that they are the ones who cursed his family. He has a basin of truth that can show the future or things related to the truth. He has used it and saw Zora desperate about something, and it turned out to be correct; it was her desperation when Kiran made Griffin face the lion.

Griffin asks Zora to peer on the basin and ask where the cup is. She looks at the basin but has a vision of she and Griffin having sex. She comes back from the vision startled and scared. Griffin sees her reaction and thinks it's bad news, but she says she saw nothing related to him. They sleep on the same bed despite Zora's worries, but nothing happens between them.

The next day, Zora and Griffin prepare to depart and he looks into the basin of truth. He's at first afraid, then looks at Zora and seems very satisfied about something involving her. She's convinced he had the same vision as her—and mortified. She has an intuition that they have to go to the Mystic Ruins, so they go there.

They find a secret chamber with strange circles and triangles on a wall, and many old human remains. There's a writing saying that the red cup is in a place where the mountains bleed, and Griffin thinks it's in a chasm in the Gravel mountains. When they are about to leave, they are attacked by soldiers, but fight their way out and escape.

Zora and Griffin spend the night together in the hammock. Although Zora is afraid of her vision, she lets him hug her, but when he approaches his face to hers for a kiss, she moves her head away because she still doesn't trust him. He kisses her forehead and hugs her tight.

Larzen, having noticed that Riadne is afraid of Kiran, pretends she is sick with a very contagious disease, making a healer lie to his brother, and hides Riadne in a small room by his. He does this to give her some time to come up with a solution. At least that's what he tells himself. Since he wants to understand what she is up to, he brings her dinner and pours a drug that can make her trust him and open up. They eat, flirt, and talk, and he confesses to her he's responsible for killing his parents. He heard that they were going to give poison to Griffin and Kiran, based on some advice from their magic master, but he put the poison in their water instead. Riadne comforts him, but then he realizes that she switched the cups and made him open up.

He receives a message that Griffin has been located and goes to the ruins with Riadne. There, she explains to him that the wall has Solana (her people) writing, and she might be able to tell him where Griffin went if he gives her secret books with triangles and circles. It's not true, she knows where they are headed, but she wants the books. Larzen hesitates at first because he believes those are dangerous books on dark magic, but ends up getting the books to her. She confesses she already knew where his brother was headed. In the morning, they leave the castle to try to reach Griffin. Larzen's goal is to help his brother escape and he's taking Riadne with him because he doesn't trust her and because she might help him find Griffin. He's also keeping her away from Kiran.

During the day, Griffin and Zora climb a tree to check the road and end up seeing Larzen and Riadne. Griffin recognizes them even though they are disguised. Zora doesn't understand why Riadne is there, but suggests that she could be a flying witch, based on her ability to sing and enchant people. She believes Riadne wants the cup. Griffin doesn't think Riadne is a flying witch, but agrees she might be dangerous.

Larzen promises Riadne that once Griffin is on a boat away from Gravel, he'll free her brother. They spend the night at a lake house belonging to the Royal family. Riadne sits to read one of the books and Larzen finds a translation, claiming that the Solanas created the curse in the royal line and that the red cup was the solution. He realizes that Griffin is after the cup to undo a curse. Up until then, Larzen had no idea his brother had been cursed. Riadne claims that Solanas don't have magic that could act through generations, but that the red cup is something they might have created. They argue because Larzen is still angry that she caused Kiran to chase Griffin and she says it's not her fault.

Griffin and Zora pass by the lake house, steal one of the horses, and send the other away. They sleep together in the hammock and embrace again.

Riadne heard Griffin and Zora but she didn't do anything

because she was angry at Larzen. She goes outside in the morning, whistles, and gets her horse back, then takes off to go to the castle, free her brother, and run away. She wonders about the red cup, and why her ancestors would have cursed a family, then an idea hits her and she turns around and gallops back to the house. She tells Larzen they have to stop Griffin.

Tris, the real Linaria princess, pretends to be sick and escapes the room where Larzen locked her and Lukas, but he feels unbearable pain and she yells for help. Kiran, still thinking he's the princess' brother, arranges for him to be treated in isolation. Lukas has a fever and strange black marks on his back.

Griffin wakes up with Zora and tries to kiss her again, but she moves her head away, even if she's still close to him. They get to the mountains and climb to get to the chasm where the cup is. They hear Larzen calling Griffin, but ignore him.

Riadne and Larzen are following Griffin and Zora. She tells him that she will die early because of the curse on her people, and also tells her that she didn't try to kill Zora.

Zora and Griffin find the cave where the cup is. She has some help from a woman's mysterious voice, who she thinks could be the Sun Goddess, even if she doesn't believe in any gods. In the cave, they find out that they need to wait for nightfall to use the cup.

As they lie down, he asks her if they're going to keep cuddling and pretend nothing's happening. She tries to still claim that nothing's happening, but then he explains to her that they need to plan what they are going to do tomorrow, and he wants to know if she wants to escape with him to another kingdom and start a life with him. He warns her that it might be difficult and that they might be poor, but says that there's something between them worth more than gold. Zora realizes that they truly like each other, she's happy because she wants to have a life with him, and they kiss.

They spend a long time kissing, but she freaks out when he's about to unlace his pants. He notices she's scared, stops, and apologizes. She explains she's afraid and confesses what her vision was. She asks him what his vision was, and he laughs at first, saying it's much scarier, then tells her she saw her having his child and that he could feel the love between them, that he knew they'd have a family. They are both excited and happy about starting a new life together, even if they don't have anything.

When night falls, Zora uses the cup and nothing happens, but after a while they hear noises and she sees shadow creatures. They go to the exit, but then Griffin fights against her, making her lose her sword. He's not himself even if his eyes aren't glowing. Larzen comes and helps Zora escape and take Griffin's sword. She hides in a small cave with Larzen and Riadne.

Riadne explains she's not Alegra and that Griffin is possessed. She also explains that the Solanas did create part of the magic confining the shadow creatures to the Dark Valley, but it was to save the kingdom. They also created the magic preventing the cursed royals from being possessed, at least until a certain age. The cup reversed these protections, opening the kingdom to shadow creatures and allowing Griffin to be possessed. Zora is angry and frustrated, but she chooses to cling on to the hope that she can find a solution and bring Griffin back.

To everyone who hopes for a better future.

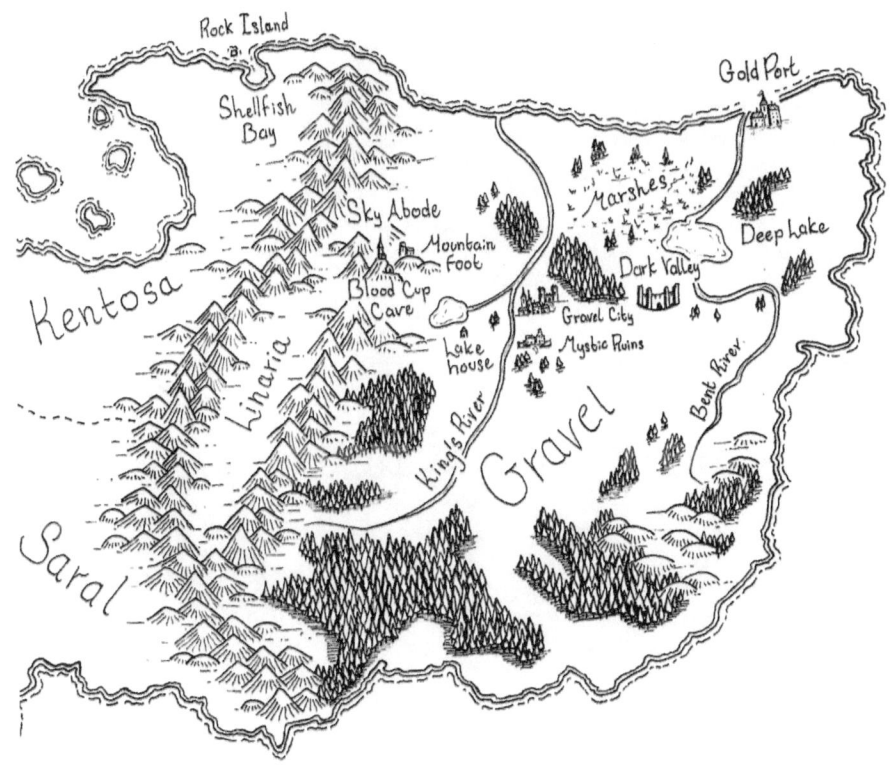

1

THE SHADOW KINGDOM

Nothingness.

Then disjointed images—memories—flashed through his mind. Among them, Zora, weaponless, facing what had once been him.

Once.

Not anymore. And he had no idea what or who he was now.

He felt no pain, no taste, no smell. No, there was a feeling; an immense sadness without a physical place to lodge itself in.

No aching chest or heart. Just emptiness.

It was as if he'd been in a timeless void.

Then his sense of smell returned. Smoke, ashes, sweat, and iron. Something rough touched the side of his face and his body.

Griffin dared open his eyes and found himself lying down over stone tiles. Outside. The sky above him was red. Or maybe there was something wrong with his vision. More than just his vision. And now he felt pain all over his body, as if it were burning from inside out. He wanted to run, escape, disappear, make that pain stop. Make it all stop.

A pair of booted feet alerted him to the fact that he was not alone. Griffin felt like hurting or even killing whoever was there. He wanted to lash out, his pain somehow turning into anger, hatred, violence, but he kept these feelings under control.

The person crouched. It was a man, wearing dark gray leather armor with intricate details on the chest. No, not a man, something. His face had a similar color as the armor, and perhaps Griffin was hallucinating because the stranger's skin looked leathery like a snake's.

At the same time, it was as if he knew that man, thing, whatever, as if he were part of an old, fuzzy memory. Was he a friend? A foe? It was all mixed. No, it couldn't be a friend. The stranger was holding something, and a reflection on what looked like a blade was enough to make Griffin get up. Pain be damned.

"What happened?" the stranger asked.

Clear Continental, with a slight, unidentifiable accent, but it was Continental, which was odd, as it shouldn't belong in that place. The man no longer held any blade—or perhaps it had been an impression.

Griffin realized he was standing on a balcony overlooking... no, it couldn't be. A sharp jolt of pain felt as if his head were exploding, then images crossed his mind, strange images, like memories that were not his. And now he recognized this place and that man. He even had an inkling as to who he was supposed to be. And yet none of that made any sense.

"Was it one of the episodes?" the man asked, then frowned. "But it shouldn't..."

"It's nothing," Griffin finally replied, realizing that his voice sounded as if it had been scrapped in the rocks.

He looked beyond the balcony and at the thousands of soldiers in their encampments. An army. They were in a ravine between two mountains. Further down stood a humongous structure, an arch, like the frame of a door, made of some strange blue stones. And indeed it was—or rather, would be—a door. A door to another world. His disjointed memories suggested that it would lead to the world that had once been his. A door through which that army was going to cross. A chill ran down his spine.

His body and head still hurt, he regretted searching that cup, and the worst part was his fear that Zora had been killed. Fear? Or certainty? As if he weren't dealing with enough pain already. But he had to put everything aside. Faced with such a threat, this was not time for lamenting the past, but for taking the opportunity and doing all he could to save his world, his brothers, Zora's beloved valley.

None of his pain mattered. He couldn't afford to make a single mistake, couldn't show any misplaced emotion. With guards surrounding him, there was no fighting out of this.

The sound of quick steps made Griffin turn. Another leathery-faced man approached, wearing a dark-red robe instead of the warrior attire.

"Your majesty, do you need your potion?" the newcomer asked.

"Leave me. I'm fine," Griffin replied with the harshest voice he could muster.

The man cowered and scurried away.

Griffin glanced at his hand; gray, like everyone's in that place. He'd better pretend well—and learn how to stop this army before they realized he wasn't their real king.

LIGHT CAME through small cracks in the improvised door, thin rays displacing darkness. Before that, the only visible thing had been the blue glow of Griffin's sword. It was a reminder of what Zora had lost a few hours before—and of her part in that loss. Berating herself wouldn't change anything, but it should serve as a lesson. A warning. No more mistakes.

Riadne and Larzen had been silent for a long time. Zora had no idea how they could have fallen asleep with those dreadful sounds outside. At first she'd thought the noise was coming from some kind of animal, but after some time she realized it was the shadow creatures. They had strange screams, like an odd mix of a horse neigh and a bird's screech, but deeper. That sound made her hair stand on end. She'd never heard it in the valley, but then, she'd never spent so much time near those creatures.

Those creatures. No longer confined by walls. That had been another reason for her lack of sleep; she couldn't shake the thought that a spider would spawn in that cave or even that a human shadow would somehow appear there. And yet none had. The rules were certainly different than they had been in the Dark Valley.

And then there was her guilt about all the people who could be getting hurt throughout the night. Unaware. Unprepared.

But the worst was wondering about Griffin, if he was alive, if he was in pain, and where he was. She looked at the sword again, as if it were a piece of him still with her, as if its glow were her hope to get him back, to restore his life.

Zora took a deep breath. Hope. There was always hope. But that was the thing; hope should be like that sword; reachable, not like a star, up there somewhere. That had been her mistake. All her life, she had clung to hope; she had tried to teach her students to hope. But what was pointless hope but a lie, a false promise? It was like believing in the Sun Goddess, believing in something outside her reach.

How could she have told herself she hoped that one day things would be different when she did nothing to change anything? That was the problem with abstract, distant hope, hope without a plan, without action. And this was what she wanted to fix. She truly believed that she could undo her mistakes and bring Griffin back. She had to trust the truth basin, had to trust that it wouldn't have shown both of them a reality that wouldn't have any chance of becoming true. But just trusting wouldn't help her achieve anything. She had to plan; she had to act.

Her biggest mistake had been not knowing enough. By the Light, she'd been so gullible. Even Griffin had been gullible and naïve, trusting that the solution for his curse was a simple cup that he knew nothing about.

Knowledge. That could make all the difference.

Hope by itself wouldn't bring Griffin back, not even hope and fury. What she needed was a plan and action, and this time she wasn't going to sit around or follow a fuzzy, obscure plan and hope it worked. She was going to get it right. No more mistakes.

That decision filled her with a sense of calm and certainty, a sense of control. All she needed now was some help.

More light came from the small cracks. It illuminated Larzen, who slept with his back on the wall. Riadne, for her turn, had her eyes open, looking at Zora, who put the sword down. So strange to be sitting with that young woman, someone who Zora once thought wanted to kill her—but also someone who had saved her life. And Griffin's life. Strange that she was not a princess, but a Solana, part of an ancient people who knew magic, and who could be the key to saving Griffin.

The false princess bit her lip. "I'm sorry we didn't get here earlier."

"Weren't you who said self-blame didn't help?"

Riadne shook her head. "I'm not blaming anyone, just wishing, I guess... that things had been different." She then looked away.

Perhaps it was an apology for a lot more than not getting to the cave in time to stop Zora from ruining the kingdom.

Zora stared at the false princess. "Help me, then. Help me fix this. If I... find more books in your writing, can you translate them? At least try to find something useful in them?"

"Why?" Riadne raised an eyebrow. "You think there's a stash of Solana books somewhere?"

"I do." The words came with a lot more certainty than expected.

"And where's that?" Riadne tilted her head, staring at Zora in a mix of defiance and mistrust.

"Where's what?" Larzen asked, still sounding half-asleep. He looked at Zora and Riadne, and then put his hands over his face, as if remembering where he was and what had happened.

"A Solana book depository," Riadne said, her voice half mocking.

Well, Zora couldn't blame the false princess's cynicism. But she was wrong.

"Rock Island," Zora said.

Riadne blinked in confusion while Larzen sucked in a breath. "Where they train the magic masters."

Zora nodded. "And where they have some rare books, magical objects..."

Larzen scratched his chin. "That place, I don't trust anyone from there."

"I know." She remembered what Griffin had told her. "The man they sent killed your parents. I'm sorry."

Riadne shifted as if uncomfortable, then she and the prince exchanged a look. It was probably a painful memory for Larzen.

"Hear me out," Zora continued. "We don't need to trust them. I'm going to go there and steal whatever Solana books they have."

Larzen shook his head and had a bitter chuckle. "They're charlatans. Why would you risk your life and waste your time on an almost impossible task? What you're saying makes no sense."

That wasn't true. "They're not charlatans. Griffin had a magical artifact. I used it."

He raised an eyebrow. "And did what with it?"

The memory came to her, vivid as if it were real, the feeling of Griffin's skin against her, the grass below her, a feeling that had been terrifying and strange, but at the same time exhilarating, exciting, beautiful.

She pushed the feeling away. "I... had a vision." It sounded silly. "A very vivid vision. And so did Griffin."

Larzen stared at her. "You do realize it doesn't prove anything, right?"

"He had rare books!"

Riadne crossed her arms. "He did have rare books. Now, if there's a place where there could be more of those books, and if they could have Solana knowledge, I need to find it."

Larzen exhaled. "The place is secret and well guarded. Nobody goes in or out. Only royal families or very rich merchants know that Rock Island even exists, but nobody has any idea where it is. All we do is send a request to the government of Kentosa."

The false princess pointed at him. "That's where it is, then."

Larzen shook his hands. "Right. As if Kentosa didn't have

7

hundreds of islands. This place is hidden, it's well guarded, and I still think they're mostly charlatans."

Zora raised her chin. "I'll figure it out." She was willing to do whatever it took to get Griffin back.

"I'm coming with you," Riadne told Zora. It was surprising that she'd be willing to help her. She seemed to notice her surprise, and added, "We've been looking for Solana books forever. If they have any, I want to get them."

Zora nodded, still surprised but thankful. Perhaps she didn't yet trust the false princess completely, but it was obvious that she wanted those books as much as Zora.

Larzen sighed. "You two do realize it's not that simple, right?"

Riadne rolled her eyes. "You think?" She glared at him, then said, her tone ironic, "Oh, I was under the impression that we'd just pay them a visit and they'd hand us the books."

"Well, what do you think it will be like?" Larzen yelled. "You think it will be a normal library you can walk in and out? You think you'll be able to get into a building guarded by the most powerful government on the continent?"

"Do you have a better idea?" Zora asked. She meant it.

Larzen paused. "We'll go to Gravel City and figure it out. We'll find a solution. I'm not letting you go on a hopeless journey for a nonsensical plan." He said it looking at Riadne.

The false princess smiled. "Great. If you have a deposit of old Solana's books, that's the time to show it. If you don't, don't you dare get in my way."

He frowned. "I'm helping you, I'm not in your way."

Riadne just stared at him for a moment, then closed her eyes and took a deep breath. "There's someone I need to check first."

Larzen's eyes locked on her. "Someone?"

His tone was... jealous?

Riadne shook her head. "Not anyone..." She stopped and glared at him. "What does it matter?"

He shrugged. "I'm just surprised."

The redhead stared at both Larzen and Zora. "The place I want to go..." She paused, as if measuring her words. "Might help us. I understand Solana's writing, but I'm not that great. We could learn more about the book I have. If it's information we need, talking to someone who knows more is only going to be useful."

That caught Zora's interest.

Riadne looked at her and smiled. "Yes." Then she turned to Larzen, then back at Zora, and her expression was serious. "But I need you two to promise you won't ever tell anyone about where we're going. I'm not joking. I mean not even anyone you trust, not even anyone you love, not even your grandchildren, years from now."

Larzen had a bitter chuckle. "You're assuming we'll survive this and live happily enough to have families. I love your optimism."

Riadne raised an eyebrow. "You can't know what's going to happen."

The prince stared at her. "And you trust my word?"

"Shouldn't I?" Riadne shrugged, then turned to Zora. "And I don't think you're going to babble away. You need my help, don't you?"

Zora imagined that they would be led to some secret hideout and, having seen the human remains in the Mystic Ruins, understood the need for secrecy. "I'll never tell anyone. Don't worry."

Riadne nodded, then turned to the prince.

Larzen raised his hands. "I'm not telling anyone either."

Anxiety was gnawing on Zora, so she got up. "Let's go, then."

The false princess got up too, tapped on the door, then tapped again, but nothing happened.

"What is it supposed to do?" Larzen asked.

Riadne just stared at him. Well, the answer was obvious. Open the door. Not door. Pile of compacted earth or something. Except that it wasn't opening.

Zora had been curious about this cave, and it was good to focus on small things so that she wouldn't feel overwhelmed by the big issues looming over her head. "How did you know about this place?"

"Saw it on the way. It's a Solana safe. There are a few in the mountains. Not that I had ever used one, or understood much of it. I mean, you could come here hiding from anything, not only shadow creatures." She frowned. "But I'm thinking I missed the part on how to open it."

Larzen banged at it with his closed fist, and nothing happened.

Zora hated what she was about to do, but she took Griffin's sword, Thunder, and hit the wall a few times. The door crumbled. She turned to the others and pointed to the sword. "It's enchanted."

They took their things and left the cave, Riadne in front of them, then Larzen, and Zora last. She kept her eyes and ears alert. Even if in theory those creatures wouldn't survive daylight, one could never know, and plus there were tons of nooks where they could hide. It was still odd to follow the false princess, but so far she had been right and had tried to warn them against using the cup. Zora sighed. There was no point looking back. For now at least, she was willing to trust Riadne, even if she had to swallow the small chunk of jealousy still lodged in her heart.

"How far is this place we're going?" Larzen asked.

"About an hour walking," Riadne replied. "Let's go. Talking won't get us there."

"Hmm, are you sure?" Larzen chuckled. "Maybe you could summon some birds to carry us."

Riadne raised an eyebrow. "I'll consider it next time."

Summon birds? They were in on some inside joke Zora had no idea about. And she still wasn't sure if Larzen and Riadne were involved or not. Not that it mattered. Well, maybe. Perhaps she was using him for some evil scheme.

Evil? She'd saved Zora three times now. Still, so many questions, so much uncertainty. Perhaps Riadne could help her, and then perhaps she was a shrewd enemy. Zora was about to figure it out—hopefully before it was too late.

LONELINESS. An odd thing to feel when Tris had decided long ago she'd never trust anyone again. Even among so-called friends, loneliness had been her only companion in the last year.

And yet she felt it again.

Strange to realize that she missed Lukas. To realize that he had been some kind of company. But now he was either dazed, yelling in pain, or asleep, and that bedroom felt smaller and smaller, suffocating her. His sudden illness had ruined their escape plans. But the worst was that he wasn't getting better and she started to fear that he could be dying. And yet, perhaps his people would know what to do. The issue was getting to them.

Tris had to do something. Enough pleading. No more asking for the healer to let her leave her confinement. Instead, she'd make her way out of that room, find Riadne, and figure out a way to get out of that castle. She ran her hands over the only knife she had. How trustful of her captors to give her that. But a knife was only one weapon, and she couldn't throw it away.

Tris didn't want to ever feel helpless again, and so she used the knife to carve and make more weapons. The edge of the bed was now thin, as she had cut sticks of wood and sharpened them. Just in case. One could never know. That way, she would have quite a few sticks to throw.

But all she really wished was that Lukas would get better and they could get their asses out of there—together. She could leave him, but if she did, remorse would kill her. Stupid remorse. Had their places been switched, would he stay? Tris sighed. This wasn't about Lukas, but about her. What was *she* going to do?

2

THE SKY ABODE

In one night, Larzen's whole world had been turned upside down. No, that was a shitty comparison. Upside down meant that there was still an order to things, that his world still made sense. But it didn't. He had no idea where his brothers were, if they were still alive, and had no clue on how to fix any of that. And he wanted to fix it. Otherwise he would think back to his parents and keep wondering what would have happened if they had lived. Keep wondering if everything he'd done had been pointless.

Riadne walked ahead of him, her steps firm. If she was really taking them to a secret place, that was an enormous display of trust. Unless she had decided to take them to a trap. No, it made no sense. Her words had been true. Her warning had been true. And yet, as fast as she and he had gone up that mountain, even braving a storm, they had been too late. Too late. So many hours lost. And yet regret wasn't going to solve anything.

What he had to do was find a way to get Griffin back, and a way to stop Riadne from embarking on a pointless, dangerous journey. He wasn't going to let her try to find Rock

Island, and he needed to come up with a way to prevent her from doing that. Soon.

They had walked for over an hour by the mountains, going north, the rising sun and the forest and valley on their right. When they got to the edge of a huge stone wall, Riadne stopped, faced both him and Zora, and raised an eyebrow. "Never tell anyone. Promise."

Larzen put a finger over his lips. "No one will ever hear a peep from here."

"Same," Zora said.

He was wondering what Riadne was about to do, considering there was no way up, and no path that he could see. Hopefully, they wouldn't have to climb or do anything too extenuating. Not that he couldn't do it—he was fit, regardless of what Riadne thought. But after a poorly slept night and all the walking, he didn't trust his body's resilience.

To his surprise, Riadne stepped inside a protrusion in the rock as if there had been nothing there, then disappeared behind it.

"Come," she said.

Larzen dared follow her. There was no stone—it was just an illusion. Crossing it was like going through smoke. They were then inside a tall hole in the mountain, like the bottom of a well, but without any water. Riadne pulled a chain, which brought down a huge metal container. It seemed to be attached to a pulley at the very far top. So they were about to step into a huge bucket. It made sense that it was the only way to go up, and quite secret, if he hadn't been able to see it even when standing right in front of it.

The "bucket" was in fact square and had a gate leading them inside. They stepped in, Riadne closed the gate, and then they were moving up inside the rock, the chains rattling and grinding with the movement. Larzen tried not to wonder too much about what he was about to see. Would there be a lot of people? Would they imprison him? And if this was a trap, his way out wouldn't be that easy. In a quick glance, he noticed that there was a hint of worry in Zora's eyes. When he turned to Riadne, she gave him a quick smile, but there was tension in her face. She was also worried. Well, she had said she wanted to check on "someone important." He didn't want to wonder who that could be. Not that it mattered. Obviously.

And then, perhaps she was nervous for some different reason. Perhaps her request for them to promise never to mention this place had been to make them compliant, trustful. Larzen was convinced that she no longer wanted to get him and his brother to kill each other. The question was: what were her *current* plans?

"Ree!" a girl's voice came from above them. A girl.

"Yes," Riadne replied. "I—"

"I had a dream, Ree," the girl interrupted her.

Their container was going up and Larzen saw the opening of a cave above them, but couldn't see the owner of the voice.

Riadne's voice was tense. "Nice. You can tell me—"

"I was flying, I was flying Riadne," the girl continued.

They reached the entrance of the cave, a wide horizontal gap leading to a shallow hole in the mountain. It was just a small platform that didn't seem to lead anywhere except for a rectangular opening on one side.

The owner of the voice was a girl of about twelve or thirteen with straight, dark brown hair, tan skin, and brown eyes. She froze when she saw Zora and Larzen, and turned to Riadne. "I didn't know you were bringing visitors."

He felt a lot more at ease realizing that they had come here indeed to check on the Riadne's loved ones. The family and friends type of loved ones.

"It's fine. Flying." Riadne had what strangely sounded like a nervous laugh. "Common dream, right? This is Zora and

Prince Larzen." So formal. She turned to them and pointed to the girl. "This is Aelle."

Aelle now had her jaw dropped, staring at him. "A Gravel prince?"

Sometimes it was odd to deal with this type of reaction. He just waved and smiled. "In person, yes."

Taking the girl's hand, Riadne pulled her away from the others. "Are you all right? How's Dada?"

The girl looked puzzled. "We're fine. Why?"

Riadne exhaled in clear relief. "I'll tell you later. I'm going up to see her. Stay here with them."

Aelle glanced at Zora and Larzen. "Are they... prisoners?"

"No!" Riadne frowned. "They're..." She looked back at him, a question in her beautiful eyes.

"Friends," Larzen finished her sentence. Somehow, he meant it.

"Exactly." Riadne had a quick smile, then turned to the girl. "Anyway, wait here." She paused. "No. Come with me." She turned to Larzen. "Stay right where you are. I'll be back in a few minutes."

Riadne pulled the girl to the opening on the side, stepped inside it, then closed a silver metal door behind her, which thumped against its frame made of rock. It was a true door made of iron and had some engravings, looking similar to some of the outer doors in the castle. This was the entrance to whatever secret place the Solanas had. Which he wasn't going to see. Well, apparently Riadne's trust only went so far. He wished he could know what was behind that door and what secrets she was keeping from him.

"Interesting place here, up high," a voice interrupted his thoughts. It was Zora. He had even forgotten she was there.

"Huh? Yes. Hard to reach."

Zora glanced at that lifting mechanism. "Not hard if you have wings."

He had no clue what she meant and snorted. "Right. Crows won't have any issue coming here."

The girl paused, then asked, "So you and Riadne... became friends?"

"Allies." The word slipped from his mouth. "There's a difference."

"Do you trust her?"

He paused. "Yes." His voice came out certain, but then why had he taken so long to reply?

"So nothing happened?" Riadne insisted as she climbed the stairs to the main hallway.

"No," Aelle said. "Why are you so worried?"

"You'll need to be careful when the sun is down. Stay in, close all doors."

"It's not like I have anywhere to go, you know?" Her voice was bitter.

Riadne gave the girl a pointed look. "You have a safe place to stay and shouldn't be complaining."

"I'm complaining? No. I was just stating facts, Ree."

Something else came to Riadne's mind. "What happened to the prisoners?"

"Oh, you're asking now? Funny. This place was a freaking inn—"

"Watch your mouth, Aelle."

"Sorry. A fucking inn."

Riadne stopped and glared at the girl. "What are you trying to do?"

Aelle tilted her head. "What are *you* going to do? Forbid me from going to Linaria? Leave me stuck here? What's gonna happen if I don't watch my mouth?"

"Linaria is an awful place for a young girl like you."

"But you went!" Aelle protested.

"And that's how I know." She hoped that was the end of the conversation and kept climbing the stairs.

Aelle was after her. "Well, what about Gravel, then? You're clearly *friendly* with one of the princes."

"Gravel's worse. And you don't know what you're talking about."

"No. I do. You get to go out, learn how to read Continental, live your life, get to know royalty, while I have to play nanny to Dada and those smelly prisoners."

They were at the edge of the main corridor in the Sky Abode. Riadne pushed the girl against a crystal wall overlooking the valley. "*Nanny*? She's the one raising you, your ungrateful, disrespectful brat."

"Ungrateful? Easy for you to say it when you're playing princess and leaving me here to suffer."

Riadne snorted. "Suffer?" Aelle couldn't be serious. No, she was serious, which only showed she had no idea what suffering was like—which was for the best. At thirteen, the girl shouldn't know anything about the real evils in this world. Riadne took a deep breath. Strangling her cousin wasn't the best way to start her visit. "I'm sorry. I bet it wasn't fun having to take care of those prisoners."

Aelle snorted. "Hum. Worse than not fun. Lots of work, that was what it was."

Speaking of prisoners... "And where are they?"

"The princess killed them."

Riadne took a moment to process it. No, maybe she'd misheard the girl. "She... what?"

"There were only two." Aelle shrugged. "She killed them. She said they deserved it."

Riadne closed her eyes. Perhaps it wasn't surprising, as horrifying as it was. Her only question was whether Lukas was making googly eyes at the princess before or after he found out she was a murderer. What a question. Of course it was after. Riadne decided to change the subject. "And you dreamed you were flying?"

Aelle paused. "Yes."

"You think it was one of *those* dreams?" Perhaps it was silly to hope that it could mean something good, a bright future, hope.

"Who knows?" The girl shrugged. "Maybe I'm just tired of being stuck here and my soul is flying away."

Riadne sighed. "You know you won't be here forever, right? As soon as you're older, stronger, you'll be free to leave."

"It's not like our lives are long, it's not like I have an eternity to experience things. You know that."

Riadne did. And it killed her. For a moment she regretted having brought Larzen here, trusting him, giving up on her plan to have the brothers kill each other and at least have a shot at a different future for her people. What were three brothers in comparison to Aelle and so many more innocents? Who didn't deserve to die early and in pain? That, if the prophecy was right. There was always that, always some uncertainty; a risk of failing she'd accepted. But now everything was confusing, and as more and more she was learning about the past, more doubts crept into her mind.

Riadne took a deep breath and faced her cousin. "You're only thirteen. I swear you'll have enough time to enjoy life and to experience everything. When you're ready."

Aelle rolled her eyes. "I'll be twenty and you'll still be saying that. You know you left for Linaria when you were younger than I am."

She snorted. "Exactly. It was so much fun."

"And yet you won't let me go," Allele protested. Did she just miss the obvious sarcasm in Riadne's voice? "And I want to learn to read Continental, like you."

"Sure." Riadne sighed.

There was so much she had never told anyone, and she wasn't certain if part of it was still some strange shame or a way to protect her cousin. She wished Aelle would never find out how evil and twisted some people could be.

As much as Riadne had gone through all that almost unscathed, she couldn't say she was left whole. A part of her had been broken. She could perhaps have told Dada, and yet, there was still that shame and regret and guilt. And that shame prevented her from telling them she had never learned to read in the Linaria castle. She wanted to bury that past together with the mounds of potato peels from the time she found refuge in the kitchens.

"Now you're angry, just because I'm telling you the truth." Aelle's words barely made any sense.

"I'm worried, Aelle, that's all." About so many things. They were in front of Dada's door, and she turned to her cousin. "I'll need some time alone with her."

Aelle puffed. "Really? I'm being left out. I'm shocked, you know." The girl turned around and stomped down the hallway.

Riadne shook her head. Since when had her cousin become so difficult? But then, she remembered when she had been younger, innocent, and full of dreams, eager to get to know more of the world. Perhaps there was a part of her still eager to make a difference, even if the world had made her jaded and hard on the edges.

"Dada?" Riadne pushed the metal door leading to her custodian's room. "Dada?"

"I'm here," a voice came from the end of the hallway.

The sound led her to the kitchen, one side of it open to a balcony without any windows between it and the valley below. Dada was sitting at a table defeathering a bird, her silvering hair tied in a loose ponytail. She smiled, cleaned her hands on a cloth, got up, and opened her arms. Riadne rushed for that familiar and comforting hug even with the sharp edges of her custodian's mangled back.

She then stepped back to look into the old woman's eyes. "I was so worried. I thought you wouldn't survive the night."

Dada tilted her head. "What happened?"

There was genuine curiosity in her tone. That was good news.

Riadne exhaled in relief, but then bit her lip. "Dark creatures. They were set free. They'll spawn anywhere that's dark, I mean, any natural place." She looked at the polished wall of the Sky Abode. "Since we are among the mountain rocks, I wasn't sure."

Dada's dark eyes were intense but calm. "There's protection here. You should have remembered it."

Riadne shrugged. "Yes, but... Some magic was undone. The protection here could have been undone too."

Her custodian had a frown. "Tell me about these creatures."

"I was hoping *you*'d tell me." She opened her bag and put the book with the history of the Solanas on a table. "A lot of it is in here, but I thought you'd know it better than me. Have you ever heard anything about a blood cup? A red chalice? The curse in the royal family? It's all here. This red thing was a Solana failsafe. It undid some old magic that prevented darkness from spreading. I tried to stop them. I tried. In retrospect, I should have tried harder." She sighed. "I failed."

Dada looked at the book, her eyes bright. "Where did you get this?"

"From the castle. A safe in the library. It had been hidden for a long time. Getting it was a lot of work, and when I finally understood it, it was too late." Strange how regret laced her words. She knew it didn't help, but she couldn't stop herself from feeling it.

The old woman opened the book and ran her hands through the pages. "I never thought we'd find any of our lost books." She turned to Riadne and smiled. "Was this the only one you got?"

Riadne shook her head. "There were other two, but they are useless." She put them on the table. "One is wise sayings, and the other is recipes." She shrugged.

Dada raised an eyebrow. "What's wrong with you? Too old to hear any wisdom?"

"I didn't mean it like that. I'm sure the book is interesting. But it won't reveal much about the past."

Dada opened the book with the sayings. "Oh, no, not the past. Perhaps the present. The future."

"I guess."

The old woman shook the wisdom book. "It's true. When you're lost, confused, just open this, and it will give you a direction."

"Oh, that's a great plan. I'll do nothing else in my life other than opening this book."

Dada chuckled. "No. You do it once a day at most." She turned to the recipe book, her eyes emotional. "This..."

Somehow, that thing grabbed the woman's attention. Perhaps it had a new way to roast crows or something, which would probably be quite useful, except that there were more pressing matters. Riadne was about to remind her custodian of that, when the woman said, "This is a treasure."

Riadne shrugged. Right. There were probably some incredible crow recipes there. "I guess."

Dada's dark eyes were on her. "You don't get it, do you?"

"No, I mean, cooking is important, right?" Riadne smiled and shrugged. "Everybody has to eat."

The woman narrowed her eyes. "These are potions."

"Po... but Solanas don't make them."

22

"Not anymore. But legend says we used to." She shook the book and smiled. "Here's proof that it's not only legend."

Potions... They could mean so many things.

The woman then said, "I'll prepare you some breakfast, then I'll take a look at it."

"I have to go, Dada. Lukas is in the castle, and I don't know what's going on there. I'm worried. And I'm not alone."

"Visitors? Or more prisoners?"

"Neither. We're just passing by. We need to get to Gravel City as soon as possible."

The old woman had a half-smile. "We. So whoever is waiting for you is working with you. Where are your manners, not to invite visitors? Call them up."

Riadne frowned. "You'd want me to reveal this place to strangers?"

"Are they in the forest below and have no idea where you are?"

"No, they're downstairs at the entrance, but—"

Dada shrugged. "Then it makes no difference."

"I... I don't want them to see you." She hoped it didn't sound offensive.

Her custodian raised an eyebrow. "Ashamed, now?"

"No, but I don't want them to judge you."

"Who's judging?"

Riadne sighed. "One of them is a Gravel prince. You know, I had plans for them."

"Plans you gave up, I suppose."

She didn't even know what to say. "Not 'gave up', just... It's all so much more complicated."

Dada chuckled. "Riadne, darling. You think I let you go, agreed with taking prisoners and your ludicrous plan because I thought you were going to succeed in your insanity?"

"I..." Wait a minute. Did she hear it right? "Insanity? Why did you agree, then?"

"I thought something would happen. Something good. Or something bad. The wheels were set in motion."

Larzen's face came to her mind, and the horrific thought of what she'd once wished for him. Riadne clenched her fists. "It's so nice to hear you'd gladly allow me to get three brothers to kill each other for no reason. Wonderful."

Dada chuckled. "Did you? Could you?"

"Almost."

"Pfh." The old woman waved a hand. "You don't have a killer heart, Riadne."

This was a bitter reminder of how much her custodian didn't know about her. Killer heart. But she'd better not dwell on that. Riadne decided to change the subject. "There's another thing. My magic is failing. I don't know what's wrong with it."

Dada raised an eyebrow. "Don't know? Or don't want to know?"

What was wrong with her custodian? This had been a real question. Riadne shook her head. "Seriously. I have no clue."

"Hum." Dada was thoughtful. "I'll tell you what. You are going to be polite and tell your visitors to come up. You're going to eat, rest, regain your strength, and leave when you're ready. I'll tell you as much as I can. The rest is up to you."

IT WASN'T JUST a whole new body, but a new mind that Griffin had stepped into. Disjointed images and memories flashed through his thoughts. In a way, it was helpful, as these memories made it easier to play the part he had to play, but on the other hand, his head felt as if it was about to split in half as he waded through all this new, and sometimes very strange, information.

And then there was the pain, regret, and loss squeezing his chest. But it was the pain that kept him standing despite everything, the pain that reminded him that this was his chance to save his people, his chance to get revenge for everything that had happened to his kingdom, to his family, to him. To Zora. He sighed. The image of Zora weaponless, standing at the edge of an abyss, was something else taking over his mind. And yet he had to push it away if he didn't want to drown in pain.

Griffin was pretending to be King Saro, inhabiting this strange, tall body, for the first time looking down on everyone else. As a young teenager, he had wished he could be taller, but this was definitely not what he'd meant.

He walked on a platform around the edge of a mountain surrounding the place where the troops were camped. There were charges around this mountain, things that could explode, probably similar or the same thing as the exploding balls in the Dark Valley.

Walking in silence gave him the headspace to try to figure out where he was and what exactly was happening. The man —or thing—well, gray man—walking with him, was the king's first in command. His name was Antelio, and he was tall and lean, also hairless with that strange, leathery skin. To be very honest, Griffin wasn't sure he could differentiate those people one from another, but this man had a red scarf over his uniform, which was helpful. If only they wore nametags or something.

So far Antelio didn't seem to have noticed anything odd, but then, so far Griffin had barely spoken other than deciding to check the charges. He wished he could do this alone, but didn't want to raise any suspicion.

He had the pieces, or at least some of the pieces, but

somehow they didn't go that well together. So the big arch would lead these soldiers into another world, his world. But hadn't they already been let in? So far, nothing indicated that anything new had happened. Maybe nothing had happened. Perhaps this place was unrelated to the dark creatures. Maybe. Then there were these explosives. All he had was a faint memory of the king giving a speech to his soldiers, telling them that they would set that new world on fire, that they were coming in armed, and yet, something didn't add up.

The small balls were set on nets all along the edge of that mountain. Very few people were allowed in the area Griffin was walking right now, which was a metal platform, apparently made to store those explosives.

But if they were meant to be taken through the gate, why were they here and not down there, in safe boxes? If anything, having them here, in these flimsy nets, was quite dangerous.

But then there was this odd, conflicting memory about these explosives. They were the game changer, they would allow them to cross over for the first time. Griffin had so many things in his mind; he felt like an aspiring juggler struggling to deal with too many balls.

The thought reminded him of the opening ceremony of the games. Had there been any jugglers? Strange; he did not know. All he remembered was a girl with wide eyes looking at everything with so much fascination and wonder that she was more interesting than all the artists the royal committee had hired. Little had he known that one day those eyes, misty with emotion, would look at him with that same fascination. Little had he realized that he'd been wanting her to look at him like that since the day in the library.

The realization shook him, but then he noticed Antelio was saying something.

The Dawn and the Prince

"What?" Griffin asked.

The strange man frowned. "Are you sure you're feeling well?"

Griffin crossed his arms. "You're a healer now? I'm fine, and I was checking to see if these are properly secured." He didn't dare say charges or balls, afraid to use the wrong word. "What do you want?" For some reason, he felt that acting rude made his impression more convincing.

"Nothing. Confirming what you're seeing. Everything's ready. The area is secured. There's no risk they would fall before the right time. We should rather get ready for our meeting, your majesty."

Meeting? Griffin had no idea what the man was talking about, but glared at him. "I'm well aware of my obligations."

"Of course. And the trap here is set." Antelio had a sly smirk.

Trap. Trap for whom? He glanced at the edge of the platform and noticed a mechanism. That mechanism... It was meant to pull the nets? Yes, that was what it was. There was something sinister going on, and Griffin wasn't sure what it was. This body didn't have visible hair, but if it had, it would have stood on end.

3

THE CRYSTAL WALL

Riadne had been gone for a couple minutes, and Larzen decided to check the door. He pulled it, and, to his surprise, it was open, leading to a wide staircase. He took a step in.

"Shouldn't we wait?" Zora's voice made him pause.

The girl frowned, as if respecting what Riadne had asked was more important than investigating her. Maybe the Dark Valley girl had spent too much time with Griffin and was about to school him on how dishonorable it would be to disobey a simple request. Remembering his younger brother tightened Larzen's heart, even if it was ironic that Griffin always went on and on about honor and yet had been the one to betray Kiran. Perhaps he was smart enough to know when to give honor a break.

Larzen put a finger over his lips. "I'll just check."

Zora still frowned, but he ignored her and crossed the door. No traps, and nobody came to check what he was doing. The stairs were made of a polished gray stone. He climbed them and was surprised at what he saw.

The wall was clear and semi-translucent, like some kind

of crystal, but thick, so that he could see the valley through it. There were more sets of stairs going up, made of a white stone. This was a palace, not simply some kind of crude hideout, like Larzen had thought at first. A strange and probably ancient palace. A set of stairs led him to a huge atrium facing that transparent wall on one side, with doors on the other side. There was a hallway in front of him.

Perhaps he should just go back, having seen what he wanted. What had even been his point in coming here? Would he find any evidence against Riadne? It was all empty, silent. All he could gather was that the Solanas had been powerful in the past, and yet secretive. Riadne's wishes for them not to talk about this place made a lot of sense, but he wondered why she'd revealed it to them. To him, of all people. Unless she was planning on having him killed once she got her brother back. No, she had changed her mind.

Probably.

Perhaps he had to stop bouncing between trusting her and fearing she had some kind of evil scheme.

A door opened at the end of the hallway, and quick steps approached. Larzen retreated to the stairs, deciding to pretend he'd never come up, partly regretting his decision.

He'd gone down four steps, as silent as he could, when he heard:

"Larzen!" Riadne was yelling, and even without seeing her face, he knew she was furious. "Stop right where you are."

He wasn't a coward, so he turned and climbed those steps. Riadne was shaking. "What. Are. You. Doing. Here?"

"You took a while. I wanted to see if you were—"

"Don't lie!" she roared.

He crossed his arms. "I wanted to see where we were. Curiosity, for one." He gestured around him. "This is... magnificent, Riadne. Then there's that little issue that I don't trust you that much."

"Well, *I* can't trust you. I ask you one thing, one thing; wait downstairs, and you can't do it. I'm wondering what you're going to do with bigger promises."

Another set of steps came from the hall. An old woman, with a hunchback, wearing a loose brown cloak, smiled at him. "Welcome. We were just preparing breakfast. Riadne here was going to call you."

Riadne closed her eyes and took a deep breath, as if trying to calm herself, but she was still shaking. She had a smile that didn't reach her eyes. "Great. I'll call our other illustrious guest."

She passed him and dashed down the stairs. Larzen was alone with the old woman, who eyed him with curiosity. He extended a hand and smiled.

"I'm Larzen. It's a pleasure to meet you."

She took it. "I'm Daviana, the oldest living Solana. But you can call me Dada."

"This place is beautiful, Dada."

He then wondered if he should go down and check if Riadne was still furious at him, or just pretend nothing happened. No, facing a furious Riadne alone wasn't a good idea. He smiled at the woman. "Can I help you prepare breakfast?"

She chuckled. "Of course. Follow me."

Zora didn't think that Larzen should have gone up without being invited. If anything, it was rude. Then there was her fear that maybe this place wasn't safe, that Riadne couldn't be trusted. Right as she was entertaining these thoughts, the redhead opened the door and glared at her.

"Come up. See? You could both have waited."

Zora felt embarrassed that Larzen had gone in without asking. "I told him to stay."

Riadne shook her head. "I know. It's not you I'm mad at." She clenched her fists. "But why couldn't he..." She sighed and smiled. "Let's go, eat, and get ready."

"Is everyone all right?"

"Uh? Oh, yes. I guess the creatures can't come here, or at least didn't come last night."

Zora exhaled, relieved that Riadne's people were fine, then followed the false princess. It was strange to be alone with her. There were some things she wanted to know, wanted to ask, but didn't think this was the right time.

The polished stairs surprised Zora, and the beautiful palace atop it surprised her even more. "How come we can't see this..." She wasn't sure what to call that transparent wall. "Window from the outside?"

"Not sure. This place is very old." Riadne's voice was still dry.

Well, Zora would also be pissed if someone came into her house without asking first.

They followed a hallway, and at the end of it came to a room with those big windows but also an opening to a balcony. There were two tables made of that white stone, a long one that could fit some ten people, and then a round one, where Larzen was cutting some fruit beside Aelle, the girl Zora had seen before, and a very old woman, who was looking at an ancient book, then raised her eyes to greet her. "Welcome."

"This is Dada," Riadne said. "And this is Zora. She's from the Dark Valley."

The woman looked at her with curiosity. Zora felt a little uneasy to be under that stare, but said, "Hello."

The woman nodded, then turned back to the book.

Larzen gave Riadne an easy, relaxed smile. "You two can sit. I'm almost finished here."

The false princess glared at him. "I didn't know you could cook."

He raised a knife. "I'm just cutting. And yes, I'm multi-talented, in case you haven't noticed."

Riadne rolled her eyes and Zora smiled, realizing that he was trying to do something nice, perhaps to make up for having come in uninvited. She sat and soon Larzen brought two plates with fruit and bread, then glasses of milk. Only then he sat down.

The girl, Aelle, did too, then turned to Larzen and Zora. "Can I come with you?"

"No!" Riadne's voice was harsh. "What are you thinking?"

The girl frowned. "I don't want to stay—"

"Listen to your cousin," the old woman said.

Aelle just looked down.

They ate in silence. When Zora finished, she looked up to see Dada sitting with them. Her face was solemn as she shook the thickest book. "I looked at it the best I could in the enormous time I was given."

"Dada..." Riadne's voice was soft, almost apologetic. "You can keep the books and examine them."

"No." The woman raised a hand. "They're meant for you. I looked at it, but from what I understand you went through the bulk of it yourself and figured that the Solanas created an enchantment to keep the darkness at bay, right?"

"Yes."

"And did you understand the reason they did it?"

Riadne grimaced. "Well, I mean, it's not that hard... Who wants to live in a place where creatures spawn in the shadows?" She turned to Zora. "No offense."

"None taken." It was true.

Dada nodded. "And you think this is the worst that this can get? This is what they were fighting against?"

Riadne frowned. "What is the worst?"

The old woman sighed. "There's a possibility that the connection to the kingdom of shadows could be open—"

That didn't make sense. "Isn't it open already?" Zora hated to be rude and interrupt, but she couldn't hold back the question.

Dada shook her head. "Not really. Not completely. Things can get worse, and that was why these enchantments were done in such a hurry. They were meant to prevent something worse from happening."

"What is going to happen?" Riadne's voice was almost a whisper.

When Griffin had been a child, he had enjoyed putting puzzles together. His mother had a small collection of artworks cut into small pieces, and it was exciting to figure out what image they would make up together. There was something similar going on in his mind now, as he tried to assemble scattered fragments of memories that weren't his. But if this were a puzzle, the picture would be blurry, and most pieces would be missing.

He had messy, often incomprehensible pieces of truth, and had to pretend he understood it all and make sure never to show doubt, confusion, or surprise, all the while trying to smother the pain he felt about everything he'd lost.

Still alive many hours after waking up in this strange world, he told himself he was doing quite well as he stood at the head of a table with some council members and military leaders. They were in a room with rough gray stone and a barred window without glass, bringing a cool breeze that made Griffin shiver. A large wooden table, smooth and unworn, contrasted with the decay of the room. This wasn't the main castle in their land, but an abandoned fortress. While the soldiers camped around it, the leaders and royalty had rooms there.

The men in front of him were not human, but had bald heads and gray, leathery skin like the others. Griffin had tried to run his hand through his hair—only to find nothing—a couple times already, and now he had to pay attention and avoid doing it repeatedly, or else it could be a giveaway that he wasn't who he was pretending to be.

Strange. His memories told him that the military leaders there were not important commanders, but young, recently promoted officers, willing to be in the frontline, willing to lead the first soldiers to cross over.

With his heart thumping in his chest, and surprised that thing had a heart, he'd asked his second, Antelio, to lead the meeting. The less Griffin talked, the easier to keep the farce. The man had a satisfied smile—probably. Differentiating between these creatures smiling and baring their teeth was something Griffin still wasn't good at, and reading their facial expressions was a challenge. He tried to keep his emotions neutral, push down everything. If his mind was clear, his face would show no doubt, pain, or fear.

Still, there was something about Antelio, and the bits and pieces in his mind told Griffin not to trust him. Another idea that came to his mind was that not leading the meeting would be a sign of weakness for these people. He'd have to turn this around somehow.

He was still trying to make sense of those explosives in the flimsy nets. And how they were the differentiating factor that would allow them to cross over. Questions kept burning in his mind as he waded through strange possibilities that made no sense.

Antelio explained to the general of the group camped beneath the mountain that they would be the first through the gate, after the explosives went through, decimating a good part of an enemy army. But there wouldn't be an army waiting for them. And again, there was no way these explosives would slide through the gate out of their own volition.

And then it clicked. Griffin clenched his fists to avoid showing any emotion or surprise. The point of the explosives was not to go through the gate, but to slide down and kill their own soldiers. Suffering and pain powered their magic, and the king and his closest advisors believed that a sudden burst of suffering would allow the portal to open. They wouldn't even need to wait for the *darkest night*, which was when they usually tried to cross.

Once the portal was open, then they would be able to cross at any time, and then more soldiers would come. Griffin took in a sharp breath. Antelio glanced at him, and was met with a glare.

But then, weren't they already invading his land? That was what had always happened in the Dark Valley. That was what had happened in his last memories while he was still himself, facing those shadow creatures in that cave. There was a bitter taste in his mouth and coldness inside him that had nothing to do with the open windows.

His questions circled his mind while Antelio lied to the men. With no hesitation or remorse, he told them that the troops in the valley would go through the gate. Instead, if this plan worked, many of these commanders would die. Griffin should be happy that so many of his enemies would be killed at once, but the wrongness in it made him feel as if he were nauseous.

The military leaders were dismissed, and then Griffin was left with Antelio and three more men, who were part of the council.

"I have something to report," a short man in dark red leather armor said. "The dark pits, your majesty, the subjects are collapsing and even dying faster. We have reason to believe that something opened."

Griffin had no idea what the man was talking about, but said, "It's not a priority right now."

The man looked down. "Understood, but... should we replace our prisoners there?"

"Follow the procedure." The man still looked uncertain. Griffin raised an eyebrow—or at least he thought he did. "Or perhaps you're not qualified for your position and don't know what to do?"

The man looked down. "I'll follow the procedure."

"But if the dark pits are open—" Another man started.

"It makes no difference considering what we're about to do," Griffin cut in. "We lose focus, we'll lose our war." Hopefully words like that would resonate even in such a strange place. "Our priority is the gate. After that, we'll see what we'll do."

The man lowered his head. "Perfect, then. We'll wait until tomorrow night."

Tomorrow night? What was happening tomorrow night? The answer came to him in a flash of a memory: they were going to cross the gate tomorrow. Griffin needed no cold breeze to feel chilled to the bone.

ZORA LOOKED at the old woman, dreading whatever she was going to say.

Dada passed the book to Riadne. "Whatever you do, do it before the winter solstice."

"Why?" Zora asked.

The woman's voice was calm as she eyed each of the

people on the table. "From what I see here, what we have right now is just a fragment of what the true horrors could be. These shadow creatures, they are easily defeated, don't usually survive sunlight, and can't do much against us, but if the gates are open, then we could face real creatures, more resistant and stronger than us, who can survive sunlight. You need to find a way to stop it."

Larzen tapped his fingers on the table. "Before the winter solstice?"

"Ideally," Dada replied.

He smiled. "Aren't we lucky? We're still four weeks away from it. Plenty of time to figure out something our ancestors couldn't figure out in what? Four hundred years? But we have to assume we're better than them, right?"

Riadne stared at him with narrowed eyes. "Hilarious."

"He has a point," Zora said, even if she knew he'd been partly joking. "We have to hope."

The false princess rolled her eyes. "Oh, yes, hope is going to solve all our problems."

"Our problems," Larzen said. "Interesting."

Riadne shrugged. "Well, if these things can attack us, it's obviously my problem too." She then turned to the old woman. "Have you ever heard about a place called Rock Island? Where people learn magic?"

Dada shook her head. "Never heard of it. But places like that must exist. If that's where your heart is telling you to go, that's where you have to go."

Riadne pointed at Zora. "It's actually *her* heart."

Zora looked down. "My heart's partly frozen. And there's a chance it could be wrong."

"Indeed." Dada's dark eyes were on her. "There's always that possibility. There's always a chance you might make a mistake. You can either let fear paralyze you, and your heart too, or you can keep going. What are you going to choose?"

The thought brought Zora such a tightness in the chest that it was hard to breathe. "All of this is my fault. Mistakes can have dire consequences. But I need to learn more, I think if I can get more information—"

The woman had gotten up and had a hand on Zora's face. "You don't know if what you did was really a mistake."

Zora swallowed a snort because the woman meant well. "Sure." But then she couldn't hold back her next words. "I mean, what are the odds that unleashing dark creatures all over the kingdom was a mistake? It's quite debatable, right?"

Dada laughed. "You don't know it all. You can't know. What you can do is keep on going."

Zora sighed. "I'm good at that."

"Well," Larzen said. "We'll go to the castle and find a solution." He turned to Riadne. "Without any traveling anywhere."

"But it might be necessary," Dada said. "We were hunted, and our knowledge was destroyed here, in Gravel. If there's a place outside where they might have some of our ancient texts, perhaps even one of our amplifying stones... It might be the answer."

Larzen had his jaw set. "Maybe there are other answers."

Riadne smiled at him. "I'm sure there were tons of answers, all over Gravel, until your great, great, great, grandpas or something decided to kill us all and destroy our knowledge. But if you do have some Solana books lying around, by all means, I'd much rather not travel to get them. Do you have any?"

He looked away. "I don't know."

Dada put the three books on the table. "Go, then, since you're in such a hurry. Riadne can keep looking into them, and maybe you'll find answers wherever you're going. When you're not sure, listen to that inner voice inside you, you know which one."

Right. The crazy voice that made people make stupid decisions. But Zora didn't say anything.

Aelle raised her hands. "Meanwhile, nobody cares what my heart is saying, and I stay here!"

"Safe, like you should." Riadne glared at the girl.

4

CAUGHT

The meeting finished—and Griffin's mind was whirling. First, he had to find a way to prevent the opening of the portal, and had too little time. Second, he had to understand what those *dark pits* were. He combed his mind for that information, but it was all confusing, fragmented, disordered. Disconnected bits and pieces about prisoners, suffering, power.

"What's your real opinion on the dark pits?" Antelio's voice got him out of his daze.

"We need to focus on the gate now. We'll deal with the pits later."

Antelio stared at him, as if still waiting for an opinion. "But if the pits are open..."

"Go on," Griffin said. "I want to hear what you think."

The man had a bizarre smile. "It's ironic that, after all this time, they should open when they're almost no longer necessary."

"Indeed. Our victory is close." Even Griffin was tired of saying empty words.

The man nodded, but eyed him for a second too long, as

if examining him. The pits, the pits... What were these pits for? They had something to do with the shadow creatures, but Griffin couldn't make the connection. He wondered if perhaps there would be a correlation between those pits opening and their king... not being himself.

Antelio nodded. "A victory as beautiful as the one we had over the storm fields."

"Or better."

It was as if something flickered in the man's eyes. A fraction of a second, and yet Griffin noticed it, pulled his sword, and pushed the man against a wall before he had the time to get any weapons. Holding his sword against the man's neck, Griffin said, "There was never such a victory, was there? And there are no such fields. What are you playing at?"

"A test, your majesty. You know it's necessary. If the pits open—"

"If the pits open *what*?" Griffin growled, but he was realizing that there was a correlation between him being here and those pits, even if he wasn't sure what it was.

"I'm supposed to test you. It was just a test."

The words didn't sound convincing. The man had been eyeing Griffin for a long time now and at this point was probably certain he wasn't their king. This was Gravel's enemy. An enemy and a killer so despicable that he was willing to sacrifice his own men. With a quick movement, Griffin pushed the sword. What had once been Antelio fell to the ground, eyes glassy.

Reality was more horrifying than any training, any stories. The weight of death was heavy on Griffin's hands, but there hadn't been much choice. He'd been his enemy. His enemy. And could have ruined his plans. But none of that changed the lingering disgust and horror in his mind at seeing that red blood. None of that changed the fact that Griffin hadn't hesitated even for a second.

He turned away from that scene and walked out of the room. Two guards stood at the door.

"Send someone for his body." Griffin's voice was firm. He then noticed that some of the generals and a couple council members were in the hallway, staring.

Griffin smirked. Or at least tried to. "He wanted to take my place leading the meeting; I let him. Gotta grant a man his dying wish."

He turned around and kept his steps steady even if he felt his heart in this strange body accelerating, fearing someone would run after him, call him an impostor, a murderer. He kept his ears perked for any approaching steps. But nobody followed. Only his own feet thumped on the rough floor.

THE WALK TO MOUNTAIN FOOT, the closest village, took about half an hour, but it might have been some of Larzen's longest thirty minutes. He was about to see the impact and destruction of the shadow creatures in his kingdom. Riadne was right that self-blame didn't help, but it was hard not to look back and have some regrets. But then, it wouldn't change anything.

Funny. Riadne hadn't pointed fingers at anyone, when she had every reason to do so. At him, for taking so long to give her the books she wanted. At Griffin—and consequently Zora —for not stopping and listening to them. Larzen couldn't help but admire that. Most people would be lashing out and blaming everyone, especially when they had clearly screwed up. Riadne wasn't most people.

But in truth, pointing fingers and arguing for what could have been wouldn't solve their problems. What could solve their problems, or at least point them in the right direction, was getting more information.

He understood the point of going to Rock Island, but he doubted they'd be able to steal anything from such a place. It was far too dangerous even for Riadne, and he didn't know how to convince her of that.

Larzen could perhaps help them, assign someone to guide them, give them the tools and resources to find whatever magic archives they had in Kentosa. And yet he didn't know if he could trust anyone to do that. He would probably need to take care of the kingdom, find Kiran, and fix so many things. But he didn't want to let Riadne go on a foolish quest, especially unprepared, with only a girl mildly decent with a sword for a companion.

A tough decision loomed on his horizon.

For now, all they needed was to find some means of transportation, and he hoped this place would have at least something.

The village was small, with about thirty houses or so, all in the old Gravel style, built with stone walls and flat roofs. From a distance, nothing had been destroyed. A cow mooed in the distance, the first sign of life from the village.

Larzen's steps slowed down as he reached the houses. Braving the tension and fear of what he was about to see was like walking through a viscous liquid. He exchanged no words with Riadne or Zora, his mind busy wondering if by any chance everyone had been killed. A horse neighed. Well, at least they'd find transportation.

Riadne stopped. "Listen!"

He tried to, but couldn't hear anything. She ran towards a house and he followed her. Behind it, a sight he definitely hadn't expected.

Five women were sitting in chairs arranged in a circle, sharing a hot drink. The sound had been laughter. They stared at them, eyes wide.

Riadne had a nervous laugh. "Uh, hello."

One of the women frowned. "Do you need anything?"

"We're travelers," Riadne said. "Do you have any horses for sale?"

Larzen didn't think anyone would recognize him that far from the castle, but it was better to let Riadne do the talking, considering the feminine audience.

Another woman pointed at the road. "Go east. The first town is Cold River. They have a tavern, and you might be able to find horses for sale there."

Sure, except that it would take them some two hours to get there.

"We can pay well," Riadne insisted while glancing at him. Larzen nodded.

The women looked at each other and shook their heads.

Zora then approached the villagers. "Did anything, uh, unusual, happen here last night?" Her voice was strained. Afraid. Of course.

"No." The first woman frowned in confusion. "Why?"

Larzen exhaled in relief. So these people had no idea that there were shadow creatures loose at night. This was almost too good to be true, but he'd take it. Perhaps the villagers had all been indoors. Perhaps the creatures hadn't reached them. In either case, the village hadn't been decimated like he'd been fearing. He glanced at Riadne, who met his eyes with a glimmer on her own. Larzen looked away. This wasn't the time to find her beautiful.

"Nothing," Zora said, her voice much lighter and more relaxed than before.

Larzen also felt more relaxed, glad not to face a tragedy.

Riadne then said, "I heard a horse. Do you know who owns it?"

A woman shook her head. "We're not a commercial stable. Maybe up north—"

A strange sound interrupted the woman. Riadne was

doing her odd singing. The villagers stared at her. Even Zora was staring at her, as if waiting for a command.

"Whose horse is that?" Riadne asked.

"My family's," the woman who had shaken her head replied.

Riadne sang again for a few seconds. "Great." She pointed at Larzen. "My friend will pay you well for it, and you'll be happy you made such a great deal, even if you won't remember much about us. Do you have a cart for the horse?"

"Yes," the woman replied with a smile, as if pleasing Riadne was what she most wanted in the world.

Larzen swallowed, uncomfortable. He knew that she claimed that her magic didn't work on him, but if it did, she could basically make him do whatever she wanted. The idea of losing control gave him shivers of the unpleasant kind. Still, there was something beautiful and magnificent about the poise with which Riadne handled her power. He'd be lying if he said it didn't fascinate him. Larzen shivered.

"Great." Riadne smiled. "Can you take us to it?" Then she turned to the other villagers. "Oh, and all of you, stay inside and bar your doors when the sun sets. Tell everyone in the village to do the same. In other villages, too."

The women nodded while Zora just stared, but her eyes looked glassy. That was beyond creepy. Riadne could be very dangerous. He knew that, even if he forgot it sometimes. She then turned to him and glared, as if she could read his thoughts. Or maybe because she noticed him staring. Well, what was he supposed to do?

The villager led them to the horse and cart and set it up. Riadne sang from time to time. Larzen would have preferred for them to ride three horses, but he didn't have the luxury of choice in such a tiny village. He did pay the woman twice what the horse and cart would be worth, to compensate for her trouble.

Larzen guided the cart as they left the village.

When they were on the road, Zora looked at them, frowning in confusion. "Hang on. What just happened?"

"I saved us a lot of time and work," Riadne said, then glared at Larzen. "Not that I got any thanks."

"Well, thank you," he replied. He turned to Zora. "Are you feeling strange or something? Do you remember what just happened?"

The Dark Valley girl shook her head. "I... I remember everything, but it is like watching something I had no control over. It felt odd. Won't the women find it strange too?"

Riadne shook her head. "They'll remember it differently. I wasn't trying to affect you, Zora. I don't know how you got caught in it."

The girl was still thoughtful. "It's quite... something."

"Right," Riadne said. "Why doesn't anyone say that it's quite helpful and you're glad we're on our way?" She turned to Larzen. "You were staring at me as if I was torturing a child or something."

What an exaggeration. "I was not!"

Riadne shrugged. "I won't use my power if it bothers you that much."

"It's helpful," Zora said. "Thanks. You've used it before to save my life. It..." She paused, as if thinking. "Can be used for good." She frowned again. "How come he didn't get affected?"

Riadne sighed. "Mystery of my life."

Larzen chuckled. "I'm that important now?"

Riadne just rolled her eyes, smiled, and shook her head, as if he didn't even deserve an answer. Quite a Riadne thing to do. Eventually they would go separate ways, and he'd miss all her Riadnesses. The thought was like a cold breeze inside him. But that was a fact, and perhaps the sooner they parted, the easier it would be.

If he stayed in Gravel City and let her go to Rock Island,

then they'd part even sooner. But that thought was more like a storm raging inside him. Larzen needed to get a grip and some reality check.

Yes, he'd wanted her when he'd been under the impression she was the Linaria princess. But since then he'd found out she'd seduced and ruined his younger brother's life, had plotted against his family, and was a dangerous enchantress. Somehow he kept forgetting all of that.

GRIFFIN WALKED AROUND THESE ROUGH, unfinished corridors searching that strange mind he inhabited for clues about where his improvised quarters should be.

Confusion, uncertainty, fear, and pain clouded his thoughts. The memory of blood, killing, and the terrifying feeling accompanying it didn't help. He could still see Antelio's eyes losing their life. The memory felt uncomfortable. Griffin had hurt men before, his own men, but it had been to defend Zora, and somehow it seemed justified then. Now he was saving himself. And maybe the chance to save his kingdom. It was worth it.

He also searched that strange mind for more important information, and perhaps what was messing him up was trying to absorb and understand so much at once.

In his scattered memories, he found the answer to what these dark pits were. Prisoners were put in dark chambers where sometimes their consciousness would cross over in the form of shadow creatures and cause suffering. Suffering was power in this place. Magical power, or explosive power that they could store in balls. Those pits were what allowed shadow creatures to cross over to his world, except that, until a day before, the only place they could go to was the Dark Valley, which was mostly lit.

Now, they could go everywhere. The prisoners died when they were killed on the other side and now they were dying at a faster rate. They were probably crossing over more often, but apparently nobody had figured that out yet. Griffin would need to find a way to destroy those pits and stop them from using them. Perhaps that could free his kingdom. He sighed. That would be just a temporary solution. He needed to find a way to break whatever connection this kingdom had to Gravel.

And then there was the crossing over the gate, which, if successful, would bring a whole lot more destruction to his kingdom. He inhaled a sharp breath, unable to imagine it, trying to come up with an idea to prevent that from happening. But how? Perhaps letting some of the soldiers know about it? If he found a way to prove it, to show those soldiers that they were meant to be sacrificed, he could perhaps incite a mutiny. But he didn't have enough time for that and wasn't sure if it could make a difference. Perhaps he could destroy or divert the explosives. That was a better idea. But he needed to come up with a strategy for that.

Still, he had to sit down at least, get some respite from being watched, have a moment for himself, gather his thoughts. Where could his quarters be? The image of large wooden doors came to his mind. He wasn't sure if it was his imagination or a memory. It was very disorienting to inhabit not only a strange body, but a strange mind.

He found a set of stairs, descended it, and then, to his surprise, saw those doors at the end of the hall. There were two guards stationed in front of it, which made sense. Griffin went through them without even sparing them a glance, and found himself in a room with a double bed and a platform with a basket or something similar.

As he approached the basket, he realized it was actually a cradle, with a baby, or rather one of those ugly creatures, but in miniature form, asleep. He hadn't considered how these people reproduced, but it made sense that it would be at least somewhat like humans.

"You came to see him," a rough but higher-pitched voice startled him.

He turned to see a person like the ones he'd seen before, without hair, except that it wore a light tunic. Not it, she. Griffin had seen women without hair before. Irene, one of his favorite commanders, had hair cropped really short, but she didn't have gray skin that looked like a snake's. So the sight of this strange woman in front of him was shocking.

But he pretended not to be surprised and smiled. "It appears so." That was the first thing that came to his mind while he tried to guess who this woman was.

He took a look back at the crib, and at the small creature under a red blanket. The red reminded him of the blood he'd spilled earlier, but the baby reminded him of his vision, the one he had thought was going to be his future. He then remembered the last time he'd seen his Zora, unarmed, with a chasm behind her, her defiant expression not masking very well her fear, despair, and disbelief.

He closed his eyes and took a deep breath.

Focus, he had to focus and find a way to deal with that gate. Regretting or reminiscing the past wasn't going to help anyone. And yet being unable to grieve while hurting was excruciating.

The woman had her eyes narrowed, examining him.

"What?" he asked, realizing he might have let his impersonation slip for a second. Much more than a second.

"Nothing." She sat on the bed, eyes wide and her posture stiff.

Perhaps he didn't know much about those people, but he could recognize fear.

Was she afraid because she suspected he wasn't the king?

Or was there another reason? Griffin was exhausted, and not looking forward to lying on that bed if he had to share it with that creature. He took a look at the room. It didn't have windows, so at least there were no cold breezes coming in. There was an armchair in a corner, where he sat down to rest. If he fell asleep there, he could say he just forgot to go to bed or something.

Hopefully the woman wouldn't expect him to... Did these people even do things like humans? Oh, gross. A memory from the previous king came to his mind and that was way beyond the amount of information he needed. Now he couldn't unsee it.

"If you're tired, you could go to your quarters," the woman said, standing right in front of him.

"I didn't ask your opinion." That was rude, but all his memories of that king were rude, and he was trying to be convincing. Plus, he had no idea where to go and wasn't going to ask where his quarters were. In fact, he couldn't believe he'd gone through all the trouble of finding this room, and it was the wrong one. He closed his eyes, not fearing any threat from that woman. Or maybe it was just exhaustion.

"I could help you." Her voice startled him. "If you help me."

He opened his eyes and saw her crouching in front of him.

"Explain," he managed to say.

"I won't tell anyone," she whispered.

He'd been caught. Again. At once feeling awake and alert, Griffin reached for his sword, but he didn't like the idea of striking someone who posed no threat, even if a small voice in his mind told him to kill her. That voice also told him to strangle her with his bare hands, and the image of those hands around her neck, suffocating her, but not killing her, came to him. That voice wasn't his, and neither were those horrifying memories.

He let go of the sword. "*What* won't you tell?"

"You're not him."

He shivered, wondering if perhaps he'd have no choice but to kill her.

She then added, "But you're not evil, are you?"

Griffin decided to listen to her and only then make up his mind about what to do. Ugh, he wasn't sure if he could kill a baby's mother. He just shrugged. "Evil is a matter of point of view."

"My name's Amina, and I'm a hostage here." That was... quite straight to the point.

He frowned. "I thought..." Her room was special, she had a relationship with the king, she had to be his wife or at least mistress or something.

"I am married to King Saro, yes," she said, as if perceiving his confusion. "But I'm from... an enemy kingdom."

"Well, you can leave." No, that was not very smart or strategic. "I mean, you can have my help in exchange for your silence."

"You need more than my silence, fake king. I can't believe nobody has found out you're an impostor yet."

Griffin wasn't sure if he could trust her and still had a voice telling him to kill her. It would be so simple. Eliminate the risk at once. Did that voice belong to his own mind? He took a deep breath. "And you can prevent me from being discovered?"

"I can answer your questions and give you information."

"And what do you want in return? To have safe passage back home?"

She shook her head. "That wouldn't solve my problem. We have an enemy in common."

"What enemy?"

She frowned. "You're completely unprepared for this, aren't you?"

"If you're wondering if I ever thought I'd be possessing a king in a strange land, well no. In fact, I have no idea what's happening."

"That much is evident." Quite cheeky for someone who was at his mercy.

"Hmm, what about you? Were you by any chance *expecting* this?"

She paused. "I wasn't expecting it, no, but we've always been prepared for this possibility."

"Who are *we*?"

"It's a long story, fake king."

He looked around. "It's not like I'm in a hurry to go anywhere."

"Well, you should."

5

BROTHERS

Tris's brother had always said that sewing was useless. Ha. She wished he could see her now.

No, she didn't wish him to see her; she wished he were dead.

Strange thought.

Stranger was the idea that she'd never again be able to share something like that with her brother, that she wouldn't be able to tell him how sewing had been useful. It was as if a part of her were missing.

She focused back on what she was doing and finished her last stitch. After sharpening so many stakes, she needed a place to put them on, a way to carry them, so she made a baldric with holes. That way, she'd always have a weapon close to her. Knife-throwing was the only thing that she could do for self-defense. It had been entertainment in Linaria.

Suddenly her mind was flooded with unwelcome memories of her time training; a warm hand holding hers, a soft voice telling her to relax her elbow, strong arms around her waist, wet lips on hers, then the cold floor of the weapon room against her back feeling warm and soft, loving words a pleasant song in her ears, as she learned to dance to that song.

But then the image was replaced by her father slapping her, calling her a slut, a whore, a harlot. Then there was screaming, screaming, screaming. Everyone screaming. The screams never stopped echoing.

She had to bury all that, bury the pain.

What mattered was that at least she had one fighting skill, and if something happened, she'd have to depend on it.

It was afternoon already, and Lukas slept, his breathing calm and steady. Perhaps he was getting better. She took a peek at his back. It didn't look like it was healing. At all. There were two black gashes surrounded in purple and even greenish bruises, as if something had been hurting him, even if he'd been lying down for two days.

Every rational part of her wanted to leave him behind. He had healers, the king thought he was the Linaria Prince, his sister would do something. But then the idea made her feel guilty. Perhaps it was just that little bit of compassion in her heart. Her mother had once told her that compassion was what made us human. How ironic. Tris still remembered her cold eyes as they hurt Krim, as they hurt her only love. Still remembered, still remembered, still remembered those awful images that were engraved deep inside her.

Tris put on her baldric. There was no point dwelling on the past. She also wore a cloak tied in the front so her spikes wouldn't be that visible. And she didn't think anyone would look too hard anyway. She crawled through the small space where they exchanged the buckets. Idiots, not to realize she could escape through there, but then, unlike their previous room, this wasn't a prison. She found herself in an antechamber, then in the hallways of the Gravel castle.

With only a vague memory of where Riadne's room should be, the issue would be getting there. Tris descended a set of stairs and found herself in a wider corridor. There was a tapestry she'd seen before. The doors here were familiar. That was where she and Lukas had been staying. After another set of stairs, she found the gigantic golden door leading to Riadne's room. A guard stood at the entrance.

"I'm going in," Tris said as she pushed it. From experience, she knew that people were unlikely to stop someone walking in with confidence.

"You can't. She's in isolation," the guard said behind her.

"I don't care."

The guard was still behind her, mumbling something, as she passed by the same room where she'd sat with Lukas and his sister, discussing her plans for Linaria. Perhaps it had been naïve to come here. Perhaps everything was pointless. She opened the door to the bedroom and rushed to it.

"Alegra." Weird to call her using her own former name, but then there was that guard behind her.

Perhaps she was asleep and really sick. When Tris was about to touch her shoulder, she realized that there was no shoulder, no face. It was just a pile of covers, as if someone wanted to pretend there was a person there.

She turned to the guard. "Where is she?"

The young man's face paled. His look of surprise was genuine enough for Tris to believe that he had no idea there was no person in this room.

"Where's the king?" she asked.

The man stepped back. "Miss, uh, you're not supposed to—"

"Where is the king? I assume I can at least request an audience. And if you don't know who I am, let me tell you, I'm the Linaria..." She almost said princess, but corrected herself in time. "... crown prince's betrothed and I want to know what happened to his sister."

The man was babbling, and Tris stormed down the hall.

If Riadne was gone, what did it mean? She looked at the long hallway, without any idea where to go, when the guard reached her. "I can take you to where you can request an audience."

She sighed. Good enough for now, but if the king took too long to see her, she'd have to take some drastic measure instead of waiting.

The guard led her to a room where a blond man sat on a table, behind some piles of papers. He looked at her up and down, and wrinkled his nose as if something smelled bad. Tris's best guess was that he'd just farted.

"How can I help you?" the man asked in a tone that was more like "get out of here before I fart even more."

Tris wasn't afraid of disgusted faces or pretentious people. "I need to speak with king Kiran. It's about the Linaria princess."

"And you are... Weren't you sick? What are you—"

Tris shook her head. "I'm fine, and what the prince has is not contagious."

The man frowned. "Who brought you here?"

She looked back, and the guard had disappeared. Coward. She smiled. "My feet. Unbelievable, right? Now if you don't wish to cause a diplomatic issue, you'd look into my request right away."

The man shrugged. "I am looking. And you'll have to come back tomorrow. It's already almost five in the afternoon."

Tris wondered if she should mention the disappeared "princess", but she had decided to try and see how much the king knew before revealing anything. That guard was such a coward that he'd probably stay silent. "I'm representing Linaria here. Don't make me wait."

The man looked at his papers and didn't raise his eyes. "Tomorrow is not waiting."

Tris sighed. She'd need to find the king, corner him, and get answers. There wasn't much she was going to achieve here. When she was about to leave, she heard a voice behind her.

"What's going on here?"

Tris turned. King Kiran was there. She'd seen him once, from a distance. Up close, she realized he was quite handsome, with full lips and long, dark eyelashes lining light brown eyes. He looked at her up and down, but with curiosity. "You are?"

"Tris Tanasia." She made up that last name on the spot. "I'm here with the Linaria Prince, and I'd like an audience with your majesty." She bowed slightly. Ugh, she hated pretending she was a commoner and acting all humble.

The king widened his eyes and had a pleasant smile. "Of course. I'd never make you wait. Follow me."

Wow, he was good looking. Funny that if she hadn't been kidnaped, she would have come here to try to get an alliance with him, and the prospect didn't look bad. At all. Except that it was all confusing with Riadne pretending she was her and everything else. And Lukas was good looking too. Not that it made any difference. Her mind was going to weird places.

The handsome king led her to a private office decorated with paintings of landscapes. A bookshelf lined a corner.

"Sit, sit." He pointed to an armchair, then sat across from her. His eyes were attentive. "What brings you here?"

"I..." She hesitated. "Have you seen princess Alegra lately?"

"She's in isolation." He shook his head. "Terrible disease. I can't risk my own health."

"Uh-hum." There was something fake about his tone, but she wasn't sure what. "But..." She took a deep breath. There was no way to do this and not reveal what she knew. "I went to her room just now. And she wasn't there."

He blinked, paused, then his lips trembled and his body stiffened, as if he was trying to control his anger. "What do you mean she wasn't there?"

"I mean..." Was there an easier way to say it? "I went there and the bedroom was empty. There was a pile of blankets on her bed."

He got up suddenly, his hands trembling and his face red. "I'll be right back. Please stay. I'd love to continue our conversation." He then stormed out of the room.

Right. So he had no idea she wasn't there. Oh, no. What if Riadne had done it herself? But then, someone had imprisoned Lukas and her. There were enemies in the castle, and from the looks of it, it definitely wasn't the king.

EXHAUSTION WAS ABOUT to take over Griffin, but what was exhaustion compared to losing everything? Not everything. Perhaps he'd lost his hope for a happy life, but his brothers and his kingdom could still have hope, and he had to do his part to make it possible.

Amina had told him that only powerful magic could destroy the portal, so exploding it wasn't going to do much. Still, he needed to get rid of those explosives and prevent soldiers from being killed. He couldn't let these people unleash the magic that could open the portal.

Griffin sought two guards who in theory could help him, who were Amina's allies. He still wasn't very clear on why she considered herself a hostage and why she didn't want that portal to open, but her urgency had sounded true enough.

The guards were doing rounds around that old fortress, and Griffin called them to accompany him. They followed with some hesitation. Weird how fear was something so palpable that he could identify it even among these strange people.

When they were alone, he asked, "What were you thinking, blue skies?"

These last two words were their code, but it didn't ease their fear or suspicion. They might have thought they had been caught. Griffin added in a low voice, "Amina sent me. Just be quiet."

Nothing changed in their posture, but he could feel less unease from their side. Either way, it didn't really matter who helped him, as long as they didn't tell anyone what they were doing.

The guards blocking the path to the side of the mountain didn't say anything when Griffin crossed them towards the platform, to "check" the nets. His plan was to tie the nets together and run some rope through them so as to keep them from completely collapsing when the lever released them. If this idea worked, the balls would roll towards the portal. Fine, even if they didn't destroy it, they still wouldn't kill the soldiers.

If his plan didn't work, it would still hinder the balls from falling and at least give the soldiers time to run. His action would prevent the killing of hundreds and, more importantly, stop whatever pain-based magic that would otherwise be used to power the portal.

Griffin supervised the guards as they worked under his directions, and kept watch to make sure nobody noticed what they were doing. He still sometimes had images coming to his mind and felt disoriented, but he forced himself to pay attention to what was happening and to how the guards were tying the nets. He hoped nobody suspected him, but then, it likely looked like a last-minute supervision from a distance. Perhaps the choice of guards could seem suspicious, since they should be doing rounds and had never accompanied the king. But then, lots of things had seemed suspicious, and since killing Antelio, Griffin had been expecting to be caught or confronted, but it hadn't happened yet.

Then something came to his mind. Gravel and the lake house, but during the day, unlike his last time there. He saw himself tracing circles on the ground. Strange, he'd never done anything like that. And why was he thinking about it?

He checked the tying of the net again. Down there, in the encampment, there was mostly silence except for a few remaining fires here and there. There was some distant, out-of-tune singing. Drinking before going to battle was a terrible idea, but the unsettling thing was to see this human behavior in these creatures. People.

Griffin kept changing the way he referred to them in his mind, unsure about so many things. He knew they were their enemies, and yet, pitied the soldiers below, hoped that his plan worked, that they could survive at least one more day. Perhaps because he was afraid that the portal would be open, but it wasn't all there was. Working alongside two of these creatures, he felt compassion for them. And yet he had to find a way to defeat them and save his kingdom.

Another image came to his mind. Gravel city, and a guard being surrounded by shadow creatures, like the ones he'd seen in the Dark Valley and in that cave, gray with sharp claws. That could be happening in Gravel right now. And he had to figure out a way to stop it. For now, he hoped he could at least prevent that portal from opening.

Tris got up, tired of waiting. There was a large window in Kiran's room, from the floor to the ceiling. So much glass, and a beautiful view of the garden below and a river at some distance. The sky was already dark blue, as the sun was setting behind the mountains separating his kingdom from Linaria, as if the sun had decided to hide there.

The king was taking a while to come back, but she wanted to wait, as she didn't want to waste this opportunity to talk to him and learn as much as she could.

After more than half an hour, when the sky had been dark for some time, the king returned. "I'm so sorry for my delay. Sit, sit." He gestured to the chairs again. He then sat across from her and sighed. "Why do I still get disappointed?"

"What do you mean?"

He shrugged. "It's obvious, right? She left me."

"Maybe someone kidnapped her. You don't know."

"Everything is possible." King Kiran took a deep breath, then ran his fingers through his hair. "I requested a high alert to find her, but I know it in my heart, I just know it. My brother, my own brother, took her from me. Can you believe it?"

"I... didn't know that." And his words meant he didn't know where Riadne was either, which was a problem.

He lowered his head and looked up at her, his long lashes lining his eyes. "Am I despicable? Am I undesirable?"

This was... unexpected, but she tried to stick to the point. "I really think something's happening, your majesty."

He got out of the chair, kneeled by her, and held her hands. This was getting insanely weird. "Not *your majesty*. Call me just Kiran. Can you give me hope? Hope for love?"

What? She swallowed a laugh, then made an effort to keep her voice steady and serious. "There's always hope, and when you look good, I mean, chances are higher, right? I've heard that being king isn't bad either, so..."

He got up and put his hands on his head. "But that's the thing. How can I know if it's real?"

As a princess, Tris had asked herself the same question a

few times. "You won't. And you have to take the chance anyway."

He kneeled by her again. "Have dinner with me."

"I..." she swallowed. "My, uh, betrothed is sick, and..." That should end this insanity.

"The Linaria Prince. Do you love him?"

"I... think so?"

He looked at her with curiosity. "How do you know?"

Tris thought about someone else, someone gone, someone who died suffering and would never come back. "My heart beats faster when I'm around him."

"But that's fear. Perhaps it isn't true love. Perhaps you could find something else here, in Gravel. Perhaps you could mend a broken heart."

Was he... flirting with her? Even after she told him she was involved with the prince? Sure, it wasn't true, but he didn't know that. But then, he was good looking. Perhaps she could still follow her original plan, but then she'd need to expose Lukas, and she wouldn't do that. And then this king was going way too fast for her taste. Way too fast for anyone's taste. She wondered if he was right in the head. But then, perhaps there were things she could still learn from him.

"I can have dinner with you, of course."

Kiran had a soft, pleasant smile. "You're a ray of light." He frowned. "Your name, you said was..."

Tris made an effort not to roll her eyes. "Tris." But then she couldn't hold back the laughter. "But you don't even know who I am."

He shrugged. "What? You expect me to ask about a title? Perhaps about your family's occupation? You think these things matter? Or what's here?" He put a hand over his heart.

"They tell you something about a person, right?"

"Something meaningless. When the only real thing that matters is what's inside. That's the part of you I want to see."

Erm... Uh. She wasn't even sure what to say and was regretting having accepted dinner. "Sure." She smiled.

No, she had to focus. What she had to do was get out of that castle and get Lukas out too. If this king wanted sweet words, she could give them.

She looked down, pretending to be shy. "I wish... I could." She looked at him. "Nobody has ever spoken to me like you just did." Well, that was true. Not enough nutcases in the world.

He eyed her intently. "Nobody has ever looked at me the way you're looking."

Like he was insane? Doubtful. But she had to keep it up. "If the prince, if the prince were returned home, I would feel more at ease to discuss these matters with your majesty, as long as you allow me to stay."

"Of course. You'll be my guest until the end of time."

Tris almost snorted, but she just smiled. It must have looked like a happy smile, because he returned it. She then said, "Do you think you can find a medical carriage to take him home?"

"Absolutely. You should have asked me earlier."

Kind of hard when she'd been locked in a room. Kiran's eyes then moved down from her face to her chest, interest spiking when it got to that area. She knew that look. No, that look came when she wore cleavage, and this time...

"What are those?" His tone was curious, as he looked at her baldric with the stakes.

Tris felt ridiculous, but pretended everything was normal. "What? Don't women here wear those?"

He had a confused frown. "No."

"Well, it's for luck, and..." How was she going to explain that crap? "It's wood. Reminds us of our connection with nature."

He smiled. "This is magnificent. All these stakes in the

holes, I'm assuming it's to remind us of our real nature. It's inspiring."

"Y-yes. I guess."

He reached out his hand. "Can I touch it?"

"No." She closed her cloak to cover it. "I mean..."

He shook his head. "It's fine, Tris. Maybe you can show me how it works? I'd love nothing else than feeling your hand—"

The door burst open and Tris exhaled in relief, as she'd been dreading what he was going to say next. Two guards were holding a handsome young man with dark hair, with two more guards trailing them.

The king chuckled. "My dear brother. There you are. Have you picked your method of execution yet?"

So that was the other prince, Griffin. Apparently they were all in a good mood, as he also chuckled. "Yes. I picked yours, *brother*."

Kiran tilted his head. "With four guards..." He then widened his eyes in shock and stepped back.

Tris followed his line of sight and took a better look at the guards. They were not guards. In fact, they were not human.

6

WHEN NIGHT FALLS

Zora felt queasy in leaving the horse in the stable, knowing what would happen at night. But then, in theory, the creatures didn't affect animals. Even in the valley, they had never harmed the chickens, but they were small. She wasn't certain about what could happen to horses.

The lake house was more like a house in her village than a palace, just slightly bigger. The interior had a large living room and dining room, with a small kitchen, then there were two bedrooms and a room with a bath on the ground floor and a mezzanine leading to two more rooms.

Larzen walked to the kitchen. "Let's see what's left."

Riadne laughed. "I had no idea you even knew how food is made."

"You wound me." He shook his head. "After I served you breakfast."

Zora should volunteer to help, but their banter was like insects buzzing in her ear, and she sat on one of the sofas, staring at the window and the lake as some orange streaks painted the sky. Just a window would be separating them from the creatures. It was true that houses also had windows in the valley, but since everything was lit, it was rare for creatures to come too close. This time... Everything about it made her feel on edge.

Riadne sat in front of her, some dried apples in her hands. "You're worried."

"You think?" She smiled, though.

The false princess bit her lip. "I swear we tried, me and Larzen, we even faced a storm."

"I know. It's my fault. We should have stopped and listened to you."

"No. You had all the reasons not to trust me." Riadne faced Zora. "I just want you to know that it was never personal." She took a deep breath. "I'm not gonna say I'm sorry, but I can say that I never held anything against you."

As if any of that even mattered now. Zora shrugged. "Right. I mean... I guess I'm glad you sent an incompetent guy to assassinate me."

Riadne tilted her head. "Assassinate you. You mean the so-called guy with the dagger?"

"And the dogs."

The redhead paused, thinking. "So it was true?"

That question was absurd. "You thought I made that up?"

"I..." Riadne bit her lip.

Larzen sat on the sofa by the false princess and turned to her, "Told you."

The redhead glared at him, then smiled at Zora. "Well, you should be pleased to know I did none of those things."

Zora wasn't sure if it was true and just said, "That's... comforting."

Riadne's eyes locked on Zora, as if examining her. "You don't believe me."

"I... does it matter?"

It was Larzen who spoke. "It wasn't Riadne, Zora." He sounded certain, but then who knows if she had used her magic on him. "And you should worry about it because it means it was someone else."

That was in part true. She'd been so focused on the false princess that she hadn't considered it could be someone else. "But who?" she asked.

He paused. "I don't know who it was, but I know who it wasn't. It wasn't an assassin or anyone hired to do that."

Zora didn't understand where this conclusion was coming from. "Why?"

He raised an eyebrow. "Nobody hires incompetent people. It had to be someone overconfident about their own fighting abilities who thought they could take you or at least scare you on their own."

That made some sense. "Maybe. And the dogs? That had to be some magic, right?" She glanced at Riadne, then back at Larzen. "Who do you think it was?"

Riadne shook her head, then turned to Zora. "It wasn't me. I did affect your horse. And locked you in the library. But none of that would have hurt you."

The cursed horse could have hurt her, but she didn't want to bring it up and sound as if she were whining.

The false princess continued, "As you well know, I was involved with someone, you were getting in the way, and I wasn't thrilled about it. But it's all over now and none of that matters."

All that belonged to another reality, a past long gone, and Zora didn't want to remember the parts about false Alegra and Griffin. She took a deep breath. "It's strange how some things can seem so problematic or so important, and then when you look back, you realize you were focusing on a speck of dust in comparison with the big picture." She paused. "But we still don't know what the big picture is."

Larzen had a half nod. "And that's a good reason you two shouldn't hate each other."

"I don't hate her," Zora said, and realized Riadne had said the same thing at the same time.

"I don't hate you," Zora repeated. "But I was wondering... what did you do to Griffin?"

The false princess looked up. "You are going to have to be more specific, because there was a long list, you see?"

Zora went straight to the point. "You can use magic to coerce people into doing what you want, right?"

"Influence. I'd say influence. And it doesn't always work."

"Did you ever use your magic on him?"

It was Larzen who spoke. "There's a lot you don't know, Zora."

Riadne shrugged. "And she might as well hear it. I went to the Gravel castle to fulfill a plan and have the three brothers against each other. It didn't work, but I tried."

It sounded believable, but quite bizarre. "Why?"

She looked down. "A prophecy. Maybe it was stupid. I thought it was the way out of my people's suffering."

That made no sense. "What does one thing have to do with the other?"

"Magic works in strange ways," Riadne said.

"But not that illogical." Zora frowned.

The false princess narrowed her eyes. "You're the magic expert now?"

"No. It's just..." Making people kill each other for a prophecy? She turned to Larzen. "And you don't have a problem with that?"

"Tons of problems, but on the other hand, she has saved Griffin more than once, she was right this last time, and she told me she had given up on that plan, right?" He stared at Riadne.

"Indeed," the false princess replied. She turned to Zora. "So Griffin, well, it was part of a plan at first, but I wasn't the one who took the initiative, mind you. Then I said, all right, why not mix business and some fun? And there you have it. But it's all over. It's as if it happened to two different people. My past self is not my present self. I'd never..." She put an apple slice in her mouth and chewed it.

Zora knew she'd need Riadne's help, but she wanted to understand what had happened. "He said he was confused sometimes, he forgot things. I want to know because we need all the information we can get. Was that you?"

Riadne rolled an apple slice in her fingers. "Well, he came to me saying I was trying to kill you. It was so absurd. And it would ruin my plans." She stared at her own hand. "Yes, I did make him confused. Yes, I made him forget you."

Zora was aghast. "Forget *me*?"

"Well, yes. He didn't think of anything else."

"Cause he didn't want me to compete."

Riadne rolled her eyes. "And you have no idea why? Really? Anyway, it all worked out in the end, so I didn't ruin anything."

Zora's throat was tight. "Nothing worked out. I don't know where he is."

"We'll figure it out. I'm even helping you. So you might want to be my friend."

"I do. And that's why I'm asking. Friends clear out the dirt between them."

Riadne shrugged. "I had nothing against you, you just stood in my way, that was all." She raised a finger. "But I did save you when I didn't have to."

"I know. And I'm thankful." Zora stopped, thinking. "So you're saying you had to make him confused because he thought you sent the assassin, right?"

"Yes."

"But..." The memory hurt, and yet... "That day, in the ruins, I saw your..." She glanced at Larzen, but there was no way not to say it. "I saw your clothes. If he was confused, he couldn't have properly, um, agreed to have his clothes off."

Riadne dropped the apple slice she was holding and glared at Zora. "Oh, gross." She got up. "What are you accusing me of?"

Zora also got up. "I'm asking."

"You're asking things you know nothing about. Nothing. Since you want to know all the details, I'll tell you. Every time we got together, let's say, physically, he was awake, alert, and well aware of what he was doing. If I dare say, he was the one taking the initiative. Now yes, maybe he was confused before, but he wasn't confused then. Did you expect me to remind him that he had this insane idea that I was some kind of murderer? And things happened." Riadne's voice got low, as if she were struggling not to cry. "He knew what he was doing. He was not a young teenager. He was never under my power, never threatened, never fearing for his life or his well-being. You don't know what you're saying, Zora, and it shows. You don't know anything about it."

Riadne ran up the stairs and shut the door to one of the rooms.

Larzen ran after her and knocked, clearly distraught. "Riadne, please, open up."

"Leave me," she yelled from behind the door.

He rested his face on the door. "Not like that, no. You're upset."

"I'm fine." Her voice was quieter now, almost hard to hear from the ground floor. "Just give me some time. Please."

Larzen got back downstairs, sat on the sofa, and rested his head on his hand.

"I was just asking," Zora whispered.

"You'll need her," he whispered back, then raised his head and locked his eyes on the stairs.

Zora sighed. "I know. I just—"

"Wanted to understand what happened," Larzen said. "Of course." He turned to Zora. "I don't agree with everything she's done, but how can we expect the world to get better if we don't give a chance to people who want to walk a better path?"

"Sure." Zora rolled her eyes. "Her remorse is touching."

"Nobody's perfect. You're young enough that maybe you don't have your dark stains, but most of us do."

Zora remembered the potion she'd given to Griffin and how it could have gotten him killed. She looked down. "I made mistakes too. But I regret them."

"We're all different."

"How did you come to work together?"

"Long story." He took a deep breath. "I found out about her plans and locked up her brother and the real Linaria princess. Now we need to go to the castle and free them."

"Oh, no." Zora put a hand over her mouth, worried about the situation in the castle with whatever was happening to Kiran. "And we'll only get there tomorrow."

He nodded. "But I think they're safe. And I didn't have much choice. I thought she could fix Kiran, that she had enchanted him or something and that was why he was acting strange. She kept saying it wasn't her fault. I brought her with me because I didn't trust her. I... wanted to keep an eye on her."

"While you tried to help Griffin." And yet the reason they didn't listen to Larzen was because of Riadne. But then, without her, Larzen wouldn't have known what the cup was really going to do.

He nodded. "What were your plans? Yours and Griffin's? After you got the cup?"

That memory was sweet and painful at the same time. "To keep going to Kentosa. Start a new life. Together." Her throat was dry.

Larzen frowned. "Without supplies, allies, or money? See, that was why I was trying to reach my brother. To help him. Running away like that would be a terrible idea."

His words made no sense. "It wouldn't. We were ready to face hardship; we're not dumb. But it would all be worth it if we were together. I know it would." Zora was surprised that she managed to say all that and not shed a single tear.

Larzen paused and took a long look at her, that strange sadness replacing his usual sly mask. "You truly cared for my brother."

"I *care for* him. And I'm getting him back." She still wasn't sure how she was going to do it, but she had to trust that she could. "Don't talk about him in the past."

He shook his head. "I didn't mean it like that. We'll get him back. I was just thinking about all that happened to him, his problems with my brother. Funny that throughout it all, he had his eyes on you."

Not on Riadne were the words unsaid. And it seemed to matter to Larzen, even if he knew all that the false princess was capable of.

Zora pointed up. "You should try to talk to her again."

"Perhaps *you* should."

She shrugged. "Well, I'm not going to apologize for asking a question. In fact, she's so offended because her answer was not a clear *no*."

"Not a *yes* either. She wasn't using magic to force anyone... You know."

"She was getting him confused, Larzen," she whispered.

"Right. Poor Griffin." He put his hands over his heart. "She must have subjected him to some horrifying ordeal. I can't imagine how much he suffered." His tone was mocking.

"It's not funny."

"No, but we can't change the past. I know that if it weren't for her, Griffin wouldn't have been on the run from my brother. Perhaps Kiran wouldn't have been acting crazy like that. You think I don't know that? But... I think she's trying to make things right, even if she'll never admit she was wrong."

Zora sighed. "And in the end, it didn't matter. Griffin would still try to get the cup. Kiran... I don't know what's happening to him. I made mistakes too, and if he's... not himself, it's my fault. I'm trying to make it right."

"Not your fault, Zora. Too many moving pieces for anyone to claim ownership of destiny."

She sighed, wondering what to reply, when she glanced at the window and saw something moving. A human shadow. And another beside it. A loud bang on the door was followed by a crashing sound. Broken glass flew through the window.

Zora unsheathed Griffin's sword. "I think they'll get in." She turned to Larzen. "Is there a safer place?"

He stared at the window, his jaw clenched. "The cellar."

Zora dashed up the stairs, sword in hand. "Riadne, come out of the room, it's urgent, we need to hide."

Larzen was beside her and pushed the door so hard it broke its lock and opened. Riadne sat on a bed and had red eyes as if she'd been crying. He pulled her hand, and they all went down the stairs, Zora first. A loud bang startled her. It was an exploding ball that went off outside a wall. It must have been a small one, and since the wall was made of stones, it still stood, but eventually the creatures would come in. Larzen opened an iron trapdoor by the kitchen and gestured for them to go in.

Zora said, "You go first."

"You go." He glared at her. "Go!" he yelled. "I'll be fine."

Idiot. But she descended the stairs, hoping he'd come right after them. Instead, the trapdoor closed with a thud, immersing the cellar in darkness.

"Larzen!" Zora yelled. "Come down here." She tried to

push the trapdoor open but heard a loud thud, as if something heavy had been put over it.

That was stupid. If he wanted to play hero, he should at least have taken the sword. And if anyone should have stayed behind, it should have been Zora, who knew how to fight shadow creatures. But even she could do little against that many.

"Larzen!" This time it was Riadne that yelled. "Get down here or I'll go up there and kill you slowly. Larzen!" The false princess then spoke softly, her voice strained, and turned to Zora. "Tell me you can open this trapdoor."

Zora pushed with all her strength. "I... I'm trying." She was afraid her answer would be *no*.

TRIS FROZE. She had heard something about the rivalry between brothers. Something to do with Riadne and whatever she had been planning, but that didn't explain why those guards had gray skin and black eyes without pupils. They wore the green royal guard uniform, but it was like a mockery, as if animals were wearing people's clothes.

"Kill him," the young prince said in a quiet voice.

The false guards advanced, something sharp in their hands. No, it wasn't something they were holding, but their own long, sharp claws. Tris stepped back, hoping somehow they would ignore her, forget her.

Meanwhile, Kiran took a chair and threw it on the creatures, who kept advancing as if he'd thrown feathers on them. He stepped back until he was touching the large window. The creatures and the prince were focused on him, so Tris took the chance to dash to the door.

Right before she left the room, she saw the glass breaking and Kiran falling down, then she heard steps behind her, turned, and threw one of her improvised wooden daggers. The young prince jumped to the floor so that it didn't hit him.

Still down, he yelled, "Kill her!"

Tris dashed as fast as she could down the hallway, then found a door leading to small spiral stairs and slid on the handrail. She opened the door and, based on smell, realized she was near the kitchen. Her mind was whirling. Creatures with gray skin. There were legends.

This kingdom had a mysterious Dark Valley, where it was said that these creatures still roamed. Something must have happened. If the legends were right, these were creatures of darkness and disliked sunlight and fire. She heard steps behind her, turned, and saw two creatures. Her aim had better be good.

She threw two stakes, hit one creature between the eyes, and missed the other. She then threw another stake and hit the other creature in its chest. They slowed down enough for her to get some distance, so she turned around, ran, and entered a kitchen. There were about ten people preparing what was probably going to be dinner.

"Run!" she yelled.

They stopped and eyed her with doubt, surprise, or even pity. Perhaps they thought she was crazy.

Tris pushed one cook away from a lit stove, took a wooden spoon, lit it, and turned just in time to see two creatures coming. There was a cacophony of screams behind her as she threw the spoon on one creature, then took a knife, a real knife, and threw it on the other.

Both creatures disappeared, only the green uniforms falling to the ground as if they'd been surrounding smoke. Her hands were shaking, but she had to keep running.

She grabbed two kitchen knives, and instead of running to the back door, to where the workers were going, she advanced to the door from where she'd come from. She had a guess that it was her that these creatures wanted, and didn't want to risk getting more people entangled in that mess. That, and she doubted she'd be able to run with a bunch of people in front of her.

Two creatures advanced in the hallway. She sent her knives flying, and they disappeared. Just their uniforms proved that they hadn't been some kind of hallucination. That everything wasn't some kind of strange nightmare.

All she wanted to do now was escape. Escape this crazy kingdom, forget about Lukas and whatever strange disease he had, forget about all her plans. Escape, escape with her life. Without realizing it, she'd gone upstairs to her hallway. Idiot. That would bring the creatures after her.

A strong smell of tinctures called her attention. The healer's office. She pushed the door, which was slightly ajar. The man wasn't there. Perhaps he'd run. Perhaps he was looking after some other patient or had already gone home or to his quarters. There were two tables and a wall with wooden shelves from floor to ceiling, with jars, bottles, and some herbs. The man's coat was over a chair. Tris took off her cloak and put on that coat. She also found a flask labeled "lavender" and threw it over herself. She wasn't sure if it would work and wasn't sure if the creatures hunted based on scent. It seemed that they'd been after her.

Of course, she'd been the only witness.

Tris exhaled. If the creatures were after her, she'd gotten them lost downstairs, and now she was doing the best she could to mask her scent. Time to run. Where? She couldn't escape in the night and face those monsters.

She ran to the end of the hall, where a heavy door took her to an antechamber, then a small revolving door took her to a room where a young man lay asleep. Her feet had brought her here even if her mind was telling her to run away. But then, it would be cruel to simply abandon Lukas.

The image of a man she once loved screaming, blood dripping down his face, came to her mind. She couldn't change the past. Couldn't even forget it, as much as she tried. But she could change the future.

Krim was gone. Lukas was here. She didn't love him. She'd never love him. But it was a young man hurting, screaming. Perhaps he'd crossed her path for a reason. Tris held on to her knives, both real and improvised, in her baldric.

Hopefully no creatures would come after her. If they did, she was ready.

7

STRANGE DREAMS

Zora had Griffin's sword in hand. The memory of him gave her the strength to wield the heavy weapon. There were creatures screeching outside, and she still feared one of them would spawn in that dark cellar.

"Larzen!" Riadne shrieked beside her, desperation clear in her voice.

But that prince playing the hero out there made no sense. It made no sense. "Riadne," Zora said. "Larzen doesn't strike me as someone who would sacrifice himself pointlessly and leave us down here locked."

"What is he doing, then?" she sounded as if she were crying.

"I don't know."

A loud thump came from above them, and then the trapdoor opened.

Larzen was there, a dish with a lit candle in his hand.

"You went to get fire?" Riadne asked, sounding incredulous.

"No. Bar the windows," he replied, his voice quiet. "Also put furniture against the doors."

"I could have helped you," Zora offered.

"I don't know. Maybe they're after you. The idea came to me when you were down here." He smiled, glancing at Riadne. "And I didn't take that long, did I?"

Riadne shook her head.

Zora was still worried. "So no creature has come in yet?"

He shook his head. "But they're trying."

Riadne sighed. "Another awful night."

The dim light of the candle illuminated some of that cellar. It had shelves with empty jars on one side, some wine bottles, and an old, dusty sofa on the other.

"We can lie down at least," Zora said. "It's a huge improvement." She had brought her bag and extended her hammock on the floor. "But we should take turns watching."

"I can go first," Larzen said, then turned to Riadne. "You can sleep on the sofa."

She grimaced. "I'm going to sneeze for a month with all that dust there."

"Don't sleep, then." He shrugged.

Zora turned to the other side. The hammock still smelled like her last moments of happiness before everything crumbled. Not last. There would be more. Embraced in the comfort of that scent, she finally surrendered to sleep, eager for the day when that embrace would be real again.

GRIFFIN'S QUARTERS were not the same as Amina's, but were upstairs, in the only tower in that fortress. She had given him the directions on where to go, and now he found himself in a room with glass in its windows. The panes looked as if they'd been attached in an improvised manner, with a rough-looking cement around them. He lay on an enormous round bed. Seriously, it could fit some four people. He wondered if it had ever fit that many people, then tried to think about something else before some dreadful, unwelcome memory came to his mind. But it didn't. In his exhaustion, sleep caught him dressed over the covers.

Strange dreams took him to Gravel. He felt as if he were in its forests, walking, then running, then taking a horse. They weren't his memories, but it was the kind of dream that felt real. He again saw himself drawing circles on the ground around the lake house. There was a point to that, but he didn't understand what it was.

He also heard a woman calling his name. It was as if the wind carried it. "Griffin, Griffin!"

It wasn't Zora. It wasn't anyone he knew. He felt it was important, but had no idea where the voice was even coming from.

At last, he saw his brother, Kiran, unconscious, lying in a pool of blood, with deep cuts on his shoulder. Dead. He looked dead. Griffin sat up, panting.

ZORA WAS WALKING in a desolate landscape, a red sky above her.

"You found it," someone said in a calm voice.

That voice... Zora turned and saw that woman dressed in gold and felt anger turning into heat and rising to her face. "Oh, not you." She ran towards the despicable woman, getting ready to punch her. "You helped me lose Griffin, condemn the kingdom, you guided me to that infamous cave to ruin everything, to make the biggest mistake of my life."

She wanted to punch, hurt, perhaps kill that woman, goddess or not, but found herself falling in a dark, bottomless pit, falling, falling, falling, unable to stop it, unable to save herself

"Zora, Zora."

Someone held her arms. Panting, she woke up, and saw Riadne, of all people, holding her.

"You were having a nightmare," the false princess said.

Zora looked around and realized she was in the dark pantry underneath the lake house. "I'm *still* having a nightmare."

Riadne didn't say anything just let go of her arms, while sitting on the edge of the hammock that had been stretched on the floor. A lonely, almost finishing candle stood at a table, casting the only light in that room, pantry, whatever.

"Is it night?" Zora asked. "The creatures didn't breach into the house?"

"They're silent. It might be day. I don't know what happened upstairs."

Zora sat up, rested her head on her hands, and rubbed her forehead. "We should go."

"Larzen's asleep."

Indeed he lay down in a corner, over a piece of fabric. It was their second uncomfortable night.

"I'm so sorry," Zora said. "So sorry for what I did. I should have waited, I should have learned more... And I had... this voice guiding me. She looked like the Sun Goddess. And that's the funny thing, I don't believe in gods like that. I do believe there's more than just this world, but not in gods or goddesses wearing gold. But she guided me to the entrance of the cave, to the temple... I..."

Riadne sighed. "You can't know what it was or what it meant. Usually what you people describe as this Sun Goddess is our spirit guide, Astrea."

Zora frowned. "Why would she want me to get that cup?"

Riadne thought for a moment. "Perhaps it wasn't her. Perhaps we still don't have the full picture. But you're right that we should get going if we want to reach Gravel City while it's still day."

"You're worried about your brother."

Riadne nodded.

"Sorry for yesterday. For those questions. I..." Zora shook her head. "I wanted to know."

"You were a rival, Zora, and I thought you had made up that story about the assassin. Perhaps I was angry."

Zora couldn't understand that logic. "Why would I make that up?"

"For Griffin's attention."

Zora rolled her eyes so much she was afraid she'd dislocate her eyeballs. "I wouldn't do something stupid like that. And plus, I didn't even like him then. I do like him now, but at that time..." Zora didn't even know how she'd felt at that time. He had been annoying, that was for sure.

"Right. I wonder why you kept gawking at him."

Gawking? "I did not."

"Then it was a wrong impression." The false princess shrugged, but it didn't sound as if she believed Zora.

"Fine. Maybe I did look at him more than necessary, but he's beautiful. Who doesn't stop and stare?"

Riadne glanced at the corner, where Larzen was lying down. "He's handsome too, and you weren't gawking at him."

Yes, sure, Larzen was good looking, and she had always thought so, but he wasn't like Griffin, he wasn't... She didn't even know. "Matter of taste." She then got serious. "But you wanted them to die?"

"I don't even know anything anymore. Right now, all I want is my brother out of that castle, and then if I can find more Solana books, I want that too." She got up. "I'll wake up Larzen."

"Wonder how my screams didn't wake him up."

"Well, it's been a noisy night." Riadne crouched by him. "Larzen."

It wasn't an impression; there was an added softness to her voice when saying his name. And it could be all part of some remaining evil plan. Or not. Zora was putting the hammock in the bag when a sound startled her.

"Larzen!" Riadne yelled from the top of her lungs.

He sat up, panting, then looked at the false princess. "What's wrong with you? Why yell like that?" His voice sounded sleepy and cranky. Well, he probably was.

"I was calling your name and you weren't listening."

"Well, no. I thought I was dreaming." He narrowed his eyes. "You think it's morning?"

Riadne pointed up. "Do you hear anything?"

He frowned. "Of course not. Your yell is still ringing in my ear."

"Oh, sure. How dramatic. The creatures are silent."

He raised an eyebrow. "Perhaps it's an ambush?"

Zora had already put her hammock in her bag, and said, "I can push up the trapdoor and peek."

Larzen yawned, stretched, then pulled a pocket watch. "Six. The sun should be up. Let me do it." He proceeded to the stairs and pushed the trapdoor. "Yes, let's go."

"Careful," Zora warned. "There could be some creatures hiding."

Riadne took his bag and they went up the stairs. The damage hadn't been as bad as Zora had expected. The main door was gone, splinters of wood scattered around the floor.

"A ball must have exploded this," Zora said. Then she felt nauseous. "If they're attacking like that..." She covered her face with her hands. No house would be safe, no village would even be left standing. "There has been a massacre tonight."

"We don't know, Zora, we don't know," Riadne said.

She pointed to the destroyed living room. "Actually, we do."

"This is here. We don't know what's happening elsewhere."

Right at this moment, a human shadow jumped at her from behind the sofa. Zora was about to pull her sword, but Larzen tripped the creature. As daylight reached it, it burned for a second, then disappeared, leaving just some smoke behind it. At least they only survived at night or in dark places. Some small consolation.

As they got out, Zora noticed that the outside of the house had many claw marks, and some black circles, as if balls had exploded there, but without enough force to break the walls.

Zora sighed and looked back. "If the trapdoor hadn't been made of iron, we'd be dead."

"This is a house for the royal family," Larzen said. "There has to be a safe place."

"Oh, really?" Riadne asked. "Why then it doesn't have a decent sofa or bed and it's covered with dust?"

The prince looked back at the house. "We hadn't been here in years." He sighed. "Let's check the horse."

Zora couldn't believe his calm. "You think it survived?"

He seemed surprised. "You think it didn't? We can place a bet, how's that?"

"No!" The thought was dreadful. "I don't want to bet on death. I hope it's unharmed, I just don't think it's likely."

"Didn't you say they didn't attack your chickens?"

"There's a difference, right?"

"We'll see."

Her steps were heavy as they approached the stable. To her relief, there was no dead horse, but then, there was no horse. The door was open and the place was empty.

Larzen turned to Zora. "See? That's what it feels to wake up and find no horses."

"It must have been scared."

"I can get it back." Riadne was looking at Zora as she said it. "I think. But if I succeed, I want you to remember how much I've been helpful."

Zora threw up her arms in frustration. "I know you've been helpful, I know you tried to stop me, I know we should have talked to you when you were here instead of taking your horses. I know all that."

Riadne smiled. "Just don't forget it, then."

She then whistled. Nothing happened. She whistled again. And again.

After a few minutes, Zora thought it was enough. "You do realize it might be too far and can't hear you, right?"

Larzen sighed. "If we walk, we'll make it to Gravel City at nightfall, perhaps even later."

"In which case, we'll definitely not make it," Zora reminded them.

The prince was thoughtful. "There's a village close by."

Riadne crossed her arms. "If you two keep doubting me, I won't get the horse back."

Larzen nodded. "Two truths, but I think you got the causality inverted there."

The redhead closed her eyes, as if exasperated. "Whatever. Do it your way. Evil, evil, incompetent Riadne."

He laughed. "I'm not saying that."

"You don't have to." Riadne started walking fast towards the main road.

This wasn't good. Zora was eager to see if Gravel City had been destroyed, and there were things she wanted from the castle. Not to mention that if they took too long, they'd need to find shelter in a village. That if there was anyone alive and any village standing. And then perhaps there was nobody selling any horses anywhere. She swallowed, debating whether to raise her concerns, but perhaps it was better to wait and see how things would play out.

When they were by the road, their horse came running towards them and stopped by Riadne. She raised an eyebrow and turned to Larzen. "Told you."

The problem was that the cart was back in the stable.

"Wait here," Larzen said. "I'll go fix the cart."

Perhaps Zora should offer to help, but she didn't know much about horses, and to be honest, was still somewhat afraid of those huge animals.

It was strange to be alone with Riadne again, and she didn't want to offend her, so she tried to make small talk. "So you have a brother?"

"Yes. You?"

"I have a sister. In the Dark Valley," she then added.

Riadne looked down. "I used to have a sister too."

"I'm sorry."

The false princess shrugged. "There's a point where you just don't care anymore."

It didn't sound like it. Her voice was almost breaking, her eyes lost, as if she were trying her best to bury her pain. But then, what was the point in allowing pain to surface? Perhaps it had to be buried.

"At least you had a sister and still have a brother. Considering you tend to..." How could she say it? "Die young. It's a miracle that you have newer generations."

Riadne looked at her. "That's because even in the hardest circumstances, even when life seems hopeless, there's that one thing we can't stop doing."

Zora thought for a moment. "Loving."

The false princess frowned, as if confused. "I was going to say something else, but I like your thought."

Zora shook her head. She would have laughed if she weren't so worried and angry.

Soon Larzen got back with the cart. They stepped in, and set off on the road.

They had to hurry, but Zora dreaded reaching the castle. Would the city be destroyed? She wanted to go to Griffin's secret dungeon and get some of his books, try to find some answers, but didn't know if the entrance would still be there. And from there, find a way to reach Rock Island, hoping it would give her even more answers.

It would be so much easier if she had a clear path, a clear obstacle. But then, the cup had been a clear goal, and look how it had turned out. This time she was going after knowledge first, and then action. If she was going to strike, she'd do it with the certainty of victory. Of course, first she had to find that certainty.

The cool wind on her face and the forest air should bring calm and comfort to Riadne, but not now, even if she was on a beautiful road surrounded by tall trees on both sides. Larzen was silent and somewhat distant, perhaps worried. His beautiful blue eyes were focused on the path ahead. He still had some of his playfulness, but there was something heavy behind it. Riadne wished she could do something to cheer him up, but then, considering everything he was going through, he was taking it all relatively well. She just... wished she could reach out to him, console him. For some reason his sadness was wrong, unnatural, and it was hard to bear.

In truth, Riadne was anxious too. She didn't know what to expect at the castle and didn't even want to wonder what was going on with her brother and if he was safe. It had been low of Larzen to lock him up. Well, considering what he'd heard her saying, it made sense. She would have done the same. No, she'd probably have done much, much worse. Larzen had been patient. But then, after that, she had helped him, she had told him she'd given up on her plans, and he still didn't trust her. He never would. It shouldn't matter, but it hurt.

The Dark Valley girl sometimes made Riadne uneasy, with her mistrustful, observant eyes. That said, it was probably hard for her to have found and used the cup, and unwittingly caused all of this. The girl loved her prince, that was a fact. Her prince. Well, Griffin had never been Riadne's, despite fooling himself that he loved her. There had never been any love there. With Zora, it was different.

Riadne felt a small pang of jealousy, and it wasn't for the youngest prince. While he had been kind of fun, it had never been anything special. Perhaps the jealousy was for that kind of love. Which was stupid, as it mostly caused suffering. Zora had felt the taste of love, but then it had become the cruelest pain. The girl tried to bury it, but her agony was like a thick mist around her.

Riadne told herself that destiny had played a hand. Perhaps it hadn't, and there was no such thing as destiny, but trusting it was better than wondering what could have been, since there was no way to go back in time.

They had to move forward, and yet, forward meant going to a castle where the king might well be possessed, forward meant facing the unknown. If only she had gotten that stupid book earlier, if only she'd gone faster. And all the time she'd spent with Griffin and never suspected a thing, never imagined he could be under a curse. And now that she was helping Larzen, it all felt awkward and she wished she had never gotten that close to his brother.

There weren't many people on the road that early in the morning, which was good. But then, depending on what had happened at night, there wouldn't be any people anywhere. That would be terrible. Eventually they crossed someone on a horse, then a cart. It meant that there were people alive, and that was great news. She even felt Zora cheering up beside her. Perhaps it had all been like in Mountain Foot. The Dark Valley girl suggested asking what had happened at night to the people they crossed, but Larzen reminded her that it was better for them to avoid getting any attention.

Another horse-drawn cart approached, and this time, it caught Riadne's attention because the conductor wore a hood. Now that she thought about it, she was starting to think that a hood wasn't a great way to go unnoticed, considering that most conductors didn't wear them. In fact, it was quite conspicuous. She was going to mention it to Larzen, but then she caught the conductor's eye. It was a girl. Not any girl.

"Hey, you!" Riadne yelled.

The girl stopped her cart and pulled back her hood. It was Tris, the real Linaria princess, brown skin and eyes, her magnificent long, wavy black hair shining in the sun. She stared at them with an expression of relief and astonishment.

Riadne didn't wait for her to say anything and asked, "Where's Lukas?"

8

REVELATIONS

After more than a day in that place, Griffin had no clue how come he wasn't hungry. In fact, he'd sensed no smell or seen any indication that there was such a thing as a dining room, and it was odd. Not that he was looking forward to eating whatever these people had.

The first place he went was Amina's quarters, eager to hear what she had to tell him. Anything he could learn would be useful. He still felt uneasy, unsure if someone would realize what he'd done to the explosives, but he figured it wasn't something anyone would notice just by glancing.

Two guards stepped aside as he entered Amina's chambers. She put the baby in the crib, and said softly, "Earlier than expected."

It was still unsettling to see such a human action in a creature like that, with its small gray baby.

"I have a lot to do, and a question. Don't we eat?"

"So you eat in your world."

"You don't?" He made an effort not to raise his voice and alarm the small creature in the crib.

"Your power comes from magic, not food. The dark pits

and prisons feed you. It's the case with the high-ranking nobles in your court. Me too, unfortunately."

"That's... convenient, I guess."

Her gray forehead contracted in what looked like a frown. "You have no idea how we get this power, right?"

"I absolutely do not. But I'm listening, in case you care to explain."

"The Void." Her voice trembled. "The Void powers this kingdom. That's why Grota is invincible."

"Grota?"

"You really don't know anything about us, do you?"

He crossed his arms and sat down. "I was under the impression we'd already established that. Are you just gonna keep asking whether I know things I certainly do not?"

She shook her head and pulled a map. It looked like a big, oval island, divided into three by rivers and some mountains. "We're three kingdoms: Grota, Kayania, and Lorel." Grota was in the middle. "Grota made a deal with the Void a long time ago, and it conquered the others. Life outside here, for the other populations, is... Hard. They're often taken as slaves."

That was horrific. "I'm truly sorry."

"It's not your fault. The overall population in Grota doesn't benefit from it. They're mostly impoverished. There is some unrest, but the king, which you're impersonating, he's invincible. Grota's power is invincible."

"Because of this Void? And what or who is it?"

"It's a person, a creature, a being. It's a he, and hides in a tower, not far from here. I cannot tell you what he looks like, as I've never been there. You will see him soon. King Saros goes to him every six days."

Wait. Six days? That thing definitely had a heart, as Griffin felt it jumping. "This Void... He'll know I'm not him. How many days do I have?"

She paused, thinking. "Three."

Three days. Three. The words barely sank in. "Well, I definitely need to hurry. I even regret sleeping."

"But no. It's your chance. It's an amazing opportunity." Her voice was way too calm for the situation. Well, any voice would be too calm for those circumstances.

It seemed that she thought that Griffin being caught could be good. Oh. He asked, "To kill him?"

"Exactly."

He thought for a moment. "Right. Now, if the king is invincible because of some magical power, I can't imagine what this Void is like."

"You'll need to learn."

"Yeah, plenty of time for that." He paused, then looked at her. "How do you know I'm the Void's enemy?"

"Well... I know you're from the other side. My father's the Lorel king. We've been trying to study Grota for some time. We know that some of their power comes from the connection with your kingdom. It's limited, but it's there. We know that the king always has a curse, a possibility that he could become something other than himself."

Griffin wondered if it was somewhat similar to his own curse. "Do you know if he's had this for some time, if there was a possibility that he would die young?"

"I don't think anything has ever happened to him before. As to dying, Grota's kings tend to live for a long time."

"But he's father dead, isn't he?"

"No. He's joined the Void," she said. "Apparently, they'll live for a long time in that tower. But as far as I know, when they are kings, there's this possibility that they could go to the other side and open the portal from there during the darkest night."

Griffin sucked in a breath. "So this could still happen? Even if the plan with the explosives fails?"

"Yes. That's what the king is supposed to do; go to the

other side and open the connection. But I think a lot of his power, and even the magic allowing him to cross over, it comes from the Void. If you kill him, I assume you'd sever the connection."

"I guess I would die, too."

"Maybe. Maybe you'll be returned to your body. This hasn't happened in so many years, it had been considered a legend, except for those of us who study, who remember."

"How did you come here? Become his wife?"

"I volunteered." She looked down. "I know it sounds strange, but sometimes you just have to do whatever it takes. I came here to bring Grota down from the inside."

"Have you achieved anything?"

She took a deep breath and shrugged. "I'm here. I'm trying. I need to find a way to defeat the Void. Sometimes I think that the kings are greedy and use him to keep their power, but sometimes I think it's the other way around, that they're somehow enslaved, influenced. And now..." She glanced at the crib.

"That's... King Saro's son?"

She nodded. "And my brother was killed, so he's the last heir from Lorel too. It would give the Void access to power from our land. And my son would be under the Void's influence. If I can stop it, I will. No matter what it takes."

Griffin was thinking. "Fine, so you don't know what the Void looks like. What do you know about him?"

"Suffering and pain power him. He makes our kings strong, immune to disease, and able to heal quickly, making them almost immortal. He gives us power, but he's recluse. Only the kings see him."

Griffin was thoughtful. "Maybe he has a weakness he doesn't want anyone to find out."

"I don't know. What I can do is give you an amulet, a magic intensifier, and wish you good luck when you go."

"What happens if I fail? If I die?"

She glanced at the crib again. "King Saro will die too, but his father can return and lead the kingdom for the time being. If he can't do it, the council will nominate someone until little Saro is of age."

"It could create unrest."

She shrugged. "It's not a bad thing. It would be an opportunity for the opposition to gather strength. Who knows?"

"So if I die, it's also good for you?"

"Not great. We'll still need to defeat the Void, but it's not bad either. I mean, not that I want—"

"No. It's fine." He shrugged. "At least if I die I can go with the clear conscience that I'm not dooming a kingdom. And it would prevent King Saro from opening the portal from the other side, so it's good. I just hope whoever opposes Grota keeps fighting and prevents them from ever opening that passage."

"Well, without a powerful king, I don't think they can open that passage."

So Griffin's death could at least give his kingdom some time. Perhaps he'd always been destined to die early. "That's good to know."

She frowned. "You don't really care if you die?"

He shook his head. "I was raised knowing it could happen, and I've accepted it. For a moment I had hope, and love, and life, but it was just a moment. It's gone now." He smiled. "But at least I have nothing to fear."

RIADNE'S HEART was beating fast, seeing the Linaria princess there, on the road, perhaps even on the run.

The girl pointed to the back. "Lukas is here."

Riadne squinted. There was nobody there.

"He's lying in the hay," Tris added.

Riadne jumped out of her cart and stood by the princess. "Is he hurt?"

The girl paused. "Sick. Not hurt."

Riadne's heart was pounding. Sick? It could be poison, it could be anything. And it could be... She closed her eyes.

Larzen said, "Let's get out of the road and talk."

They went to the side of the road, among trees.

Riadne climbed the princess's cart, to take a look at her brother, who was lying down on his stomach, a blanket over him. She removed it and saw his bare back and on it, clear black marks. This was it. Her brother was dying. Riadne sucked in a breath.

She'd accepted it. She'd known it was bound to happen, and yet, it felt too soon. It always happened too soon. It always felt unexpected, even if they knew it would eventually happen.

"Why is he unconscious?" she asked the girl.

"He yells in pain when he's awake. Do you know what he has?" To her credit, at least she managed to look worried.

"Yes." Riadne sighed. "And there's no cure."

Tris put a hand over her mouth. "Oh, no. What is it?"

Zora was by the cart. "Is it his wings?"

How dare she mention it so unceremoniously? "No. It's his death."

"He's sprouting wings," Zora repeated, as if it hadn't been heard the first time. "Right?"

Tris frowned in confusion.

Riadne took a sharp breath. "No. He's sprouting big, dark things that are going to grow inwards and pierce his lungs. Wings are freedom; they let you fly. This is an aberration."

"We could take him to the healer in the castle." Larzen was by her side, and his voice was soft, laced with worry, as if he cared.

"We were there," Tris protested. "The healer was seeing to him, but all he did was give him sedatives or potions for the pain." She looked at Riadne. "I was hoping you'd know what to do."

"You were in the castle?" Larzen asked.

Tris glared at him. "Locked in a room. Where else would I be? Do you happen to know who locked me up there?"

"It was me." His voice was soft, and the confession surprising. "To be honest, I didn't mean to lock you up, I just wanted to imprison Lukas. I heard Riadne's plan and wanted to make sure she didn't do anything... I don't know." Tris widened her eyes, and Larzen looked down. "But you and Lukas were together. What was I going to do?" His voice then became softer. "When did you leave the castle? Do you know what's going on in Gravel City?"

Tris took a deep breath. "Is there something I should know?"

"Shadow creatures," Zora said.

Larzen then added, "Creepy-looking, humanoid—"

"Yes," Tris said. She looked down and took a deep breath. "It was horrible."

"What?" There was urgency and anguish in Larzen's voice.

The Linaria princess looked at Larzen. "Your brother... The youngest prince—"

"Griffin?" Zora asked, and there was no hiding the pain in her voice.

"It's three brothers, right?" The princess asked. "So yes, Griffin. He came in with guards, but they were not guards. They were, I think they were these shadow creatures. And..." She took another deep breath. "I was in the king's office, talking to him, when they came. The king..." She swallowed and glanced at Larzen. "Was attacked and fell down the window."

"Attacked?" Zora asked, as if those words hadn't made sense.

"Yes," Tris replied. "Griffin came in to kill his brother."

Zora looked down, thinking. Larzen's face was still like a mask, but Riadne noticed the pain showing behind it, the way his eyes dimmed. He'd done so much to save his brothers, and now had to see this.

"Maybe he survived?" Riadne asked.

Larzen turned to Tris. "The big window? The one right in front of his door?"

"Yes."

He shook his head. "It's the equivalent of six floors. There's a lower garden, by the basements, beneath it. I don't think..." He closed his eyes.

Riadne put a hand on his shoulder. "Larzen." She had no words. She wanted to say she was sorry, sad, that this was terrible, but what could she say? And she was losing her brother too. But then, the difference was that she'd always known this moment would come with Lukas. Larzen had never expected this, and he certainly hadn't poisoned his parents thinking that his brothers would live so little.

He put a hand over hers and looked down. They shared a moment of silence, a moment of common pain, that hand seeking comfort and comforting at the same time. And then she wished she could hug him and comfort him even more, she wished she could rest her face on his chest and cry for her brother.

Riadne pulled her hand. If she fed these feelings, she'd become vulnerable and weak, and would eventually get hurt, even more hurt than she already was, seeing her brother about to leave this world.

"Was he normal?" Riadne asked the princess.

"Who?"

"Both of them, I guess."

Tris sighed. "The king was very flirty. I know men are flirty, but he was quite... something. And he didn't even know who I was."

"He's normal, then." Riadne rolled her eyes.

Zora nodded.

Larzen was thoughtful. "We don't know. We don't know if and how he was affected and if that was his true normal."

"Maybe. And Griffin?" Zora asked.

Poor girl. It must have been horrible for her to hear about him transformed into someone or something else.

Tris shrugged. "I'd never seen him before. He came with these creatures, told them to kill him, then told them to kill me."

Zora frowned as if confused. "He could talk?"

"Yes," Tris said.

Something caught Riadne's attention. "You said he told the creatures to kill you? In Continental?"

"He did," the princess replied. "And they obeyed."

Zora was thoughtful. "I wonder how many creatures he can control."

Tris shook her head. "I don't know if he can control them, or if they just listen to what he says. I know he wants me dead."

"Because you saw Kiran falling," Larzen said.

"Probably," the princess agreed.

"How did you escape?" he asked.

"I waited until morning, then put Lukas on a blanket, and pulled him. Then I gave some coins to the first attendant I found to help me and not ask questions. I stole this cart and here I am. It sounds much easier than it was."

"Wait," Zora asked. "You said he told the creatures to kill you. How did you survive?"

The princess opened her cloak and showed a strange baldric, where she had sharp pieces of wood. "I know how to throw knives, so I threw these and ran." The girl had some ingenuity and guts. She continued, "The ones who were following me disappeared when they were hit enough times. In the morning, there were no creatures, but I was afraid that the prince would find me."

"He's not the real Griffin," Zora said. And it was true; that was likely the shadow king or something.

Tris shrugged. "Whoever he is, I don't want to cross him."

"We were going to get you out," Larzen said. "I thought you'd be safe in your room."

"Lukas wasn't getting better," the princess said. "So I wanted to secure a carriage to take him home. I thought his people would know what to do." She glanced at Riadne. "The king still thought Lukas was the Linaria crown prince, so I figured that would be worth something. But then..."

Larzen was very grave and looked down. Riadne wanted to put a hand on his shoulder again, let him know he wasn't alone, that she knew how much he was suffering, how much it hurt to hear about his brother's death, but she feared he'd hold her hand again and didn't want to feel that connection anymore.

After some silence, Zora turned to Larzen. "You're the king now."

This wasn't the time to bring it up, but then, the girl had no idea what he was going through.

He exhaled and put a hand over his brows, then turned to Tris. "How was the castle? Were more people attacked? Did you see any houses on the way here? Were they standing?"

"I only know what I saw," Tris said. "But the attendant in the morning was oblivious, so I'm assuming it wasn't that bad."

Zora looked at him. "I... I understand you might have to make sure false Griffin is not controlling the kingdom. Can you just... not hurt him? We don't know what could happen if you do. I'm going to find Rock Island regardless and I'll bring back what I can."

"Hold on." He stretched a hand. "Let's get to the castle and grasp the situation. Then... I'll see what I can do."

"Good luck," Tris said. "I'm taking Lukas back."

"You won't make it," Zora said. "You can't travel at night."

"I still think we should take him to the healer in the castle," Larzen suggested.

"He was there!" Tris yelled. "They thought he was the Linaria prince. You think he wasn't getting the best treatment possible?"

"I know a better healer," Zora said.

Riadne wanted to punch someone. She hated that they were still pretending this was some silly disease, still trying to find a solution, still trying to fan the hope that she'd buried a long time before.

"You don't understand, do you?" She glared at the Dark Valley girl. "There's nothing, nothing, nothing that can be done. We're not stupid, we're not incompetent. If a healer could fix our ingrowing wings, it would have been done before."

"So they *are* wings," Larzen said.

"They should be. But they're not!" Riadne yelled.

"Riadne, listen," Zora said. "I went back to the Dark Valley, and I had an arrow wound. My parents treated it. Griffin said it was the fastest cure he'd ever seen, and that I would never have healed so fast in the castle."

Riadne shrugged. "He could have been trying to flatter you."

"He's not the flattering type!" Zora protested. She looked at Riadne and Larzen. "And I bet you both know it. If he said my parents are better than the healer in the castle, he meant it, and it means that's her brother's best chance."

Riadne was making up her mind as to who she wanted to

punch, and rolled her eyes. "So they're better than generations of Solanas."

"Well, we have potions, you don't," Zora said.

Riadne paused. That was true.

The girl continued, "Perhaps it's old knowledge, from the
time before the Dark Valley was created, from the time when
your people could still fly."

Riadne looked down. Hope led to disappointment.
"Maybe."

"So we could try," Zora said.

She sighed. "Yes, but we have a kingdom crisis to deal
with, you need to find some magic answers to get your prince
back, and…"

Larzen's expression was calm. "Let's get to Gravel city, see
what happens, then I can hire someone to take Lukas to the
Dark Valley. It's worth a shot. Anything to try to save at least
one brother."

Tris looked down. "So you're taking him back? I need to
escape."

"Come with us to Gravel city," Larzen said.

Riadne didn't understand why he was suggesting that.

The princess scoffed. "Where they're trying to kill me?"

"We'll avoid the castle and guards," he said. "I know my
way. I know a place where we can hide and rest. Then we can
plan, and I'll help you escape properly, not alone like that,
risking being on a road at night when shadow creatures can
attack you. I won't have you returned to Linaria as a fugitive."

Tris narrowed her eyes. "Pretty words for someone who
locked me in a room."

"A comfortable room. And circumstances were different
then."

The princess sighed. "I don't think I have much of a
choice."

Riadne remembered Larzen telling her that he'd been

manipulating Zora because he was interested in a princess from a kingdom of gold, the princess she'd been pretending to be. Now that the real, gorgeous Linaria princess was here, Riadne wondered about Larzen's motivations. No. What was there to wonder?

She felt as if the fruit she'd eaten was revolving in her stomach. Stupid feeling. Larzen was a prince, no, a king, and would obviously do whatever was necessary for his kingdom. And Riadne had absolutely nothing to do with it. And didn't care. At all.

They set off to Gravel city, Larzen guiding the cart the princess had brought. Tris lay on the back, to keep watch over Lukas and because she was exhausted from a poorly slept night.

Behind them, Riadne traveled with Zora. It was a weird choice, but the girl wasn't good with horses or carts, and Larzen had suggested they travel together so as not to be alone. Perhaps he wanted them to start bonding or something, but they rode in silence.

Riadne was stressed and plus she didn't think Zora's idea to take Lukas to the Dark Valley would work. It would be wonderful if it did, of course, but Riadne had lived through too many disappointments to allow herself to be fooled. She just hoped nobody let him suffer more than necessary out of a misplaced hope that there could be a way out. Riadne would need to go to the Dark Valley and talk to them, before trying to reach this mysterious Rock Island. Larzen would probably stay in his kingdom, dealing with his *kinging*. Perhaps it had always been his destiny. But it all felt weird, uncomfortable, and unreal.

9

UNEXPECTED MEETINGS

Anxiety gnawed on Zora as they approached Gravel City, dreading facing death and destruction. But they didn't get to the city and instead left the road, then took a path in the forest, going around the castle. Larzen indeed knew his way very well and assured they wouldn't be spotted by city guards.

Zora was still trying to grapple with the thought that Kiran was probably dead. She felt bad for Larzen—and Griffin—but didn't feel sad that the king had died, and was wondering if she was a horrible person. He'd been responsible for some of the worst moments in her life, when she'd seen Griffin almost getting killed in that arena, and when she'd been locked in that room. Perhaps it hadn't all been his fault. Still, her main feeling was relief that she wouldn't need to fear the king and his craziness.

The top of the castle and some city buildings came into view at a distance, as they reached some fields by it, close to where Zora had practiced once.

Larzen eventually stopped in front of a decrepit wooden

shack. The windows had broken glasses, with missing panes here and there, and part of the roof was collapsed.

"Charming," Zora said to Riadne, just because there was nobody else to share her impression with. Riadne shrugged and grinned.

If this was the safe place Larzen had been planning for them, he was nuts. No way this house would withstand the night. Withstand the night. She still had no idea how the city had fared.

Larzen got out of his cart and approached Zora and Riadne. "It looks like you don't like my lovely shelter."

"Of course I do." Zora smiled. "Didn't I just say it was charming?"

Larzen nodded. "Bucolic, right? Like part of a painting." He was joking but there was some strain in his voice.

Her voice probably wasn't any better. It was hard to forget everything that was happening, forget the fact that Griffin was gone, but perhaps what mattered was the effort to keep going.

There was a barn across the shack, which was also decrepit, but it was bigger than it looked, and the horses and cart fit in it. Depending on the state of the shack, Zora would suggest switching places with the horses and sleeping here. Well, no, they needed solid doors and walls. Not that the house had any. Was Larzen going insane too?

When they entered the shack, Zora was stunned. It was the complete opposite of the outside. The walls were made of solid stone and light came from a window in the ceiling. This house was almost as big as the lake house, with a large living room and three doors, which she assumed were for a kitchen and two bedrooms. There were purple sofas, and the walls had many paintings, mostly purple. The middle of the room had a fluffy purple rug. It was all very sophisticated, glamorous, or perhaps just kitsch. At least Zora was glad to be in a place where she could rest, even if she wasn't sure what would happen at night. The entrance door was made from thick metal, and would probably withstand the creatures, but she wondered how thick those walls were.

Larzen came in carrying Lukas, who was awake and moaning in pain. Poor guy. He was laid down on one of the sofas and Tris sat by him.

He then turned to Zora and Riadne. "Charming, right?"

"More than charming," Zora had to admit. "But how can this be the shabby shack we saw from the outside?"

"The wooden house is a structure built outside this one." He smiled. "What's the point in a secret house if it's going to call attention?"

"But it's bigger than it looks."

He cocked his head. "Just an illusion. The windows outside are oversized and give that impression."

Riadne was also taking a look at the house. "So you have a secret dungeon, secret rooms, and now a secret house."

"Perhaps I like secrets." Larzen smirked, then looked back at Riadne's brother and his expression darkened. "I'll put him on the bed."

"No," Riadne said. "He's calm now. Better leave him."

Tris was sitting by him and nodded in agreement.

Larzen also nodded, then opened a door leading to a room with a large bed and dark red walls. "This is the only bed in the house. If anyone wants to rest while I'm gone."

Riadne narrowed her eyes. "You think we're going to be sitting around, or rather, lying around waiting?"

He took a deep breath. "I hope so. I don't know what exactly is happening in the castle and I'd rather nobody risked their lives unnecessarily."

The false princess put her hands on her hips. "Must I remind you, I'm the one who's been saving people here?"

That was true.

He shook his head. "I'll go in and out. Just to check what's going on, get some supplies. Then I'll plan my next move. Stay with your brother."

Riadne rolled her eyes. "Sure. He might dream of me."

Zora didn't plan on sitting in the house either. "I also need to go to the castle," she said. "I need to fetch some things in Griffin's basement." She was thinking about his rare books, maybe even some magical objects. Perhaps Riadne could make sense of them.

Larzen frowned. "They'll find you, Zora."

"There's a secret passage. And... a secret room," she explained.

"Looks like secrets run in the family," Riadne said.

Larzen stared at the false princess and snorted. "As if you didn't know about his—"

"She didn't," Zora interrupted. "Nobody knew about it. Other than him."

"And you think you'll find answers there?" Larzen asked.

"I don't know. But it's worth a try." She then glanced at the open bedroom door and something called her attention. "Why is there a mirror on the ceiling?"

Larzen paused, then blurted, "Nightmares." He paused again. "Imagine you have a dreadful nightmare, one of those where you think you're somewhere else and something awful is happening, then you wake up terrified. You'll see yourself on the bed and know it was just a dream."

"Oh." Zora had never heard of anything like that. "Interesting. But I think I'd be so afraid that the mirror would fall on me, I wouldn't even dare move on the bed."

Larzen raised an eyebrow. "Well, that would definitely be a problem."

Riadne snorted a laugh. Zora usually felt silly or suspicious when people laughed at something she didn't understand, but their mood had been heavy since the news of

Kiran's death, and a bit of laughter was welcome. Even if it was at Zora's expense, which kind of sucked.

"So tell me, Larzen." Riadne had a mocking voice. "How often did you have *nightmares* here?"

Zora had an inkling that she wasn't talking about bad dreams.

"Lovely." He smiled. "We're already confessing all our secrets? I haven't heard yours."

"You have," Riadne said. "You know my worst secrets."

He looked at her, as if thinking for a moment, then raised a finger. "First, I don't owe anyone any satisfaction about when or how often I *have nightmares*. Second... Not really second, but... I don't mind telling. I haven't been here in over a year, and even before that, I used this house very rarely. One of those things you think is going to be useful, but ends up not being the case."

"Glad to hear you've been sleeping well," Riadne said, still in a mocking voice.

"I was. Before it all happened." His voice was tight.

Zora looked down. There had been a *before*, when all she'd wanted was to win the Blood Cup, even if she had no idea what it was, when Griffin had been himself, free, a prince. His smile came to her mind, that smile she had always thought was fascinating and magnificent, even before getting to know him. And that was why she had to find as much information as she could, as fast as she could, and find a way to get him back. Not a way. The right way. She wasn't going to make any mistakes again.

"I'll make it right," Zora said, surprised to hear true confidence in her voice.

"I'll help you," Larzen said.

Zora was stunned. "Even to Rock Island?"

He sighed. "If that's where you need to go, I'll help you, but let's... let me see what's happening first."

Then Riadne said, "And I guess I'll save your asses when it all goes rotten."

Larzen turned to her. "I hope you stick around, then. Who wants a rotten ass?"

"Exactly." Riadne smiled. "That's why I'll go with you to the castle."

He raised an eyebrow. "Because of my ass?"

She smirked. "Can't help it. It's just that appealing." She then turned to Zora. "It's a joke."

"I'm not saying anything." Well, Zora was wondering how much these two were flirting and if Riadne's plan was indeed to seduce the three brothers, but she didn't think she'd been grimacing or anything.

Riadne shrugged. "*I'm* saying. I don't want people thinking I'm flirting when I'm obviously not."

"Nobody said anything about flirting." Larzen pointed at her. "You're the one thinking about it."

There was something sweet about seeing these two teasing each other, and sad, too, as it reminded Zora about what she had lost. And then there were some creepy possibilities, as she still didn't trust Riadne, but Zora had more important things to do. "I have to get going. I'll leave first, if you don't mind, since we're going separate ways."

"That makes sense," Larzen said. "Can you cover your hair?"

"I have a wig." She looked inside her bag and her heart tightened. "There's another one." She handed it to Larzen. "Maybe you should take it."

He took it, adjusted it in the mirror, then turned to Riadne and Zora. "Unrecognizable, right?"

Riadne snorted. "Right. With your eyes bright like two beacons, hair isn't going to make a difference. I could recognize you among a thousand people."

Did she realize what she'd just said? It could fit in a bad love poem.

Larzen paused for a moment, as if to catch his breath, then smiled. "Such a great visual memory. Not everyone's like you."

Riadne shrugged. "Can't help it."

Zora, for her turn, thought about Griffin wearing that wig, how it was then that she had started to really trust him. And started to like him. She hung on to the image of them together, a future that had to be possible. Hope. Hope was part of the fuel that kept her fire, and she had to keep it burning.

LARZEN WAS in the area behind the castle, away from the city. The secret entrance he had chosen was the safest one, and yet Riadne was going to learn about it. But then, as much as he could come up with good arguments as to why it would be a bad idea for her to see it, he wasn't that worried about her. Perhaps he was coming to trust her. Still, he wished he were alone, but for different reasons. One person was always easier to slip by and make a quick run. On the other hand, it was also true that her powers could eventually help him in a tough situation.

His heart was beating fast, perhaps with the faint hope that Kiran would still be alive. Many of the words he'd never said to his brother circled his mind. Larzen had loved and admired his older brother, and yet, why was it that he'd never shown it properly? And yet he still cringed thinking about his brother's actions in the previous days, unsure if it had something to do with this Shadow Kingdom and a possible curse.

Riadne was the only person who knew what Larzen had sacrificed to keep his brothers alive. It felt like yesterday that he'd given his parents the poison destined for Kiran and Griffin. The idea that it would all be for nothing was crushing him. There could still be some hope for his youngest brother. Maybe. But if Kiran was dead, then this was it.

They were in a tunnel to the castle, dark gray walls illuminated only by the orange fire of his torch, when Riadne touched his arm, her delicate hand sending shivers through his body.

"Are you sure about this?" she asked.

It was a little late for that question. "Why do you think I'm here?"

She shook her head. "Couldn't you send some spies first, gather some information? I don't like it, Larzen." Her voice quivered, and her eyes were wide, luminous as they reflected the fire. It was odd to see her afraid.

"You can wait here."

She exhaled a sharp breath and put her hands on her waist. "That's worse!"

He sighed, then decided to explain why he was rushing into the castle like that. "Gathering information is tricky when I'm not sure who's still an ally, and it takes precious time that we don't have. I'll stick to secret passages; I know what I'm doing."

"Let's hope that's the case. I still don't like it."

For some reason he wanted to put his hands on her shoulders and kiss her forehead, telling her that it was all right. It obviously made no sense considering they weren't anything. Not even friends. Too much lack of sleep, that was his problem.

They reached the inner hidden hallways in the castle.

"Shadow creatures could hide here," Riadne said. "You know that, right?"

"They'd need to get inside these passages first, and I don't think they know how to."

He was regretting having agreed to bring Riadne. It wasn't as if he needed to add any more worries to his list.

When he got to the passage to his bedroom, he observed it through the back of the mirror. It was empty, and the door closed. He had feared that there would be guards or even shadow creatures waiting for him, but it wasn't the case.

This was good; he'd be able to reach his safe. After that, he'd need to check the meeting room and the healer's office to see what he could learn. Probably not a lot, but it was a start. Then he'd need to decide what he was going to do.

The way into his room was a crawl space in a cabinet. It felt odd to enter the castle as if he were an intruder. Well, that was what his younger brother must have felt a few days before.

He listened again, heard nothing, then went in. His plan was to be fast and silent. Riadne was right behind him—about to learn more of his secrets. Eventually he'd need to stop and think why he was allowing her to have so much information. Eventually. Now he didn't have much time to think about it.

His safe was inside what looked like a vase, but with a false bottom. He turned it, pulled it open, then took all the money from there and a few other important objects. By the Kingdom, he'd need to find another place for all that. The house had a safe too. Perhaps he'd put some of it there.

He turned to leave. Riadne was by the cabinet with the entrance, her face still tense, until her eyes met his. Her frown was gone, and he couldn't hold back the smile, especially when she returned it. And it wasn't a sarcastic or cold smile, it was rather soft, innocent even. Riadne was always beautiful, but that sweet expression made his heart jump.

Right then, he heard a sound behind him, and turned to see a guard stepping from behind an armchair, and three more entering through the door, pointing their swords at him. They were not any guards. One of them was Irene, the commander Griffin had raised from nothing. She was a good fighter, and had three more guards with her, two female and one male. Larzen was outnumbered, and the only weapon he had was his dagger.

He turned back to Riadne and felt heat rising up to his head. Two male guards held her, and she was gagged with a strip of cloth that had something in her mouth. Her eyes were wide with fear, and she mumbled and tried to wiggle free, but the guards held her tight. Her strength had never been in fighting.

Irene was unlikely to be bribed, so he had to find another solution.

Larzen raised his hands. "Stand down. I'm unarmed and I'm still your prince."

The woman sneered. "You're not *my* prince, vermin."

He inferred that Irene was quite angry. Still, he tried. "There are some things you don't know."

She narrowed her eyes. "Let me guess. You're going to say Griffin is not really Griffin."

He nodded. "Competent and well informed, as always. No. Really, he killed or tried to kill Kiran, and—"

"*You* tried to kill him. Griffin saved him."

Larzen exhaled, relief washing over him. "He's alive?"

"Sad?" She turned to a dark-skinned guard. "Isabelle, shackle him."

The girl moved in his direction, manacles in hand.

Larzen still had his hands up. "We can talk. I'm unarmed. And I'll go where you want. There's no need for chains."

They pretended he hadn't said anything. A glance told him that they were about to shackle Riadne too. She shouldn't have come. Now if something happened to her, it would be his fault. Larzen had to think, think faster than ever. He didn't know if he wanted to hurt these guards, but the biggest problem was that he didn't even think he'd be able to. Unable to fight or talk his way out of this, he'd need to find another solution. In less than one second.

THE SECRET ENTRANCE to Griffin's dungeon was in a back alley in the city, and she found it by going back the way she had left in what felt like an eternity before.

As Zora passed through a small street, every muscle in her body relaxed. There were people going about their routines as if nothing had happened. Buildings were still standing; they hadn't been destroyed like the lake house. She'd been a lot more scared than she realized. Horrible images of destruction and death had been circling her mind, and so far there had been none of it. She felt her eyes burning with tears of relief, but she didn't want to cry. If tears of relief turned into tears of sadness she had no idea how she'd keep herself together. But she was glad to see the city alive, normal, glad to know that the destruction she'd caused hadn't been as horrific as she had feared.

Hopefully no guards would be looking for her anymore, but she couldn't be sure. Head down, with a dark brown wig, she hoped nobody would recognize her. She opened a wooden door leading to an abandoned house, then, downstairs, opened another door, which led to a tunnel. Thank the Light that she still had the key. Perhaps she should be thankful that she'd only lost her sword, not her bags.

The floor of the tunnel was compact earth, and the walls were rough stone, with a damp and somewhat moldy smell that strangely felt comforting, as it reminded her the last time she'd been here. When she reached the final door before Griffin's dungeon, she took a deep breath. Weird how she needed courage to face the reminder of good memories, as if they could trigger the trauma of their loss. After pushing the door slowly, she found everything the way they had left a week before. So nobody had been there.

Zora glanced at the bed and remembered how she'd been afraid of Griffin, perhaps not afraid of him, but afraid of what was going on between them, afraid of where it might have led her. Such ridiculous fears, now that she looked back. She moved to the corner shelves, picking the books that she thought would be useful. There were no books with Solana writing though, and that meant that Griffin had read everything that was in here. But then, it was one thing reading these books before, when they didn't know as much. Perhaps there would be something there she could use. Not very likely. Why had she decided to come here?

The truth basin was on the table. It was about the size of a small plate. Could she bring it with her? Or maybe she should use it. Was it the reason she had come?

Beside the basin, there was some empty space on the table, where she had enchanted Griffin's sword, Thunder. Somehow she could imagine a younger version of him with that huge sword giving it what sounded like a powerful name. So Griffin.

She had put so much feeling in that enchantment, hoping that the sword would hit true and remain strong and sharp. Her idea had been to protect him. Well, her plan now was to use this sword to get him back. She laid it there, then took her ingredients, plus a couple feathers to make it lighter. As much as she had gotten used to its weight on her back, she didn't want it to impact her fighting. This sword was for Griffin, and she was going to save him—or at least avenge him. No, she was going to save him. The visions had to be true.

The ingredients were being absorbed when she heard steps on the stairs, picked up the sword, and turned.

Zora trembled and had to focus on her grip, as she almost dropped Thunder.

In front of her was Griffin, and yet not Griffin. It was the same beautiful face, the same shiny dark hair, but there was a coldness in his eyes that gave her chills.

10

ABOUT THE PORTAL

Zora stared at that strange thing, or creature, wearing Griffin's face. Griffin's body. How dare he?

"Put that toy down," false Griffin said. "You don't want to hurt this," he pointed at himself, "do you?"

It was so horrible to hear Griffin's voice and not his voice. She was so angry. "I want to rip your heart out like you did to me, and if I have to kill Griffin, so be it."

"Your heart is still beating. And we can be allies. We want the same thing."

"You tried to kill me."

He looked away, and then back at her, as if impatient. His face was still beautiful, which made her even angrier.

"The transition is disorienting," he said. "I wasn't really myself. The fact that you're standing there should be proof enough of that."

"What do you want?" she snarled, still pointing Thunder at him.

"I want my body back, the same way you want this body back."

Zora paused. Could he be saying the truth? She couldn't

hide the eagerness in her voice. "There's a way to reverse it? To get Griffin back?"

"See? We want the same thing."

"How?"

"He'll find you—"

"He's here? Is he one of the creatures?" She felt her eyes stinging. It couldn't be possible. Perhaps it was some strange joke.

"He's not here. Yet. But things will change. You'll know when they do. He won't look like himself, but I believe he'll look for you."

Griffin here, looking for her. That was almost too much to ask. But she couldn't trust this shadow king, and she had to know what he wanted. "And then?"

"Bring him to me. If both of us step into the portal at the same time and agree to undo this," he pointed at himself, revulsion clear in his face, "we'll be reversed."

It sounded too easy, and maybe it was a trick. Maybe all he wanted to do was kill Griffin.

She tried not to sound suspicious and keep the eagerness in her voice. "Really? That's it? And where's this portal?"

"You'll learn about it soon."

Cold dread took over her, but she smiled to cover up her feelings. "What's going to happen?"

"A surprise."

Probably a horrendous surprise, and she couldn't figure what could be worse than what was already happening. "But would you really want to get your body back? You'd no longer be a prince."

"I'm still a king, and so will be your lover."

"In Gravel? Isn't Kiran the king?" Unless he was dead. But she couldn't reveal that she knew that.

He waved a hand. "Gone. Now it's just one more to go. Easy, right?"

So Kiran was indeed dead. Her heart was beating fast, but she tried to sound happy about the news. "Really? Kiran's dead? I won't have to fear him anymore?"

"I threw the body in the King's River. He isn't coming back."

Keeping her voice sweet took a lot of effort. "That's great. And I guess Larzen's next? So Griffin will be king?"

"I have no intention of sharing my plans with you." His tone was drier this time, and he glared at her with a coldness that again chilled her to her bones.

Still, she had to learn as much as she could, and smiled. "Right. Of course. I'll do my best to bring Griffin to you, but... Not that I'm doubting you, but how can I know you won't hurt him?"

False Griffin looked at her as if she were stupid. "That's easy. He has my body."

"Right." It made sense. She risked one more question. "And the creatures... do you control them?"

His eyes were narrowed and his nose crinkled in disgust. He managed to make Griffin's face almost ugly. "Go or I'll change my mind and kill you too. There are other ways of securing my body without your help."

She pretended not to have noticed his threat. "I understand, and I'm leaving. I'll bring you Griffin once whatever needs to happen happens."

Zora was trembling as she grabbed the basin of truth and the jar with the black liquid and stuck them in her bag. That king made it clear he was no longer going to answer her questions, and she still had no clue how he knew so much, including the entrance to this basement and the name of a river. Perhaps he'd been spying on Griffin while still not possessing him. Then she wondered about what was going to happen, but it was indeed best to leave.

Zora opened the door to the tunnel and waved. "See you later."

False Griffin nodded. She walked, then ran away as fast as she could.

ALL RIGHT. It was time for a quick decision. If Larzen were caught, he doubted he'd survive this day. And he didn't even want to wonder what the Griffin impostor would do to Riadne, who didn't deserve to suffer for any of this.

The guard named Isabelle approached him while two more guards had swords drawn.

If he made a mistake, he'd be doomed, but there wasn't much point in fearing it because if he didn't try anything, he'd be doomed regardless. Larzen pushed Isabelle while at the same time drawing his dagger. He turned, giving his back to the guards. Hopefully the movement was unexpected enough that they'd take precious seconds to react. Larzen reached Riadne, and while one of the guards who had been holding her pointed his sword at him, he cut the cloth around her mouth in one swift stroke, and understanding sparked in her eyes.

That awful sound of Riadne singing reached his ears, but it didn't seem as if it had an immediate effect. A guard pushed him, and he was starting to think he'd need to find a miraculous way to fight six people at once, when they stopped.

Riadne paused her singing and addressed the guards. "You're confused. There was nobody here, it was just an impression."

She then sang again, as the guards left the room. Riadne and Larzen entered the secret passage through the crawl space, but he made sure to bar it from the outside.

They were in the tunnel when Riadne finally spoke. "So, happy you brought me?"

"Your company is always appreciated. Not sure why you ask."

She grimaced. "Perhaps because you didn't want me to come with you."

"Past me was foolish."

GRIFFIN WALKED towards the balcony of the fortress. For his personal guard, he had added the two men appointed by Amina, but he couldn't get rid of his regular ones. Well, at least he was well protected, which was exaggerated, if he was invincible or almost immortal. Well, he wasn't going to change things.

The red sky was disorienting. There was a sun, but its light was diffused, as if it had been covered by a thick, red blanket. But time passed in day and night cycles, and it was afternoon now.

The soldiers in the valley below stood in formation to march through the arc, the portal. Griffin had studied military strategy, but had never seen anything like that. Gravel was peaceful and had mountains separating it from the rest of the continent, so it had never faced a real war against other kingdoms. He had never thought he'd see troops like that, and in fact, had never wanted to see that.

The tension in the valley below was palpable. Of course the men were afraid to march into unknown territory. And yet they had no idea what the real plan was, how they were meant to be sacrificed. Griffin didn't even know if this body had a stomach, but he felt it turning. This was a reminder that he didn't know much about their anatomy and how to kill them. And what about this Void? He had no clue what he even looked like.

Before going to the Void Tower, he was going to try to find and sabotage these dark pits, and do everything he could to help Gravel gain time, hoping that one day a final solution could be found.

So much to do. So little time. Far in the distance, on the platform in the mountain by the valley, he spotted what he thought were some members of the council and many guards. The lever to pull the nets was huge, and looked as if it would take several people to pull it. His heart was beating fast, unsure if his sabotage was going to work, unsure about what could happen if he were discovered. And yet he could do nothing but stand on this balcony and hope his plan didn't fail.

As he stood and waited, a jolt of pain rattled his entire body. He clenched his fists to prevent any strange movement. Pain, so much pain that he wanted to collapse and yell and cry, but he stood. The pain was just physical. There were worse pains. Then an image came to his mind. Zora. Zora in his basement, wearing the same wig they had worn when they escaped the castle. That was a worse pain, and everything together made it unbearable.

But there was something different about her. Was it his memory? Well, she was enchanting Thunder, doing her strange magic that somehow affected the sword's blade. He remembered that, and yet, there was something about this image, something, something... So much pain, and if he only let go of the vision, it would stop, but he couldn't let go.

Zora turned, but her eyes were different, so different that she didn't look like his Zora. There was hate in that look, hate that he'd never seen before. Griffin understood. He was accessing a vision from King Saro.

It meant... Zora was alive? She'd survived the attack in the caves? But this vision then became agonizing, as she was in terrible danger and he couldn't do anything to help her.

Then suddenly his point-of-view changed, and he could look at the scene as an outsider. Zora was speaking to the impostor, but she knew that he wasn't him. He told her that Griffin could get his body back. Her eyes changed, a glimmer of hope in them. No, he could be tricking her. But what if it was true? It sounded true.

So there was a way for Griffin to get his life back, his body back, his Zora back. There was a way. There was hope. But that meant opening the portal and letting this kingdom invade Gravel. Opening the portal, which was what he was trying to avoid right now. It could ruin the kingdom, but it could give him his life and his dreams back. Griffin knew what the right thing to do was, but it didn't make it hurt any less. Knowing there was a way, and at the same time knowing it would be wrong, was tortuous. But there was something to be glad in all that. Zora. She was alive. Saving Gravel meant saving her, and if he could find a way to end the suffering in the kingdom, in her Dark Valley, she would still be alive to see it. It was worth it. It made it all worth it.

A loud clack startled him. "Please roll to the gates," he mentally pleaded to the exploding balls. He didn't want that portal to be powered, Gravel to be invaded, he wanted to make sure everyone there was safe, or at least as safe as they could be for now. And he would keep fighting and do whatever he could.

The lever had been lifted. But nothing happened. Perhaps something was stuck. That was good. It meant the balls were not rolling to the valley. So far.

Then something snapped. The balls were about to roll. The question was: in which direction?

ZORA WAS STARTLED and shaking when she stepped into the streets of Gravel city again. But at the same time, she was relieved. It was possible to get Griffin back! Not only that, it was also what that king wanted. That part seemed to be true, considering the way he had been sneering and looking disgusted. Perhaps his plan was to kill Griffin afterwards, but it meant Griffin was alive somewhere. It meant that her hope wasn't pointless. Far from pointless; there was a way to bring him back.

That false Griffin had mentioned a portal and she wondered where it was. Could it be that more creatures were coming? That things would somehow get worse? That part she didn't like. And he was a king, he'd told her so, and had sounded sincere. Perhaps even the Shadow King, but she would wait for him to be back in his body to rip out his heart.

And Kiran was dead for sure. She still didn't feel bad about it or had any sympathy for the former king, but his death made her wonder what false Griffin's plans were. No, there was nothing to wonder. He'd said Griffin would be king, and all it took was one more, probably meaning one more death. Larzen was in danger. Oh, no, and in the castle or headed to it right now.

But Zora couldn't do anything about it; she didn't even know the entrance Larzen had used. Hopefully Riadne would protect him. What a bizarre thought.

As she headed to a small alley that would lead her outside the city, Zora looked back, wondering if she'd been followed. That false Griffin had been too nice and let her go too easily. Could it be that he thought—correctly—that she could lead him to Larzen?

In theory nobody was after her, and she had a wig, but she went in the opposite direction she had to go, just in case. Hopefully she wouldn't get lost. She found herself in a narrow street with houses stuck together as if they were just one building. In the distance, she saw an extremely tall man. Not only tall but also bald and muscular. She knew who it was; Mauro, the Marshes champion, who'd been a good friend to her during the Royal Games.

She debated mentally whether to talk to him or pretend she hadn't seen him, not that she disliked Mauro, but she didn't want anyone inquiring too much about what was going on. While she thought, a sight caught her eye. It was a poster with drawings of Riadne, Tris, and Larzen. The title said: *wanted for treason.* Then, below, in smaller letters, it claimed that Larzen and two "witches" had attempted against Kiran's life, and, by using dark magic, had unleashed creatures in the kingdom. The reward for bringing Larzen in was five-hundred thousand crowns, and the prize for the "witches" was fifty-thousand. That was a lot of money as far as Zora knew.

Larzen would have a hard time leaving this city, or even getting back to his safe house, unless he could somehow challenge false Griffin and get support. But how?

"Zora!" a voice broke her thoughts.

She turned and saw Mauro walking towards her. Unlike during the Royal Games, he was wearing an eyepatch, covering his missing eye, and he didn't look as menacing. Perhaps it had been a strategy then. His head was entirely shaved, like before.

"I thought you'd be back," he said. "How are you?"

"I'm... good?" She smiled and tried to sound casual. "And you? What brought you back here?"

"Came to visit." He frowned, as if worried. "Did something happen?"

"No, why?" She tried another smile.

"I saw that Prince Griffin was back and I thought you'd be with him. But..." He paused. "I guess you're not."

"I'm not." She felt guilty for not telling him the truth.

"I'm sorry, Zora." He sounded genuinely sad. "If something serious happened, you'll find someone better. Broken hearts hurt but heal. But if it was something small... For what it's worth, he was always trying to protect you during the games."

It was surprising that he knew that they were involved. Or maybe it had been obvious and Zora had just been really slow to catch up. "I know."

"I hope you'll work it out, then." He smiled. "Storms are just clouds. The wind soon carries them away."

This time Zora didn't have to force a smile. "I missed your sayings."

"They're not mine." He then pointed at the poster, showing Larzen, Tris, and Riadne. "Do you think it's true?"

Zora shook her head slightly.

He sighed. "There's something big happening. I was hoping maybe you'd know what it is."

She shrugged.

He looked around and then whispered, "I dreamed about a red sky and an army marching on us. That's why I'm here. I want to help the kingdom. Did you know six guards were killed last night?"

"No."

"Do you want to grab some late lunch? Early dinner?" he asked.

"I..." She was going to say she was busy, but his talk about this dream and the killed guards got her curious. "Yes. No." She then whispered, "I think someone could be following me."

He nodded, then asked, "What do you mean you don't have a place to stay?"

She frowned in confusion, then realized he was trying to help her. "I just got here."

"There are some free rooms in the inn where I'm staying. Do you want to check it out?"

"Sure."

She followed him into the city. There were fruit stands, stores, and even artists in the streets, as if nothing had happened. And something had happened, considering what Tris had told her and that six guards had been killed, but at least most people didn't seem to have been affected. Zora didn't look back to see if anyone was following her because she wanted to act natural and unconcerned.

They got to a building with thick wooden doors. It looked like a restaurant at first, with many tables, but then, on a corner, an old lady sat behind a counter by a set of stairs. This was the inn. The woman didn't smile when Mauro approached. If anything, she stepped back, as if afraid of him. Rude.

"My friend needs a room," he said.

"I'll need payment in advance," the woman said in a very unfriendly tone.

Oh, no. Zora had no money with her. She was about to tell Mauro, when he pulled a pouch with coins and put some of them on the counter. Zora had almost told him not to bother, but it was true that there could be someone following her, and she was trusting his plan. She'd need to ask Larzen to pay him back.

He said, "She'll need two nights. Get her one of the suites with a private bath area, if there's any available."

The woman glanced between him and her with a malicious smile, then handed Zora a key. "Room 23, second floor. I believe your generous sponsor can show you the room." She then turned to both of them. "Remember this is a respectable inn, and none of our guests wants to hear any noise. Be quiet."

Zora frowned, annoyed.

"She's my friend, madam," Mauro said. "And I have my own room."

"It's a reminder for all guests. We respect silence here," the woman said.

As they were going up the stairs, Zora couldn't help herself. "Wow, at least the staff here is really nice."

He laughed. "Actually, most of them are all right, and this place is comfortable and affordable."

"I'll pay you back," she said in a lower tone of voice, now wondering if by any chance he was really thinking that she needed a place to stay.

"Don't worry about it." He opened her room, then pointed to a window. "Come check the view."

It was an alley, facing the back of a building. "It's... interesting."

He then whispered in her ear, "Bar the door from the inside. In five minutes, when there's nobody looking, climb out the window and enter one of the wooden boxes. You'll be moved. Don't get out." He then stepped away. "Hope you like it. See you later. If you want to go down to dinner with me, I'm in room 28, just knock at around six."

"Sure."

She barred the door right after he left. That bed was calling her, inviting Zora for some much-needed rest, but this wasn't why she was here. She moved the blanket to make it seem that she had slept there. In reality, she'd probably sleep over the covers, but it would still mess up the bed.

She understood that Mauro's idea was to make whoever was following her think she was going to stay at the inn. The worst was that she didn't even know if anyone was following her. But then, if false Griffin had control over the guards, it wouldn't be difficult to enquire where she was. At least they would think she was here. For some time, at least.

There was no clock in the room, but she waited a little,

then opened the window and climbed down, holding onto the windowsill. She tried to find a place to put her feet, but there was none. There was a pipe by the window, and she reached out and grabbed it to support her descent. Still, she fell down ungraciously with a thud. Carrying a bag with books and a strange basin didn't help. There were wooden boxes by a door, which was probably the back of the inn. Zora found a large, empty box and got in. Mauro's plan was starting to make sense. Sort of.

The box had a strong smell of wine, and her heart was beating fast as she waited. After a while, she felt it being lifted, and then moving as if on something on wheels on rough terrain. She really hoped it wasn't a wine merchant thinking the box was filled with bottles. No. They would notice it was too heavy. The ride was quite bumpy for her taste, and she hit her head a few times.

After some time, he lifted the top just a little, and whispered, "We're far from the city, and I think near where you were going. We weren't followed. You can go now, and don't worry about paying me back. But if you want, you can take me with you. I dreamed about it, Zora, and I think it wasn't a coincidence that I found you. There's something happening and I want to make a difference, no matter how dangerous it is. If you can trust me."

Zora felt bad. She understood what it was to want to make a difference, to want to be a hero. All her teenage years she'd dreamed about being a ranger and fighting shadow creatures in the valley. She ended up not becoming a ranger, as she realized that she could make a bigger difference as a teacher. Still, she knew that yearning. And yet, the house wasn't hers, and she wasn't the one for whom there was a prize.

"It's fine," he said. "I hope I was able to help you today.

You can go." He then added, "Unless you trust me enough to let me take you to where you're hiding."

Zora had to make a decision. She sort of trusted Mauro, but she didn't know him that well. And Larzen's safe shack wasn't her secret to keep—or reveal. Then she remembered what Dada, the old woman in Riadne's strange palace, had told her.

THE SOLUTION

G riffin felt as if even the wind had stilled, waiting for what was going to happen with the explosives. They didn't move at first. Then something snapped. On the back, away from the portal, balls rolled down the mountain right on the soldiers. He kept a passive, stoic expression as he watched the men try to run away from the balls. Some saved themselves, some were hit by explosions that carved holes on the ground. There were murmurs of shock down there. Here, on the balcony, nobody was surprised. Perhaps their only surprise was that the rest of the balls were taking so long to fall.

Then there were more snaps. Oh, no. So many things could go wrong. Perhaps someone had checked the nets after Griffin had made the changes. But the exploding balls didn't slide down the mountain. Instead, they slid forward like he'd planned. They clanked against each other but didn't explode until they fell down in the valley. Some of them detonated in the portal, some kept rolling. At least it looked realistic that the plan was to send them against their enemies.

Down there, no sign that the portal had been activated.

There would be something visible, like a light in its middle, but there was nothing. Nothing. The passage hadn't been opened. Griffin exhaled. This was a good enough victory for today.

His next step would be to check those dark pits.

RIADNE HELD her brother's hand. He had a tissue in his mouth and was making a lot of effort not to scream.

Tris shook her head. "I gave him the same draught he was getting at the castle. I just think that the sedative is not working anymore."

It hurt so much to see Lukas suffering and not be able to do anything, to look in his eyes and see the fear of death, fear of pain. It stirred years of anger that she tried to keep down, like a monster inside her about to wake. But what could it do?

Larzen sat by her and ran his hand through his hair. For some reason this simple gesture always made Riadne catch her breath. As if this was time for that. And maybe he was sitting there to be close to Tris. She closed her eyes and took a deep breath. No, Larzen wasn't trying to get close to the princess. Riadne had to stop imagining things—and focus on their other problems.

She finally voiced her concern. "Zora is taking too long."

Larzen bit his lip. "She didn't say how long it was going to take."

Riadne exhaled. "She said all she needed was to pick up a few things. Nobody takes that long to go in and out of the castle. If she's been caught, then we'll also be caught soon, depending on what methods they use to interrogate her." That was a chilling thought, but true. Larzen's face was grim. She then added, "Perhaps we should find another hiding place."

The prince—no, king, dammit, she wasn't going to call him king—Larzen, sighed. "I still think she's coming back. And it's not that simple to go somewhere else carrying a screaming man."

She pointed a finger at him. "Don't you dare blame my brother."

Larzen shook his head. "I'm not blaming anyone. I'm stating a fact."

Riadne sighed. "Leave us then. Hide. They're after you the most."

He scoffed. "Don't be ridiculous. If they get to you they'll get to me."

That made absolutely no sense. "No. Not if I don't know where you are."

Larzen shook his head again.

Lukas screamed, then removed the cloth and mumbled, "Kill me. Just kill me, sister."

His eyes were pleading, and she could almost feel the agony behind his death wish.

Tris then stared at him. "I already told you no, so it's no. Not unless there's no other option."

"It might not take long." Riadne's voice was almost failing her. She then turned to Larzen. "Please. Go. Hide. I'm begging you."

He smirked. "But then who's going to save my ass?"

Riadne shook her head. "I don't have a good grasp on my powers, Larzen, and if I use it like I did, it takes a while for me to regain my strength. I... can't guarantee I can defeat large numbers."

He narrowed his eyes. "Just say you hate my company then, go on."

She took a deep breath. "I absolutely abhor your company and I want you as far away from me as possible, Larzen. Does that convince you?"

Larzen stared at his nails. They were cut short, but clean and well styled. What kind of guy stared at his nails? "No," he said.

She turned to Tris. "Are you sure there isn't any more pain reliever?"

"A little, yes, but I'm not supposed to give him too much."

Riadne turned to Larzen. "Let's say Zora doesn't get back in, I don't know, one, two, three hours, whatever you find is enough to realize something happened. What do we do?"

There was uncertainty in his face, which wasn't something she'd ever seen before. He looked down, resting his chin on his hand. "I'm trying to think."

The distance between them felt wrong. Riadne again had the bizarre urge to sit by his side and comfort him somehow, and had to figure out what was wrong with her. Perhaps it was just fear. Those awful moments in his room, when she'd been helpless and he'd been surrounded, had been engraved in her mind together with the terror she'd felt then, fearing that he'd be imprisoned and perhaps killed while she watched, unable to do anything about it.

A sound in the door washed away her tension. Toc, toc, then toc, toc, toc, which was their signal. The Dark Valley girl was finally back. Larzen got up, but Riadne did the same, and put a hand in front of him. "Let me open. Just in case."

Riadne peered through the door and almost closed it again. Had Zora gone insane or was she just incredibly dumb?

"WE CAN TRUST HIM," Zora said before Riadne closed the door on her face. "And he helped me avoid pursuers."

The false princess frowned. "You were followed?"

"Can we talk inside?"

Mauro came in after her, carrying the empty box just in case someone passed by the shack.

Larzen widened his eyes when he saw Mauro. Tris just glanced at him. Poor Lukas was lying down and moaning.

Zora turned to Riadne and Larzen. "He can help us, and I trust him." That's why she had brought him; she had decided to trust her heart, and her heart had told her that Mauro was a good friend and could be a good ally.

"If you say so." Larzen shrugged. He didn't seem bothered.

Riadne rolled her eyes. "Yay, what a great time to invite guests."

"I can go," Mauro told Zora.

Larzen glared at Riadne, then turned to Mauro. "No. You're here, you're here. And who knows, perhaps we could use your help."

Riadne waved a hand. "It was a joke. But I *am* surprised." She turned to Zora and tapped her feet on the floor. "What happened?"

She sighed. "A lot."

"Who was following you?" Riadne asked.

Zora didn't even know how to answer that. "I'm not sure if there was anyone following me, I just thought it could be a possibility, and took every precaution." She pointed at Mauro. "With his help." Then, wanting to change the subject, she asked, "Did you see the posters?"

Riadne frowned. "What posters?"

Surprising. "You didn't see anything?"

Mauro sat on top of the wooden box, which contrasted with the fancy decoration of that room. "They're offering prizes for you three." He pointed at Riadne, Tris, and Larzen. "Saying he's responsible for attempting against King Kiran's life with two witches, and that you caused some dark magic to be unleashed. There are portraits and all." He glanced at Tris. "Not perfect, but still."

Larzen raised an eyebrow. "How much?"

"It makes a difference?" Zora asked.

The prince waved a finger. "It actually does."

Zora tried to recall the amount. "Five hundred thousand for Larzen, fifty thousand for Tris and Riadne."

"What?" Riadne protested. "They think he's worth ten times me?"

Tris shrugged. "And me. It means they don't know who I am."

"Right." Riadne rolled her eyes. "I'm obviously worthless, considering I'm not a royal."

Mauro frowned and stared at the redhead. "I thought... Aren't you princess Alegra?"

Riadne sighed, as if annoyed.

"I can tell you all later," Zora said, wanting to prevent some kind of impolite outburst. "For now," she pointed at the false princess, "this is Riadne," then she pointed to the real Linaria princess, who shook her head slightly, perhaps afraid of having her identity revealed, as if she hadn't done it herself a few seconds before. "And this is Tris, a friend." She pointed to the young man lying on the sofa. "That's Lukas, Riadne's brother." She then pointed to Mauro. "And this is Mauro. He's a friend."

Tris smiled. "Pleased to meet you."

"Same." He returned the smile.

Zora then turned to Larzen. "What difference does the prize make?"

"First, it reminds me how immensely valuable I am. But second, it tells me how much I'll need to bribe for help."

That made sense. "A lot, and it's a problem, right?"

He nodded.

Zora then turned to Mauro. "Can you tell us what

happened? With the six guards? And what you know about this… Griffin?"

Mauro grimaced. "What do you mean *this Griffin*?"

"It's an impostor," Zora explained.

"Oh." Mauro looked at everyone. "I'll tell you what I know. This morning six guards were found dead, but they had just underwear. Their uniforms were gone."

"The creatures that attacked me!" Tris said. "That was why they were dressed as guards."

Mauro frowned. "You will have to explain it all to me, but it's fine for now. Anyway, Prince Griffin, or not Griffin, came to the city on a heavily guarded carriage. He went to the central square and gave a speech."

"Did you see it?" Zora asked.

"Yes." He nodded. "He was saying Larzen was a traitor, that he had tried to kill Kiran and had unleashed some kind of dark magic in the kingdom. He told us to avoid going out at night, that there might be creatures, and that it was Larzen's fault. And he urged anyone who knew Larzen's location to inform the city guards."

"Did you believe him?" Zora asked.

He paused, then said, "Yes, at the time, yes."

"Great!" Riadne smiled. "Now you can go and try to be six hundred crowns richer."

Mauro looked down. "Of course not. Griffin left the city with Zora. If she's saying that's not him, it's true."

"You know what surprises me?" Larzen asked. "That anyone would believe my younger brother could give a speech."

That wasn't true. "He spoke in the opening of the games. And spoke well."

Larzen sighed. "Well, yes. I guess. Still, it's too much money. I don't even think we have that in our coffers, but I doubt he plans on paying anyone." He sighed. "But he claims Kiran is alive?"

Zora heard the hint of hope in his voice and looked down.

"Yes," Mauro said.

The prince was thoughtful. "I guess one piece of good news."

Erm... not really. And Zora wasn't sure how to tell him that.

Larzen then asked, "How did people react to false Griffin?"

The huge warrior paused.

Larzen snorted. "Don't say it. They were determined to kill me for the good of the kingdom, completely convinced that honorable, righteous Griffin couldn't possibly be lying."

"That's pretty much it," Mauro admitted.

"Commoners like Griffin. He dresses like them, he comes down and trains with the soldiers, competes against regular people..." Larzen sighed and put his hands on the side of his head. "If they think it was him, this is a nightmare." He then shook his head. "What I don't understand is how come this... thing would know how to corner me so well, would know how to speak to our subjects. Unless it's really my brother and he's being... manipulated or something." He shrugged. "I mean, I'd be happy to know he's alive—"

"It's not him," Zora cut him. She'd been hesitating, wondering if she should tell them everything, but if they were in this together, it made no sense to keep secrets. "I went to his dungeon, picked up some books and a couple objects, then, when I was almost leaving, he showed up." Chills ran down her spine as the memory came to her mind. "The impostor."

They were all looking at her with surprise. She continued, "He looked just like Griffin, of course, but the facial expressions weren't the same. There was a difference, but small, for sure. But he didn't try to kill or hurt me."

Riadne grimaced. "Why?"

"He said he wanted his body back, so it's as if they switched. According to this impostor, if both of them came to some kind of portal at the same time, they could undo the change. So he asked me to bring Griffin to him, when and if he shows up."

Larzen widened his eyes. "Show up? What do you mean? Where is my brother?"

"I don't know if what he's saying is true, but he also said something was about to happen, that I would know when it did, and that then Griffin would show up, but that he wouldn't look like himself." She took a deep breath. "It's as if... something's about to happen, and it doesn't seem to be anything good."

They were all thoughtful, looking at her, except Lukas, who was still lying down and moaning.

Zora continued, "Other than that, he knew a lot about Griffin, because he found the entrance to his dungeon, and he also knew I'd be interested in getting him back, you know?" She looked at Larzen. "He also said that he's a king, so I guess he's the Shadow King or something. And that..." She paused. "He threw Kiran's body in the King's River. Then he said it was just one more death and then he'd be king. I guess he wants you dead, Larzen. Perhaps because of some magic, I don't know. And I'm sorry."

Larzen bit his lip and looked down, a vacant expression on his face.

"He could be lying," Riadne said.

That was a possibility. "For sure."

Riadne's brother then emitted a loud groan of pain.

Larzen shook his head. "Tris saw him falling from a pretty high window. What could have happened? This Shadow

King found him and took him to a healer? If he did, it's obviously with some nefarious intent." He closed his eyes. "But that's the kind of thing that's complicated, messy for this Shadow King. What if Kiran starts talking? And Tris said the order was to kill him, right?"

She nodded.

Larzen continued, "So he's dead. It makes sense that this impostor would say Kiran is alive. Considering he's pretending to be Griffin, it gives him legitimacy, the impression that he's working with the king. If he says Kiran's dead, he'll come across as a usurper, and then I have a rightful claim to the throne, which could put into question his accusations against me. Simple as that. We're dealing with a smart enemy."

"I'm so sorry." Riadne sounded truly upset.

They were silent, except for Lukas, who moaned again.

Mauro bowed. "Your majesty."

Larzen shook his head. "Don't. Just Larzen. Or even some other name for the time being."

"Are you..." Riadne hesitated, then asked Larzen, "Are you going to try to get the kingdom back?"

"How? How am I going to buy any help when mercenaries are not trustworthy? Any of them might turn around and decide to bank the five hundred thousand crowns, because people get dumb when greed is involved. And then there's the part of the guard that's actually loyal to Griffin. I don't want to face them, hurt them, kill them. I don't want to. I'll go with you to Rock Island and we're going to find answers."

Riadne's jaw dropped. "You? But why?"

Larzen smiled. "Riadne, dear, if you keep showing such eagerness to travel with me, people will think you're flirting."

"But it's not safe!" Riadne yelled, ignoring the teasing.

"Nowhere is safe for me. Well, actually, the farther from

Gravel I am, the safer. Plus, I gave it some thought." He looked at everyone. "These creatures were defeated before with magic. And that's what we'll need to look for." He sounded certain.

Zora nodded.

"A *magic* solution," Riadne said, her tone sarcastic. "Sounds feasible."

Larzen looked at her. "You got a better idea?"

"No. I'm just saying." She shrugged. "The solution's magic." She smiled.

Larzen glared.

Mauro was at ease sitting on the wooden box and asked, "Where is this Rock Island?"

Zora hesitated, unsure of how much they'd allow him to know.

It was Larzen who replied, "Away from here. Right?"

"You're gonna have a bit of a problem," Mauro said.

"No kidding." Riadne rolled her eyes.

Larzen tilted his head. "Tons of problems, but I'm assuming you mean something specific, or am I wrong?"

Mauro nodded. "They're posting guards on all roads. Not only that, they're encouraging people to watch in case you try to run away."

Larzen closed his eyes. "And I thought these dark creatures were mindless."

So did Zora. Then something Mauro had told her came to her mind. "What did false Griffin say about the night?"

"To avoid it," Mauro said.

"Well, that's it, then." Zora smiled.

Larzen waved a hand. "That's definitely it; we're totally screwed. I just don't understand why you look happy about it."

"Because that's our solution."

12

MAD ESCAPE

The idea had sounded quite logical and even smart in Zora's head. But now she was starting to wonder about her mental state. And her companions'. Crazy ideas didn't usually feel crazy when other people agreed with them, but this time, it wasn't working that well.

Lukas was sitting, and had even eaten. Although he still moaned in pain sometimes, he seemed a lot more alert. Zora was happy that her potion, which had been just a simple, regular potion for the pain, had worked and was helping him. It made her confident that taking him to the Dark Valley was a good idea. Even Riadne and Lukas himself were more confident, and he had stopped asking to be killed. It was a win.

Riadne was going through the book that was supposedly about potions, but they were hidden in recipes as some kind of sauce or seasoning. This was probably quite important information to have been hidden even though it was written in Solana. There was a "wing cake", but the "icing" didn't look like any potion Zora knew. It mentioned some kind of black table, but Zora couldn't be sure if it was a regular potion surface. Even then, she wrote it down in Continental so that it could be given to her parents. Some of the potions were somewhat similar to potions Zora knew, so it was possible that it would be a real potion. The issue was that there were many ingredients Zora didn't know and some things Riadne couldn't understand. Lukas was not that good at reading Solana writing, not to mention that he was in no condition to do that, so the book would remain with his sister.

It felt odd to work with Riadne checking these potions. Zora knew what had happened between the false princess and Griffin in the library, when searching for books, and had to focus and push those thoughts away. At least Riadne had been truly searching for books in a foreign language. What Zora didn't understand was how come they decided to move on to *other activities* after not finding anything useful. Well, it didn't matter now, and she should try to wipe all that from her mind.

Zora slept a little, on the corner of the living room, lying over her hammock, and the others slept in sofas or on the floor. Lukas took the bed because of his condition, and Riadne slept on the floor by him. Zora had no idea if and where Larzen slept.

At least there had been some time to bring Mauro up to speed with what was happening. He just listened, never seeming surprised or horrified at anything, then said, "I'll help you save the kingdom, Zora. Trust that sometimes things happen for a reason."

She smiled. This idea of greater meaning for why things happened was more and more sounding like a way to dodge responsibility. *Yay, let's blame destiny! Not stupidity. Nope, not at all.* But again, there was no point berating herself.

After putting the finishing touches on another analgesic potion for Lukas, she took a deep breath and closed its bottle. It was night outside, but the shack hadn't been attacked yet. It probably meant that false Griffin had no idea where they were. Also, thinking back, she realized he'd probably guessed that Larzen would spend the night at the lake house and somehow had set up something or directed the creatures to attack them. It had been close. Tonight she still heard the occasional shrieks in the distance, meaning that there were human shadows outside, near the city. Hopefully people had indeed stayed indoors.

When it was almost four in the morning, Larzen led them all to the bedroom, where he opened a closet.

"Time to choose your poison," he said.

Inside, there were a few bows, some crossbows, swords, darts, and knives.

Riadne grimaced. "Unfortunately there are only weapons." She was the only person there who didn't know how to fight physically and perhaps felt left out. As if she were forgetting about her creepy powers.

Larzen turned to Riadne. "You'll be guiding the horses. It's the most important job, and that's why you won't need a weapon."

She rolled her eyes. "Right. Super important."

The truth was that her powers didn't work on shadow creatures, so it meant she would be defenseless. Zora didn't envy her. Still, Riadne had agreed with the plan. They all had, which, again, was now making her question the mental state of her companions.

Mauro reached out to a bow. "I'm a good archer."

"Sure you don't want a crossbow?" Larzen pointed to the smaller weapon. "Easier to aim."

Mauro pointed at the weapon in his hand. "Faster to recharge."

Larzen nodded. "Yes, but we'll need to be careful, as I don't have that many arrows."

Zora counted at least a hundred on the bottom of the

closet. But yes, now, thinking about it, if they were four people using bows or crossbows, that would mean some twenty-five arrows for each. It was nothing.

Lukas took a crossbow. "I'll try to help." He looked far from well.

Larzen nodded. "If you can. If your pain is too much, stay in the middle."

"I'm not gonna lie down while you fight," he protested.

How quickly he'd forgotten how he'd been lying down and screaming a few hours before.

Tris opened her cloak and showed her improvised baldric. "I'll use my knives and stakes because I know I can aim well with them."

Larzen pointed to the closet. "There are a few knives here, but you're going to throw them away, aren't you?"

The Linaria princess nodded.

He shook his head. "I never understood people throwing weapons to their enemies." Still, he gave her the knives he had.

"Arrows are weapons too," Tris said as she arranged her baldric. "And it's just a sport in Linaria, not something used for real fighting." She shrugged. "But I never prepared for any fighting."

Larzen then tried to hand Zora a crossbow, but she shook her head. "I'm a terrible archer. And I trust my sword more."

The prince tilted his head. "But then you'll need to wait for the creatures to get close."

Zora touched the hilt of Griffin's sword on her back. "If they do, this is much more efficient."

"Carry both," he insisted.

"How am I going to change weapons like that?" Zora asked. "And plus, I don't want to waste arrows. I'm bad."

Larzen raised an eyebrow. "I thought you had archers in the Dark Valley."

"Only rangers get advanced archery training, especially the ones who go to the observation towers. Regular people use swords because it's faster for self-defense and lets you fight more than one creature at a time."

Larzen sighed. Zora didn't like the unease with which he looked at her, as if she were going to be a dead weight or something, but she had to trust her gut.

"She's right," Mauro said. "A weapon you don't master is a gift to your enemy."

Larzen frowned. "I have a better saying: a knife is better than nothing."

Maure replied, "Not if your enemy takes it from you or if it distracts you. And she's got a sword. That's better than a knife."

"All right, let's get philosophical," Larzen replied. "If you don't want your enemies to get close, you should use ranged weapons."

It made sense, but Zora still thought she should keep her sword. "But if something happens and they do get close, somebody needs to be ready to fight them fast."

"Fine." Larzen pointed at Griffin's sword on Zora's back. "Let's hope you don't get to use it."

"Let's." In reality, she thought she would end up using the sword, and that he was delirious thinking things would be so easy that they'd only shoot them from a distance, but didn't want to bring that up.

Larzen then took a sword, and handed one to each of the others, except Riadne, who said, "I thought you preferred daggers."

He had a smile that didn't reach his eyes. "I do. And I also prefer not to fight or have to defend myself at all. Unfortunately, it seems that life's not being good at granting my wishes."

Zora took a deep breath. "There's still time to change our minds."

"Then what?" Riadne asked. "We wait until someone finds us?"

"We could maybe try to leave the city in barrels, boxes, something." She looked down. "They'd probably expect that, I know. And traveling at night was my idea." And that was why it was suddenly bothering her, as she knew that if anything went wrong, it would be her fault.

"Don't be so smug." Larzen smiled. "The only way to deal with a smart enemy is to do what they don't predict. If you hadn't suggested leaving the city at night, another one of us would have. "

Zora exhaled. "That makes sense."

Larzen then took three quivers, filled them with arrows and gave two of them to Lukas and Mauro. Everyone had their bags ready.

"Time to go."

"Wait," Zora said. "I have a potion for us. Not a lot, though." She picked a closed bottle. "Night vision. But we'll have to share."

"Still. Useful." Larzen chuckled. "Funny you never mentioned you could brew magic potions."

That wasn't true. "I always said I could make potions."

"Potions. We think they're like regular healer potions, not magic..." He gestured to her bottle.

Zora shrugged. "They're just potions."

Larzen nodded, then asked, "How long does it last?"

"One hour or so."

He was thoughtful. "Maybe we should save it for later."

"We can take a little now and then more if we need," Zora said.

She put a drop on the palm of her hand and licked it, and the others did the same.

Larzen then opened the door, and so far no creature showed up, so they all followed him.

Mauro and Larzen took the lead, with Riadne and Tris in the middle, and Lukas and Zora at the back. She tried not to get offended that she was there. Then perhaps she should be flattered, as she was alone with a young man who was in a less-than-ideal state.

Zora heard it before she saw it. Not the screeches, but steps. Human shadows somehow sounded different, lower, as if they had huge, muffled feet. Two creatures were coming from behind the house.

"I'll get them. Run."

She had her sword ready when something hit one of the creatures on the head, then the other creature, and both disappeared. Lukas had shot them. Perhaps Zora wouldn't use her sword after all. They reached the barn, and a human shadow ran towards them from inside it. Mauro killed it with his sword. Earlier during the day, he had arranged the cart to fit the two horses. Amazing work to have been done so fast.

Zora jumped to the back, together with most of the group, then Larzen and Riadne were in the front as they left the house. They headed to a country road surrounding Gravel city, the horses trotting much slower than she would have liked. What worried her was not so much the human shadows, but the shadow wolves. They could easily outrun their cart and jump on it, and that would be when a fast sword would come in handy.

The city was empty and silent, except for some sounds coming from creatures. It was a relief to be getting away from that castle and from that horrible Griffin impersonator. They took a smaller road leading away from Gravel City, not yet in the direction of the Dark Valley, but going south. The idea was to avoid the main road and also mislead pursuers in case they were seen. The road going east also had a big outpost, where Larzen feared there could be archers and watchers and where they could be caught by guards.

The castle and the lights of the city were fading behind them, Zora barely believing that they were leaving, that they had hardly been attacked by shadow creatures. Once in a while they crossed a human shadow. Larzen, being in the front, got most of them.

Then they took a small road and finally headed east towards the Dark Valley, where Lukas was going to stay. They had decided that it wasn't so far out of their way, and it would be good not to head straight to a nearby port, as it would be a too-obvious escape route.

Running away at night had been working so far. The whoosh of an arrow brought her back to the present moment, as she saw a creature heading towards them, then disappearing after another arrow hit it. Larzen had shot it. So far, all arrows had hit their targets.

"You're all great shots," Zora said.

Mauro and Lukas mumbled thanks, while Larzen said, "Of course I am."

Arrogance definitely ran in the family.

"Yeah, most people have trouble when trying to hit a moving mark," Mauro added.

Zora shrugged. "See? I'm right to leave the arrows to the pros."

But in a way it was embarrassing, as they had been out for over half an hour and Zora had done absolutely nothing. Tris had kept her knives too, which made sense, as they were better for short range and the creatures, thankfully, were still far. Riadne wasn't supposed to do anything other than guiding the horses, and she'd been doing that.

Lukas moaned in pain again.

"You should rest," Zora said.

He shook his head, still holding his crossbow. Tris cast him a worried glance, then looked at Zora and shrugged.

Then she heard it: shadow wolves. The effect of the night vision potion was wearing off already and it hadn't been strong enough in the first place. The creatures were ahead of their cart, and Zora moved to the front in time to block one creature with her sword, while the other landed by Larzen, then disappeared, a wooden stake in its chest. Tris had been fast. One of the horses reared up and the cart shook, but Riadne regained control of it.

The prince was shook, his breathing heavy. "They're fast."

Zora nodded, then looked around for signs of more of those.

"Stay here helping to guard our front," Larzen said. "In case they jump on us again."

He cast a worried glance at Riadne, who, for her turn, had her eyes focused straight ahead.

More shadow wolves followed them, but Mauro shot the creatures. The few human shadows they crossed posed no threat, as Larzen was quite skilled with his crossbow. Still, Zora couldn't help but notice that they were using up their arrows. She wished she could make the sun rise earlier. Or else they could have left later. But they had planned it this way to be far from Gravel City by the time anyone could see them.

Then Zora saw something rolling towards them: a ball. If it exploded in the cart, it would not only ruin their means of transportation, it could kill them.

"There!" she pointed, trying to get Larzen's attention. He shot it twice and it exploded away from the cart, a loud thud that scared the horses and made them run faster. A shadow wolf jumped on them and Zora cut it in half, killing it.

Then she heard another boom, and the cart went up and down, then dragged on the ground. She looked back and saw

Tris, Mauro, and Lukas away from the edge of the cart, which had black marks of an explosion and was catching fire. Tris threw a blanket to smother the fire, but it didn't change the fact that they were going much slower now. A shadow wolf ran towards them. Mauro shot it, and Zora finished killing it as it tried to jump on the now slow-moving cart. She heard another boom and realized that a small ball had gone off by another wheel in the front and they were slowed almost to a halt.

"We need to get off this cart or it will go down on fire!" Zora yelled. "And it's not even moving."

Riadne reached out to the horses' harness. What was she doing? Oh, she unclasped them. Larzen stared at her, wide-eyed.

"What?" the false princess asked. "She's right. We aren't going anywhere like this."

"We can't go anywhere without horses, that's for sure," Larzen said.

No, they couldn't. With few arrows left, without any shelter close by, they were about to be swarmed by shadow creatures.

"THE ANSWER IS SIMPLE," Griffin said. "There is a traitor among us."

He was back in that dreadful meeting room with the open windows and chilly gusts of air, facing the Grota council. They were older men, not that Griffin really saw any difference, but they exuded experience and confidence.

There were whispers that they were unhappy he had dismissed the troops so quickly. They wanted to try to open the portal again, or wait for the Void's advice, and that was exactly the reason Griffin had dismissed those soldiers. If they decided to open the portal again using the same strategy, it would take a while to gather such an army again. Apparently, gathering all these explosives also took a lot of time, but he didn't want to take any chances and wanted to gain time.

"Was it Antelio?" one of the men asked.

Interesting question. "He was one of them, but we clearly have another." Griffin met the eyes of each of the members. "Among us."

They looked at each other, somewhat rattled. Good. These men were like Antelio, smart, experienced, and they knew the king and all the secrets about the magic in Grota. By making them suspicious of each other, they would focus their attention elsewhere, not on him. It would also give him a great excuse not to talk to them.

He continued, "But I'll find the truth soon. Meanwhile, I suggest you keep any important information to yourselves. This is all for now."

After the meeting, he went to Amina's quarters. She had a small bag and wore a traveling cloak and boots.

Griffin glanced at the bag. "That's it?"

She smiled. "It's just a short visit."

It wasn't. If everything worked out well, she'd never come back, but it was true that nobody should know about it. And then perhaps she didn't want to take home much from here.

Amina extended a pendant with a pink stone. "Here. Take it."

Griffin took it. "This will amplify my magic?" Nonexistent magic, but he wasn't going to say that.

She nodded, then took little Saro from the crib. Such an innocent little thing. One more reason to hope that the Void could be defeated.

"Thank you," he said. "I'll do my best."

She looked down. "I feel like a coward, running."

That made no sense. He gestured to the baby. "You have a good reason to run. And you've helped me a lot already."

She sighed. "Good luck." Her tone was still sad, resigned, as if she truly wished she could do more.

He nodded, then opened the door and called the guards who would accompany her. Like that, his only true ally in this place left. But he didn't think there was any other choice. Griffin could be unmasked as an impostor at any moment, and if she wanted to go home, he had to help her do it while people still believed he was the king. It wasn't going to last.

Perhaps all that he wanted was to remove a baby from harm's way, even if that baby would eventually become the king of this wretched land and have some strange connection to the Gravel royal line. Even then.

Rolling the pink pendant in his hand, he stared at it. She seemed to think it was important. Perhaps it could be helpful for someone who had any magical knowledge, but he had no idea what good it could do to him. Still, refusing it would have been rude.

Strange. He felt tired, and his first thought was to wonder if he'd been drugged, then he remembered that he didn't eat or drink, so it would be highly unlikely. Still, he sat in the armchair.

A strong flash of light startled him, and then he was no longer sitting, but walking in a bright meadow.

"Griffin," the woman's voice called to him, but this time her voice was clear.

He felt that he was dreaming, but felt that it was real at the same time.

"I'm here," he said.

A woman dressed in gold appeared in front of him. It was hard to distinguish her features because she was too bright, as if she had a light inside her.

"So you see me now."

He frowned. "Are you real?"

"It depends on your definition of real. Are *you* real?"

"If we're going to debate definitions, nothing means anything."

She chuckled. "Your grief. It was like a dark mist around you. I couldn't find you. You still have a lot of grief, but it isn't as suffocating."

"Yes. And?"

"Something funny happened to you, Griffin."

"Oh, yes, something hilarious, you know? I thought I was happy, with my problems solved, a life ahead of me, then it was all taken away. So funny."

She tilted her head. "I meant funny as in strange. But maybe not strange, but good."

"Right, excellent."

The woman shook her head. "The fact that you were in love when you switched bodies made all the difference. Your heart had no anger, fear, or greed—just love. What it means is that you can never be under Void's control."

"For the next two days, for sure."

"Even after. He might discover who you are, you might be physically imprisoned, but your mind will still be free. The way this curse works, you would have been affected, influenced by him, but you, he can't reach you. Not your mind."

"Well, I guess that counts for something. Now, you're all shiny and look powerful, can't you defeat the Void?"

"Under some conditions, yes, but for now, I can only give you advice. It means a lot that your mind is free. Free from your body. Free from this dimension. You can dreamwalk."

"Can it help me defeat this thing I don't even know what it is? Save my kingdom? Get my body back?"

She tilted her head. "Perhaps. Dreamwalking will allow you to contact people you're connected with. It means you can make plans together and act from both sides at the same time. That will be your weapon."

"Dreaming?"

"Talking to the ones you love."

"Knowing I might not go back to them? Do you realize how painful it could be?"

"No. Dreaming of the people you love can be wonderful. Tell me you don't want to meet the girl you love?"

"In the real world, not..." What he wanted was to go back, go back and restore all the future they had once planned together, restore that moment of happiness, make it last, make it forever. And yet... here he was.

"One thing will lead to another," she said.

It still didn't make much sense, and the woman started to disappear. Great. He asked, "Are you leaving?"

"You have all the advice you need for now, Griffin."

"No, no, no." He had to save his kingdoms, his brothers, Zora. "Tell me about the Void. What's his weakness? About the pits? Tell me how to prevent Grota from opening that dreadful portal." The woman was almost invisible now, and he yelled, "Tell me."

"Next time. If you have better manners." It was only her voice now, her image completely gone.

She couldn't be that petty. "Tell me now. Help me. Please."

He sat down and banged his fists on the ground. Why would this shiny person appear to him if she wasn't going to help him? Perhaps she wanted to taunt him. Zora had said she'd heard a voice, and he wondered if it was the same voice. Perhaps it wasn't even anything good. And still, this idea of dreamwalking made some sense. He had seen memories from the king inhabiting his body in Gravel. At first he'd thought it was because they were somehow connected, but perhaps there was more than that.

Zora. He did want to see Zora. He heard the sound of

heavy breathing behind him, turned, and saw her. Lying down, trembling from exhaustion. She had some cuts in her hand and a bruise on her forehead.

It couldn't be real. "Zora?"

He was so surprised that he opened his eyes and found himself in Amina's quarters, his hand still clutching the pendant.

13

RISING SUN

"There!" Zora pointed to a large rock by the road. "We'll have a better chance if we have the high ground."

"The cart is high," Larzen said.

"But it's wood, it's flammable. Go!" Zora used the commanding voice that worked even with her nine-year-old students, and everyone was running away from the rock.

Two shadow wolves ran in their direction, but Mauro and Larzen got them. Zora saw a ball and did what she knew was the best thing to do: grabbed it and threw it really fast, before it exploded. It landed away from them and the cart. They all climbed in the rock, Riadne and Tris with some help. It was barely large enough for them all to stand on it, but at least it gave them a better vantage point.

The creatures no longer targeted the cart, and instead came towards them. Mauro had replaced his bow with a sword, cutting the creatures that came close. Sometimes Zora bumped on him or on Lukas, who sat in visible pain, and yet still shot from his crossbow. It wasn't like fighting with Griffin, with whom they could almost predict each other's movements. Anyway, at least they were alive so far. Tris and her knives proved useful. Riadne, for her turn, stood in the middle.

Perhaps remaining in the same place acted like a beacon for the creatures, as more and more came in their direction. Zora jumped down from the rock to face two shadow wolves and a human shadow while they were far enough from them.

"No more arrows," Larzen said.

This was bad. Zora got back up on the rock. Their higher ground gave them an advantage against human shadows and shadow wolves, but she was getting tired of attacking with the sword and it felt as if night was never going to end. And she couldn't see well in the dark anymore, and there was no time to get more of her vision potion.

Attack, slash, and then another human shadow was gone. By her side, Tris threw a knife on a creature at a distance.

Never in her life, Zora had fought so many creatures for so long. If she hadn't enchanted the sword to be lighter, her arms would be dead by now. Heavy breathing by her side told her that Mauro and Larzen were exhausted too. Lukas was crouched in the middle and yelling in pain. Zora wanted to tell Riadne to give him the potion, but there was no time to explain, no time to show her where it was, no time to think about anything other than defending themselves.

A ball came rolling towards them. No, two. Tris hit them. It was as if that nightmare would never end. Right then, she noticed a hint of blue in the sky. Zora focused on the creatures, focused on keeping herself alive, as the sky turned lighter and lighter until eventually, creatures in the distance burned and disappeared. Zora collapsed on the ground, exhausted.

The others went to the cart to check it.

"I think I can fix it," she heard Mauro saying. But what

was the point, without horses? Zora wanted to close her eyes, sleep, disappear.

"Zora." She heard a familiar voice calling her.

For a moment, she felt terrified that false Griffin would be there. No, there was a softness in the voice. It was Griffin. She sat up, looking around, but there was nobody there other than her travel companions. No real or false Griffin anywhere to be seen. She was imagining things, probably having some stress-related hallucination. And yet the voice had sounded so real.

RIADNE HAD FEARED for her life before, but never like that, for so long. It was like cold; she could face almost-freezing temperatures in the Linaria mountains even with a light dress, if she spent just a couple minutes in the cold. But long exposure made the cold unbearable. That was how she'd felt, unable to do anything, feeling useless, and seeing her brother close to dying, Larzen doing his best fighting, and the others too, trying their best. She'd almost taken a sword and tried to help, but it was true that she'd only get in the way.

Creatures and creatures and more creatures. And now they had a broken cart. Mauro was trying to fix it, saying that the explosions had only dislocated the wheels, not destroyed them. It turned out that Zora's friend had been quite helpful so far. Perhaps it had been destiny that he'd run across Zora. But then it would have been destiny that their cart had been broken. Well, broken, not destroyed. There was still hope. Ugh, she was starting to sound like Zora.

Lukas was lying down on the ground and took the last potion for the pain. She hated seeing him like this and knew that he was feeling even worse, especially not being able to help much, being a hindrance to the group, and having to be taken care of. Funny how being vulnerable was so uncomfortable. Riadne herself hated it.

Tris approached them. "But what are we going to do without the horses?"

"They'll be back," Riadne replied.

The real princess frowned in confusion, but then nodded.

They were all exhausted, sitting or lying on the ground. It was weird to see Larzen not his usual cool and composed self. In fact, it had been even weirder to see him using a crossbow and a sword. It wasn't that she thought he couldn't fight. Well, indeed, she didn't think he'd be good at it, but it turned out he could more than hold his own. Still, now he sat down, eyes closed, arms trembling slightly, and yet even in this state there was something fierce and proud about him.

Well, they had escaped. The sun had risen, and they were far from Gravel City and the castle. They were perhaps a lot more tired and worn than they should, but they had succeeded in the first part of the plan. The issue now would be getting that cart to work.

"Ready to go," Mauro said.

"What?" Riadne asked.

"I fixed the wheels," he added.

Riadne took a look. It was true.

He was checking the cart. "They aren't as firm or as smooth as before, but still..."

"This is amazing. Amazing." She was surprised. "Great work."

Mauro smiled. "Thanks."

"Thank you." Riadne returned the smile, now really trusting that destiny was working their way.

She turned, whistled, and whistled. At least this time neither Larzen nor Zora were going to doubt her. The others were tired or busy. She glanced at the prince, who was now sitting down, looking at her. When their eyes met, he smiled, as if saying "I trust you." Riadne smiled back, a warm feeling of joy in her chest.

Perhaps it was just that it was good to receive some trust. That was it. Riadne wasn't prone to idiotic feelings and she wasn't about to start. She turned back to the road and whistled again, a stubborn smile still on her face. It was relief, relief and joy at being alive, at being able to try to do something that mattered.

She even had a thin hope for her brother and perhaps for herself. But if she died soon, at least her short life wouldn't have been in vain. Gravel also depended on her, and she was doing her part. Ironic that she'd once wanted to see the royal family destroyed, and now she was helping them—or at least some of them. Perhaps it was destiny too.

The horses got back, and they soon set off to the Dark Valley, using a smaller road to avoid Valerianville and any place where there could be more people. News didn't travel that fast, but it had been almost an entire day since the Griffin impostor had accused Larzen of being a traitor. Long enough for people in this area to be aware of it and have learned about the prize for bringing him in, so it wasn't a good idea to risk being seen.

Mauro guided the cart, sitting by Lukas, who was feeling better. Her brother wore a loose cloak not to hurt his back and to hide the marks. Riadne didn't know how long her brother had to live. The rest of the group was in the back, so that they could hide if necessary, as they were approaching the Dark Valley. The walls surrounding it were much higher and more imposing than she'd imagined. It was indeed a large prison, and she felt bad for Zora.

The cart stopped far from the gates and the outpost.

"Are you sure this is a good idea?" Larzen repeated.

Riadne exhaled. "I think we've established that I can take

care of myself. Unless it's against shadow creatures, which isn't the case now."

Mauro then got off the cart. "I'll go with you. They aren't looking for me."

"We don't know," Riadne replied.

"I can stay away and watch you from a distance," he said.

Larzen nodded. "That's wise. Thank you, Mauro."

Sometimes he gave orders like a king, which was annoying. Well, he was a king now. But still, Riadne had trouble coming to terms with the fact.

Zora gave some final instructions to Tris and sent her a basin, which apparently was some magical object. The Dark Valley girl was staying back just from fear that someone could recognize her. The fewer people knowing where they were, the better.

Tris, Lukas, and Riadne walked towards the gate, followed by Mauro. Hopefully there would be no extra forces waiting for them. And hopefully whoever was at the gate would respond to Riadne's magic.

There was one guard by the gate. It didn't seem that they had noticed that things were different outside and inside the walls. It would probably take a couple more days for people to realize that.

Riadne focused on control and used it in her song. The guard looked at her as if expecting orders. Phew. For a moment she'd been afraid he wouldn't respond to her magic. She then told him, "Open and let them in. You'll forget you saw anyone. You'll forget you opened this gate."

As the bars went up, she looked at her brother. As much as she wanted to give him a big, tight, hug, she knew it would hurt his back, so she didn't. "It's been an honor being your sister. Whatever happens, I'm glad to have shared some time with you."

She wiped a tear from her eye.

"It might be the end." He kissed her cheek. "You are an amazing sister and a great person."

"I'm not." She was sobbing now.

"You are. And you'll keep trying to find a solution for us. I know you will. You're a fighter."

"So are you."

"I'll fight for my life or else I'll face my end with my head high."

"I know." She took a deep breath. "See you later. Here or on the other side."

"Later, then."

The gate was up and he and Tris turned to enter. The princess just waved goodbye. She had decided to stay, claiming she'd had enough excitement for a lifetime. And it was a good idea for her to hide while false Griffin was looking for her. Larzen had offered to try to get her to Kentosa, from where she could also return to Linaria, but the girl was obviously tired of running. Or perhaps she wanted more time with Lukas. He seemed happy. Whatever happened, if they found a miraculous way for him to live, or if he passed to the other world, he was happy, and that was what mattered.

Riadne stepped back and sang again for confusion and memory loss as she stepped back, then joined Mauro to get back to the cart.

"Don't tell anyone you saw me crying," she said.

He frowned. "There's no shame in it. Only dry souls don't have tears to shed."

"I am a dry and tough soul, Mauro, that's the thing. But it might have been the last time I saw my brother." She had to hold back the tears not to choke on these words.

"Only someone heartless wouldn't cry. But I'll let you pretend you're heartless, if that's what you want."

"Thank you."

ZORA HAD DOZED in the cart a few times, and still sometimes heard Griffin's voice. It just gave her a tight feeling in her heart, a certainty that she had to get this right. Perhaps it was a reminder that he was still alive somewhere, that there was a good chance that he could come back.

The idea of seeing him again as himself made her heart speed up. She couldn't even imagine what it would be like to kiss him again. She wanted to smack her past self who kept refusing his kisses for so long. Well, her past self deserved some smacking for much worse reasons; using that cup being the worst of them. She closed her eyes.

The Dark Valley was far behind and they were heading to the Bent River, near the Marshes, a place she had never dreamed she'd visit. She wished she could have stopped and seen her parents, her sister, but it was better to cause the least possible fuss. Having two strangers in the valley would be enough to cause a stir; she didn't want anyone babbling to the guards that Zora had been there.

In fact, hopefully Tris would follow her instructions and come to the back of her house. Her parents would be surprised, but they would know what to do, and maybe even find a way to help Lukas. Zora couldn't imagine what it would be like to live with the knowledge that death was coming so soon. She glanced at Riadne, who guided the cart. She had to live with that. Somehow that thought made Zora pity her.

A lot of the next steps in the plan depended on trusting Mauro, as he said he knew someone with a boat that could sail both in the river and in the sea. That would mean they wouldn't need to stop at any port city for a boat out of Gravel.

They got to a very simple wooden house near the river. Its thin walls gave Zora shivers, considering the shadow creatures were now everywhere in the kingdom. As she waited, her eyes closed.

Zora was walking in a strange valley surrounded by two steep mountains on both sides. The strangest part was the sky; it was red. There was a fortress behind her. No, ruins of a fortress, and in front of her, a large stone arch.

"There you are," a woman said.

Zora turned back and saw that woman dressed in gold. That woman who had led her to the blood cup. Zora buried down her anger, thinking that it was better to learn as much as she could. She smiled. "Well, hello, if it isn't my lovely guide."

"Your guide? Oh, I'm flattered. Your manners have improved so much."

"Who are you?"

"You got it right. A guide. But you don't understand things and you're angry at me. You do realize you didn't need me to find anything you found, right?"

That was possible. Maybe. Even then... "I would have at least taken longer. Riadne would have stopped me."

The woman nodded. "Yes, well. I'm glad I helped, then. Time is a luxury, Zora."

"What do you want?"

"This..." she pointed to the valley around them. "It's a vision. It's not real. But it's just so you know how lucky you are. Of course, you won't understand any of that."

"And you're going to explain it?"

The woman exhaled and shook her head. "No. You don't trust me, so it won't do any good."

"Why are you showing me this, then?"

"You called me, asking for help, and I had nothing else to do."

Zora couldn't prevent her grimace. "I called you?"

"Why? You think I'd spook people randomly or something?"

"I don't even know who you are."

"It doesn't matter. You need help, you get it, even if you don't trust me. You're strong enough to face the storm that's coming."

"What storm?"

THE DARK VALLEY had always seemed something out of a legend to Tris, the kind of place that couldn't possibly be real. She'd grown up hearing stories about Gravel, their neighboring kingdom, and how it had a place where monsters spawned in the dark. It was quite terrifying, for her, as a child, to hear about it. At that age, she'd always feared that the same thing could happen in Linaria and monsters would appear in shadows. Her parents and caregivers obviously had always told her that it wasn't something that happened. But it was! And there was an entire valley to prove that it was possible. And the idea chilled her.

"But that's beyond the mountains, beyond walls, in a place you'll never set foot on," they said.

And yet here she was. She'd learned that the real monsters stood tall and proud in daylight. And yet she'd seen the shadow creatures and all the harm they could cause. But they were no longer confined to this valley, so there was no point in fearing going in.

Tris followed Zora's direction, going to the forest bordering the wall to go around the village. Lukas moaned as quietly as he could and walked slowly. Ingrown wings. That had to hurt. She'd had an ingrown toenail once and the pain had been unbearable. She couldn't imagine what it was like to have something fifty times bigger than a nail ingrowing on her back.

Yet he was walking. She knew and he probably knew that there was a huge chance that Zora's parents wouldn't be able to do anything, but so far, the girl had been the one to provide the best care, and the only one able to alleviate his pain. At least here he wouldn't suffer as much, even if he ended up dying. She didn't like that thought.

When she saw a house that was taller and bigger than the most, she rushed to it and tapped on a window, like Zora had told her to do.

A blond woman appeared, looking startled. "Who are you?"

"I'm Zora's friend," Tris said. She pointed to Lukas. "He needs medical attention and she said you'd be able to help me."

The woman frowned. "Where's Zora?"

"She's... busy. She's with Prince Larzen."

"With *another* prince?"

Tris shook her head. "Not with him, as in with him romantically, but she's doing something important. For the kingdom." The woman looked at her, thinking. Tris then added, "You're Lorena, right? Her mother."

The woman nodded.

Tris pointed at Lukas. "He really needs help. And fast. And I can't be seen."

Lorena opened the window some more. "Can you jump in?"

She turned to Lukas. "Can you?"

He nodded while grimacing.

They entered a bedroom then were taken to another room. A man was called in, probably Zora's father.

Lukas was put on a high bed, and Lorena checked the marks on his back. "What happened here?"

"He has..." It sounded crazy and she hoped they believed her. "Wings." She smiled. "They're growing, but wrong. Inward. His people, they always die when their wings come out, but Zora said that maybe you'd be able to help. At least give him something for the pain."

Lorena didn't seem bothered by the fact that a person growing wings was beyond strange. She just turned to the man. "Maybe we could try to remove them?"

He was thoughtful. "It could kill him."

"I don't care," Lukas moaned. "Just make it stop."

"We'll do our best," Lorena said.

Tris then remembered something. "Wait." She pulled the paper Zora had written and handed to her. "It's a potion. It should help. I... don't know anything about it, and neither does Zora. It's from an ancient book."

The woman looked at it and frowned, then turned to the man. "Get him some pain draught." She turned to Tris. "You'd better leave, unless you don't mind seeing blood."

"Blood gives me nightmares."

Lorena walked her to another room, then said, "Are you sure there's nobody who could know what to do?"

"There isn't. His people, they'd just let him die. They've been dying for generations."

"And Zora thinks we can do better than them?"

"Your valley has some ancient knowledge. Nobody knows how to brew potions in Gravel anymore. It could make all the difference."

She nodded. "We'll do our best, but we can't promise anything."

"I know."

"Do you want to go back and say some last words?"

Tris shook her head. "I wouldn't know what to say."

Lorena nodded, then rushed back to the room. At least they seemed a lot more competent than the healer in the castle. Tris wondered if she should have said something to him, but it was true, she didn't know what to say. And she also thought it was bad luck. For now at least she was going to believe that he would come out of this alive, and then she'd tell him all she had to tell. Once she figured out what it was.

14

THE BENT RIVER

Somebody touched her shoulder. "Time to go," Larzen said.

Zora couldn't even remember where she was. "Where?"

He rolled his eyes. "We're headed somewhere, remember?"

Yes, now that he mentioned it, she did remember that they were about to get on a boat. She also remembered her dream and her question: *what storm?* There were probably many storms ahead of her, and it was true that Zora wasn't going to trust anything that woman told her. But that place... Either way, she had to focus on the present moment.

She got her bag and jumped out of the cart, wondering how long they would have to wait. Instead, Larzen walked by the house, without entering it, and they reached a small wooden pier, where a large boat was attached. Behind it, a river much wider than Zora had imagined; it could fit some six boats side by side.

She turned to Larzen. "I thought you were going to negotiate or something."

"We did. I guess you were sleeping."

Zora had never been on a boat before. In fact, she had never seen a big river like that. Larzen led her to a cabin with six thin bunk beds, three on each wall, without much room between them. Riadne was already there, sitting on a bed.

Zora put her bags in a corner. It would be nice to finally sleep on a bed, no matter how small. The boat also had a cabin in the front, which had more beds and a table. Outside, a mast had a sail rolled on it. The owners of the boat were a couple in their forties, a brown-skinned man with shaved hair called Manee, and a woman with black hair and light brown skin called Lia.

"They're saying the wind is on our side," Mauro said as he entered the cabin. "We can reach the sea by nightfall."

Nightfall. "So we'll be able to pass by a port city when people will be indoors." Zora was thinking. "The creatures only spawn in natural spaces, and I don't think they can swim."

Mauro nodded. "Then we can stop at an island, as Manee and Lia will need to rest."

That didn't make sense. "Wouldn't an island have shadow creatures too?"

"If they're not in Gravel, they won't have them," Riadne said. "It's something in Gravel that allows them. Sort of like they used to spawn only in the Dark Valley. It's the same now, but in the entire kingdom."

It made sense. Partly. "But without a wall, they could go elsewhere."

Riadne shrugged. "They're not gonna swim, at least not that far."

Zora nodded. Of course. It was just... It seemed almost too good to be true. "Then soon people from Gravel will start leaving the kingdom." She paused. "They probably will."

"The ones who can, sure," Larzen explained. "But there aren't that many boats, and not everyone can pay them. Also remember that until now, the creatures haven't attacked villages that much."

Zora sighed. "I wish we could tell them, make sure everyone stays indoors."

Larzen's expression darkened. "We'd never reach the entire kingdom. Trust the word of mouth, that people will tell each other."

"After some dreadful accident or death." She closed her eyes.

"It is what it is," Larzen said. "You think it doesn't pain me to leave the kingdom when it needs me the most? But the thing is, I need to know how to fight these shadow creatures, this Shadow Kingdom. I won't be able to do much if I stay and fight blindly."

"You're doing the right thing," Zora said.

Riadne narrowed her eyes. "No. He should take care of his safety."

"I'm doing both," he said.

Zora was so tired, she wanted to rest and leave Larzen and Riadne to their arguing. "Can I take this middle bunk?" she asked nobody in particular.

"It's yours," Mauro replied. "But if you sleep you'll miss the lake. It's huge."

"Well, hopefully I can come back here some other day. I'm exhausted. I'll try to get some sleep."

Zora went to her bed. Mauro was tall and would have an easier time getting there, but she feared he'd be too heavy for the small bed that looked more like a shelf with a thin mattress. It had a wooden board on its side to prevent a fall, thank the Light.

It was odd to be going in a direction based on a hunch. But it was a logical hunch. She had no idea what she was going to find, but didn't let her hope fade. She was going to

fight until the end, fight to undo her mistakes, save the kingdom, and get Griffin back. She had to.

THE COUNCIL and all the nobles were leaving that dreaded
fortress, headed to the Crown Castle, where the king and
his entourage lived. Griffin was packing the king's personal
belongings. Apparently it was something he did it himself,
if his memories were right. There wasn't much. A small
notebook, with writing very similar to Continental. This
could be useful, or maybe not so much. The king had never
written anything about secret plans, like the one to open
the portal. There were few notes written, mostly about
army numbers, enemies, things that Griffin still had to
grasp.

He wasn't going to the castle, but rather to those pits. He
had a very good reason and excuse to do that, considering
there was news about subjects dying faster, whatever that
meant. His goal was to figure out how to destroy or maybe
neutralize them in the two days he had before having to
present himself to the Void. Then he was going to tell the
guards who were aligned with the rebels and hope someone
did the trick. His other plan was to try to find information
and memories in his mind about this Void, but strangely, it
was as if it didn't exist. He couldn't even picture the tower
where this creature lived. Perhaps the previous king had
blocked those memories or there was something preventing
him from accessing them. He didn't know.

Then there was this idea of dreamwalking. He wasn't sure
how useful it could be, except that if he had his way, he would
do nothing else. And yet, seeing his kingdom, seeing Zora,
that could make a difference, maybe at least quiet his heart
knowing that everyone was all right. There was no time to

sleep, but he figured he could try to do the same thing he'd done the previous time.

Griffin sat on the bed and held the pink pendant, the gift that Amina had given him. If dreamwalking was his magic, and if this thing could amplify it, then perhaps...

After a deep breath, he closed his eyes, and like that, he was no longer in Grota. Relieved to be back in his body, even if it was in dream form, he found himself on a boat on a river. It had to be the Bent River, with its strange curve, and he didn't quite understand why he was there.

He entered a cabin and saw Larzen in a bed, sleeping peacefully. His brother, alive! It was as if a rain of relief dissipated another dark cloud around Griffin. Above him, on a bunk, princess Alegra. He had no clue what she was doing there. No, he remembered now that she'd been with Larzen, chasing him and Zora when they were after the Blood Cup. Perhaps he should have stopped and listened to them.

On the other side, the Marshes champion, Mauro. Griffin liked him and remembered how he'd been a good friend to Zora. On top of him, on the bunk, having what looked like a troubled sleep, was Zora. His Zora, wiggling on the bed with a slight frown. She was alive, very alive, and this felt so real, it could only be true. He didn't know if he could touch her or if it would wake her up, but he didn't like to see her struggling in her sleep.

He ran his hand through her pretty, soft brown hair with blond tips. Or tried to. His hand went right through her hair and head, and then he was no longer on the boat, but on that cave, the cave of the red cup. The cave where there had been just the two of them, ready to start over, when having each other meant being rich beyond measure. His throat tightened.

"Griffin?" a voice asked behind him.

He turned and saw Zora, dressed in her usual leather

armor, her jaw dropped, and her eyes getting misty. She'd always been beautiful, but now she looked sublime, luminous, glowing.

"It's you," she said, her voice filled with emotion.

"It is." He then wrapped his arms around her, glad to realize that she felt solid and real against his chest. He wanted to hold her and keep on holding her, and never let her go.

"I'm so sorry," she said.

He broke the hug and looked at her. "No. Don't. It's... It had to happen."

She frowned. "No, it didn't."

He shook his head and touched her face. It felt so good to feel her soft skin again. "I don't know how long I have here. With you."

There was so much he had to tell her, perhaps ask her, but she was looking at him with those beautiful eyes, and he had to kiss her. And then there was nothing but her lips, her kiss, her body against his. Memories of their last time in this cave flooded him, his fingers unlacing her top, his lips kissing her collarbone, then moving down with more and more kisses. Her taste and feel were still on his tongue. Then he remembered her wide, scared eyes, and how he regretted having gone so fast. And this wasn't the time for any of that.

Griffin broke the kiss and stepped back.

"What's wrong?" She was breathless.

"I need to talk to you. I'm in the Shadow Kingdom."

She ran her hand over his face, her eyes filled with concern. "Are you all right?"

He took a deep breath, basking in her touch, and nodded. "Yes." He looked in her eyes, such calm eyes. "I'm doing the best I can. They... they were going to open the portal, but I stopped them."

Her hand paused. "I've heard about a portal. But if it's closed, why are there creatures everywhere?"

"It's something else. Some dark pits." He kissed her temple. "I'm going to look into it."

She caressed his hair. "I'm going to find a way to bring you back. Don't try to do anything dangerous."

He swallowed. There was very little time to try to save him, and he didn't know if it would be possible, but he didn't want to smash her hope. At least not yet. Not like that.

He kissed her forehead. "I'll be careful." He then stepped back and looked into her eyes. "I know that you saw the shadow king, the one impersonating me."

Her eyes were wide. "How?"

"I can see some of his memories."

"Oh." She looked down, thinking, then said, "And I think he sees yours. That's how he knew so much about Gravel."

Griffin nodded. It made sense and was quite dangerous. "Maybe. But what I need to tell you is that this shadow king, he can open this portal from your side, and then it will make things much worse. I don't want you to take any risks, but maybe... tell my brother, try to have them stop him, even if he has to be killed."

She frowned. "But no. He said that you can get your body back."

"Zora." He didn't hide the warning in his tone. "We would need to open the portal. I'm sure you don't want that."

She looked down. "I don't. I want to find another way." She looked at him and had a faint smile. "There has to be one. But I'm not gonna let anyone kill that shadow king while he's taking your body."

He nodded. Perhaps he would need to try to contact Larzen in his dreams. His brother surely wouldn't mind killing him for the good of the kingdom. And yet it hurt to leave Zora. He ran his hand over her face, wishing to keep the memory of every feature, every smile, every look, every touch.

"Fair enough," he said, leaving out so much for which there was no time and so much that she wasn't ready to hear. "Maybe there could be a way to destroy this portal."

"Do you know where it is? In Gravel?"

"No. In Grota, I mean, in the Shadow Kingdom, it's in a valley, near an old fortress."

Something sparked in her eyes. "An abandoned fortress?"

"Yes, why? Do you know any place like that in Gravel?"

"I know very little, Griffin. It's just, I think I had a dream about it, but not in Gravel, in this Shadow Kingdom, and it was in a valley, near a fortress."

He ran his hand through her hair, wondering if he'd ever do this again for real. "There should be something similar in Gravel, like a big arch, but it can't be destroyed the way you'd destroy a building. I have no idea where it is, though."

"I can try to find it," she said.

He then remembered where he saw her sleeping and asked, "Why are you on a boat? Where are you going?"

She shrugged. "We want to find some books with magic. Riadne had a Solana book. She was trying to stop us, you know?"

He didn't know what she was talking about. "Who's Riadne?"

"Oh, she was pretending to be princess Alegra. It's the redhead you..." She had a little grimace. "You know."

Embarrassing.

Zora continued, "She's a Solana, one of the flying witches."

He frowned, confused with the mix of old legends and whatever she was doing. "Flying witches?"

"Yes. They exist. I know it's odd." She chuckled. "Riadne is one of them. She found a book in their writing. That's how she found out that the red cup would undo the spells keeping the Shadow Kingdom contained. She was trying to stop us."

He closed his eyes. Why couldn't he have listened to Larzen? But then, he wouldn't be here. It was all so confusing.

Zora continued, "Now we're trying to find more of those books, more information."

"Where?"

"Rock Island."

The words hit him like a punch. "WHAT? Zora, you can't."

Griffin was trembling, sitting on his armchair in the king's room in the old fortress. He still held the pendant. With eyes closed, he tried to focus, hoping it would let him connect with Zora again, dreamwalk again. *Zora, Zora.* He had to talk to her.

Nothing happened.

Perhaps the only way to do it was when he relaxed, and there was no way to relax after hearing that. His heart was racing so much that his chest was aching.

No, Zora.

And yet he had no way to plead.

Zora opened her eyes and found herself in a strange, dark room. Not a room; a cabin on a boat.

Zora, you can't. Griffin's words rang in her ears.

But it had been just a dream.

Had it? It had felt real, and yet it was all mixed. Something about a portal. A portal, a big arch like the one in that other dream. And yet, was any of this real? Or her mind playing tricks on her?

This wasn't the first time that the memory of them in that

cave came to her mind. She'd been so happy and eager then, sure that everything was going to work out well.

Then they were together, and it always played out differently, without fear. To be fair, she'd never had a dream where they stopped kissing to talk about portals. But then, there was so much she had to find out, she was so worried; it made sense that she'd dream about him. She missed his beautiful face, his smile, his calm, level-headed temper. And yet her last image of him had his eyes almost popping out in horror. *Zora, you can't.* Well, dreams were weird sometimes. But she could still feel his kiss.

She sat up and got out of the bunk. Larzen slept on the other side, and Mauro on the bed beneath hers. Riadne wasn't in the cabin. Zora stepped outside, where the cool wind brought a fresh smell of trees—and something more. The ocean? The sun was halfway down, so at least in theory they were about two or three hours from the coast. Zora had never imagined one day she'd see the ocean. She'd be happy and excited if the circumstances had been different.

Riadne was sitting on a bench on the back of the boat, one of her books in her hand, and looked up. "Zora?"

"You didn't sleep?"

The redhead shrugged. "A little, but I wasn't fighting shadow creatures at night, like all of you. I'm trying to find useful potions in this book. But I need your help."

"Maybe you could try to make them." It was strange that Riadne thought Zora would have more success with ancient Solana potions than her.

"Maybe, but still, you could help me. Here, there's something for strength. It says it needs blood and pepper on a black surface. Does that look like anything you know?"

"The usual strength potion uses iron and pepper. I still don't know what this black surface is. Maybe it's just a potion table, but with a different name? You think I should make a potion for strength?"

"No," She flipped the pages. "There's another one here. Balsam of truth."

"What for?"

Riadne bit her lip. "I think... it makes the person who takes it speak the truth."

"I can see how it would be useful if you want to question someone, find a secret, I guess." Zora wasn't sure why she was bringing this up.

The redhead sighed. "I was thinking... Could you make it and give it to me?"

That made no sense. "To you?"

Riadne exhaled, as if annoyed. "Well, yes. I don't want Larzen or you looking at me with mistrust, you know? I understand you have good reasons not to trust me, but... I just want to prove I..." She paused and pinched her lips. "It's not that I changed. It's not that I regret anything, even if I'm not sure if what I was doing was wrong, it's just..." She looked down.

"I trust you, though. I mean, I'm pretty sure you want the books as much as I do, and I don't think you want Gravel to be taken over by shadow creatures. I think Larzen trusts you too."

Riadne looked away, at the river.

Right. The problem was Larzen. But he trusted her. More than trusted.

Zora said, "You know, sometimes you need to open up and tell people how you feel."

Riadne looked at Zora. "It's not how I feel. It's what I mean." She looked down. "For the record, I am sorry for..." She looked away. "Griffin. And you. And getting in the way." She closed her eyes.

Zora was taken aback at the apology, but wondering why

Riadne was saying it. And perhaps that was why the false princess wanted to prove what she said; to avoid all this wondering about her motives.

"For a potion like that," Zora said, "The only way it would be useful would be if we were sure that it worked."

"You could test it."

Zora grimaced. "On me?" The idea was horrible.

Riadne smirked. "Got your secrets too? I thought you were all pure and perfect."

Zora crossed her arms. "I'm neither of those. And I don't make potions for people who tease me."

Riadne shook her head. "I'm not teasing. I mean it. I doubt you've ever done anything evil in your life. So I'm surprised you'd have any secrets."

"Everybody has secrets."

The redhead opened the book and showed a page with those strange triangles and circles. "It's here. Lemon, orange, and clove. Sounds simple, but if I were to mix them, it wouldn't make a potion."

"You have to set a table and do it like a potion, not like a drink."

Riadne paused, thinking. "So you need the intention."

"I guess. Is there anything else? There should be proportions, you know? And I'm not sure this boat has these ingredients."

"There's a small storage cabinet. They have it, I checked. The proportion is equal."

"That's gonna be a lot of cloves."

Riadne shook her head. "No, one clove. Three drops of the others. You put the drops in a drink."

Zora took a deep breath. "I can try. But someone else needs to take it too, to prove that it works, otherwise it won't do much. Not that I think you need to do that. Like I said, we've been trusting you."

"Yeah, *we've been trusting you.* You say it as if it was a great concession that I don't deserve." Zora was about to protest that it wasn't true, but Riadne extended a hand. "I know, I know. I understand why you do it. I just wish you could really trust me."

Why did it matter to her? Perhaps because of Larzen. And then perhaps it was some kind of machination, some kind of plan. That potion could do anything.

And there she was again doubting Riadne, and she understood the false princess' point. "I'll try it and we'll see what happens."

"Thank you. I promise I'll do everything I can to help you bring your prince back." Riadne squeezed Zora's shoulder, got up, and entered the cabin.

Funny how Riadne always said *your prince*, perhaps to make it clear that she was no longer interested in Griffin and that he was Zora's. Sometimes she wished she wouldn't say that.

Zora had kissed and planned to spend a life together with Griffin, but that been when he was no longer going to be a prince. She just wanted him, title or no title. Just Griffin, not *a prince.* And what she wanted most was to give him his life back, regardless of whatever ended up happening between him and Zora. So much could change. So much had already changed from that moment on the mountain when they had decided to keep going and start over.

She looked at the side of the boat, moving fast against the water, passing trees and river banks. They'd all need to go inside if they passed a village, but she assumed the owners of the boat would tell them.

Steps drew her attention, and she turned to see Mauro, who stretched his arms.

"Got some rest?" she asked. By the Light, he deserved it. She had no idea how he could have fixed the wheels after fighting for an entire night. As a matter of fact, she had no clue how he'd fixed the wheels.

"I did."

"So you grew up near this river?"

"A little west, but close by. It's after where it bends and meets the lake."

Zora had seen this river on a map. "It's funny how this river curves."

"Some say that hundreds of years ago, it didn't. It went straight to the ocean, then something happened, and it bent. That even the lake moved."

"Do you think this story is true?"

"I don't know, I wasn't around back then." He laughed, then got serious. "I heard you talking."

"And?"

"She wants to make things right. She saved your life. You know that, right?"

"I do. And I... kind of trust her. It's just, this idea of making a potion sounds more convoluted than necessary. Sometimes all we need is time to trust someone."

He shrugged. "It doesn't hurt. It won't kill anyone. I mean, I hope that's not the case. You can give it to her first, just to be sure."

Zora shuddered. "She can't die. Who's going to translate the Solana books?" She caught herself. "I mean, and I obviously wouldn't want her to get hurt or anything..."

"You said there was an old woman in the place Riadne's from. She could translate them. In fact, weren't all Solanas supposed to die or something?"

"Riadne said Dada, this woman, is a rare exception and had a great healer or something." Zora tilted her head. "And I don't want Riadne to die."

"Of course!" He nodded, thoughtful. "Isn't the potion made of lemon, orange, a clove? How can it kill someone?"

"I doubt it could kill, but still... Potions have special prop-erties. They're not like some juice or normal drink. I mean, you could, at least in theory, have a killing potion with common, non-lethal ingredients."

Mauro looked at the cabin where Riadne had retreated. "She doesn't strike me as suicidal."

Zora sighed. "I'll see if I can do it. I can try to make regular potions for us too, I don't know... Strength? But I doubt we'll face any enemies soon."

He thought for a moment. "Seasickness. We might need something against that."

The list of known potions passed through Zora's mind, but there was nothing even similar to that. She bit her lip.

Mauro chuckled. "Oh. I doubt you'd need something like that living encircled by walls, far from the shore."

"Maybe something for regular nausea? Maybe. I'll see what I can do."

Perhaps it would be a good idea to focus on something that she could do right away instead of agonizing over what would happen on Rock Island, and whether they would be able to reverse the spell in the kingdom. And then if she reversed it, she wondered what could happen to the Dark Valley...

And how she was getting Griffin back.

15

UNDER THE STARS

A few stars appeared in the darkening sky, and Riadne could also see some lights from Gold Port emerging far in the river. They were about to cross the city, making it one of the most dangerous parts of their journey. Of their river journey, at least.

The night trip had been dangerous enough and no doubt people on Rock Island weren't simply going to let them walk in and steal their books. Still, they had to avoid guards or any attention that could draw the Shadow King's eyes to where they were going.

Lia, the boat owner, led Riadne and Larzen to the main cabin and lifted a plank. "Here. I'll call you out when it's safe."

Larzen went through the hole, then reached out a hand to her. Only the two of them were going to hide. At first, they had debated that Zora and Mauro should hide as well, but then thought it would be even more suspicious for Lia and Manee to be leaving with an empty boat. At least that had been what the prince said. A small part of Riadne wondered if he wanted some time alone with her. That was the kind of stupid wondering that made women make fools of themselves.

Riadne jumped in without his help, then heard a thud, and was immersed in darkness. The floor was the bottom of the boat, curved and slippery.

"Do you have a light?"

"It wouldn't be wise," he replied. "We'd better be quiet."

Of course. They were hiding. What was she thinking? "I know," she whispered.

It was just strange not to see anything. Riadne sat on the bottom, even if it had some beams that made it quite uncomfortable, but if she fell it would be worse. She heard Larzen sitting across from her. Even with the water outside and the wind on the sail, she could hear his breath. So far and so close. The urge to reach out to him was overwhelming. In another time, another place, if they both had been different people, with different histories, would they have a chance?

So much pointless thinking, just because of his pretty blue eyes. It wasn't the eyes, it was him, it was having gotten used to his presence and even learning to trust him. She could think that she'd have done everything differently if she could go back in time, but then she wouldn't be here. Perhaps she'd never even have gone to the Gravel castle.

There was no point wishing things were different. All she could do was hold down those thoughts in that special place for absurdities. It was fine to conjure nonsensical ideas, it was fine even to wish them. Riadne had learned not to censor her thoughts. But she could, she should, and she would censor her actions and words. And wouldn't feed these thoughts with stupid, unrealistic hope.

She was fine. Larzen was attractive. Really attractive. They had spent time together. He was nice. Of course it messed her mind. It didn't mean anything.

Riadne exhaled. Even in the dark, she could feel his eyes

on her. She did wish he could trust her more, though. She wasn't sure if the idea of the truth balsam had been silly. The Dark Valley girl seemed to think so. Riadne just wanted to prove that she wasn't going to hurt Larzen, and that she had long given up any wish to see his family destroyed. All she wanted was to make sure they would work well together. Mistrust didn't help, and their journey was hard enough as it was.

And yet she could feel Larzen's presence in front of her, an uncensored thought wishing he would come near, yearning to hear his breath from up close, by her ear. Perhaps it was just that it had been a long time since she had been with anyone. But it hadn't been *that* long.

Yikes.

She wanted to forget her last time, which felt all wrong now. If she could turn back time, she'd never allow Griffin to touch her, that was for sure. Looking back, it felt awkward, and it had been completely unnecessary, even when she'd been set on her plan. Not that he'd ever done anything wrong or bad or unpleasant. Well, it had been the opposite of unpleasant, in fact. He had quite the talent, and sometimes she wondered if it ran in the family.

Great. Now her mind was making it all a thousand times more awkward. Ugh. Oh, well, regretting wasn't going to change anything. She needed to find a way to at least erase all that from her mind. She'd need to ask Zora if she had a potion for that, without explaining the reason, of course. So. Awkward.

Thinking of potions made her thoughts turn to her brother. Goodbyes had stopped hurting a long time ago. At least if they had good potions for the pain in the Dark Valley, he'd go without suffering. He was so happy just to have Tris by his side. Funny what even unrequited love did to a person, even someone dying.

Death.

Soon Riadne would face her own end. She'd need to get some of those good potions or learn how to make them. She glanced at where Larzen was, even if she couldn't see him properly, wondering if she would die without kissing him. Probably. She wasn't going to beg for a kiss, and she wasn't going to act like a silly girl in love. Self-respect mattered more than those silly wishes. And it was silly.

A powerful Solana like her should bring men to her feet, not the other way around. Larzen was an oddity; not only he didn't respond to her magic, he didn't notice her. Oh, well, some people were just weird and there was nothing she could do about it.

A thud brought her back to the present moment. Someone lifted the board on top of them.

"Are we clear?" Larzen asked. Sometimes just hearing his voice brought chills down her spine, and this was one of them, maybe because of all that time alone with him in the dark wondering things she shouldn't be wondering.

"Out in the ocean. Nobody even stopped us," the man called Manee replied.

Larzen pushed himself up, then extended a hand to help her. This time Riadne took it just because going up was harder than going down. She'd definitely turned into a silly girl, as her entire body trembled with the touch. She turned away from him and looked outside, at the lights on the coast far from them. Her heart was beating fast, and she took a deep breath to calm down.

"Are you all right?" It was Zora who was asking.

"That compartment below isn't the most comfortable, that's all."

She looked at the girl to see if she'd give any sign that she'd considered making the truth balm, but she just nodded. Perhaps she'd forgotten it or thought it was silly. Perhaps the idea *was* silly and useless. And then perhaps what was silly was caring about what these people thought of her. At the end of the day, it didn't matter. If they failed, they'd probably die soon. If they succeeded, they'd eventually all go their separate ways. Not that she had any clue what hers was. And she'd probably die soon regardless of what happened.

Funny that she'd always thought that a boat would rock a lot on the ocean, to the point one wouldn't be able to stand on it, and so far it hadn't been that bad. Her imagination had probably exaggerated what it would be like to be on the sea. The smell was so different from the mountains, as if there were salt and fish in the air, and then so much nothingness and darkness on the side away from the land. A quarter moon shone in the sky, its rays reflecting on the waves.

Riadne sighed. They should start planning, preparing, except that they still didn't know much about what they were going to find. She felt someone approaching, turned, and saw Larzen.

She caught a breath, then asked the first thing that came to mind. "Have you ever been out in the ocean?"

He shook his head. "I saw the world through maps. As much as I planned for this, I never left Gravel." He closed his eyes. "By this, I mean traveling, not..."

"I know."

From what he'd told her, he had never thought his older brother would die, never thought he'd be king. Funny how people sometimes avoided seeing the obvious, or at least the very likely.

He leaned on the side of the boat, looking at her. "We're getting to our stop."

The moonlight made him look so good that she felt her face flush. At least it was dark. Riadne turned around. "I'll see if they need help."

Her heart was thumping in her chest as she walked away,

Of course the couple didn't need help, at least not from Riadne, who'd never before in her life been on a boat.

When she got to the front, she realized they were getting to a small island. The boat moved slowly to that piece of land that didn't belong to Gravel. Technically, they were in Kentosa waters, even if it would be another day to reach a port city on the shore of the kingdom.

Slowly, the boat approached a sandy beach. Lia threw an anchor, then the couple called them to have dinner.

They all sat at a small table in the front compartment. The couple served marinated raw fish and bread. Apparently it was a typical dish in Gold Port, probably because it was easy to make and store on a boat and didn't need fire. Riadne sat at the edge of the table, by Larzen, and she really had to stop obsessing about him.

Mauro opened a bottle of wine and filled their cups, or at least put a little bit in the case of Zora and Manee, who didn't want to drink much.

"I propose a toast," he said.

"To?" Zora asked.

Mauro smiled. "Being alive."

Larzen raised his cup. "Succeeding in the first part of our plan."

"Having great food," Zora said.

That brought a reaction in Manee, who smiled. He and his wife had a quiet complicity. Riadne tried to avoid it, but she sometimes felt jealous of people who could get old, especially the ones who got old together.

Riadne raised her cup. "Having friends."

Her words were meant to be polite and pleasing, but as their glasses clanked, she realized it was true, in a sense. Almost dying together was a powerful shared experience. She'd never have guessed that she'd consider someone from the Gravel royal family a friend. Larzen's eyes met hers, as if also taking the meaning of her words. There was still so much to do, so much that could go wrong, but it meant something that they were all there, eating together.

When she finished, for some reason she felt as if everything around her was a blur and the sounds distant. The only thing she was aware of was Larzen by her side. Again she could hear his breath, and it must have been her imagination, but she thought she could hear his heart beating. For a moment it felt as if nothing else existed, just the two of them, everything else dissolving into nothingness.

Riadne took a deep breath, trying to ground herself again and pay attention to her surroundings. Instead, she felt his hand holding hers, feeling a sudden emptiness in her stomach as if she'd just fallen.

"Come," he whispered in her ear. "I've never been to an island." He turned to the others. "We'll be right back."

Lia might or might not have said something about danger and pirates, and they jumped on the shallow waters of the beach, getting her feet and the bottom of her dress wet. The water was warm, contrasting with the cool wind.

They got away from the beach, walking among trees, but soon were on the other side. Here, thunderous waves hit the sand and rock with fury and power. A calming, hypnotizing sound. The dark waters reflected the moon until that light got lost on the horizon. That was a pleasant sight, but Larzen looked even better.

Her heart was beating as if it wanted to burst out of her chest. She didn't know what to say, but the silence was stretching for so long that it was getting unbearable.

Riadne faced Larzen. "Any—" How could she say it? "—reason you brought me here?"

He let go of her hand and caressed her arm up to her shoulder, while tucking a strand of her hair behind her ear with the other hand. "I missed being alone with you."

She smiled. "Same." It felt good to say that, to admit so much in one simple word.

From her hair, his hand moved to the nape of her neck, his other arm pulling her closer. Riadne looked up and met his eyes, then he lowered his lips to her. The feel of his tongue meeting her was like a spark casting a fire on her. Perhaps it was just revealing the fire that had always been there. She wanted Larzen, and had wanted him for so long it ached. Now that she was kissing him, she wanted all of him. Every part of her body had this ache and want and yearning.

She pulled him back to the soft sand. She wanted him now, she wanted him yesterday. Any more second without him was almost painful. He pulled up her dress, and she raised her arms as it came off. He then fumbled with the back of her bodice. Why was she wearing that thing? It seemed that he was as impatient as her, as he pulled his dagger and cut it.

She put her hands under his shirt, and he took it off. His torso was marvelous, so firm and tight that he looked like a work of art. It felt wonderful to touch his chest, his hard stomach. She then tried to open his belt with some difficulty. He pushed her hands away and opened it.

He was everything she wanted, everything she needed. The truth was that she loved him. She loved Larzen. Loved, loved, loved him as madly as anyone could love anyone. Perhaps more. There was nobody else, there would never be anyone else but Larzen, Larzen, Larzen.

The fury of the waves hitting the rocks was nothing compared to his fury pounding her like a ram. And she wanted it. She wanted him to break all her walls, shatter all her shields, bring down all her defenses. Break her, break her, break her. Tear it all down, until all that remained was her love, her light, her fire, burning bright for him. He was entering her body, her heart, her soul. Breaking all her walls.

THE NIGHT WAS BREATHTAKING, with so many stars reflected in the ocean. Darkness was beautiful, and it was an experience Zora had never had in the Dark Valley. She sat by the edge of the boat, immersed in that beauty, when Mauro approached her.

"Feeling anything different?"

It was a weird question. She said, "Darkness is always different to me, but I like how things change from colorful to tones of gray. I had never seen it while growing up."

"It's almost hard to believe that there are no creatures on this island."

"I really hope there aren't, for their sake." She thought about Larzen and Riadne. "They're taking long, aren't they?"

He shrugged. "Must be settling their differences. Finally. See? Her idea was good."

Zora frowned, confused. "What do you mean?"

"Aren't you feeling a bit more truthful?"

"What? No." Yes, she had made the potion, but she had put it aside. "Wait. What did you do?"

"I put the truth balsam in the wine."

What? Zora could barely believe him. "You should have told me, you should have told her!"

"Then what's the point? If you know you're being forced to say the truth, you'll try to control what you say."

"Still not right." She shook her head, then something came to her mind. "You took it as well."

He smiled. "Yes. Want to ask a question?"

"Well, no, according to you it won't work."

"Just try it."

"Why are you here?"

He paused, then pointed to the eyepatch covering his missing eye. "I got this when I was five."

Zora covered her mouth, remembering the children in the valley. "I'm so sorry."

He shook his head. "No. Pity is the worst, you know? Maybe second worst. Derision, disgust, those are the ones that hurt. And I was a child, it was not my fault. But I guess the other children were too young to understand." He shrugged. "My parents always told me it didn't matter what other people thought. But it's not true, is it?"

She bit her lip, unsure how to answer.

He continued, "Well, I thought being the champion would change things, but it didn't. It didn't. Maybe being a hero will change things, maybe doing something that matters for the kingdom."

She sighed. "We could fail. And it's possible that nobody will learn about what we're doing."

"I'm trying. Maybe it's for myself. I don't know."

Zora nodded. "I always wanted to be a hero, do something meaningful. I did—or tried, and I ruined the kingdom. I want to be more careful this time, make no mistakes."

"You can't guarantee that. You gotta do your best."

"I have to. And it's for Griffin too. I miss him every second."

He smiled. "You love him very much."

"I do. You have love too, don't you? Perhaps you shouldn't... be risking your life."

"I have love. And yes, it's great. But it's not everything, Zora. It's like we have many compartments, and they all need to be filled. Love is just one of them."

"But it's a very important one."

"For sure."

She glanced at the beach again. "They're taking too long."

He smiled. "They must be finding the truth."

She sighed. "I guess." Then she heard a scream and stiffened. "It's Riadne. We have to get them." Zora turned to go to the ladder.

"Wait." He was suppressing a laugh. "I don't think she needs help."

Another scream. Oh. It sounded as if someone was torturing her, but then it sounded like she was enjoying it, as if it was some kind of pleasant torture. A ridiculous description, of course, but it was all Zora could come up with. It meant that Riadne and Larzen... Well, that had been fast. Another scream. She had no idea it could be so loud. "Is it normal? That much noise?"

He shrugged. "I'm not an expert on women, but I think so. Sometimes."

Zora wondered what made it noisy or not, but that was way too much to ask a male friend. And perhaps it varied from person to person, just like when someone was stitched. No, it wasn't good to compare it to pain, but she didn't know what else to compare it to. She thought about Riadne and Larzen, and how they'd been eying and teasing each other for so long. "At least they're being truthful to each other."

Mauro nodded. "Just imagine how much more focused they're going to be from now on."

"I hope so."

16

THE MORNING AFTER

Griffin almost threw the pendant away, but then he remembered it could still be useful. Why couldn't he contact Zora again? Or his brother? That Sun Goddess or guide or whatever? Nothing. And he'd been trying for hours.

Going to Rock Island. He didn't know who had put that stupid idea in Zora's mind, but he already wanted to strangle whoever it was. Why? Why? He felt cold inside, and empty.

Two knocks on the door drew his attention. He didn't even know if he wanted to leave again. Perhaps he'd try to sleep and see if he could see her. What would it take for that? Getting drunk? Asking someone for a sleeping draught? Did these people even drink?

Another two knocks.

"Yes?" he roared.

Nobody opened it, so he got up and opened the door himself. Bruno, the guard, was there, and he bowed. "Your majesty. The time—"

"I know." His voice was calmer now, Griffin pushing down his anger, then he almost ran his hand through his hair, but he had no hair, so he just ran over that leathery weird disgusting bald thing and sighed. These guards had no fault. And he had to check the dark pits. "I'm coming."

He had decided to travel with just Bruno and Samuel, the guards loyal to Amina. He hadn't told them he wasn't the real king, and had no idea what she'd told them, or if she'd told them anything, but it was the best he could do for now. Perhaps the council or other nobles would be suspicious, but he didn't have time to waste. He had to find these pits as soon as possible, and, if he could, figure out a way to destroy them. His scattered memories told him very little other than it wouldn't be easy. Well, nothing was easy.

Perhaps once he got tired, he'd be able to sleep and dreamwalk. And perhaps he was overreacting. What were the odds Zora would even find that dreadful magic island?

RIADNE WAS FLOATING above the ocean, facing the rising sun. No, that was a dream. She felt rough sand under her body, and something hard, like a weird leather-covered iron pillow, under her head. The hard thing was Larzen's chest. Riadne was leaning on his naked, perfect-looking body, but it felt so unreal.

He pulled her closer, still asleep. What had happened? The memories came slowly, like a thread being unveiled. Walking to this beach, and then... She looked around and saw her bodice—cut in half. She closed her eyes in disbelief. What she did remember was a whole ton of "I love you, Larzen." *Love you, love you, love you*, echoed in her head. Had she said that?

A nauseous feeling came to her with the thought that she was placing her happiness in someone else's hands. She'd seen women in love before, in love with men who didn't want the same, how they humiliated themselves for scraps of affection. And there she was, hungered, desperate for his affection, his love, feeling foolish and weak. Up until then, she'd been in control over her feelings, her happiness. Now she depended on someone else.

Last night she had let down all her walls, all her protections, and offered her heart out. Out to be stabbed. No, it made no sense. She was a powerful Solana; she could stab first. And then, perhaps she could enchant him and make him forget all that happened, make him think it was an illusion. That would be easy—if he responded to her magic. She had to undo what she'd done, be back in control, but she wasn't sure how.

He opened his eyes, looked at her, smiled, and chuckled. She wondered what he thought was so funny.

LARZEN HAD Riadne in his arms. Riadne; the woman he'd always thought was the most beautiful in the world. Undressed, under the rising sun, she was a lot more striking than he had ever imagined. But her expression was thoughtful, perhaps even angry.

"Something wrong?" he asked.

"No. Why?"

Her voice was cold and distant, and felt like a bucket of cold water.

A tinge of panic came to him, as he wasn't sure what he'd done wrong.

"Nothing," he said, then ran his hand over her head, but she looked away. He added, "We'd better get dressed." He had no clue what else to say.

He sat up and turned to his clothes, trying to recall the previous night, until slowly the memories became clear. Well, now he wanted to dig a hole in the sand and hide there forever. First, he glanced at her destroyed bodice. Then he remembered how things had happened and cringed.

In his opinion, intimacy between two people was like a fine dinner, with appetizers and drinks, something delicate, sophisticated, to be savored slowly. Last night he had acted like a starved dog. That should be enough to piss her off.

He put on his pants, then turned to Riadne, who already had her dress back on, but without undergarments, he could see the shape of her breasts, and all he could think was to get that thing off her and start it all over again. Great. Now he was feeling like a horny young teenager.

He looked up at her and sighed. "Last night, I..." How did one apologize for acting crazed like that?

"Forget about it." She tilted her head and smirked. "It's meaningless, and you know that."

That wasn't exactly what he'd been thinking. "Meaningless?"

"Nothing. It's nothing for you. It's nothing for me." She smiled. "Doesn't need to happen again."

Right. It *had been* terrible. "It was rushed, and I'm at fault here." Apologizing was humiliating, but sometimes it was necessary. "But I care about you. If you can forgive me." These words had taken all his courage to come out and he felt naked, exposed.

"I care about you too." Her voice was cold and didn't match the words. "We have to work together, right? I've already forgotten about last night." She got up.

Forgotten? She could forget it like that? Perhaps that was what she meant by meaningless. But he had to remember that she had an abrasive personality, and he was probably misunderstanding her. He stepped in front of her, wrapped his arms around her waist, and kissed her cheek. "We can start over from scratch. Do it right."

He moved his mouth and met her lips, which opened for

a long kiss. At that moment, he knew that his worries were silly. There had been so much love last night. He felt it then and he felt it now, and his only certainty was that he wanted to have her by his side forever.

After a few seconds, she pushed him. "Larzen, no."

"What?"

She rolled her eyes. "Just because we did it once it doesn't mean I'm available to you any time you want."

He stepped back, astonished, not even sure how to address what she'd just said, so he tried to change the subject. "It wasn't once. It was what? Four, five times? I lost count."

"Counts as one for me and it's still nothing. You have no feelings for me and I have no feelings for you."

He swallowed. "Don't speak about my feelings."

"Then tell me about them." She was staring at him with her beautiful brown eyes, but they were cold.

He wasn't even sure anymore. For a moment he'd thought they understood each other, he'd even gone as far as to think that they were in love. "Why? So you'll mock them?"

She shrugged. "I'm curious."

"No idea why, since you're so good at guessing, aren't you? Now me, I can't ask about your feelings, since you don't have any, do you?"

Riadne rolled her eyes. "I have lots of feelings, Larzen. None of them has anything to do with our activities last night."

A horrible sinking feeling of humiliation was taking over him. Still, perhaps he was misunderstanding her. "It was just relief, right? It could have been with someone else."

"Maybe."

She turned and started walking back towards the boat. He held her arm. He was going to ask her if it really had meant nothing, if it had been an impression, if the feeling he'd seen in those eyes had been an illusion, but her face told him everything he could know.

He was so angry, so humiliated, so he covered it all up with a smile, or perhaps a smirk. "Thank you. For last night. Really. After all the fighting," he let her go and rubbed his hand over his right arm. "My arm was really sore. I wouldn't have been able to do it myself. With you it's not quite the same, but it's close."

She stared at him for a moment, and he felt a wicked satisfaction at the delayed flash of fury in her eyes when she finally understood what he meant.

She smiled. "Yeah, extenuating circumstances demand extenuating sacrifices. I was glad to help."

The truth was that the more they talked, the worse it got. "Can we never mention it again? Just pretend it never happened?"

"What?" She had a confused frown. "I don't remember anything. Do you?"

"Don't know." He scratched his chin and smiled. "What were we talking about again?"

In truth, he remembered every detail, every touch, but he was obviously the only one who did.

THERE HADN'T BEEN any more dreams about Griffin, just his voice calling her. But then, what was the point in dreaming? If she wanted to see him again, she'd need to make it become a reality, and not count on dreams.

She got out of her bed and saw Larzen and Mauro sleeping, but no Riadne.

The redhead was outside, holding the book with the Solana potions, running her hand over it, her face wistful. There was sadness there. Zora sighed. She and Mauro had agreed that they had to tell Riadne the truth, but now she was second-guessing it.

She raised her eyes and gave Zora a thin smile.

"Reading?" Zora sat by her.

She looked at the book. "Wing cake." She had a bitter chuckle. "Is it too much to hope that somehow our solution could have been in a book all this time? Or is it ironic that it could be so simple?"

"You're worried about your brother," Zora said.

"And myself too. Maybe I'm wondering what's going to happen." Riadne bit her lip, then looked away, at the ocean, her eyes lost.

Zora was wondering if Riadne would ask again about the truth balsam, give her an opening to mention it, but she didn't. Zora would need to bring up the truth. She took a deep breath, then said, "I... made the potion you asked me."

"Hum. Yes, maybe it could make a difference." Riadne didn't sound interested.

"I... it wasn't my fault," Zora blurted. "It was an accident. It was Mauro, but he didn't know you were going to drink it—"

Riadne frowned. "Say it."

"It wasn't on purpose, but... there was some of the truth balsam in the wine yesterday."

The redhead froze and stared at Zora. "In the wine?"

"Which you drank." Zora bit her lip.

"What?" Riadne got up and put her hands on her head. "You know what it means?"

That Zora was a horrible person? But she just shook her head.

"I could be misunderstanding this book. It's over four hundred years old. Words change. Meanings might have changed. What you gave me was likely some kind of..." She paused. "Stupid decision potion."

"It could be the truth."

Riadne rolled her eyes. "No." She chuckled. "Definitely not."

"I'm sorry."

She waved a hand. "It was my idea, in a way. I'm sure you meant well." Still, Riadne's voice was tight. She was angry.

"Did something bad happen? Between you and Larzen?"

The false princess shook her head. "Nothing happened. Nothing important, at least."

"Should I tell Larzen about the potion?"

"Oh yes, that will be wonderful." Her tone was sarcastic. "Then he'll think I forced him like I did with his *baby brother*."

"Nobody said that."

"Say whatever you want." Riadne picked up the book and walked away.

Zora had no doubt that the false princess and Larzen had gotten together the previous night. In fact, Riadne had admitted as much. What she didn't understand was why all of a sudden it seemed like a problem. Perhaps it had been the potion that made it all wrong somehow. Damn Mauro. And Riadne. And everyone.

But then, the important thing was getting to Rock Island. So far nobody had quit, and that was what mattered.

King Saro's horse was a black stallion and, like his owner, didn't need to drink or eat. Quite convenient. Griffin sighed. Of course not, if the price was whatever they did to people in the dark pits and being dependent on an evil creature.

Bruno and Samuel's horses weren't as lucky—or as cursed, and they ate hay and some brown vegetables that looked like carrots. It was interesting to realize that this place had food. He even wondered if he could eat if he tried, but preferred not to risk poisoning or any other complication.

Griffin had been traveling with the guards for half a day. He didn't feel tired and his legs didn't cramp for sitting for so long. Not *his* legs, that thing's legs. He still barely dared to look at himself in the mirror, and often tried to contain his disgust. Strange because his revulsion by the guards had stopped, now that he was starting to trust them. He hadn't been repulsed by Amina and her baby. Well, at first, yes, but not later, after she helped him. Perhaps it was just the disgust in wearing someone else's skin, someone else's body, and an enemy's body on top of that.

He was still worried about Zora and her insane decision. Really, who had told her to do that? Larzen? The stupid not-Alegra flying witch, whatever her name was? Griffin would need to try to contact Zora and explain the danger of trying to go to that dreaded island. He would do it tonight, after he checked his first dark pit.

The jumbled memories in his mind didn't have much on those pits, other than the fact that they existed and were scattered in the kingdom. Prisoners and criminals were taken there, where they remained until they died. He didn't think the king had ever personally visited any of them. Why bother? They worked. They had existed for a long time, long enough that it seemed like forever.

The king had known that it was possible that these pits would start producing more energy and having prisoners killed faster if the gates opened. Apparently he had some notion that there could be a different circumstance where this would happen, but he hadn't been sure about it.

Other than that, the king had known that it would be possible to pass on to the other side, from where he could open the gates for his kingdom to achieve more power, but it didn't seem that it was something he'd been expecting, and that he connected it clearly to the pits.

It was interesting for Griffin to have the time to let these memories come to him. A ride in silence was the perfect opportunity to investigate the information in his mind. There was nothing about the Void, just perhaps some... fear? Fear of something much more powerful than the king, but at the same time a sense of trust, reliance. Those were the only impressions that reached Griffin. He found no memory of visiting his tower, and still had no idea what this Void looked like or what his abilities were.

"We're getting close." Bruno was beside him.

Griffin saw a stone building with just one floor that didn't look like much. It had to have some six rooms at most. "That thing?" He pointed at it.

"That's the station, yes," Samuel said. "The pit is beside it."

"And they have Lorel prisoners here?" Griffin wasn't afraid of asking stupid questions.

"Lorel, Kayania, some local," the guard said. "Anyone who's an enemy of the kingdom is sent to these prisons."

"But there are other prisons, right? For lesser crimes?" There was something about it in the memories in his mind.

"A few, yes. Criminals can be sent to prisons. This is more for treason. In theory. I mean, they can basically put anyone here."

Griffin nodded, thoughtful. If these soldiers were loyal to Lorel, they could be sent here if discovered, and they probably knew people who had been sent to these dark pits, to suffer until death. This kingdom was horrible.

There was a tall, circular wall by that building, around what he surmised was the pit. And apparently it was indeed a pit.

They dismounted, and Griffin turned to the guards. "Stay here."

"Are you sure?" Bruno asked.

No, he wasn't sure about anything, but for some reason he decided it was better to approach alone. He had an odd feeling. Perhaps it was because that place gave him the creeps, and he didn't want to expose the two men unnecessarily.

Griffin approached the building, and a short and broad man came to greet him, then widened his eyes and bowed. "Your majesty. How may I serve you?"

"Is there anything worth reporting here? Perhaps something different happening?"

The man was still bent over. "Yes, your—"

"Stand straight and look at me." He wasn't going to talk to someone staring at the ground. Griffin didn't even know if the rudeness was his or some memory he was accessing.

"Your majesty. The subjects are dying faster, and we're making more energy."

Griffin didn't want to ask stupid questions, so he just said, "I see. I would like to inspect the premises."

The man widened his eyes. "You? Your... Yes, yes, your majesty. I'll provide an escort."

The man went to the building, and then called four guards. They all wore thick leather armor with some metal plaques in the chest, and had helmets too. The armored guards led him to a heavy iron door at the wall and opened it. What was inside was a spiral ramp descending a circular hole so deep that Griffin couldn't see the bottom. The ramp didn't have a rail separating it from the chasm, and he felt a little dizzy stepping on it. This was dangerous. One little push and he would be gone. Who knew if whatever strength he had would allow him to survive a fall? If that thing even ended somewhere.

Down below, there were cells with iron bars, but they

were empty. Perhaps this was a stupid question, but he had to ask, "Why isn't there anyone here?"

Silence.

"Can you talk?" Griffin repeated.

"Y-yes," one of the guards said. "This is the overflow area. The prisoners are down there in the pit."

They kept going down, and a guard lit a torch. Even though they weren't far from the surface, it was dark as if it was night. Moans and screams came from below. From what he understood, some of these prisoners would become the shadow creatures in Gravel.

"Is there anything different that you see here?" Griffin asked.

"They're more silent, it's as if they're transitioning more often, and aren't really here."

Right. Because now they could go to Gravel. Griffin had to find a way to destroy these pits, and yet this oppressive darkness gave him little clue. Perhaps if he freed the prisoners. No, they'd just fill it with more people. He had to undo whatever magic that allowed this to happen.

"That's fair. I think I've seen enough. We can go back."

He turned around, and they went up the ramp again. He would need to stop and think, maybe go to the real castle and try to find books, information, try to find something in his memory. Two days. How could he do all that in two days?

When he stepped outside the wall, there were some seven men standing around the gate.

A man, who seemed older than the others, dressed in thick leather armor, stepped forward and bowed. "Your majesty. We're here to escort you to see the Void."

Griffin thought that he was part of the council, but wasn't perfectly sure.

"That's admirable, but I know my way."

"We insist," the man said. Yes, he was one of the council

members. Griffin didn't recall his name. He didn't, but then the memory came to him. It was Krasan, one of the oldest members, someone who had known King Saro's father well.

Griffin smiled. "I'll go there tomorrow, Krasan, there's no need to worry about it."

The council member and his men exchanged a look. Some of them had strange dark crossbows.

"Your majesty," Krasan said. "You know it's for your own good. There are certain conditions under which you're supposed to present yourself to the Void, and this is one."

"And I'm going tomorrow." Griffin pointed behind him, to the gate. "Or do you want these pits to go unchecked?"

"I'm going to ask you," Krasan said. "Politely. To come with us now. Remember these are your own orders."

"Well, I'm changing my orders. I'm going to ask you. Politely. To leave me alone." No way Griffin was going to let them shorten his deadline. Not when he hadn't learned anything. And if they were already suspicious, there was no point in trying to act natural.

"That won't do." The man raised his arm, then closed his hand.

Four men ran at him at once, with some kind of black paddle in their hands. Two men aimed their crossbows.

They wanted a fight? Well, good. Griffin had been wanting a fight for some time now.

17

THE PRETENDING GAME

Tris had been there for one day and there was no sign that Lukas was getting any better. Zora's parents had tested her blood, and asked her to give it to Lukas. It was so strange. She'd never heard of it, but she sat by him while Lorena injected her blood on Lukas. They hadn't yet removed the wings, but had to make some cuts, and it never stopped bleeding. According to the woman, that much bleeding wasn't normal.

They had been trying to do the potion Zora had given them, without success. Tris had told them about the shadow creatures outside the valley, and they had difficulty believing her. They had even more difficulty believing that the Dark Valley wasn't like before, and that shadow creatures wouldn't spawn in any small place. She'd showed them, using an upside-down bucket, and even then they'd told her it was a fluke.

She hoped they'd find a solution, hoped Riadne and the others found a way at least to defeat the impostor in the castle. If the worst happened, Tris would need to use her status as a princess and bribe a guard to get her out of the valley, and then back to Linaria. But it was a long way, and as long as there was a prize on her head, she wasn't going anywhere. She hadn't even left the house, and spent her time with Lukas, when there wasn't too much blood, or reading.

Sometimes she regretted her decision to go to Gravel City. But then, if she hadn't done that, she'd be in those caves. Probably alive and free. But Lukas would be closer to dying. Perhaps there was a reason this was happening to her. Perhaps this was just some bad luck. She was much farther from her goal of getting revenge on her family, and questioning if it was really worth it. Her brother at least hadn't hurt Krim, he'd just dealt the final blow. Perhaps it had been mercy. Perhaps she should think about forgiving him. That, if she ever left this place.

THE LAND WAS NEAR. Kentosa. A new kingdom. Much farther than Zora could have imagined a few months ago. And yet she would give everything to be arriving through the mountains with Griffin. Well, at least she was on her way to get him back, and she knew for sure that he was alive and that there was a way for him to return to his body.

Zora could feel the heavy atmosphere when they sat at the table to discuss their plan. Larzen and Riadne didn't even look at each other and were both serious. For all their faults, they tended to be light and playful, especially the prince, but right now there was none of it.

Larzen drew an improvised map of the Kentosa coast. The kingdom had a huge bay with many islands in it, but the prince pointed at the ocean, outside the bay.

"I think Rock Island is here," he said. "Kentosa Bay has more than one hundred islands, but they're close together. I don't know if that's where you'd keep a place supposed to be secret. My hunch is that they'd pick an island out in the ocean."

"It could be something like your shack by the Gravel castle," Zora said. "Inconspicuous from the outside."

He paused. "Not impossible, but the thing is, there will be people, and especially goods coming into this place. The magic scholars are well regarded, and I assume well paid, so there must be someone delivering luxury items, and especially fresh fruit and vegetables, to this island." He pointed at a dot near the outside of the bay. "We're going to this village, Shellfish Shelter. It's a fishing village. They get some visitors too, so we won't stand out that much. We'll need to try to talk to people and find out about any suspicious boat traffic. I mean, people have to get to that island somehow, and more importantly, they have to be getting some kind of supplies."

It made sense.

Larzen then grimaced as if he'd eaten something sour. "Me and Riadne will need to pretend we are married."

"Why married?" Riadne asked.

Larzen sighed and closed his eyes, as if he'd been expecting the question. "Noble ladies don't travel with friends. You don't want to draw people's curiosity."

She pointed at Zora. "*She* can pretend to be your wife."

He exhaled, visibly exasperated. "I'm not going to pretend to be married to my brother's beloved. It's creepy."

For some very bizarre reason, his words warmed Zora's heart, as she realized Larzen recognized her and Griffin as a couple. It also made a clear differentiation to Riadne, who, by all accounts, had been much closer to him.

"Plus," he added, "we'll need two of us to try to watch the fishermen. Zora can pass as a commoner."

"I *am* a commoner," she said.

Larzen stared at her. "You're highly educated, Zora, and I

doubt you have ever known hunger a single day of your life. You don't look, talk, or act like a peasant."

It was true, sure, but it was strange to hear that.

"Still," he continued, "wearing leather armor and with a sword on your back, you don't look like a noble lady either, so we can use that to our favor." She pointed at Mauro. "You two can pretend you're siblings. Mauro is our protector, and you're bringing your little sister along. You look the part."

"Oh, so *they* can pretend they're siblings." Riadne glared at Larzen.

"They're pretending to be commoners, we aren't." Larzen glared back at her. He then rolled his eyes. "I find the idea as loathsome as you do, Riadne."

Zora rested her head on her hand. She'd been sure that the previous night would help these two find some kind some kind of common ground, but instead it only made it all worse. But then, they were still focused on finding Rock Island. Whatever happened or did not happen between them was none of her business.

GRIFFIN FIGURED that those black paddles were something magical. These people couldn't possibly be thinking of killing him, for a variety of reasons. But then, who knew? He had his sword ready, even if it was that ridiculous, flimsy thing that King Saro carried. He missed the balance and weight of his sword Thunder.

"Stand down," Krasan said. "We don't want to hurt you."

"I suggest *you* stand down," Griffin said. "I don't mind killing you all."

The man laughed. "No need to be so dramatic, and in fact, it has never been your style."

Griffin was paying attention to the archers, and noticed

when one of them loosed a strange dark arrow. He jumped to the ground, threw his sword up in the air, then, leaning on one hand, rolled his legs in such a way that he tripped the four men with the paddles. He grabbed the sword, got up, jumped the men, found the second archer, pushed him in front of him, then stabbed his back, killing him.

Griffin dropped the man, then ran to the other shooter, punched his crossbow away, then turned to block a blow from one of the paddles. He pulled the man by his hand and threw him on the ground. There was no time for pity. Krasen had a sword ready, but Griffin disarmed him quickly, then nicked his neck with his sword, deep enough to kill him. He turned and saw two of the men running, then another one with his hands up, and another with a dagger. Instead of trying to attack him, the one with the dagger inserted it into his own neck, and dropped dead.

Griffin sighed. The broad officer and the four armored guards stood at a distance, staring.

"Do you want to defy me?" he asked. He then pointed to the man with his arms raised. "Put him in the pit."

"No! Please," the man begged.

Something in his pleading eyes got to Griffin. "Go then, run."

The man instead took a sword and ran through his stomach.

One more death. Among so many. He looked at the bodies around him. They bled red, like people, and the guards and even the council member were probably just following orders. Yes, order from a king who condemned his subjects to suffering for life. The men taking care of this pit were following orders too, which didn't mean what they did wasn't horrific. Griffin couldn't have any pity.

He turned to the armored men and the officer and smiled. "I was in a good mood."

Riadne looked at Larzen. "Our clothes look terrible. We're not gonna convince anyone."

"Oh, we will. We're worn travelers who lost their luggage and need to buy new clothes. Spending money will make people cooperate with us."

"Or we could just find some boat owners and let me sing to them."

He nodded. "That, too. But we need a sense of things first, and perhaps have an idea where to look for information and who we need to convince. Plus, c'mon, shopping is fun."

"You like shopping?"

"Who doesn't?"

"Erm..." Did she really have to state the obvious? "Most men?"

"I guess. I'm not most men."

"I doubt we'll find anything *worthy of a king* in this wretched village." She was testing him, trying to understand his nonsensical logic.

"Good thing we're only pretending to be minor nobles, Riadne."

He got off the boat and offered his arm. She took it because she had to, but tried to keep her mind steady and ignore whose arm she was holding, ignore all the feelings and memories that touch gave her. Easy for him to decide that they should pretend to be a couple; he probably didn't feel anything.

Their boat had been attached to one of many piers in the village harbor. Most boats were shoddy, but there were a few in better condition, which might have belonged to visitors or to richer merchants.

A rock-paved road led to a group of about a hundred houses, all made of wood. They surrounded a circular plaza, with a well in the middle. Among it, an inn and one tavern, a couple buildings that looked like they were some kind of stores, and some merchants selling goods in tents outside.

During the whole time they walked, she felt Larzen's arm around hers. She wondered if he was doing this as some kind of mockery, as a cruel joke to hurt her. But then, she had said some pretty hurtful things. But he'd been the one who started. And the truth was that she didn't want to be vulnerable, weak, didn't want to have her heart at his mercy. Perhaps this was a good opportunity to train her strength and to show him that he didn't affect her. That was probably it: he thought that walking arm in arm with her would turn her into some foolish lovesick teenager. Well, he was wrong.

They passed a few tents with grains, fruit, and vegetables, until Larzen stopped and they entered what looked like a shop, with some simple linen clothes. On a corner, a counter had some rings and accessories. She scanned the place to see if she found any adequate undergarment.

A middle-aged woman with graying blond hair approached them. "Well, visitors! What a surprise!"

Riadne leaned her head on Larzen's shoulder. "Recently married. Discovering the world. Amazing, right?"

"Great, great. Where are you staying?" She had a big, genuine smile, making Riadne feel bad for the lie.

"We have a bed in our boat, but there's an inn here, right?" Larzen asked. "Do you recommend it?"

"Hum... Maybe. I won't say it's terrible, you know?"

Riadne ran her hand over Larzen's arm and smiled at the woman. "I'm guessing you won't say it's good either."

The woman shook her head and laughed.

Larzen turned and kissed Riadne's temple quickly. She shuddered, surprised. He then pointed to the counter and let go of her arm. "Do you have any rings there?"

"A few, yes."

The woman moved to the counter and Larzen followed, then turned to Riadne, who stood back. "Beloved sweetheart, come see those."

Riadne glared at him for a second, and the corner of his mouth tilted. The prick was holding back his laughter and having the time of his life.

She walked towards him and caressed his hair. "What is it, husband dearest?"

"I thought my beloved sunshine would like some of these beautiful rings or necklaces."

The woman was still smiling, her eyes wide staring at them. Right, they'd obviously get a whole lot of information acting like some weirdos.

Riadne cast a glance at the rings. They were mostly made of silver, with different gemstones, and were not bad at all for a tiny fishing village. She smiled at the woman. "They are beautiful. Do you make them yourself?"

The woman returned the smile, showing the satisfaction of recognition. But she shrugged. "Oh, yes, I get the gemstones here and there, and then I put the pieces together."

"I bet you travel a lot, to buy these beauties," Riadne said.

"No. There are sales people coming by. We get..." She paused, then had a nervous laugh. "We get visitors here, right? So merchants pass by."

Larzen kissed Riadne's temple again. "Pick whatever you want, my love."

She wanted to strangle him, especially because she was about to ask about these merchants, and he interrupted. She also felt a stab of pain with the thought that he'd say it to mock her.

She pointed at a ring with a pink stone. "Can I try that one?"

"Yes, I knew you'd choose this." The woman passed her the ring.

Riadne put it on and it fit. She showed it to Larzen. "Do you like it, my honeycomb critter?"

Yep, she was calling him a drone, even if she was not sure he'd get her meaning.

He raised an eyebrow and again his mouth curved, but somehow, this time it didn't make her angry but amused. "My queen bee, it's almost as resplendent as you." He turned to the woman. "How much is it?"

"Four hundred fish scales," the woman said.

Riadne had no idea what she was talking about.

Larzen paused. "I have crowns. You surely use them in Kentosa, don't you?"

"Six hundred crowns."

She heard Larzen catching his breath. The woman wanted to rip them off.

Riadne took off the ring with the pink stone and pointed at a simple, silver one. "What about that?"

The woman shook her head and showed the ring with the pink stone. "You want this one. It's love quartz."

Right. She was definitely out to swindle them. Riadne smiled. "What a curious stone. Never heard of it."

"It's magic and it's rare," the woman said. "Only someone truly in love would choose that."

Riadne closed her eyes, in an effort to keep from rolling them.

Larzen rubbed his hand on Riadne's back. "It makes sense, considering our love is so huge and gigantic and magical. And that's my point. What do you mean magic?"

"Pink magic. Rare." The woman whispered. "I have a son. He knows these things. I can't say how or where. He's been gone for over a year, but he still sends me gifts like this."

216

Riadne felt Larzen squeezing her shoulder lightly. Yes, they were getting some information.

She turned to the woman. "It must be sad having a son far away, though. Does he visit sometimes?"

"He's not that far. But he's happy." She looked at Larzen and Riadne. "One day you'll understand."

Larzen kept caressing Riadne's back, but more softly. He turned to the woman. "We will. Now, as much as I would love to get this ring, it's more than I can pay. Unless you give me a better price, and explain what it does."

The woman looked at them up and down. "Hum... One hundred crowns." She made it sound like a great deal, but it was still a lot for a trinket like that. "Final price. It shines when your love is near."

It wasn't shining, though. Riadne just pretended to be confused. "I don't understand. It should have been so dazzling it was blinding when I tried it, then."

"It's not like that," the woman explained. "It shines when you need it."

Right. Obviously. Riadne refrained from rolling her eyes. "How does it know—"

"I'll take it," Larzen said. "Your offer is very kind. Do you have any more magical objects, by any chance?"

The woman paused. "I'm afraid you can't afford them."

Ouch.

Larzen smiled. "You never know about the future. Today's beggar might be tomorrow's king. And then he might remember that marvelous object he saw at that little store in the fishing village."

The woman sighed. "All right. I don't have them with me, but if you or anyone you know were ever interested, I could maybe find something. It depends on what you need. I could find you a basin of truth."

"Wow, really?" Riadne tried to sound impressed. Zora had

left one in the Dark Valley, taken from Griffin's secret magic room or something, and she said it created visions, but she wasn't sure how to use it. "How does it work?"

"It's a basin." The woman sounded eager to talk about it. "You put clear water, then drip octopus ink. The forms you'll see will tell you what you need to know. It can show you the present, the future, and even the past."

"It shows you visions?" Riadne asked.

"No. It forms shapes in the water," the woman said, then added, "But they are true."

"That's... fascinating." Larzen actually looked truly impressed and interested. "And how would I acquire such an object?"

The woman had a small smile, then, in a firm voice, said, "Two thousand crowns. Five hundred in advance. Then give me up to two weeks."

Larzen paused, as if thinking. "It's not that I don't trust you, but how can I know you won't run with my crowns?"

The woman smirked. "The ones you don't have, right? Well, I live here. You can follow me if you don't have anything better to do."

"And how will I know it's real?" he asked.

"Trust me. You'll know."

That woman had a lot of confidence. It probably meant that the artifact was indeed real, or else that she was sure it would pass as one. Interesting.

Larzen nodded. "It's something to think about. Will you be here tomorrow?"

"I'm not going anywhere. But I assume you're taking the ring for now."

He took some coins from a bag and put them on the counter. "Of course."

She handed him the ring. "You have to give it to her as a symbol of your love. To make sure it works."

Riadne extended her hand as he slid the ring in her finger and said, "Take it as a small representation of my infinite love."

"That you bargained for." She didn't hide the sarcasm in her voice and didn't care what the woman would think.

He kissed her forehead. "Absolutely. Because I'm in the habit of getting more value than I give, or else I'd never have you."

She couldn't let his fake words get to her, and rolled her eyes. "Beautiful words for a miser."

"Not as beautiful as you."

He looked at her and she didn't know if he was teasing, trying to flirt with her for real, putting a lot of effort into pretending something for the woman, or what.

Riadne chuckled and turned to the woman. "Men. So original."

The woman's eyes turned sad. "Rejoice love while you have it. Some of us part quickly." There was pain and longing in those words, the words of someone who probably had faced loss in her life.

Riadne almost wanted to apologize, but she also knew that her own life was probably going to be short. She'd gotten used to the idea and had learned to accept it, but sometimes the truth cut like a knife, and this was one of those times.

Larzen wrapped his arms around her and brought her close to him, maybe to pretend, maybe to comfort her, she didn't even know anything anymore.

"Thanks," he told the woman. "It's a good reminder."

They remained like that for a couple seconds, and she'd be a liar if she said she didn't like it. Well, hey, she *was* turning into a lovesick teenager. Riadne stepped away. "We should check more shops, my dearest most beloved husband."

"Of course, sunshine of my night." He turned to the

woman. "Thank you so much. And we might come by tomorrow."

Riadne had the ring on her finger as they stepped back outside.

"Great shopping, water of my desert," she said, half joking, but also quite glad at their discovery. They had found a great lead, and maybe if they kept searching, they'd find even more.

"Amazing." He'd spoken in his natural tone, all pretense gone. Then he smirked and added, "Salt of my river."

She chuckled. From annoying, their pretense had turned amusing. In fact, there was always something to be amused with Larzen. The thought gave her a slight feeling of panic, knowing well that this was bound to end eventually. She pointed at a tent with clothes. "Let's see if they have bodices. I'm in dire need of a new one."

"Anything for the queen of my hive."

This was too close to the truth to be comfortable, and an unwelcome reminder of his current title. She shook her head. "Never queen."

"Always queen of my heart."

His tone was unsettling, without his mocking intonation and at a low enough volume that it sounded just for her. She stared at him. "Fine. My most beloved drone."

He chuckled again, happy, amused. He looked so good that her chest hurt, and yes, she was aware that the cause-effect here made no sense whatsoever.

ZORA WALKED by the beach with Mauro. She had her sword and even her bag with her, just because she always liked to have her potions, even if she had left a lot of things on the boat. Other than the boats in the piers, there were a few boats anchored near the beach and Zora and Mauro were checking them, as well as the area. But the problem was that all the boats looked the same to her, wooden with small compartments, and she had no clue how to know if they were for travel, fishing, or transporting goods.

"I feel a little lost," she confessed. "I've never seen a boat before, let alone the ocean. I wouldn't know what's different or not."

"The ocean is new for me too, and plus this is a different kingdom. But sometimes things jump at us." He paused. "Other times they don't."

"Don't you have some saying for that?" she asked.

"Hum... Sometimes even the untrained eye can spot the obvious?" He laughed. "Nah, I made that up. Can't think of a saying."

Zora shook her head. "You almost fooled me." She then glanced at the sun setting behind the hills by the shore. "Night's coming soon."

"It's odd for you, isn't it? To be out like that?"

"I almost got used to it, but then..." She looked down, overwhelmed with painful memories of her mistake.

"We'll fix it."

"Of course." She rolled her eyes. "Aren't we so much better than generations that came before us?"

"I don't think they tried to do anything. At least we're trying. That makes us better already."

"I know. But it doesn't mean it isn't overwhelming." And scary too, as she grappled with the small possibility that she wouldn't find a way to defeat the Shadow Kingdom, or locate that portal. Sometimes she wondered if she would run to the Griffin impostor for help to bring real Griffin back. But no, that wasn't what she was supposed to do.

"You miss him," Mauro said.

Zora nodded.

He added, "I know it must hurt, but at least you have someone to miss, you know? Someone to look forward to meeting again, and—"

He fell backwards, and Zora didn't understand what was happening, until she realized that there was some kind of net around him. She heard steps behind her and drew her sword.

18

THE MAGIC TEMPLE

Zora and Mauro were being attacked. She heard someone coming up behind her, turned back, and elbowed that person, a young man, and he crouched. Another guy was coming up in front of her, and two on her sides. She had seconds before they advanced on her, and used them to rip the net holding down Mauro. She then heard a whoosh like an arrow behind her and turned to cut a net that had been thrown on her. A young man recharged an oversized crossbow. She ran towards him and cut his weapon with her sword.

The young man had wide eyes and raised his hands. "Don't kill me."

Zora stepped back, somewhat stunned that he'd think she'd do something like that. She still had no idea what was happening, but heard steps behind her, turned, and was too late to parry a sword blow, so it scraped her shoulder. This was a teen boy, short and skinny, no older than fifteen. Zora disarmed him easily—but then was pushed from behind. She fell forward but turned in time to use her sword to block a punch from the young boy, causing a deep cut in his hand. He stepped back yelling in pain.

Zora got up quickly and swung her sword to make sure the boys would keep their distance. Mauro was by her side, not holding any weapon. He wrapped his arm around the young man who had the crossbow and made him faint. Or killed him. Hopefully only incapacitated him.

He turned to the young boy with the bleeding hand. "Who are you and what do you want?"

The boy stepped back, then turned around and ran. He was fast, but Zora was faster and tackled him. With her sword on his neck, she asked, "What do you want? Why did you attack us?"

The boy sobbed. "I... it was not my fault. Don't hurt me. We weren't going to hurt anyone."

"Just answer my question!" Zora didn't feel very patient then.

Mauro then said, "Hold him while I'll secure the others."

She nodded, then turned to the boy. "Answer!"

He was bawling and didn't seem inclined to say anything. Zora sighed. Apparently, it was the opening he needed, as he pushed her back, got up, and turned to punch her, but then stepped back to avoid her sword.

"Want to lose a hand?" she asked.

Mauro approached them. "Try to run again and I will cut off at least one of your fingers." He sounded as if he meant it, and even Zora shuddered with the threat.

The boy raised his hands. "Giant blood. We wouldn't hurt you. They pay well. They won't hurt you, just take some blood."

Giant. They meant Mauro. Ignorants. "Giants don't exist."

"They pay," the boy said. "Giant blood. We're hungry, we meant no harm."

Zora clenched her fist on the sword. "You're hungry? Get some fish!"

"No boat, no boat." The boy sobbed again.

"All right," Mauro said. "If you want to get out of this alive you're going to tell us who these people are and what they want. We might even pay you more than they do. But you have to help us."

The boy looked around, then yelled, "Hel—"

Mauro's hand was on him in a second, then he wrapped his arm around his neck. He was suffocating him.

"Stupid kid," he said.

Zora pointed at the young man. "Aren't you afraid you could kill him?"

"This rarely kills." Mauro then looked at her. "But what do you want me to do? You hesitate, you know? That could get *you* killed one day."

"I don't hesitate."

"You do."

Perhaps he had a point. "Well, it's unsettling, you know? To hurt people. Young boys, to make it worse. This one reminds me of my students, even if he's a little older."

"He wouldn't hesitate to hurt you, Zora. Sometimes it's you or them."

Mauro then dragged the boy back to where the others were. They had been secured with a net like the ones they had thrown, and were unconscious.

"They'll wake up soon," Mauro said. "And we need to put them somewhere more discreet."

Zora looked around the small beach. It had all been so sudden. Night hadn't fallen yet. "I wonder how nobody saw it. Should we put them on the boat?"

"How are we gonna get them there without anyone seeing?"

There were some bushes by the beach. "There, maybe?" She pointed.

"It works."

Mauro dragged the four of them at once. They were quite silly to think they could go against him and Zora. But then, the net was quite strong, and maybe if she hadn't ripped it, and if Zora hadn't carried a sword, perhaps they would have a chance.

"Strange that they would be talking about giants, isn't it?"

Mauro looked down. "There are some superstitions." He took a deep breath. "Some think that people tall like me are descended from giants, or else that even if we're not, there's some magic in our blood."

Zora knew that he'd had a tough childhood, and bet that these superstitions didn't help. "I'm sorry."

He shrugged. "It's fine." He then paused. "Let's see if one of his friends is more interested in talking. We might have found our map to Rock Island."

"Or perhaps our ride. Remember they wanted to take us there. Unless it's a different place."

"Well, it's a place where they have money and study or practice magic. If it's not Rock Island, it might still lead us there."

She nodded. "Talk about jumping on us... I'll go get Larzen and Riadne. When we get back, perhaps one of them will be awake and into talking. You can take care of the four of them, right?"

"Absolutely."

"You're an amazing fighter, you know that, right?"

Mauro shrugged. "I guess." Lovely false modesty.

Zora smiled. "Thank you for being here."

She then ran towards the village.

LARZEN HAD no clue what he was doing anymore, but for some strange reason, coming up with more and more outrageous endearments was fun.

This was the third shop they entered, as they felt that salespeople would be more willing to talk inside buildings than outside in the tents. This shop owner was an old man with a pronounced belly, who looked at them with wide eyes and sometimes had to hold back his laughter. Unfortunately, like in the previous shop, this owner didn't seem to have any relatives who could smuggle magical objects, but if they left the shop too quickly, it might be too obvious.

Riadne was looking at a blue dress. "Oh, this color is so pretty. But of course, no blue can ever match the fire in your eyes."

"The fire is because I'm looking at you, pollen of my leaves."

She grimaced for a moment as if the nonsense had gotten too much even for her. Then she smiled and shook her head. "You exaggerate, salt of my river."

"Never. Always as true as a mirror."

The salesperson pulled the dress from her hands. "This is a respectable place." Riadne was stunned, and Larzen felt heat rising to his head. The man continued, "You want to declare your love, declare it in your room."

He wanted to punch the man, but it wasn't a good idea to antagonize the merchants in the village. Instead, he took a bunch of coins from his pouch and waved them in front of him. "Look at what you're not getting. And I declare my love wherever I want."

Riadne pulled his hand. "We were leaving anyway."

Larzen pulled her towards him and kissed her lips. A fast kiss, but she looked at him with wide eyes full of surprise and something else. He wasn't sure what it was, but felt that it was inviting him for another kiss.

"Out! Out of my shop!" the man yelled.

Riadne rolled her eyes, which was quite normal for her to do, but it meant she was no longer looking at him. The moment was gone.

"With pleasure," Larzen replied. "Tons and tons. Unlike you."

When they were outside, Riadne laughed. "C'mon, someone had to tell us how ridiculous we were getting." No mention of the kiss, not even to complain about it.

He smirked. "But it was fun."

She shook her head and looked away. "Playing pretend is always fun. There's nothing to lose."

Pretend. Yes, it was all a pretense. A ridiculous one, in fact. And yet it felt so good to turn to her and tell her he loved her and she was his, even if he was doing it in the most obnoxious way. How much of it was fake? He was still angry. No, he should be angry after all she'd told him, and yet he wasn't.

Riadne stared at him. "Looks like you left your tongue in the shop."

"It's here. One of my most prized organs, in fact. It's just sad I failed to show you all its artistry and skill."

"It's always weaving sharp words. I never failed to see its skill." She smiled. Despite her words, her face showed that she'd understood his meaning. And she wasn't angry that he was bringing it up.

He'd thought about it, and forgetting wasn't something that was going to happen. And yet he didn't know where to go from there, wasn't quite sure about his feelings, her intentions, and even if he could ever trust her.

"Riadne." He sighed.

She put a finger in front of her lips. "Shush. I prefer it when you're playful."

He smiled. "Moonlight of my day, I..." He had no idea what to say.

Something behind him caught Riadne's attention. He turned to check what she was looking at, and saw Zora beckoning at them from a distance.

RIADNE AND LARZEN were led to the beach near the piers, as the Dark Valley girl explained that she and Mauro had been attacked.

Larzen was thoughtful. "You think they can lead us where we want to go?"

"I think so."

"We might have a lead, too," Riadne said.

"But it could take two weeks," Larzen added.

Zora seemed curious. "What is it?"

He lowered his voice. "A woman wants to sell us a basin of truth."

"A basin..." Something flashed in her eyes, like a memory, then she changed her tone and laughed. "Well, I left one in the Dark Valley. Maybe you could get just the manual on how it works."

"Clear water and octopus ink," Riadne said.

Zora nodded. "Nice. Who knows, that could be helpful."

"Yes, but we were more interested in trying to figure out from where she was getting these magical objects." He pointed at Riadne's hand. "She sold us a magic ring."

Riadne laughed. "Sure. If this is magic, then Larzen's a virgin."

He shrugged. "You never know."

"Can I see it?" Zora asked. Riadne extended her hand, and the Dark Valley girl shrugged. "Looks like a normal ring to me, but then I'm not a magic expert."

"The basin they wanted to sell us could be fake too," Larzen said.

Zora nodded. "But the people who wanted to kidnap Mauro because he has so-called giant blood are real."

That was very convenient. He smiled. "We could just all be captured and convince them to take us where they wanted to take Mauro."

"Or two of us could be *captured,* and two of us could follow them," Riadne said. "Or we follow these people and see where they go."

"And then what?" Zora looked thoughtful. "We need to get inside access to this Rock Island. I think we could just let them take us, the four of us, then Riadne does her singing, we grab whatever we need to grab, and make a run for it."

Riadne bit her lip and looked uncomfortable. "I wouldn't make a plan depending on my ability to enchant people. My powers have limits, and it could go very wrong."

"Mauro and I can fight," Zora said.

Larzen rolled his eyes. "I'll pretend to ignore you just excluded me from the fighting crowd."

"I meant *fight well,*" the girl added—as if it made it any better.

They got to the beach, and Zora pointed at some bushes. "Here."

She then stepped back, as if scared.

There was something red on the sand and moss. Larzen stepped forward and saw four bodies with sword wounds.

LARZEN SHUDDERED and extended a hand to tell Riadne to stay back. As much as he'd seen bodies of crime victims before, the sight of death was never something easy to deal with. At least Mauro wasn't among the dead, but he was nowhere to be seen either.

"No, no, no!" Zora sounded desperate.

"These were your captors?" he asked.

"I..." She closed her eyes, then approached the bodies, peeked, and looked away. "Yes. They were unconscious. Mauro had choked them or something, but it didn't kill. He was with them. I shouldn't have left him alone."

Larzen tried to calm her down. "They need his blood, and you said they wanted to take him alive. They're unlikely to kill him."

"Let's get out of here," Riadne whispered.

"There's blood. There should be a trail," Zora said.

"Let's go," Riadne insisted. "I don't want to have to face whoever defeated Mauro. And killed four teenagers."

She had a point.

"We'll figure it out," he said, hoping Zora would stop looking at the ground in search of a trail.

Instead of turning to walk away, she unsheathed her sword and yelled "Watch out!"

Larzen pulled his dagger, even if he didn't see anything, then he heard Riadne singing.

Four people jumped from the trees. They all wore black leather pants and jackets, and tight leather hoods over their heads with holes only for the eyes and part of their noses. Two of them had crossbows, one of them had a sword, and one of them had a strange flask in his hand.

The attackers just stood there, looking at Riadne—she had saved them—again.

"Who are you and where is our big friend?" she asked.

"We serve the Magic Temple," they all responded at once, which was creepy.

"You." Riadne pointed at one of those men. "Just you. Answer. Where's our friend? Where were you taking him?"

"The Magic Temple."

She sang again for a few seconds, then asked, "But where's he now?"

"Our boat." He pointed to the sea. "We're taking him."

"Can you show us where this boat is?" she asked.

"There." He pointed at the same place, a patch of sea where there was nothing.

She looked in that direction, then turned back to him. "I don't see anything."

"Of course you don't. You're plain."

Riadne arched an eyebrow. Larzen assumed this was the first time someone called her plain.

She smiled. "Indeed. But there's a boat there?"

"Yes."

She glanced at Larzen. A boat that couldn't be seen would probably indicate some magic. Then she asked the man, "Were you planning on killing us or taking us with you?"

"We didn't want witnesses, but maybe some of you could be useful. We hadn't made up our minds."

Riadne pointed to the bushes, where the bodies were. "Why were those young men killed?"

"They were causing trouble and would eventually get us caught."

By the Kingdom, these were disgusting and despicable people.

She nodded. "How many people are in that boat right now?"

"Three. Plus the giant."

She sang again and the men were all frozen, eyes lost, still standing. She turned to Larzen and whispered, "What now?"

"We can try to get him back and then follow them, or we can ask them to take us there."

"Follow an invisible boat?" Zora asked. "I'll go there. You two can follow. It will take us to Rock Island."

Riadne swallowed. "I'll come with you. And let's hope my singing works." She turned to Larzen. "If we take more than two days to return, go back home. Don't risk your life for us."

If she had punched him, he'd be less surprised and offended. "No. I'm not staying back."

"Please. I'm begging you," Riadne pleaded. "Please, please, please, please." Her eyes were wide and she sounded sincere and afraid.

Larzen didn't understand if she was saying that because she cared about him, or if she was pretending to care because she thought he would be useless. Well, even if she cared, she didn't want him to go because she likely thought he couldn't defend himself or help them. He hadn't expected that from Riadne.

"We'll need him," Zora said. "He brought us here, to this village, and it turned out to be the right place. Plus, his knowledge of diplomacy and royalty could come in handy."

Riadne shook her head. "No. If my singing works, we'll be in and out in no time. He doesn't need to come with us."

She didn't need him. Charming. But the worst was that she was ignoring him. "Hey, I'm here, and I believe my opinion matters. Oh, actually, more than matters. In theory, you're supposed to do what I tell you. And I'm telling you I'm coming with you."

Riadne looked at him. "Please, think. C'mon, you're smart and realistic. You know staying back is the right thing to do. Don't take unnecessary risks. I'm begging you, Larzen."

"And I'm refusing your request," he replied. "Let's go. Can you convince them to take us all with them?"

Riadne sighed. "I can." She sang again, and then all the men looked at her. "Take us with you. We're important and you'll bring us all inside." She then glared at Larzen and looked down.

Two men whistled, and a large rowboat appeared as if

from out of nowhere. Three men were in it, and he didn't see Mauro.

"Where's the giant?" Riadne asked.

"Sleeping," one of the men replied.

They pulled the boat onto the beach, and the huge warrior was indeed lying down there.

Riadne sang again, enchanting the newcomers, but their eyes didn't look glassy and lost, like the attackers'.

"We'll take these three as well," one of the men told the others.

Riadne, Zora, and Larzen got on the boat. It was a simple rowboat, without any compartments, but it was large enough that it could fit some thirty people on it. This Rock Island was a lot closer than he'd imagined.

They left the beach and then soon were out of the small Shellfish Shelter bay. Still not out in the open ocean, they already faced waves that seemed gigantic in comparison to the height of the boat.

Riadne was stiff, looking outside. He reached out and was about to hold her hand when he remembered their pretense was over. He also remembered that she didn't need him here and didn't want his help, and probably thought he was useless and couldn't fight. And all they had done was meaningless for her. Somehow, he couldn't forget it, couldn't explain it away by the fact she had been angry. And yet he'd said some hurtful things too. And he shouldn't be thinking about that, but about whatever they would find on Rock Island.

They had no plan, but how could they plan when they didn't know anything about that place? Perhaps they could have spent some time investigating it, but time was what they were most short on, considering something could happen soon in Gravel, and considering they had to act before the winter solstice.

His hope was hanging on Riadne's magic, but she'd proven to be powerful before. It was strange to admit it, but, despite everything, he trusted her. At least for this. He trusted that she wanted more information about her people and even that she wanted to defeat the Shadow Kingdom. He didn't trust her as a potential romantic partner. Not that she could ever be his partner. Perhaps she was after the crown. So many questions. But then, it wasn't as if she'd been putting any effort in seducing him. What had happened that night had been more of an accident than anything else. But did she consider it a happy or sad accident?

Larzen took a deep breath and paid attention to his surroundings and the direction they were going. All of that could be useful when it came time to escape.

Riadne sang a little, but quietly, as if she were singing to herself. Perhaps she had varying intensities or ways to enchant people. He'd need to ask one day. Maybe he'd even understand why she never affected him. And yet she did affect him in so many other ways.

The boat was heading towards a small island with a light-house. That couldn't be it, as it was too close to the village and way too obvious. The men kept rowing, hitting the water in an unsynchronized rhythm. A seagull cried overhead.

Instead of going straight ahead to the island, the boat turned, so that it circled it. Its side was all made of rock, standing high above the water, without a place where a boat could dock, but the island was deep and much bigger than it had seemed at first. But that rocky wall probably meant that this was in fact Rock Island, just because of the name. Then again, quite obvious. The boat kept circling that protruding rock wall in the ocean, and then approached it and entered a small tunnel, which had been imperceptible up until then, almost like the entrance to Riadne's Sky Abode. Inside the island, the boat stopped at an inner dock.

One of the men woke up Mauro, who got up, but looking groggy as if he were completely drunk. He also had his hands bound. This was bad. If by any chance they needed to fight, he wouldn't be able to help them.

Two men walked ahead of Mauro and two by him, in front of Riadne and Larzen. Zora was behind them, followed by the remaining men. On a natural wall, a man pushed part of the rock, which retreated, revealing a passage. They climbed worn, moist stone steps and came to a corridor with dark stone walls leading to large, circular stairs made of a blue stone. When they were on the upper floor, Larzen was stunned. They were in an indoor garden with pink blossoming trees and flowers. This was the atrium of a tall building, with one of its walls made of glass. One of the sides was open, leading outside. The other side had six floors with balconies overlooking that garden, connected by spiral staircases. In front of them, large stairs led to a huge golden double door.

He wanted to reach out to Riadne's hand again, but he obviously didn't. The place was beautiful, well lit, and with white floor and walls, and yet he had an eerie feeling about it. Perhaps it was the fact that they were surrounded by these men with covered faces, perhaps it was the sheer size of the building and the number of people they'd need to fight to get out of there.

Larzen then noticed two guards by the golden doors. They wore dark red robes with hoods and were young, in their early twenties at most. The only weapons they had were swords on their belts. Still, the two guards plus the seven men around them would not be easy adversaries, especially when Mauro was partly incapacitated. Riadne would have to sing and convince someone to lead them to a library or perhaps a vault with rare documents.

The issue was that she'd been using her powers for over

an hour now, and according to her, controlling a lot of people at the same time wasn't that easy or something that she could sustain for long. Still, they could probably at least get to the documents, then improvise an exit, maybe on the same boat that had brought them. He sighed. So many maybes. But if there was a place in the world where they could find information on how to defeat the Shadow Kingdom, this had to be it, and they needed it, otherwise they'd strike blindly and be sure to fail. He wanted his younger brother back, he wanted his kingdom to be free of these creatures, he wanted so many things. If Kiran was indeed dead—part of him still resisted the idea—then it was Larzen's duty to find a real solution for his people. But it didn't look like it was going to be easy.

The man in the front spoke to one of the guards, who walked in, and they waited. His heart was thumping hard in his chest, but it shouldn't be. Riadne would have it all under control and deal with whoever was behind that door. He glanced at her, but her eyes were focused. True, she had to concentrate. And yet not sharing a look with her felt wrong. Their distance felt wrong, even if they weren't more than an arm's length apart.

They waited in silence for several long minutes, until the doors swung open, revealing a large circular room with a skylight on top. Larzen could hear their steps echoing on white marble as they walked in. Some people sat on large wooden chairs on a semi-circular raised platform. They wore dark red robes, but with some special kind of gold embroidery with geometrical symbols. One of them was a woman, the rest were all men, five of them now that he counted, and seemed to be between twenty and thirty-five years old, fairly young. In the middle, a man with an even darker robe, black hair, and green eyes sat on the biggest chair in the room. It was funny how size correlating to power was something used everywhere. That man was likely their leader. This looked like some kind of council, and many chairs were empty, which likely meant that not all members were present.

The leader remained sitting down, and asked, "What's the meaning of this?"

One of the men who'd brought them, the one who'd been in the front, kneeled and said, "I believe these might be important blood sources, Master Smyr. Together with the giant."

The man, this Master Smyr, eyed Zora, Larzen, and Riadne with his nose wrinkled, and an expression of disgust. "I don't see the need for an emergency meeting."

Then Larzen heard it; Riadne's singing, and exhaled. He waited for the eyes of their capturers to turn lost and glassy or for them to do her bidding, but the singing was taking longer than usual.

Master Smyr narrowed his eyes, then, after a while, burst into laughter. "Is that meant to be some kind of enchanting singing?"

Most of the other leaders or masters on the platform snickered. Larzen trembled. This didn't look right.

Riadne kneeled. "Yes, my lord." Her tone was formal. "I'm one of the last Solanas from the kingdom of Gravel. My people have been almost exterminated by their king. I'm here to ask for help. I believe that with your magnificent magic and knowledge you'll be able to help me find a cure for our people, and a way for our wings to grow. I can translate texts in our language and help with your studies, and I assume you'd also want to study me. All I ask is for support and protection. As a sign of my loyalty, I'm bringing you a giant, a king, and a virgin."

Larzen had been too stunned to understand what was happening. Was she doing it to gain time? To betray them? And it was true, she didn't need Larzen to find her books and her knowledge. She didn't need him. Had she been planning on doing that, and had begged for him to stay back as an act of mercy? Or had been a way to trick him into coming? Larzen still had his dagger, and he believed he was good enough to fight more than one opponent, but not five or four of them. Or seven. Or Twelve. He wasn't sure if the council members would get up from their chairs.

"No!" Zora yelled and raised her sword.

In half a second, the men were advancing on her, and Larzen yelled, "Stop!"

The girl glanced at Larzen and stopped her movement, her sword still raised. Riadne was still kneeling and looking forward as if he didn't exist. As if none of them existed.

The leader gestured for the men to pause, and smirked at Zora. "That's a big sword for you. What do you plan to do with it?"

Zora threw the sword on the floor, smiled, and said, "Look! I can enchant objects. I thought... I could learn some magic too?" She then kneeled.

Larzen shrugged. "Gravel king here. At your service. I'm sure we can come to a decent—"

Master Smyr made a small gesture, and then Larzen was gagged and his hands bound. Riadne didn't look at him even once during all that time. Not even a glance. When they put a blindfold over his eyes, he almost felt relieved. At least now he had a great excuse for not seeing the obvious.

19

ASPIRANTS AND APPRENTICES

Zora was trembling and unsure of what was happening, and hating letting go of Griffin's sword. She wasn't sure if Riadne was trying to gain time or if she had changed her mind. No, it had to be a trick; her singing hadn't worked. She wouldn't have asked for a truth balsam if she were lying. But then, who knew what that potion really was?

Larzen and Mauro had been carried away. This was so unfair to her friend, who was only trying to help. But not unfair to Zora, considering it had been her idea. Perhaps she should be happy that they got inside? The issue now was getting out of there. With the information.

That man, Master Smyr, got out of his chair or throne or something, and stood in front of Riadne and Zora.

"Get up."

Zora stood, glancing at the sword he was now holding in his hands. Griffin's sword. "This is interesting." He looked at Zora. "We might have some use for your tricks." He then eyed her up and down. "Yes, we'll find some use for you." He then addressed his guards. "Take her to Barna."

Two guards approached Zora. "Follow us."

Follow. So she wasn't exactly a prisoner. As they led her to the door, she turned back to take a last look at Riadne. Smyr held her chin, a large ring with a black stone glistening in his hand. "Yes, you'll be most welcome."

For some reason, his tone gave Zora chills.

NEITHER THE OFFICER nor the armored guards stopped Griffin from leaving. As he stepped away from that dreadful dark pit where people were tortured until death, he wondered if those guards would say anything, send someone to follow him, but perhaps it was already too late to worry about that. Someone *had* followed him and brought reinforcements to capture him. Talk about being impatient. Couldn't these people wait a day? Griffin's plan had been not to attract attention and to go to the Void as if he were King Saro, to try to have the highest possible chance of killing him. Right. He didn't even know what that creature looked like, let alone how to defeat it.

He walked back to where the two guards accompanying him had been left—and they weren't there. They could have maybe escaped or perhaps have been captured or killed. As he looked around, he heard steps, and saw the two men.

"We got the two guards who were escaping," Samuel said.

Griffin hadn't seen the need for that, as they posed no threat. Or perhaps they did, if they were to run somewhere and inform someone of what had happened. But then, technically, all that happened was that the king had been challenged and reacted. It shouldn't be that abnormal that King Saro would refuse to be taken somewhere.

"We couldn't get to you and help you," the guard added. "We're sorry."

Somehow, he felt something off about it. Of course, it was

probably a lie. The men likely hadn't wanted to try to defend him and die in the process. Or worse.

"No problem," he said.

He looked back at the small outpost and the wall encircling the pit, which was high, but not imposing or anything that looked impossible to climb. The memory of the walls of the Dark Valley came to him, these walls that had kept Zora and so many people contained for so long. His mind came back to the present moment.

"If there are enemies and traitors there," Griffin asked, "Shouldn't the security be higher? In case anyone attempted a rescue?"

The two guards paused and looked at each other.

"We fear the pit itself," Bruno said. "That it could swallow us. I don't think anyone would attempt to go there."

"Those guards do." Griffin pointed.

"Yes, but... I don't think anyone envies their position."

Griffin recalled the dreadful feeling when he went down just a little on that ramp. He remembered the screams. It was all so horrible. "How many pits are there? In the kingdom?"

The two men were thinking, then Bruno said. "Some fifty? One hundred? I know where some of them are, not all."

How in the world would he destroy them all before being caught? But that was the point; he couldn't try to destroy these pits. It would be like trying to bring down a tree by cutting its branches. But then, if enough branches were cut, the tree would die. Or it would keep growing new branches, and there would be no time to stop it. Griffin had to get to the Void, even if he had no idea how. Still, he looked back and felt guilty. He hadn't been raised to support torture or cruelty. Of course, freeing the prisoners there or destroying one pit wouldn't make any difference.

No, it would make all the difference for those who were there.

"I'm going to free those prisoners," Griffin told his guards. "Do you want to help? Or do you want to stay back?"

The guards exchanged a glance, then Samuel asked, "Are you sure?"

Perhaps it was foolish, but since Griffin had been found out anyway, at least he could destroy one pit. He had a feeling that the Void already knew that he wasn't King Saro, and therefore there was no point pretending.

THE GUARDS LED Zora out of that room. She noticed that a man dressed in red robes was also following her. Nobody held her arms, and she didn't have chains. Perhaps they were really thinking that she wanted to study magic. That was good, except for the fact that she didn't know what could be happening to Larzen and Mauro.

She had imagined that they would go up the stairs, but no, they went down, but it was a different set of stairs. Instead of ending in that interior river, they were in a corridor with stone walls, illuminated with torches.

They opened a heavy wooden door, and Zora found herself in a room where some thirty young women sat in a circle, an older woman walking around them. This was a classroom. A very gloomy one, without windows. The woman came to them.

"She's supposed to join the group," the men in red robes said.

The woman frowned. "This late? And where's she from?"

"She showed up, and Master Smyr thinks she could be useful," the man said.

The woman eyed Zora up and down as if she were an unwelcome stain in a new dress. "Well, sure." She extended a hand. "I'm Barna, and I'll help you go through the picking. I'll explain it later." She then had a smile that didn't reach her eyes. "Welcome to the Temple of Magic."

Zora tried to give her a convincing smile. "Thank you."

Barna then turned to the group. "Sarina, come and help her get dressed and proper. She'll stay in your room."

A petite blond girl got up and smiled. "Of course." She then got in front of Zora and smiled. "I'm so glad to help you."

The man turned to Barna. "Can you take it from here?"

"Oh, yes, don't worry," the old woman said.

The man and the guards left.

The woman then turned to Zora. "Follow her and do what she says. You'll join us for dinner in two hours."

"Thanks." She tried another smile. If anything, she had to convince these people that she truly wanted to study magic here. And it was an amazing opportunity to try to find some books and more information.

The girl walked down the hall in fast steps. Zora wondered if this would be a good opportunity to ask questions, but she had to get to know the girl a little better.

They got to a room with four beds. The girl smiled. "Our bedroom."

She then handed her a white cotton dress, identical to the ones everyone was wearing. "You'll wear this." She pointed to a corner where there was a curtain. "You can bathe there. It's from the morning, but it shouldn't be too bad."

Zora approached the curtain and saw a bathtub behind it, still full of cloudy water. So they shared their water. All right. It made some sense. She didn't want to complain, and instead undressed quickly, put her clothes on a stool, and entered the chilling water, suppressing a scream. It was so cold.

There was a bar of soap on a dish by the tub. When Zora was about to pick it, she felt her head being submerged in the water, something heavy pushing it down.

THE BROAD OFFICER and one of the dark pit guards lay dead on the ground, as they'd tried to stop Griffin. The others said they were happy to help the king, whatever his wish. These were smarter. They were indeed opening the cells, as prisoners were coming out. Most of them were extremely skinny, their eyes hollow with dark circles.

One of the armored guards came up to him. "What about the ones who are asking for a merciful death?"

These people were really into dying. He glanced at Samuel, who said, "They've likely suffered too much and don't want to suffer anymore, or there isn't any more hope for them."

Griffin sighed. "Go with them and make sure that's really the case. You can give them the merciful death if that's what they wish."

One of the prisoners, who looked at least somewhat healthy, asked, "Are you going to free all the prisoners in the dark pits?"

"As much as I can, yes. I'm going to them one by one and undoing them." He smiled. "That's my plan for now."

They sat by the building, and some of them had difficulty walking. It would be a lot of work for them to leave there. There wasn't any town nearby, and in that state, without transportation, they would take a long time to find any place. Perhaps the forest would give them some refuge. Perhaps Griffin had condemned them to death. Either way, it wasn't as bad as Bruno, for example, had suggested. He had said that the prisoners would see him or the guards as enemies and try to fight them. None of that happened. It's as if time in that horrible prison had sucked life away from them.

And then the memory came. It wasn't that the void was in the bottom of the pit, but that he was somehow connected to the land in Grota. Suffering anywhere could power him, but the downward funnel shape of those pits worked like an amplifier, giving magic to the Void and creating magic within the pit, magic that allowed them to come to the other side like shadow creatures, usually like human shadows, but sometimes like shadow wolves. The spiders were the spiders in the pits. The balls were the balls generated there. They rarely crossed over, but sometimes they did. There was some connection between Grota and Gravel, a connection related to the land. Griffin had to figure what it was, and how to undo it.

Once all prisoners were freed, he was thinking of throwing some balls and exploding that pit, but then it would only make an even bigger hole. It wasn't the pit itself that generated the magic, but the suffering in it. Once empty, it generated no more magic. But then, it would be easy to repopulate it. Griffin took some balls and threw them on the ramps. That would make it at least more difficult to repopulate this pit.

They rode away from the place, and when they were very far, he asked Samuel, "Do you know a place where I could get information on your history, your magic?"

"Your castle?"

"I want someplace that's not obvious," Griffin said. "They probably think I'm going to the dark pits, which is good, but now I can't go to any of them anymore. And I don't want to go to the castle or the..." An image came to his mind. "The great library. It's too obvious."

The guard narrowed his eyes. "You're not him, are you?"

Griffin had the feeling that they'd known this for a while, but he didn't want to give them any details. "You know the answer. Just help me. I'll face this Void very soon. I'll try to delay it as much as I can, but I don't know for how long I can elude him. Anything that I can learn about him, about this place's history, the connection to the other side, any of that might help me."

Bruno approached them. "There's a place in Lorel that might have the information you need, but getting there won't be easy."

"Well, nothing's easy."

The guard nodded. "Yes, but if we want to get there and avoid busy roads, we'll need to cross the swamps."

Griffin shrugged. "I got no problem with swamps."

"Me neither," Bruno said. "The swamps are fine. The issue is the creatures living there."

"I can fight a few creatures," Griffin said. "What are they like?"

"Giant lizards."

"Let's go." It didn't sound any worse than facing the Void.

ZORA'S first thought was that something had fallen over her, but then she felt that her head was being held down by a hand. That was strange. Zora immersed her head deeper in a fast movement, meaning to slide forward to get away from the grip, but she felt her hair being pulled.

She punched the hand holding her down and gripping her hair, but it didn't move. She was considering pulling the hand and making the girl fall on top of her, but they could both get hurt. No, that wasn't smart. This girl was unlikely to want to kill Zora. She was just trying to scare her. The more Zora struggled, the more she'd use up her air. Instead, she just relaxed.

"This," the girl, Sarina, said. "Is so you don't get any ideas. You come from nowhere. And you need to understand who leads here."

This was very strange. Why make a speech to someone

who could barely hear what you were saying because of the water? Zora was running out of air—and out of patience. She held on the edges of the tub, then bent her body, pushed her legs back, and kicked the girl, who let go of her hair. Zora was out of the water and the bath in two seconds, then pushed the girl on the ground, holding her two arms with one hand and her throat with the other.

Zora chuckled. "What did you say? I didn't quite catch."

Sarina's face was pale. "I... was joking."

"Really? Why?"

"Let go. It was just a joke."

Zora did let go and stepped away, waiting to see if the girl was going to try anything.

Sarina stood there, arms crossed, her dress wet. "It was just a prank. No need to get all violent. Everyone goes through this. If I tell Barna she'll expel you, you know?"

Nope. Zora wasn't going to be threatened, and raised an eyebrow. "Only me?"

The girl shifted. "You'll lose your chance. You should be glad they let you in, considering we're almost done with the picking."

Zora wanted to ask what this picking was, but figured that it was better to understand things a little better before asking questions.

She smiled. "True. I'm thankful. And I'm sorry if I hurt you. I'm that... competitive." She extended a hand and forced a smile.

Sarina took it, a fake smile on her face too.

Zora exhaled, more annoyed than relieved. "Can you let me get dressed now?"

"Sure." The girl then walked away from the curtain and back into the bedroom.

Zora sighed, then took a towel and the white dress and put it on. The fabric was soft, and the underslip was comfortable. Zora always felt weird wearing skirts, resulting from a life in the Dark Valley where a spider could spawn in any shadow. But she had to get used to life outside her valley. Life everywhere, if it was true that the magic within the walls that surrounded her village had indeed gotten weaker.

Despite Sarina's smile and the guarantee that it had all been just a joke, it didn't change the fact that this prank or whatever had been meant to humiliate and scare Zora. Humiliating, for sure. Scary? Nope. Zora had seen and faced much worse than a girl trying to intimidate her.

But it was better to keep an eye on Sarina. Tiring. Hopefully, Zora wouldn't stay long here. All she had to do was figure out where they kept the rare documents, how to take them, where Larzen and Mauro were being held, how to free them, and then how to leave that island where they had dozens of guards. Her odds sounded horrible, and yet, she had to find out at least a way to free her friends. Sarina's stupid competition was so far from being a priority that it wasn't even funny. But Zora would need to watch out for the girl.

RIDING IN SILENCE, under that eerie red sky, accompanied by two guards that he would have considered monstrous creatures until a few days before, Griffin had all the reasons to feel ill at ease, but there was something else nagging on him. Sometimes he wondered if the Void had eyes or could feel the entirety of the kingdom, in which case Griffin was definitively screwed. Perhaps that was how that council member had found him.

They were at the edge of the swamp. When he thought of swamps, he remembered the Marshes in Gravel, flooded for some time of the year, with forests adapted to the water. This looked nothing like it. There were crooked trees here and there, looking more dead than alive, spaced far apart from each other. And he couldn't see far beyond the whiteness of a thick mist.

He had to cross it to get to Lorel, to a place where they would have more information. Neither of his guards knew what the Void was like nor how long he'd been in this land. But if Amina knew that someone from "the other side" could possess the king, they did have a lot of knowledge, or at least some knowledge.

A strange screech sounded above him. He'd been wondering what these giant lizards would eat in a place that seemed dead, but perhaps there was life.

Griffin and his companions moved at a slow pace, avoiding making any sounds so as not to attract any predator. He touched the grip of his sword, even if he still wasn't used to it. He missed Thunder, especially when after it had been enchanted, when it had felt sharper, faster, more precise. In reality, what he really missed was the person who'd enchanted his sword. Zora. Trying to get to what was likely the most dangerous place on the continent. Why? *Why, Zora?* And he couldn't do anything about it.

The mist closed in to the point he couldn't even see what was beside him. The plan was to go straight, but "straight" could easily bend. A horse neighed behind him. Strange. He had the feeling that the guards were beside him, or even slightly in front of him. Or else...

He pulled his sword and turned to face whatever—or whoever—was coming. Through the mist, he saw a horse, only one, very similar to the one he was riding, and another of those gray men, but he wore a helmet covering his face.

"Saro. It's time for your visit. Don't make me force you. If that's even you."

Griffin frowned. "Don't make me kill you."

The man laughed. "Amusing. You don't even know who I am. What a negligent son."

Son? Oh, no, the memory came to him in a flash. That was the previous king.

"Why?" Griffin shrugged. "You think I won't kill you?"

"I think you're not capable of it."

Griffin had never trained to fight on horseback. He knew that they practiced it in other kingdoms on the Continent, but in Gravel, riding was just to get them from place to place. "Get down and let's duel, then," he suggested.

The man laughed again. "I don't think so. Fire."

It took Griffin half a second to understand what the man had meant. Fire? But he wasn't talking to him, but to someone behind him. The understanding hit Griffin at the same time as the first arrow, then second. If this body was invincible, perhaps almost immortal, the arrows shouldn't hurt or kill him. They were made of a strange black material. Like the paddles. Perhaps to make him fall asleep? His mind went black, like the arrows.

20

DREAMWALKING

Zora walked to the dining hall with her new roommates, Lea, Alma, and Sarina. Sarina was the most delicate of the trio, which was weird considering she tried to pick a fight with Zora. Alma had brown skin and straight black hair, and was also short, and Lea was tall with brown hair and eyes and tan skin.

After spending some time in the classroom with all the girls, Zora understood that they were in some sort of selection process, and that only a few of them would be chosen as apprentices. The others would find positions in the *maintenance of the temple*, meaning that they would become servants, until the following year, when they could try again. A few would be sent home.

The teacher told them that all the positions were honorable and that serving the greatest magic temple in the world was a privilege. Well, maybe, but it didn't seem that the girls saw it this way. It seemed as if failing to be picked was as bad as dying or something. Zora bet some of these servants would be bitter. If she could find one that would talk to her... But then, perhaps they would be hoping for a chance and trying their best to remain loyal to this creepy temple.

Plus, she had a feeling of being watched at all times, with guards in the hallways and girls who were assigned to watch the others. The girls didn't seem bothered, though. In fact, her three roommates were excited about a ball the following evening. Apparently it was a big deal and an opportunity to have a greater shot at the rank of apprentice.

Zora had so much to figure out and so little time to waste. She had told them that she was from Gravel, and had come looking for this temple, eager to learn magic. It didn't explain why the council of magicians, which was what those people with red robes with gold embroidery were called, had allowed her to join the group so late.

The hall had low, unfinished ceilings, and looked like a cave. She wondered how come it didn't all flood from the ocean, but perhaps this was all within the rock that was above sea level. There were many small, circular tables in the room, and it looked more like a tavern than a palace or school. In the Dark Valley, they had long tables with benches in the school kitchen.

They had to line up with cups, then they got a thick soup that looked like it was made of carrot and had some kind of fish in it. Carrot and fish. Hardly one of the worst things happening to Zora right now. Griffin came to her mind, and the fish and bread they had shared. Her chest tightened, and she pushed the pain away. It should only give her the resolve to figure this out and get back to her kingdom with answers.

Zora sat with the girls, glad for a chance to talk and try to learn more about the place. Sarina had been super sweet and kind since after the incident in the bath. Zora wasn't sure if it creeped her out, or if it had been just a misunderstanding and the girl was actually nice. Hopefully that was the case, as she felt uncomfortable disliking people.

"So you saw some of the magicians?" Sarina asked, sounding impressed.

Magicians were apparently the leaders there. Zora wasn't great at lying, but even she knew that it was always best to make it as close to the truth as possible. "I mean, I went to a circular room where some people sat, and they looked important. They were not old, though, and then they sent me here." In fact, none of it was a lie.

"The room with the big golden doors on the ground floor?" Alma asked.

"Yes. But some chairs were empty. Do you know what that place is, or who they are?"

Lea snorted. "You don't know that? And you want to be an apprentice?"

Zora shrugged. "No." She didn't want them to think of her as a threat. "I don't care. I just want to be here, in this... uh, magical place."

Sarina didn't seem to mind answering. "The magicians wield magic, for real, and yes, they aren't old. But they're very wise. They can take apprentices, but it's rare. You'll more often be paired up with a higher-ranking apprentice or put in a group."

"And..." That was something that had been nagging at Zora. "How come some people are turned away and sent back? If in theory nobody leaves this place?"

Lea rolled her eyes. "You think anyone would go around admitting their shame?"

"They could put a nice twist on it," Zora said. "Sell the secrets of the Magic Temple or something."

"I have to agree with Lea that they're too ashamed," Alma said.

Zora wasn't sure if that made sense. Surely some of them would want to profit from their experience. But something else came to her mind. "What if they are sent to the prisons?"

Sarina frowned, confused. "Prisons? In Kentosa? I've never heard of anything like that, and it would be quite complicated."

"I mean the prisons here. Some people are kept here, right?"

The girls looked at each other, then looked at Zora as if she were crazy.

"Of course not," Sarina said.

Zora felt her stomach lurch. So if nobody knew about where Larzen and Mauro had been taken, anything could happen there. Plus, it would be much harder to find out where it was.

Still, since they were in an answering mood, she asked, "And what about the magicians who go to other kingdoms, become advisors?"

"That's different," Sarina said. "And they're not magicians. They're high apprentices who are trained for that. And they usually don't get to learn all the secrets of the temple. But someone like us, if they're turned down, they don't know anything. You do realize we're underneath the temple, not in it, right?"

"I see." Zora was thoughtful. "And the ones who go to the shore to buy things, bring people, who are they?" Perhaps she was trying to figure a way out.

"I'm thinking you want to leave." Lea had a smile. "All you have to do is ask, you know?"

"I'm trying to understand, that's it."

Lea was staring at her. "Maybe you should have come in earlier and understood it when it was the right time."

"The crossers are special guards," Sarina said. "It's part of their apprenticeship. It's a great honor and great responsibility."

Yeah, so honorable. They were cold-blooded murderers.

But Zora just nodded, then asked, "And what's the ball tomorrow night about? Is it to celebrate who's selected?"

"Not really, it's a chance for some of us to meet the magicians," Sarina explained. "Our process finishes in two weeks."

"But only a few of us got to be invited," Lea added.

"Are you going?" Zora asked.

Sarina pointed at her two friends and smiled. "Yes. The three of us got in."

"Congratulations." Zora's smile was genuine. Well, she did like to see that the girls were happy.

"We'll tell you all about it," the petite blonde added.

"Yes, please do."

The girls then looked at the other side of the room, at a group of some six young women who had just entered. They had cotton dresses similar to theirs, but pink. Zora's heart skipped a beat when she saw Riadne among them. "Who are they?"

"The apprentices," Lea said, then rolled her eyes. "They think they're so much better than us."

"You'll probably be one of them in a few days," Zora said.

"But I'm not gonna act like that," the girl replied, then said, "That one's new." Lea's voice called her attention. "The redhead." She meant Riadne.

Sarina frowned. "Strange."

Zora glanced at the recently arrived group. Riadne was smiling and didn't look in her direction. Perhaps she hadn't even seen her. Was she still interested in helping Zora? Or playing her own game? Zora wished she knew the answer, and she didn't even mind what it was, it was just that she would like to plan things properly.

"They don't get new apprentices?" Zora asked, trying to understand things a little more.

"They usually have to go through the picking process, like us," Sarina replied.

Zora had no clue why Riadne was there either. "Maybe there are exceptions?"

Sarina looked thoughtful. "Perhaps. If one of the magicians themselves chooses to appoint her. But where did she even come from?"

Zora kept her mouth shut. Perhaps she should say something, but she didn't know what. In fact, she knew way too little for someone who wanted to steal precious documents and break two people out of a prison that nobody seemed to know existed. Mess, mess, mess.

THAT WASN'T A CELL, it was a cage, not even tall enough for Larzen to stand up in it. He and Mauro had been brought to a tunnel underneath the castle. At the time, he had thought they'd go to that river, but instead he was down below, in what looked like some natural cave systems.

He was put in a hole separated from the main corridor by iron bars. There were guards monitoring the prisoners, but they didn't have the keys. Only men wearing red robes opened or closed the cells, which meant very little trust placed on the guards. This wasn't good.

Larzen had no idea, absolutely no idea what was going to happen to him and if and how he'd escape. What hurt more was Riadne. Really, couldn't she at least have looked at him? Let him know it was a plan, that they were still working together? He wanted to believe so, but still... There was a cold feeling creeping up on him.

Mauro had been put in a different hole, far from his. Left alone, Larzen sat and took a deep breath. There was no reason to panic. At least not just yet. What he needed to do was observe. And plan. And then escape.

In his hours since he'd been brought in, Larzen had

found out a couple things; first, the guards indeed didn't have keys to the cells or even the hallway, second, they didn't expect anyone to leave this place alive. Faint screams echoed in the distance and Larzen figured that however method they used to collect blood wasn't as benign as one might think.

Two guards passed carrying a young lady in chains, followed by a man wearing red robes.

The girl wore a white dress and was crying. "I'm sorry, I'm sorry. I just wanted to go home. I won't tell anyone—"

The man in red punched the back of her head. "Silence or it will be worse."

The girl grunted, but then sobbed quietly.

This was horrible. Larzen felt something cold inside him, wondering if Riadne was risking something similar, wondering if she was in danger, while he was here, unable to do anything. Well, that was stupid. He was the one already imprisoned. Now he was afraid she would have the same fate as his? Not even one look back. She hadn't been capable of even looking back at him once.

He also felt bad for the girl and for everyone who was there—but felt worse for himself. He'd thought that he'd be able to wiggle his way out of that situation; promise a good bribe or a good position, but there hadn't been any opportunity to speak to a guard, and even then, what good would it do if they didn't even have the keys? His money hadn't yet been confiscated, and he had coins in an inner pocket, stuffed with fabric around them so as not to jingle. Still, they were Continental crowns, and it didn't seem that was what these people used in this area. And he didn't think they'd be willing to take it. This was the kind of thing that should be done one-on-one, and the men in red robes were never alone and didn't seem to be the type who needed money.

If they were going to try to take his blood, that would be his only opportunity to try to fight his way out. And what about Mauro? Perhaps he'd need to fight his way out too. Was that what their group had become? Free for all? Each one for himself? Had Riadne betrayed them? That question had been echoing in his mind, even if he'd tried to ignore it. And then there was Zora. The girl was unlikely to free them on her own. He thought back to the girl in white who had been brought in chains; this was likely the danger the girls were against. All because Riadne's singing hadn't worked. Or because she'd refused to make it work. If that had been the case, at least she had tried to warn them.

GRIFFIN WASN'T in his body. Well, that wasn't new. He hadn't been in his body for a few days now. He thought he'd been dealing with it quite well. But this was different; he wasn't in Grota or Gravel. He was nowhere.

Then he had the sensation of dreamwalking again. Zora. He found himself walking on the ocean. There was a red wall, like the glass of the red cup, but it was as wide and tall as he could see. Somehow, he knew she was behind it.

"Zora!" He banged his fists on the wall, but nobody answered.

He heard splashing steps behind him, turned, and saw that Sun Goddess or whoever she was. "You."

She smiled. "Such a warm greeting."

"I'm trying to... I need to talk to someone. Do you know how to go through this wall?"

She stared at him. "Why don't you use this time to spend your energy where it's needed? Didn't you want to find answers?"

"But Zora—"

"Is a smart grownup who'll deal with her own challenges.

You want to see her, do what you can to see her in the real world."

Griffin sighed, and then he was at a meadow in Gravel, far from the castle. The woman was still there, so he asked her, "Do you know what this Void is? How I can defeat him?"

"You'll find some answers in the past. Why don't you go there?"

"Why don't you just answer me?"

"I don't have those answers. You can see your ancestors. I can't."

Griffin took a deep breath. "I just want to save Gravel."

"Then perhaps you should understand what happened."

"What happened?"

"I don't know. But I believe you have someone far down in your family who does. Don't you want to talk to them?"

How? He didn't even get to voice his question, as he felt he was walking in that swamp in Grota, mist surrounding him. Four men put chains around the body of King Saro, then placed him inside a fortified metal carriage.

But that was not Griffin's body, just the body he'd been inhabiting last. He found himself falling, then in the meeting room in the Gravel Castle. He saw himself, or rather, his real body, dressed in a ridiculous white shirt with some lace and embroidery in the cuffs. It was something that Larzen could wear and look good, but on him... His impostor, who had an awful taste for clothes, was speaking to Stavos.

"There has to be an arch somewhere, or someone who's seen it."

"There are no accounts, your highness," the blond man said. "We have sent four scout parties to all sides of the king-dom, to try to find such a monument."

The king wearing Griffin's body rested his head in his hand.

They were looking for the portal on Gravel's side. And it

was true, there wasn't such an arch anywhere, at least as far as Griffin knew.

Could it be that it had been destroyed? Or maybe hidden somehow. Maybe if it was by the edge of a mountain, perhaps they could put rocks, earth, bury it? It still didn't make that much sense and didn't seem feasible. But it was good. If all it took to open Gravel to Grota was the king to go there and do something, then the fact that this portal was lost would allow them to gain time.

The Griffin impostor then asked, "Any sign of the fugitives?"

"No. It's as if they left the kingdom."

"Someone somewhere should have seen them."

"Nothing so far."

"What about Zora?"

Why was his impostor asking about her?

Stavos crinkled his nose in disgust. "The Dark Valley champion? What about her?"

Griffin didn't like the man's tone or his expression.

The king glared at him. "You're not to question my orders. I want to know if she's been found."

"That's not going to be easy without issuing a request for her to be detained. Or a prize for information about her."

The king shook his head. "She needs to think she's free."

"Of course, your highness. I'll ask for reports."

Stavos was highly incompetent at any discreet information. That was also good. But then, the reason Zora hadn't been found was that she'd left the kingdom. What a terrible idea. And Larzen was with her. He still hoped they'd never find that cursed island.

Griffin had to get more information. About the Void. And Gravel's past. Not about Larzen and Zora, as much as he feared for them. Perhaps he should trust that they were smart enough not to go to a place from where they couldn't get out.

Larzen wasn't someone who would rush into danger, and if he was with Zora, Griffin had to believe they would be safe.

The past...

What was there to learn from the past? So much. There were so many questions and he didn't even know from where to start, or if it was even possible to find out any of that, to dreamwalk to a time long gone.

He found himself in a room with stone walls. There was a window with small panes of glass, in an ancient style. He looked outside and saw the valley in front of the Gravel castle. This was the castle, and it wasn't. The gardens weren't the same, the usual trees weren't there.

Griffin turned and saw two men discussing while staring at a map. One of the men was about forty and had black hair and blue eyes. That was Jarren, one of the past kings. He wasn't sure how exactly he knew that. It was almost the way he was able to capture memories of the Grota king.

"But then the kingdom will be shredded apart," Jarren said.

"The alternative is a bloody war," the other man replied.

"But if we let them, let whoever wants to declare their own kingdoms do it, will it have an end? Will it ever stop? What if they start fighting amongst themselves? What if they decide to attack us?"

Griffin had read that Gravel had been formed by unifying smaller settlements and regions. He also knew that there had been some friction, some inner squabbles, but he'd always learned that they had been minor, that the people of Gravel as a whole enjoyed being one kingdom. Perhaps it hadn't been exactly like that. Perhaps the history he learned was like his parents' portraits; somewhat similar to the truth, but without the wrinkles.

He found himself in another room, some kind of reception area for visitors and small meetings.

King Jarren turned to an assistant. "Let's hear what he has to say."

"Without guards? Are you sure?"

Jarren just stared, and the man left. An old man walked in, wearing simple, old linen clothes, looking like a peasant. But he wasn't one.

"So, you're the famous Collector," King Jarren said. "And you have something for me."

"I have something to sell. It's up to you to decide if it's for you or not."

"And what is it?" Jarren's voice was cold and it was hard to decide if he was curious about the object or just wanted to know what this man wanted.

"It's a ring. It will allow you to communicate with the void."

Griffin wondered if the men meant the Void, like the Void in Grota, or if it was something else.

"And what will it do for me?" Jarren asked.

"Knowledge. Power."

"You've had this ring for how long?"

"Ten years, your Majesty."

Jarren scoffed. "Well, I can see how powerful you are. I'm quite impressed."

"No, no." The man shook his head. "He'll only talk to a king."

"Right. And I'm assuming you've tried to sell it before, and for some mysterious reason, no king bought it."

"I didn't try to sell it before. I came to your majesty because I saw the opportunity. You need it."

Jarren stared at the man. "I can try it, but I'll only pay if I see any result." It was clear that the king didn't completely believe in that ring, but was willing to give it a try. "Would that work for you?"

The man bowed. "That's a fair compromise."

Griffin felt as if he was hit by a strong wind, then he was following Jarren as he supervised a construction site.

Workers were piling up stone slabs in a valley, forming two columns. Oh, it was a stone arch, very similar to the one in Grota. So that was how the two kingdoms had become connected. Griffin wished he could recognize where this place was, but he had no idea.

He still didn't understand the connection between the ring and the man, how the Dark Valley came to be, and how the royal family became cursed. There was little to see in that scene, but Jarren's face was calm, satisfied, without the previous strain when discussing and looking at the map. It was as if Gravel's conflicts had been solved. Perhaps Griffin would need to try to look back and understand more.

Understand more. For a moment, he saw a little house by a river, then he felt a buzzing sound in his ears and opened his eyes. He was back in King Saro's body, but his two wrists were chained up to a wall. A stone wall, inside a tall circular room illuminated with torches.

That man, the previous Grota king, was there, without his helmet. His face was old, but not like old age, it was as if the upper layers of his skin were shedding. Perhaps it was something that happened to these creatures.

"So you finally decided to come," a voice said.

Just a voice. Oh, of course. The Void. The Void didn't have a body. Chills ran down Griffin's spine. Killing someone while chained to a wall was hard enough. How could he kill something without a body?

21

NIGHT STROLL

After dinner, the girls tried on dresses for the ball in a large room. It reminded Zora of the balls in the castle, of Griffin puking by her shoes. Why had the memory suddenly turned endearing? She could still recall the feel of his hair in her hands. But she had to focus.

What she gathered about this area was that it was a big underground corridor, with rooms and bathing rooms on one side, and bigger halls on the other, including the dining hall, the classroom, and now this dressing room.

A seamstress adjusted dresses on the girls, but some of them, like Zora, only watched. She could see them glaring so hard at the other girls, and wondered how come they hadn't yet punched holes in the dresses. Zora smiled and complimented the ones who acknowledged her. In fact, a ball where those magicians would be occupied was the perfect opportunity for her to hatch an escape plan, and she was glad she'd have this opportunity to roam free in that building.

She then came to her room with Sarina, Alma, and Lea, wondering if it was even safe to fall asleep there. Sarina's open hostility might have looked unusual, but these girls were all competing against each other, and under the impression that Zora was also against them. There were easy ways to get rid of a competitor.

The room was gloomy, with only one candle lighting it, making it so dark and with so many shadows that Zora shuddered. But she had to learn about this place and about any chance she'd have to find books and an escape.

"So," Zora asked. "What do usually you do at night?"

"Sleep," Sarina said. "Barna takes away our candle and they watch for any sound."

"Oh. Can't you smuggle a candle or something?"

"Of course." Sarina smiled. "If you want to be sent home."

"How would they even find that out?" Zora asked, not that she wanted to light a candle, more that she wanted to figure out the security in that place.

"The hall is dark. Everything is dark. They'd notice a faint light sipping from under the door."

"Right. But if it's all dark, what happens if we need to, I don't know, go to the bathing chambers at night or get some water?"

"There's a chamber pot under each bed."

"Yikes. In the dark. That's gotta cause some accidents."

Sarina shrugged. "You get used to it. And it's not like you can leave anyway. An apprentice passes by and locks our doors at night."

"From the outside?" Zora glanced at the lock. It was a normal lock with a keyhole. "And we don't have the key? What if the room catches fire or something?"

Lea then said, "It sounds like you have some interesting plans involving a smuggled candle, Zora."

"I don't. I just don't like to be locked in, that's all." Especially when she planned to run away, but she wasn't going to mention that.

Sarina shook her head. "This is the Magic Temple. There

wouldn't be secrets if aspirants like us were allowed to roam free."

"That's true." And horrible. "But what if something happens?"

"We can call someone." Alma pointed at a rope that led to a small bell.

Interesting. Zora also noticed that there were some chains hanging on the top of the door, making jingling sounds. This was probably also to prevent anyone from leaving the rooms.

Insane that these girls hadn't yet realized that they were in a prison. But then, they were so focused on the small chance of getting out of there that they didn't care for the way they were being treated. Oh, well. What Zora had to do was to plan.

"I guess I'll go to sleep, then. Goodnight."

Zora sat on her bed and opened her bag. She could barely believe that nobody had inspected her belongings, and that she still had everything—except the sword.

It bothered her because it meant she was defenseless, and also because it was Griffin's and she liked to keep this memory of him and their last time together. It gave her courage and resilience—and perhaps some recklessness. Way too much recklessness, when she considered not only the position she was in right now, but also what could be happening to Larzen and Mauro.

But at least she still had a few potion ingredients and even some night vision leftover. Night vision. She wanted to kiss those bottles. The security of this place was betting a lot on the fact that nobody would do anything in the dark, and this was her chance. From what she gathered, Barna removed the lights, but then someone came later and locked the doors. She'd need to plan this right. Any mistake could be deadly. She had to remember those young teens murdered on the beach. This was a dangerous place.

Someone walked in the hallway, opening doors, and Zora, under the covers, chugged down a bottle of night vision potion and put on her dark cloak. Then the door to their own bedroom opened, with its jingling sound. Barna walked in, a tray in her hand, where she put the candle.

"Good night, lovelies," Barna said, with the softness of a caring mother.

"Good night," all the girls answered, including Zora.

The woman walked away, leaving them in darkness. Caring mother. Right. She was their warden. But then, chances were high that she was, in her own way, a prisoner too. Not that Zora pitied her, as this had been her choice. But it had been the girls' choices too, and she didn't know against what they had chosen this path. Anyway, she would hopefully be gone before she had any chance to find out.

Slowly the shapes of the bedroom became clear to her, so she pulled her bag, stepped away from her bed, but threw a bottle on it so that the sound of it hitting the mattress would make the other girls think she was still lying down. She even slowed down her breathing, then took a chair, put it in front of the door, climbed on it, and tied the jingling chains.

She then removed the chair and looked under the door. There was no light coming in. This was great. She timed throwing another bottle on her bed, and then opened the door slowly and walked out.

Her heart was beating fast and it made it hard to breathe slowly and silently, but she'd managed it so far. What she needed now was to find the person who locked the doors and try to steal the key, as she doubted she'd find everything she needed and get everyone out in one night, so she would need the key to come back and pretend she'd never slipped out.

The wall had some recesses, and she found one where she could hide and wait for the apprentice who was going to lock them up, hoping she'd only bring a faint light that would not illuminate Zora.

After a couple minutes, steps echoed in the hall. A young man in a dark red robe walked in the hallway and locked the doors while holding a faint candle in one hand. Odd. Zora had thought it would be a female apprentice. It was as if this was someone whose rank was above Barna, and perhaps they didn't trust her that much. The man had just one key, so it was the same one for all doors. That was good. She hoped the darkness, the depression in the wall, and her dark gray cloak would be enough to protect her from view.

Click. The man locked Zora's room, then passed her without noticing her presence. He then put the candle on the floor by another door and extinguished the flame. The hall turned completely dark, except that she could still see because of the potion.

What was he doing? He then entered the room. Zora's heart sped up. Would he take one of the girls and imprison her? But no sounds came from the bedroom. Zora dared approach it, and found another depression in the wall. Silence. How was she going to steal the key now? Still silence. And time passing. Then she realized something; this door didn't jingle or make any noise when opened. She could see well with her night vision, so she pushed the door carefully.

The man kissed a girl on her bed, more than kissed based on the way they moved under the sheets. Zora looked away quickly. His clothes were on the floor, with the key in the pocket! This was so much luck. It wasn't that hard to move unnoticed in this room, with the couple's ragged breaths. She wondered how the other girls didn't say anything, but noticed the other beds were empty. Interesting.

Zora left the room in silence. Where to go? To the entrance, from where she'd come from. Eventually she'd find some light and need to hide. Odd how darkness, which was something that she had feared for so long, now provided a cover for her. But then, in a way, it had been the shadows that scared her, and now that everything was dark, there were no shadows.

She walked carefully to the end of the hall, where there was a heavy wooden door. Unlocked. She considered locking the door and leaving that man in, but he could then cause a ruckus. He could already cause a ruckus when realizing the key was no longer there. But then, he wasn't going to assume somebody had stolen his key. He'd most likely forget about it or try to find it in the morning or something. Hopefully. She wasn't going to give it back.

Zora opened the door slowly and saw that it led to a set of stairs, which probably went up to that inner garden. But this part wasn't dark; there was a candle—and someone on a chair. A guard. Well, of course. She closed the door. The guard hadn't looked, but if he'd seen her, she'd be caught.

An apprentice should come out of this door. Wearing a red robe. Like the one she'd seen on the floor. Keeping her steps silent, she went back to that room and opened the door. The young man was still in bed, and she didn't look to see if they were still doing anything or not. In fact, Zora didn't even know how long that took. A few minutes? An hour? Well, she had the key and the clothes, and there would definitely be a ruckus in the room, but she had no choice.

She put the robe over her gray cloak. It was too long and dragged on the floor, but all she had to do was pass the guard.

Zora opened the door and headed to the stairs, her steps firm. A sound of steady breathing made her think that the guard was perhaps asleep, but she didn't want to look back and check. After two flights of stairs, she found herself in the interior garden with those beautiful pink trees.

She bet that if there was a library or something, it would

be on the upper floors, but then those stairs were so visible...
And this part of the building wasn't dark anymore. There
were lanterns and then there was the light of the moon and
stars coming from the transparent wall. How much could her
red robe fool people?

She took a look at the balconies, wondering where a
library would be. It would probably have big doors that
wouldn't go unnoticed. But on which floor?

It was a matter of finding it. There were some guards and
apprentices walking in that atrium, so she hid behind a tree
and waited until there were fewer people. After a long time,
she went up the stairs, trying to mimic the naturality and
confidence of an apprentice and ignore the dragging hem of
the red robe she was wearing.

After going up the stairs, she found herself in a large hall
with wide columns, leading to many hallways, and with two
sets of stairs going up. She wondered if this could be like the
Gravel castle, with smaller passages for servants. Well, no, it
seemed that everyone was watched here, and they didn't have
real servants, but failed aspiring apprentices or something.

She didn't think the library would be on this floor. Somehow, she thought it should be bigger, more noticeable, so she
went up again. There were four large doors in a hall similar to
the one underneath. There was some laughter and light
coming from behind one of the doors, as if they were having
some kind of party.

Zora went up again and saw a long hallway with two
guards sitting by a large door. There was a table with a candle
in front of them, which was the only source of illumination.
This large door looked like it could lead to the library or
archives, but the issue would be passing through these
guards.

She walked by the hallway before the guards saw her.
Perhaps she could use the darkness to her favor—again. But

the issue was getting to that candle. Or else she could just walk there and pretend she needed to enter. No. These guards here would see that she wasn't an apprentice.

Perhaps the darkness could still hide her. She took the red robe and put it in her bag, then moved slowly to the wall, facing it, so that only the dark gray of her cloak was visible. The light of the candle still didn't reach her. She moved slowly enough that nobody would notice the movements, and it might have taken minutes for her to get near the candle.

When Zora was close enough, she blew it. The men cursed and complained, and she took the opportunity to pass them and go to the door. But it was locked. The key looked similar to the one from the bedroom, so she tried it. At least the men were still talking, so that they didn't hear the click, the door opening, and Zora entering. When she was inside, she saw a thin ray of light coming from underneath the door. They had lit the candle again.

Although the room was completely dark, Zora could distinguish shapes in black and white, thanks to her potion. This was not really a library, but some kind of research room. Still, one of the walls had books from floor to ceiling. Other than that, there were what looked like cages with objects or books inside them, and, on the other side, desks with papers and drawings. One of them depicted a sort of big basket with something round on top floating in the sky. There was also a table with anatomy illustrations, much more detailed than what she'd seen in the Dark Valley.

In the display cages, she saw an object that looked like a basin, a crystal, and an ancient book, lying open. It wasn't a Solana book, as it had some other kind of writing, not Continental, but it wasn't those circles and triangles that Riadne could read.

On the back, a heavy iron door had a huge keyhole. The

door had wood engravings attached to it, depicting skulls and snakes. If there were Solana books in this building, they would be there. She took the key she had stolen, but it was too small for the hole.

Zora peeked through it, and although it was also dark, she saw shelves and shelves, some with books. Great. Now she had to figure out a way to find that key or to destroy that door. Perhaps with some explosive ingredients? She'd never done anything like that, but studied about it. The issue was the risk of destroying not only the door but also the books, which would render their trip here useless.

No. She had to figure out where that key was, and a way to steal it.

She then felt some faint light coming into the room.

"Anybody there?" a male voice asked.

GRIFFIN WAS USED to being handcuffed, but it was one thing to do it himself. Now his arms were high above him, in an uncomfortable position, but the most uncomfortable was knowing that he'd been caught by the Void—who didn't seem to have a body, to make matters worse. King Sarro's father watched him in silence.

Griffin smiled. "Well, hello, I'm obviously here." He glanced at his wrists. "But no wonder you don't get visitors, considering how you treat the few ones you get."

"Very true," said the Void. "And you have no idea how glad I am that you're here. But you still shouldn't have defied me."

"If you explain why, maybe I'll reconsider it." Griffin wanted to gain time, wanted to understand his situation. He was going to keep trying to find a solution, a way to save his valley.

"Father King," the voice said. "Cut one of his fingers."

"But that's your son's finger," Griffin told the man, barely believing he had to bring up this obvious fact.

The man approached him with a dagger, took one of his hands, and cut the little finger. The moment the pain hit him, Griffin saw himself away from that scene, looking at it from outside that body.

And then he was no longer there, but flying over a small house by a river, and then in a bedroom, where King Jarren sat, looking at a ring with a black stone. A chill passed through Griffin's spine—his father had worn a ring just like it, which Kiran had now. But it was an heirloom, and there was nothing odd about it. Well, actually, there was, as Jarren addressed the ring.

"The portal is almost complete. I still need to see the benefits that it will bring to my kingdom, master."

"You're a king." The voice was coming from the ring. "Gravel is united. I've been keeping my part of the bargain."

"And then once the portal is built, I'll have access to riches on the other side?"

"So greedy."

"No, I'm just thinking about my people."

"Obviously."

King Jarren still stared at the ring. "And my line will keep the throne."

"Yes, the throne will be passed down to all your generations."

"The only cost is destroying the Solanas."

Solanas... like the false Alegra, the ones whose books Zora was after.

The voice from the ring then said, "That's the only thing I require in exchange for the instruction and the power I'm giving you. And they're not only my enemy, but yours too. These witches could undo everything you're fighting for."

"Killing them could cause unrest and problems. They are well regarded in the kingdom."

"But that's what you need to change. You don't start by killing them. You start by destroying their reputation, making people fear them. It's easy, isn't it? Aren't they monstrous already?"

"Most of them look normal. They clip their wings."

"Don't let them do it. Find who does it. Find who teaches them how to do it."

Griffin could notice that Jarren wasn't totally convinced, and yet, based on his previous memory, he was building the portal. He probably thought that there was no harm in building a stone arch, even if there were no results.

But it made sense that he would be reluctant to kill people. Not people, flying witches. But they were people too, in a way at least. Griffin remembered the witch pretending to be princess Alegra. He'd never guessed she wasn't human. Well, they were likely just a different type of human.

Jarren nodded. "Give me a sign, then. If you're all-powerful, give me something to believe you can do what you can do."

"You demand too much, little king. How easily you forget how desperate you were not even two months ago. But I'll give you a sign. How would you like to have more physical strength?"

"It's not that useful for a king. But I'll take it as a display of power."

The voice from the ring laughed.

And then something pulled Griffin away from there, but he wasn't back in Grota, chained to a wall, missing one finger. He was flying over an island.

ZORA CROUCHED. The person who opened the door had just a candle, looked around, then got out and closed it. It was almost as if they were expecting some light or something. Darkness had provided cover for her again.

But she had other problems. She'd found the place where the books were probably kept, and that was great, but she didn't have the key, and doubted it would be that easy to acquire. But her most immediate problem was that she was in a room with only one exit, and there were two guards outside. This time, there was no way to blow the candle before leaving the room, not even any way to walk out naturally wearing the red robe.

One solution could be to hide here until morning, then sneak out once there were more people. A very dumb solution. She'd be caught before even getting to the garden. Plus, someone would notice she hadn't been in her room. And with an apprentice with a key missing... She had to get back.

As she thought about it, she noticed that one of the ladders by the wall with the books led to a trapdoor. It didn't hurt to check.

Zora went up slowly not to make any sound. If someone walked in, she'd have a hard time hiding while in the middle of a wall. The trapdoor had a lock, and the key she had wasn't exactly the right one, but with some jingling, it clicked open, allowing her to climb up.

Her first feeling was disappointment. She'd expected that this room would have more books, perhaps even some rare objects, and instead it was an empty, dark chamber, with a flight of stairs going up. She took a better look around and realized there were other trapdoors. This wasn't bad; this was excellent. I could lead her out of that library. The question was where those trapdoors would lead her. And then there were those stairs. Zora decided to check. She climbed them, tried the door, and was surprised to see that it was unlocked.

She was outside, on the roof of the building. From there she could see the ocean surrounding the island and feel the wind on her face. It felt good to be out of that prison. In fact, this could be a possible escape route. A very convenient one, considering it was right by the secret books. But she had to find the key first—and a way to free Larzen and Mauro.

The roof had a parapet around it, and something behind the door that led her there. It was like a huge hammock over something. It didn't make sense. Parts of it had ropes tied to metal hooks on the floor. And then she realized it might have been the flying thing she'd seen in the drawing. This was their experiment. Part of her thought that only someone highly suicidal would embark on something like this, but a small part of her did wonder if this could help them escape. Right. She had no idea where Larzen and Mauro even were.

The roof had a raised platform. She climbed it and saw a large crystal in its middle, like purple or pink, she wasn't sure. It was cylinder-shaped, as tall as her forearm, and wide like the trunk of a young tree. This stone was right on top of the temple, in the center of the roof, and had to mean something. She'd better stop wondering that, as she wasn't here to steal magical artifacts, just take home some historical records.

"Zora." A voice called her. *That* voice.

She knew he wasn't really here; it didn't make sense. But she also knew she wasn't imagining things and wasn't crazy.

"Griffin?" She wished she could see him, touch him, but listening was good enough for now.

"You can hear me?" There was surprise in his voice.

"Yes. Where are you?"

"I'm in... the Shadow Kingdom, but I'm fine. What about you? Please tell me you didn't try to go to Rock Island."

Strange. Couldn't he see where she was? Perhaps not. "Why?"

"My magic master... I know he ended up killing my

parents, but he wasn't bad in the beginning. He told me that he actually escaped the Magic Temple, and also told me about some horrors that happen in that place."

It sounded right, based on what she'd seen so far. She wanted to ask him a thousand things, tell him how much she was going to fight to get him back, but at that moment, she decided to ask for something more practical—and urgent. "Any tips? I'm not saying I'm going there, or that I'm already there, but let's assume by any chance I ended up in this Rock Island... Any tips for me to get out?"

All she heard was the wind. Even incorporeal Griffin gave her the silent treatment when pissed off. Perhaps he was going to walk away again.

"You're there." So much pain in his voice. Pain that she was causing him.

"We want to find answers about the past and what happened," she rushed to explain. "And they have old books."

"I can find out about the past. I... I can see things. I'll find the answers and I'll tell you, Zora. I see you're outside the building. Just get out of there."

How would she explain that his brother was there? Better not to mention it. "I will," she said. "Don't worry."

"I... couldn't reach you before. Something was blocking me. I can't... stay. Zora, please be careful." His voice started to fade. "With everything wrong that has happened, let me at least know you're safe back in Gravel." She barely heard the last word.

"I'll bring you back," Zora said.

No reply. This time she didn't think he was giving her the silent treatment. He was gone. Griffin.

And then it was hard to breathe and her eyes were stinging with the river of tears she had pushed back. She took a deep breath, taking in the pleasant smell of the ocean. Why cry? She was going to find an answer; she'd come here for that, and she wasn't leaving without it.

She tried to think. So something blocked Griffin. It could be the building, and it could also be that stone. Could it have blocked Riadne's magic? She went to the place where the stone was, but it was well stuck to the roof. Well, she could break it, like she'd done with the cage in the Royal Games. But she didn't have a single tool to do it.

She needed time to plan and think, but for now, the best she could do was return to her room. She went to the door that should lead downstairs—and found it closed. It had a lock, but it was one of the big keyholes. No way she was bringing down that door. She took a look at the wall surrounding the building. It looked fairly smooth, with stone blocks placed close together, but she was going down; all she needed was something to slow down her fall. And there was grass down below.

The wall had parts that were roundish and stuck out like beams. Zora took the gray robe in her hands, so as to ease the friction, hung herself from the parapet, wrapped her legs and arms around the beam—and let go. She slid down super fast, but not so fast that she hurt herself.

By the garden and the entrance, she moved from tree to tree, looking to get to the stairs leading to her dormitory. She even put the red robe back again.

While sticking her neck out to see if there were any guards, someone grabbed her from behind and put a hand on her mouth. This was bad.

22

AN OFFER

The cells were immersed in complete darkness at night. If only Larzen still had some of Zora's night vision potion. For what? To look at the same walls he'd seen for hours? But there was one thing he could do. He doubted it would work, but it didn't hurt to try. He pushed his shoulder between two bars and twisted his body to try to force them apart, pushing against them. He'd always been stronger than most people, but this was an exaggeration even for him.

Still, it seemed to be working. He needed to think. Once this was done, there was no going back, and here he was, unarmed, with no idea how to get out of that place, and not knowing anything about Riadne. Perhaps she would ask those leaders to free him. Maybe she had a plan. And then maybe she didn't. And yet, *he* had no plan. That was the most dreadful part.

"Stop wriggling, Zora, it's me." Riadne.

Zora relaxed, then whispered, "What do you want?"

"Hmm, what a question... Some cake, maybe?"

"What?"

"Freaking stupid question, Zora. We have to get out of this place. Tomorrow, at the ball, we make a run for it. I'll be there and we'll arrange our escape."

"I'm not going to the ball."

"Of course you are," Riadne said.

"I'm not. They didn't give me a dress."

"Cause yours is going to be made at the last minute."

"I found where they keep the books," Zora told her.

"Forget books, Zora. Let's get out of this place and never turn back."

"But then coming here will be useless. Aren't you worried about Gravel? Your people? Maybe there's a secret for your wings, Riadne."

"Zora." Her tone was a warning. "I don't give a crap about any of that. I'm leaving tomorrow and getting Larzen out, and if the entire kingdom has to perish, so be it. If all the Solanas die, so be it."

The issue was Larzen, of course. But he wasn't the only person Riadne loved. "Even your cousin?"

Riadne sighed. "I can't do the impossible."

"It's a door with a big keyhole, it's a big key, then there are old books. I'm not leaving without them."

"A big key." Riadne paused. "Master Smyr, you know, the leader who took us in, he wears a key like that around his neck. If you really insist on your nonsensical plan, get to his bedroom and take it."

"How am I going to get in there?"

"How?" She was still whispering, but it felt as if she was yelling. "Sometimes I don't know if you're stupid or if you're just pretending."

"I'm not stupid."

"Sorry. I'm angry. Sorry. But... it's not that hard to get into a man's bedroom, is it?"

Zora then felt her face get hot. What was the false princess suggesting? But that wasn't even the main problem. "I bet half the girls in that ball will be willing to go there. It doesn't mean he'll pick them all. Or me."

"Oh, I think he'll pick them all if he gets the chance. Either way, figure it out. Or else forget about it, or find another plan. But be there at the ball, and do what I tell you."

"What are you planning?"

"I'm not sure yet, but the cells are down below, and so are the boats. We have three decent fighters counting you; we'll improvise. But I'm not joking, Zora, I will leave you behind if you get caught up in getting these books."

"I can leave on my own later." She was thinking of going to the roof and then sliding down. It didn't solve her problem of lack of a boat, but it got her out.

"Fine. We'll see what happens. Keep your ears sharp. And wait some five minutes. I don't want anyone thinking we're together."

Riadne disappeared in the shadows. Shadows. The garden was getting dark, even for Zora's eyes. Oh, no. The potion was running out. Plus, she still had no clear plan on how to re-enter her hall. This time she wouldn't be able to give her back to the guard. She needed a plan, fast.

Zora remained hidden behind the tree for a few minutes. It was obviously a terrible hiding spot if Riadne had found her. How had she found her? The only plan she came up with was to just go the way she'd come.

Without a weapon, she took a big twig. Right, this was awful. But she wasn't that terrible as a fighter. She put on the red robe again and descended, hood down, the twig partly hidden in her sleeve. The guard didn't look at her, she unlocked the door, and found herself in the hallway, which was still immersed in total darkness. She decided to get rid of the red robe, even if it was a good disguise. What if someone searched her room and found it? Still under some effect from the potion, she found the room where the apprentice had entered and left it in the hallway outside.

She then found her door, opened it carefully, and went to her bed. The other girls were asleep.

So far, luck had been on her side. But the big night was tomorrow.

GRIFFIN WAS BACK in King Saros's body, his wrists chained to a wall, one of his fingers replaced by terrible pain. And yet perhaps what hurt more was learning that Zora was in danger, in a different realm, and being unable to do anything about it, with his hands literally tied.

But he smiled and looked at the hand with the missing finger. "I have nine more, you know? I mean, not me," he turned to the older king. "Your son."

The man showed no reaction. Strange.

"You seem to think you're amusing," the Void said.

"I don't think. I'm sure." Perhaps his bravado was fake. His world was collapsing, and he saw no way to get his life back. But allowing his suffering to overwhelm him wasn't going to solve his problems.

"Indeed," the Void said. "So certain. But I have good things to offer you, young prince."

"Wow. No, no, no. Please don't tell me you are going to want to negotiate. Not after you cut this finger. It's not mine, but still. You don't cut someone's borrowed finger and then expect them to be nice to you."

"I could cut your tongue."

"How are you going to get a reply to your amazing offer?"

"There are many ways, little prince."

"Calling me little is not helping you either." Griffin truly hated that.

"Father King, cut another one."

The older king then approached him with a dagger again, aiming at the other hand, and held his middle finger.

"There we go," Griffin said. Then blinding pain reached him.

And then again he observed the scene from the outside. He wondered if in this state he could see this Void, maybe find where he was, or what he was, but instead, he was pulled somewhere else.

Griffin was again back in what he assumed was Gravel a long time ago. Jarren sat in a bedroom, stared at his ring, then said, "The portal's about finished. Are you going to say anything?" He waited. "Just silence? Great."

The king sighed and put the jewel on his nightstand. A woman with long, light brown hair came in.

"Were you talking to someone?" she asked.

"No." His face changed, and most of his worry was gone.

That had to be his wife. Seeing older couples, this calm domesticity, always got to Griffin. Growing up with his curse gave him little hope that one day he'd have that.

She sat by him. "You're worried."

"No, I... It's just a monument." He smiled and shook his head.

"It means unity between all the people of Gravel. Maybe you fear that your monument might be as fragile as our peace."

"The monument is solid. I'm not worried about that."

She smiled. "You know that's not what I mean."

He hugged her. "Everything is fine. And perfect."

Griffin was then taken out of there, which was a relief. He didn't really want to see what his many-time great grandparents were up to in the bedroom.

The scene changed and then he was by that strange arch, now complete. Griffin still had no idea where it was. King Jarren lit a fire underneath it, in some kind of ceremony. Griffin dreaded seeing what was going to happen next. But nothing happened.

The king, his wife, and a young man who seemed to be their son got in a carriage.

"I don't understand," the young man said. "If this is supposed to represent unity, why didn't we invite more people?"

The king stared at him for a moment, contempt in his eyes.

"It was just a question, father."

"Don't question me." The king's voice was different, his eyes were cold. Oh, no, Griffin knew what was happening and now dreaded even more seeing this.

The young prince looked away. The queen put a hand on Jarren's, or rather, fake Jarren's shoulder. "Are you feeling well?"

He glared at her at first, then seemed to realize that it wasn't the right thing to do. "I'm fine."

She looked at him. "Do you know my name?"

He paused. "What kind of question is that?"

The queen shrugged and smiled. "I would like to hear it from your lips."

He frowned. "You don't make demands here."

She looked at the window, took a deep breath, then faced him. "You're not yourself today."

The king widened his eyes for a second, then took his sword and plunged it into her chest. Her eyes were wide with surprise and maybe disbelief while she bled. Jarren, or rather, his impostor, turned to the prince, but the young man was ready and had a dagger in his hand. The king was stabbed in the neck and died before he could do anything.

"Stop, stop," the prince yelled, then went to his mother and checked her pulse, tried to stop the bleeding, but her eyes were already distant. Dead.

The carriage door was opened from the outside. A guard stood there. "What's wrong, my—" He put a hand over his mouth in horror.

The prince dashed past him, tears running down his eyes. He collapsed on the ground, sobbing.

A guard approached him. Not a guard; his clothes looked nicer. A general or something. "My prince."

"King," he hurled. "He killed her, he killed her. He was crazy. Then he killed himself. It was the Solanas, I know it was. They... messed with his mind. I hate them. I swear I'll hunt and kill every single one of them."

The prince then turned to Griffin, as if he could see him. "You. What are you looking at?"

"It wasn't..." Griffin tried to explain, but then he wasn't there anymore. He didn't know if that prince could hear him, but he would still have tried to tell him that it hadn't been the Solanas, warn him about Grota and the Void, warn him about the ring, but the scene dissolved.

He then saw the young prince inside a room in the castle reading a letter, and tried to yell at him, tell him to be careful, not to kill the Solanas, but he had no voice anymore.

"Who sent this?" A young woman asked him.

He shook his head. "The messenger didn't see it, or doesn't want to tell it, but I know it's from the Solanas."

"What do they want?"

He snorted. "It's... some mockery. It's saying that in each generation one son is open to the darkness, that the darkness is contained within the royal family, but held back until they come of age. To be undone, a champion must wield some Blood Cup. Not anyone, but the winner of an open contest for strength, courage, skills, and smarts. Sealed with a blood sacrifice. The champion will find the cup which can undo the magic embracing the darkness."

"They are offering a solution," she said.

"But why?"

"You expect witches to be logical?"

He shook his head. "I don't think there's even any curse on the sons. They're just threatening us."

"Let's hope that's the case."

Griffin again wanted to scream, but then he was no longer there, but back in the Void's tower.

"You seem to evade the pain," the voice said.

The body Griffin was using had two missing fingers now. "Maybe. Now, you said you had an offer. After such a nice display of goodwill, I'm quite inclined to hear it." It was true that he was curious, but also true that he would refuse whatever the Void proposed.

"You're a hard one to figure out. You lack greed, anger, hatred. Makes you quite boring."

It was annoying that the Void didn't have a physical presence for Griffin to glare at. "Oh, I have hatred."

"Such a pure heart. So filled with love. But you know what? It's even better than greed. It's easy to give you what you want." The Void's tone was clearly mocking, but then his voice became harsh. "Wardens, bring her in."

Griffin's heart sped up. Who could it be?

THE ROOM WAS STILL IMMERSED in complete darkness when Zora heard a click on the lock. She wasn't sure if it was morning already and if the other girls were up. After some minutes, the door opened, bringing with it a bright light. Well, not that bright. Just a candle in the hands of another woman, not Barna.

The woman then stopped to look at the door. Oh, no, the jingling chains were still tied. How could Zora have forgotten them?

"What happened here?"

Zora had to think quickly. She could just pretend she had no idea what had happened, but they would still suspect her.

"It was me," she said. "I was afraid they wouldn't let me sleep. I was going to untie them, but it was so dark..."

The woman narrowed her eyes.

"I'm truly sorry. Please don't tell anyone," Zora added.

"Untie it. Before anyone sees it."

"Sure." Zora rushed and took a chair, making the maximum amount of noise possible, then climbed on it and untied the chains.

The woman was older than most people there and eyed Zora up and down. "Don't do anything like that again. Or you'll be sent home."

"Thanks."

When the woman left, Sarina turned to Zora. "Faria is too nice." She sighed. "If Barna were to learn about it..."

Her tone was nice, but Zora hadn't forgotten the threat in the bathtub. "Well, she could want to punish all of us, just in case." She smiled and added, "So it's a good thing she didn't say anything. Plus, it wasn't even me, but I thought it was better if I confessed it, you know, since I'm new."

None of the girls seemed to believe this last lie, but it was hopefully enough to plant some doubt and prevent them from ratting out Zora to Barna.

She smiled. "Which one of you tied it?"

Lea rolled her eyes. "Zora, don't be ridiculous. We know it was you. The question is *why*. And when."

She shrugged. "Well, I don't know."

Stupid Zora. She had passed guards and then ended her night with such a silly mistake. And now Riadne wanted her to go to that ball. The one she hadn't even been invited for. But she could still take the opportunity to sneak around and try to find Riadne.

And what about the key? So many questions in her head. This was what she got for jumping into a plan head first. But then, did anyone outside this island have any idea what went on here? There would have been no way for Zora to figure out this place before getting in.

Despite some sideways glances, her roommates were nice to her as they walked to the dining hall. It was hard to believe that it was day, as the corridors and rooms were illuminated only with candles and torches, and no sunlight came in.

They lined up to collect two loaves of bread, a glass of milk, and cheese. When Zora had barely finished eating, someone tapped on her shoulder. She turned and saw the woman who had brought the light, Faria.

"Come with me, please."

"Is this…"

Faria put a finger over her lips, and Zora got up. As she left the table, she noticed that Sarina had a smirk. That girl was dangerous. Or perhaps dangerous was whatever was going to happen to Zora. If they questioned her, she would deny it all.

They entered a small and obviously very dark room, lit by only a candle, where a servant held a dress.

"This was last minute," Faria said. "So it might not fit you perfectly, but it was the best we could find on such a short notice."

"For the ball?"

"Of course. Your name is on the list."

Riadne had been right.

"Just try it so we see if it needs any adjustment."

There was no dressing room or curtain. "Here?"

Faria raised an eyebrow. "You could go out in the hallway,

if you wish."

Zora decided to take it as a joke and smiled. These people had no concept of privacy or modesty. She took out her cotton dress, leaving only the underslip and bodice on. The key was inside the bodice, as she didn't want to take any chances and leave it where it could be found, but it wasn't visible, and the women didn't notice it. She then put the ball dress on. It was dark red and made of a soft, velvety fabric. The color stunned her, considering it was similar to the color of the apprentice's robes. The previous day the girls had blue, yellow, orange. The closest to red had been pink.

The servant took some measurements of her waist. "I'll just tie it a little here." She smiled at Zora. "You'll look great. Don't forget us down here."

Her stomach churned. She wasn't even sure if she could escape with her friends, let alone do anything for the dwellers of this place. Still, she asked, "What do you mean?"

"She means nothing," Faria said while glaring at the servant.

"You think I'll be promoted to apprentice?" Zora asked, trying to fish for more information. "If I am, I can come back and say *hi*." As if she even knew these people. "And I'll still be in the temple."

"Of course." Faria smiled. "And we'll be down here, working hard to make sure everything is in order."

Since they were just the three of them, alone, she decided to voice her curiosity. "Why do you think I'll be accepted? I just got here."

"Your dress."

"Who sent it?" Zora asked.

Faria shrugged. "That, we do not know."

She could be saying the truth or not. It was hard to gauge these people. And then Zora asked something else she was curious about. "Are you happy here?"

"Extremely." Faria had a smile that did not reach her eyes.

"Very much," the servant added.

"Get dressed now. You have classes to attend," the old woman said.

Zora put back her cotton dress and rushed to the dining hall. The girl who had gotten the apprentice's visit the previous night was there, eating with other girls and looking normal, which was a relief. It would be horrible if the girl were to pay for Zora's actions.

They were ushered to a classroom, again very dark. She sat by Alma, and asked, "Why aren't there any windows here?"

"It's symbolic. We're still plain. We'll see the light when we are knowing."

"What about the people who work here?"

"They don't spend all their time down here." She stared at Zora. "You seem to disapprove of this place?"

"No idea where you got that impression. I mean, spending days without windows is super healthy, right?"

The girl shook her head. "You understand so little." Her voice was laced with pity.

But what she said was true. If that temple had a logic, it completely eluded Zora.

"Quiet, now," the girl added in a whisper, as if to shut down any other questions.

Zora remained silent. Tonight, again she would rush into action without a clear plan. She had rushed headfirst into things before.

The night she had taken Seth's place and decided to go to Gravel and compete as the Dark Valley champion, she had no idea what was going to happen. But at that time, there had been so little to lose. Now, her kingdom, her life, her love, everything was at stake. But she was going to keep her hope.

23

PREPARING FOR THE NIGHT

Griffin couldn't imagine who they were about to bring in. Well, actually, he feared it could be Zora, but it didn't make sense. All he knew was that they were planning something that would scare or disturb him.

Two men wearing helmets came in bringing another Grota person. A woman, gagged, her two arms being held. Her eyes were defiant, but she glanced at Griffin and winked. It was Amina. Why? She had nothing to do with any of this. And he had been under the impression that she had escaped. But showing that he cared would only make things worse.

He frowned, as if confused. "You do realize she's real King Saro's wife, not mine, right?"

"Oh, don't worry, silly boy," the Void said. "She's here just for a demonstration. What we'll do to her, we'll do to the one you care about."

Griffin flinched, but tried to remain calm. "You know nothing about it."

Amina struggled her arm out of a guard and removed her gag. Facing Griffin, she said, "The Void needs to be invited. He wants you to invite him into your kingdom. But it's yours.

It's yours. The kingdom's yours." Then her throat moved, as if swallowing something, and she no longer looked at Griffin as she said, "You'll never torture me."

She convulsed, then struggled to breathe, as if suffocating, then collapsed in the guards' arms. Why her? Griffin remembered her little baby in her loving arms, eyes all full of innocence and love, even if he was gray and strange like all the people here.

But she had a message for him. *Invite him to your kingdom. But it's yours.* It sounded obvious, but must have had some deeper meaning. It almost looked as if she had let herself be caught to send him the message. Or at least waited until swallowing whatever poison she had in her mouth. Not all warriors wielded swords.

"It seems you're sad," the Void said.

"Should I be happy to see an innocent woman, a mother, be killed?"

"She did it herself," The Void said. "Not my fault. Why would I kill her that fast and waste all the screams and suffering? But I can still use her for a demonstration of what I'm going to do to the one you love."

Could the Void know where Zora was? Could he reach her?

Still, for now Griffin wanted to avoid some gruesome spectacle involving an already dead body. "I don't need a demonstration. Your point is quite clear. Just tell me what you want."

"Exactly what she told you. No idea why she went through the effort."

"You want me to invite you to Gravel?"

"Exactly. But under some conditions. You'll need to be king."

"You're out of luck, then."

"Oh, no, not at all. The rules in your kingdom are quite

easy. All you'll have to do is kill one person. I'm sure you can do that."

So the Void expected him to kill his own brother? Griffin rolled his eyes. "Right. Super easy."

"And invite me to connect to the land in your kingdom. I'll help you and your line stay in power."

"I don't even care about power."

"Very true. But you have love. That might be an even greater weakness than ambition, pride, or greed."

"But I love my brother."

"Put that love on a scale. I have a king under my control in your land. And he can reach the one you love. Then we'll start killing her slowly."

The conversation between Zora and the Grota king pretending to be him crossed his mind. He didn't doubt she could look for that impostor, and then... He didn't even want to think about what could happen. The idea of letting them hurt her was unbearable. But he couldn't let his entire kingdom suffer either. He couldn't invite The Void to Gravel. He had to think, had to gain time.

"What else do I get?" he asked.

"More? You'll be protected. You and all your great-grand-children can live happy lives. All I'm asking is that I be allowed to go to your kingdom and help it gain power."

"Power from pain and suffering."

"It doesn't need to be from Gravel's subjects."

Griffin was trying to think. Amina's words came to his mind. *The kingdom's yours.* Hang on. Her point hadn't been that he shouldn't accept the invitation. It was as if there was a way to make it work, there was a solution.

He said, "Fine. I'm considering it. But you said I need to be king, right? I understand what I have to do, but I'm not even sure if my brother's in the castle—"

"I can give you some time. But if I send you back, you'll be bound by your words."

"How?"

"You'll have ten days to become king and invite me to your kingdom. If you fail, you'll be brought back here, and so will the people you love."

But that would give Griffin time. He could tell Zora to run away, to hide. He could try to make a plan with Larzen. No, when the Void said that they would be brought back, it meant bringing them to this kingdom, so he would be condemning them to a horrible fate. He couldn't let it happen. Instead, Griffin could try to dreamwalk and reach Zora. Warn her. Keep her away from danger. He didn't need to accept this deal. And yet Amina's words rang in his mind. She clearly wasn't telling him to refuse the proposal. But why?

"Can I have some time to think?"

"Of course. Meanwhile, we'll carry on our demonstration. Wardens."

The two men who had been holding Amina's body let her fall to the ground. One of them took a dagger. The idea of them desecrating her body was horrible.

"Stop it. I accept your offer. I accept it. What happens now?"

THE CLASSES during the day ended up being useful, even if sitting in rooms without sunlight was uncomfortable. All the girls attended the classes, since the ones not selected for the ball with the magicians would attend a ball with the male apprentices.

Barna and another woman taught them how to dance, how to hold a cup, and how to behave in a ball. Well, that part wasn't that useful. Zora had been to balls in Gravel and didn't think she had made a fool of herself. Perhaps she hadn't smiled as much as they were suggesting or something, but doubted it was such a big deal.

The useful part was that they had portraits of all the magicians and explained who they were. The idea was that the magicians shouldn't have to go through the trouble of presenting themselves. Zora appreciated having this information, since it was important to know as much as possible about this temple.

There were fifteen magicians in total, fourteen men and one woman. According to Barna, that female magician was a reminder that the opportunities were equal for male and female apprentices.

Zora had to hold down a snort. She looked around to see if the other girls were also in disbelief, but it didn't seem to be the case—or else they had gotten good at pretending. Hopefully that was it.

Barna didn't explain what each magician did, or what they did as a group, for that matter. This explanation might have been in a lesson Zora had missed. Still, the excitement in the girls about the possibility of meeting them showed that they were admired here.

Zora, for her part, assumed that they had some hand in keeping these aspirants in dark accommodations, so she couldn't share the excitement. The only thing she was excited about was getting the key from Master Smyr, but it wouldn't be as easy as Riadne believed. The master was like a god to these girls, and, based on whispers and looks of admiration, a good part of that group would gladly go to his bedroom. Zora just wanted a key, though. Perhaps there was another way that was not Riadne's way.

In the end, Barna said, "So behave well and make sure you're pleasant. Your performance in the balls tonight will impact your chances of being selected. If you're not going to the main ball, don't despair. You will have other chances. Your performance will determine if you'll continue as an aspirant, become a servant, or, in very rare cases, be sent home. But that's very rare and I don't want you to be scared. Just make sure you don't antagonize anyone, and you will be fine. This is your first socializing event, and the apprentices can open wonderful doors to you."

The girls clapped, and Zora joined in a few seconds too late. The whole thing sounded very wrong. The male aspirants weren't selected based on their performance at a ball. She remembered Kiran offering her a position as a potion master, but insinuating that she would need to do things not related to potions. But they weren't insinuating any of that here. This was just a horrible place that treated girls like crap and had secret prisoners. Her heart got tight thinking about Larzen and Mauro. But Riadne seemed to have a plan.

It was late afternoon when the girls got back to their bedrooms, based on the time it had been since they had lunch. Zora wasn't totally sure, as she hadn't seen any clocks and there was no natural light. A servant brought them their dresses.

"Why did they bring this for you?" Sarina asked Zora.

She hadn't told them that she was actually going to the main ball, and she would need someone to talk to and act normal, or else she would need to stand by a corner on her own. No, wait, she had to talk to the magicians. It was fine if the girls hated her.

"It turns out I am going to the same ball as you," she said. "I hope you're fine with it."

Lea shrugged. "Makes no difference."

"True." Zora smiled, even if she noticed the hint of fury in Sarina's eyes.

After hearing the classes today, she understood these girls

a little better. They had little hope for their future and felt that they were competing against each other. But it was sad.

They should instead demand better opportunities for girls like them and fight not to have their futures depending on frivolous balls. But then again, the reason they didn't stand up and demand something better was that they didn't want to ruin their chances of getting it. Zora had no idea if there was a solution for the way things were in this temple. Perhaps it was too much to hope that the solution should come from people who were put into such difficult conditions.

In a way it was like the Dark Valley; they were so focused on defending themselves from shadow creatures that they could never stop and try to come up with a solution. Here the girls were so afraid of being sent home that they never thought that things could be different.

And Zora was thinking too much. All she had to do was get that key, get the books, and get out. It wasn't up to her to change circumstances she didn't really understand. The girls looked happy. Perhaps nothing had to change.

How could anyone sleep with those screams? Echoing in the walls of his cells, making him shudder. Larzen had waited long enough. Based on what he had witnessed here, their method of extracting blood would be worse than uncomfortable.

Of course Riadne wasn't coming for him, of course she didn't have any plan to release him. Zora, poor Zora. As much as she was brave, well-educated, and even smart, she was a naive girl raised in the most isolated place in the kingdom. His chest tightened thinking about Griffin, who cared about her. But at this point, his best chance would be to return to

Gravel, claim his place as king, then try to use diplomacy to rescue Zora.

Of course, there was the little issue of fake Griffin and the prize on his head. He'd need to find a way to work around that. Work around so many things. And leave Riadne behind. The hardest part would be to get her off his mind.

What he observed was that the red-robed men with the key came in rarely, and in fact there had been none of them today. There were always two guards, but they walked back and forth in the hallways. From the time they passed his cell, it was three hundred seconds, or five minutes, until they returned. His plan was to get his cell open, find Mauro, then get out. The two of them together should be able to disarm two guards and make a run for it.

He just had to focus and make sure he made no mistakes.

THE FIRST THING Griffin felt was the absence of any feeling. No smell, no sight, no touch, no sense of time or physical body. This wasn't like dreamwalking, but something else. He could hardly believe it was true, that he was about to go back to Gravel, go back to his body. And then, perhaps the price would be too high, but he had to take this chance, he had to try.

What he felt then was physical pain, as if his entire body were on fire, and difficulty breathing, as if something were compressing his lungs. It felt wrong and strange. There was a table in front of him, so he held on to it so as not to collapse, then found a chair and sat.

He was in Kiran's office, in front of a table with a map of Gravel. A blond man stared at him. Stavos. Griffin still remembered seeing the crown assistant's glee in capturing

Zora, and how he wanted to capture him, and didn't quite understand how he had come to help his impostor.

The man frowned. "Feeling well?"

It was as if he had to find again his lips, his mouth, find the way he spoke. Finally, he said, "It must be something I ate."

"Well, I know I'm not supposed to give you health advice, but all these cakes can't be good for you."

"True." Cakes? The shadow king had been eating cake in his body? Well, he had never eaten before.

Griffin ran his hand through his stomach and noticed it was slightly more pronounced. How could the king have gained weight in his body in only what? Five, six days? He wasn't even sure about time anymore. He then looked at his arms and noticed that he was wearing a long-sleeved shirt. That part was fine, but the problem was that the shirt was made of shiny silk—yolk yellow. Over it, a red vest, paired with blue pants. Griffin might as well join a circus.

But what pissed him off the most was that nobody had noticed it wasn't him. In Grota, Griffin had been very careful not to wear different clothes, not to call attention. Meanwhile, here, his impostor had been eating cake and dressing like a clown, and it seemed nobody had batted an eyelid. In fact, for some reason, Stavos seemed to approve and respect him more.

Griffin turned to the blond man. "I'm sorry. Could you just go back a little and repeat what you've been saying? I think these cakes are really getting to me."

Stavos raised an eyebrow, then said, "There have been talks about Larzen being here," he pointed to a village near the mountains. "After that, we had two reports, from this village, and this one." He pointed at two villages that were too far apart. "Nonsense, of course. Now, the Dark Valley girl." His nose crinkled while mentioning her.

Griffin didn't say anything or react because he wanted to see where this was going.

The man continued, "She has been seen on a boat, leaving Gravel. We're trying to contact spies in Kentosa to check if they've spotted her." He got serious. "She will be brought back and imprisoned, correct?"

"Maybe." Griffin was trying to think. This was information he knew already. He knew she was in Kentosa, on that horrible island, and he had to come up with a plan soon to get her and his brother out of there.

But there was something else bothering him in Stavos. Griffin had to test him. "You know, I'm very thankful you've been loyal since I returned. Even though we've had our differences."

The blond man shook his head. "I was under orders. My loyalty is to Gravel and the crown, and it will always be. And I'm glad to make things go back to the way they were. Traditionally. Like it was in your parents' time."

Right. When Stavos had a lot of power and influence. The truth was that he would be loyal to whoever allowed him to have the most power. The king impersonating Griffin had read the man well, which was smart. Stavos was easy to manipulate if he got his way. Plus he loved to talk, and probably enjoyed explaining obvious things. Interesting.

Griffin nodded. "And you believe we should imprison the Dark Valley girl?"

"Well, it's your idea. I know you said she should be brought in as a hostage and not harmed, but I'm glad you're over your obsession with her. It was her dark magic. Those people in that valley, they should never be allowed to leave. That little witch is dangerous."

Witch? Then a memory came to him: Zora, scared, coming to his office to ask for help, trusting him to protect her, to find her assailant. Griffin then had most people in the castle examined for knife wounds. But he missed the real suspect.

"Stavos. Can you remove your shirt, please?"

"Excuse me?"

"Remove your shirt. It's an order."

The man frowned. "What for?"

"It doesn't matter. I'm saying so."

"Your highness. Our agreement was that I would represent king Kiran's interests, therefore I do not need to heed your orders, even if I tend to do it out of civility."

"Are you going to remove it or do you want me to do it?"

Stavos sighed. "This is humiliating. And unnecessary. As far as I know, you're not a healer."

Once his shirt was out, then Griffin saw, clear as day, a mark on his shoulder, and another on his ribs. He had been the one to attack Zora. "Why?" Griffin asked.

"Why what? I don't understand what your highness is implying."

Griffin was usually calm. That was not a natural disposition, but the result of focus and effort. His mother had always warned him against losing control, fearing he could transform into something else. Now he knew it was nonsense; the curse didn't work like that, but still, it had been a useful skill he had learned.

But he wasn't going to use it now. Griffin dropped the crown assistant on the floor and put his hands around his throat.

"Did you send my dogs after her too? Why?"

"I did nothing." Stavos's voice came out with difficulty.

"Explain. Or die. If you live, you'll get a fair trial." Griffin loosened his grip on the man's throat.

"The dogs can be trained to attack using scent. It's easy. And I never meant to harm her, just scare her away. Our games were getting ridiculous with those pointless, easy tasks. Your highness was getting ridiculous with your obsession with her. It was for the crown."

"My dogs? You dared use my dogs?" He pressed his hands against the man's neck.

"They weren't hurt," Stavos whimpered.

"She could have killed them."

"Nobody was hurt."

"Guards!" Griffin yelled.

The door opened, and two guards entered.

Griffin said, "Take him to the dungeons. I'll deal with him later."

He had a lot to deal with later. He needed to check the state of his kingdom, find out if Kiran was really dead, undo the prize on Larzen's head, and maybe declare war on Kentosa. All this in less than ten days, when he'd need to find a solution, or else condemn Zora to a fate worse than death.

24

THE BALL

Zora lined up with the other girls to go up to the magic temple. There was excitement all around her, some nervous giggles and whispers.

All the female aspirants were very pretty, and they were gorgeous in their dresses. She counted; there were only nine of them. It meant that most of the girls would go to the other ball.

They went up the stairs to the garden, then climbed up to the first floor and entered a ballroom that wasn't much larger than their dining hall in the basement. There were lots of couches, a table with some appetizers that Barna had warned them not to touch before the other guests, and some empty space in the middle, which she assumed would be used for dancing.

Big windows faced the ocean and the starry sky. The laughter Zora had heard the previous night seemed to have come from this room, so it wasn't that special. There was no place for a band anywhere, only what looked like a large music box on a corner. It made sense that they wouldn't bring a band to such a secret place.

The aspirant girls mostly sat on couches. Zora stood by the window. The door opened after some time, and three female apprentices came in, Riadne among them. Of course she didn't even glance in Zora's direction. Eventually they'd need to talk, if they were going to plan anything. No magicians had entered yet. Zora had the odd feeling that the girls were there for display like the food on the table. Fantastic.

Riadne stopped by the window, by Zora, then whispered, "Ignore me and pretend I'm not talking to you. Don't spend time in large groups of girls. Don't look at him too much, but when you do, stare in his eyes."

Zora didn't understand who Riadne was referring to, but then realized she was trying to tell her how to flirt with master Smyr.

She continued, "Touch him lightly in the arms, but don't stay too long near him. Pretend you don't care whether he's interested in you or not. Men are competitive. Try to get attention from other men, so that he sees you as a challenge. Never doubt that you can get his attention. Good luck. You might have to kill him. Then find me here or by the stairs going down. I won't wait for you past midnight." She then walked away without even glancing at Zora.

It was only eight. Still, how was she going to get that key and the books before midnight? But it was true that they had to get Larzen and Mauro out as soon as possible. She went over what Riadne had told her about getting to master Smyr. She almost sounded like Larzen, pushing Zora on Kiran. What he hadn't realized was that Kiran didn't require any effort; just existing was enough to get him interested.

The doors opened again, and six magicians entered, all male. Then some five male apprentices, who must have been highly ranked, came in. Then more male apprentices dressed in red entered carrying trays with bottles and cups and serving drinks. Zora took a glass of wine to blend in, even if she wasn't planning on drinking it. But she had to be flirty. Two magicians were by the table. She remembered their names from the lesson and approached them.

"Lovely to be here." She looked into their eyes.

One of them nodded politely, and the other turned away without looking at her. Well, Barna had told the girls not to approach them, but then how was Zora going to get to Smyr if she stood or sat by herself and hoped that he noticed her? Still, she told herself that she had made a great impression on them. And then maybe it was just that they weren't perverts.

The door opened again, and all eyes moved there. Smyr himself was among them. He actually looked good for someone his age, assuming he was thirty-something or so. Zora found him too old for her taste. All the men there were creepy, and this place was horrible. Right. But she couldn't be thinking that. Still, what she did wonder was how come there were no old magicians there, or no old people other than Barna and Faria, and they weren't older than fifty at most.

More things that shouldn't be in her mind right now.

A magician stood by her. "You are the new girl."

She smiled. "In person."

"We will want to discuss your enchantments once these..." He gestured around him. "Trials are over."

"I was glad to join in." She smiled. "Thanks." She then moved away, but not without giving him a lingering look.

She found Alma standing at a corner, looking serious. "Are you all right?" Zora asked.

The girl had a fake smile. "Me? So excited! This is such a great celebration." Her tone was far from convincing.

There wasn't anyone around them, so Zora whispered, "You're afraid."

"Who isn't afraid of being sent home? Or maybe of staying." She smiled again. "But fear is just a little thing."

"Why did you choose to come here?"

"Why did *you* choose?"

"Me?" Zora asked. "For learning." That was true, in a way. "You?"

"The chance for a better life. A better life for my family, too." She then changed her tone. "Well, nice talking to you." The girl walked away, perhaps regretting having confessed her fear.

There was no way these girls had come here knowing what really went on. And again, Zora had to get to Smyr. He was sitting on a couch, talking to two girls.

Zora didn't know how to flirt, but then she had a wonderful idea: she was going to pretend she was Riadne. What would she do? Zora took a deep breath, imagined she was the super confident redhead, then walked to Smyr and sat on his lap. He was startled, then smiled. She looked in his eyes, noticing the rays in his irises, which had mixed green and brown. "I've been here for two days and still haven't shown you how I enchant a sword."

"In a hurry?" he smiled.

"Not me." She tilted her head. "But the sword will get lonely."

She ran her hand over his arm, got up, and walked to the table, where she left her glass. When she turned, she saw him looking at her. Zora smiled and approached an apprentice, as the magicians were all surrounded by people. Now, hopefully this one wouldn't shun her.

"Delightful wine, isn't it?" That was stupid, but people said stupid things at a party.

"I've had better. You? Got your fill? Enjoying your learning?"

"It's great."

He nodded. "Good to know. Your name?"

"I'm Zora."

"You're the one, the new..."

"The enchanting one."

"That's right." He put something in his mouth and swallowed it.

On one corner of the room, Riadne was sitting among three magicians, and they were all laughing as if they were having the greatest time ever. All three of them looking at her with puppy eyes. She was good at this. Or maybe it was some magic.

But perhaps Zora wasn't that terrible. Master Smyr got up and was walking in her direction, except that he ended up looking at where Riadne was, perhaps wondering what Zora was staring at. He then changed direction and walked towards the false princess.

"Do you have plans for after the party?" the apprentice by her side asked.

"It depends. What do people here usually do?"

"I don't know about people, but I'm quiet. I'm an adept of the three Bs."

"Which are?"

"Bath, books, and bed."

"Silence and solitude are great for learning."

He shrugged. "Company is good, too."

"I'm sure you'll find amazing company. If that's what you're looking for."

"Maybe." He took something else and put it in his mouth.

Zora took the opportunity to walk away. Master Smyr was whispering something in Riadne's ear. She punched him lightly in the chest, smiled, then whispered something back. Perhaps she'd try to get the key? Well, she was much better at it than Zora.

Smyr and Riadne got up and seemed to be walking away, but then they passed by Zora, and Riadne pulled her hand. "Come. You'll love this."

And then she was walking out the door and up the

stairs, then they entered a huge set of doors and found herself in a large bedroom, almost as large as the ballroom downstairs, with one huge bed, three sofas, a small table, a big dining table, bookshelves, and a desk. The ocean and some lights from the continent far away could be seen from two large windows. Neat. These people did appreciate sunlight.

On a wall, she saw Griffin's sword and couldn't help walking towards it. When she realized what she'd done, she exclaimed, "Oh, it's here! I can tell you about the enchantments."

He smiled "Oh, you're so cute. We will discuss all types of enchantment, don't worry." He then started unbuttoning his robe.

Zora's stomach chilled, and she walked to the window so he wouldn't see her face, which was probably pale. "I love the view here."

She then felt hands around her waist, and his face by her ear, whispering, "And what else do you love?"

He started to move his hands up. Zora was trembling and didn't know what to do, but he screamed behind her and let her go. She turned around and saw him facing Riadne, a dagger stuck on his back, between his ribs, right on the back of where his heart should be. That should have been a fatal wound.

Riadne was smiling and laughing, as if delighted, clapping as if she'd seen the greatest magic trick in the world. "This is wonderful. It's so amazing to see it for real!"

"You tried to kill me," he snarled.

"Don't be silly." Riadne still looked calm and was smiling. "You can't die, can you?" She cocked her head and pouted. "I thought it was exciting."

He put his hand behind his back and pulled out the dagger. There wasn't even blood. Zora wasn't sure if he bought Riadne's story or if he was just stunned at her reaction.

Riadne pouted again and put her hand on his chest. "It's not every day I meet someone immortal."

While he was staring at Riadne, Zora walked towards the wall with the sword, without giving her back to Smyr.

He held Riadne's wrists. "It's not every day I meet someone claiming to be a Solana. Except that your magic doesn't work here, does it? But we can dissect you and examine your wings."

"Hmm," she said in a whispery, seductive voice, ignoring his threat. "I'm actually looking forward to being dissected. Why do you think I'm here?"

Zora climbed a chair and took the sword.

"You!" Master Smyr yelled, and he was now facing Zora. He moved his hands as if modeling a ball in front of his stomach, and some red light appeared in it.

Zora dashed to him as fast as she could, and in fact, it was a great thing that his hands were down. She swung the sword and beheaded him. His head rolled far away, and his body thumped on the floor. No blood came out.

Zora should be shocked or disgusted, but she wasn't. She was relieved, for one, and that bloodless body didn't strike her as human. It felt like killing a shadow creature.

Riadne was now wide-eyed and trembling, and said, "He might come back."

"He won't." Zora took the head and threw it out the window, then crouched by his body and took a chain with a large key.

"You might be right," Riadne said. "How did you know how to kill him?"

"Well, the head commands the body, right? Unless there's something else commanding both. Still, it's going to take some time for them to find each other again, if that's the case."

Riadne covered her face with her hands. "I was trying to get the jailer to show me the prisons. He was one of the magicians I was talking to."

"All right. There's a big stone on the roof of the building. I think that's what blocks your magic. I'll get the books, then go to the roof and remove it. You'll try to get as close to the cells as you can, then do your singing."

"I'm not betting everything on my magic again, Zora. We don't even know what these magicians are and if they respond to it."

"Fine. I'll still remove the stone. Just in case. Do what you have to do. Get them out and leave without me. But get Mauro out."

"You've decided to stick around or something?"

"There's something on the roof. I think it floats and could get me to the beach at least."

"No. We all leave together. Hurry with the books and the stone and meet me in the ballroom. If not there, in the garden."

Zora was stunned that Riadne cared about her, or at least pretended to do so.

"Fine."

"Then go."

RIADNE TOOK a deep breath and walked downstairs, back to the ball. She'd done a lot of research on who was who in this place and knew that the magician who usually took care of prisoners was a red-haired, young-looking man. She would have considered him cute if she didn't know that he was old enough to be her grandpa at least.

She walked in, her posture and face relaxed and light. Her plan was to dare him to show her the prisoners. Shitty as far as plans went, but male egos were male egos, and she thought she could convince him. He was in a corner, talking to a blonde aspirant who looked so scared she probably was thinking he was going to eat her. Imagine if she learned that he was in fact some kind of immortal monster. Well, the good news was that the girl was no competition for Riadne, who stared at him. He noticed it, looked in her direction, and smiled. So far, so good. She just had to push down the horrible images of the beheaded thing upstairs, and the realization that this magician would be just as dangerous as Smyr, and then play her game.

But then he looked away, at a young guard who entered the ball and whispered something in his ear. The magician left and didn't spare Riadne a single glance. Rude. Wait. Hang on. She could follow him. When she reached the door, two guards stepped in front of her.

She pointed to the jailer magician. "I'm with him. Just... want to talk to him."

"He'll come back and call you if he wants you," one guard said.

Ruder than rude. And now she had to figure out a way to leave that stupid ballroom.

THE GUARDS PASSED BY LARZEN. He had five minutes. Enough waiting, or else he would risk being the one screaming. He pressed himself against the bars and pushed. They seemed to be moving, but very little. There was a high possibility that he had overestimated his strength. But it was this or death. Or being tortured. He gathered all his force, pushed, and then opened it enough that he could slide through. For once he was thankful for his relatively slight build.

He had heard Mauro's voice before and had an idea about its direction. As he passed some cells, he gestured to the prisoners to be silent. His plan was to free Mauro, and only then confront the guards, so that they would have superior strength to counter their weapons. And he wanted to free the other prisoners too.

When he passed the cell with the girl, she yelled, "Help me, please."

"Shut up," he whispered. "Or the guards will catch me."

"Set me free or I'll yell," she threatened him.

"I need to get the key."

"A prisoner escaped! A prisoner escaped!" she yelled from the top of her lungs.

"Well, thanks," Larzen muttered, then he dashed away from her cell in the direction from where the guards were coming. If anything, he didn't want to give his back to them, and knew that they would be expecting someone running away, so he'd have a small surprise advantage doing it this way.

He crouched against the bars of an empty cell, since they were slightly retreated from the stone bordering them and would provide him some cover. He also thought that the guards wouldn't expect him to crouch and hang around.

Larzen was dreading what came next. Not only he wasn't a great fighter, he hated violence, and couldn't stand the sight of blood. He had been trained for diplomacy, which meant doing all he could to avoid a confrontation. But it wasn't his fault that nobody here even tried to listen to him.

When the steps approached, he reached out his leg and tripped the guards. One of the swords was dropped in front of them, Larzen took it, then stabbed the chest of the guard who was getting up, and got the other one in the back. The blood and deaths made him sick.

But then he remembered the young men on the beach, killed mercilessly by people from this temple. Not these guards, though. But then, they watched as prisoners were brought in for torturing. Larzen had no idea how much of a choice they had in all that, but they were in a deadly place regardless. He rushed to where he thought Mauro's cell was.

The girl yelled, "Help, help!"

He hoped the red-robed men outside would consider all this noise normal. He got to Mauro's cell and saw him lying on the floor.

"Mauro, can you help me escape?"

He sat up with difficulty and had a bruise on his forehead. "You have the key?"

"I am the key."

Larzen leaned on the bars, realizing perhaps too late that this would be much harder than his own bars, considering the prisoner's size. Sweat was dripping from his forehead when he thought he'd bent the bars enough, but Mauro tried to pass through, and the gap was still too small.

"Maybe you can free someone else to help you? Then come back," Mauro said.

"The problem is that I don't trust them, and I need someone skilled. We don't know what we're going to face."

Larzen put all his effort this time, pushing hard against the bars, even if he was getting out of breath from the effort and felt more and more sweat in his face. This time, Mauro passed through.

"Thank you," he said.

Larzen shook his head. His voice came out with difficulty, between ragged breaths. "We... need..." By the Kingdom, he was already exhausted. "To wait... for the man with the key... then open all cells."

Mauro frowned. "This will get a lot of attention. We won't be able to have a discreet escape."

"Distraction."

"Many will die."

Larzen shrugged and gestured around him. It wasn't as if anyone there was going to leave anytime soon. At least the confusion would give them a chance.

Mauro paused, then said, "Rest a little. I'll deal with it."

Larzen sat on the ground and nodded.

A door opened. Mauro had two swords and could deal with up to three or even four guards or apprentices. Their chances were pretty good. But there were no sounds of steps. Mauro went to the corner to look at the door and the main corridor.

"They threw something," he said.

Crap. It was probably something explosive, and Larzen was sitting here. He closed his eyes for impact, but nothing happened.

"It's..." Mauro continued. "There's some black smoke coming from it."

The sound of coughing came from the cells near the door.

"Poison." The word came out of his lips before Larzen had even understood its implication. "They're going to kill us all."

25

POISON IN THE AIR

Zora could barely believe that she had that key in her hand, even as she tried to forget the harrowing moments before she got it.

Even now, the image of that head wouldn't leave her mind. But the worst was the feel of his hands around her waist. So gross. And perhaps the worst was that she didn't feel a tinge of regret for having killed him.

She went up the stairs quickly, realizing that she looked odd wearing a dress and carrying a sword. It felt weird to carry it like that, without a baldrick. Her plan was to try to trick the guards. But she was lucky—there was nobody by the door to the archives. It was locked, but she still had the key that opened it. There were two candles still lit in two corners of the room, providing it with some light. She went to the door on the back and tried the big key. The lock clicked open.

Opposite two small desks, there was an entire shelf with books. She wanted the ones with Solana writing, but if she opened each book, it would take too long. She tried to remember the book Riadne had been reading and what its cover looked like. It was some old kind of leather, but all the books here were old and had leather covers.

She put the sword aside and decided to pull random books from different shelves. They would certainly be grouped by theme or language, so that she didn't need to check each one, but try to find the group that had the books she wanted. The first ones she opened had a language that looked like Continental, with similar letters, but the words were different. Then she found something with strange letters, but still written in lines.

After searching for some five minutes, and messing the shelves, she found a book with those strange triangles and circles. She checked the books around it and found four more. She sighed. Hopefully these would be useful and this trip hadn't been in vain.

She wished she had her bag to carry them. After a quick glance, she noticed that one of the desks had a large leather bag. Zora emptied it, then put the books there. She glanced back at the shelves and all the knowledge that was stashed there.

There could be so many important things, stories and recipes and more from different countries, different cultures, so much that could help Gravel and the entire Continent. Instead, they were kept here, in the dark, just adding to the power of monstrous creatures who exploited and imprisoned young men and women. But there was nothing she could do right now.

If the corridor were still empty, she could go down and rejoin Riadne. The issue was getting into the ball carrying a bag with books and a sword. Well, that would certainly be a huge problem.

And then she still felt that the stone in the roof was blocking Riadne's magic, and, without it, their chances of escaping were too slim. Zora would need a tool, and she didn't want to risk damaging her sword, so she used the key, opened one of those cages, and took something metallic that resembled a shovel. It would have to do. After climbing the ladder, Zora ended up in that strange, empty room. Although it was still dark, she remembered well where the stairs and door had been so that she could still find them without seeing much.

The door was open again, and she checked that her key worked—and it did, then she rushed to the stone to try to remove it. It had been attached to a hole in the roof with some kind of cement. She used the almost-shovel to hit the part where it was attached, but it didn't do much, so she also used the sword. The enchantments in it made it quite powerful.

After hitting, hitting, then pushing the stone, it was wobbly. She kicked it with all her might, even if she was wearing some silly, delicate shoes.

Then it came out.

It wasn't that heavy. Not heavier than two books. Zora put it in her bag. This was stealing. The Solana books technically belonged to the Solanas, so it wasn't really stealing. But this...

Well, how wrong was it to steal from these horrible people? And she didn't want them to put it back. Zora then heard steps behind her, grabbed her sword, and turned.

Four guards stood there, their swords pointed at her.

"Let go of the weapon and come with us," one of them said.

Zora swallowed. Bells rang somewhere in the building. This was probably a warning, the same way they had gongs in the Dark Valley. All their security would probably start looking for them.

And here she was, cornered and outnumbered against a

small fraction of all the guards this temple had, with no idea how to get out of this.

"This way," Mauro said.

Larzen followed him until they reached a metal door, and Mauro kicked it open.

There were two empty tables and a chair with restraints.

"They brought me here before," Mauro said, then he pointed to a cylindrical structure on the rough floor. There was a grate with a lock covering it, but it led to a tunnel going far down. "They threw things here," he added.

This was a possible escape route, or a route to a fatal fall, considering the height. They would need to push their feet and hands against the tube to slow down their descent. And remove the grate first.

Larzen then looked back at the door leading to the tunnels and the other cells. He felt his eyes getting misty. "I wanted to help them."

"You know you can't, so there's no point berating yourself." Mauro then went to the grate and pulled it loose. "I suggest you take off your shoes."

Larzen nodded. Of course, so that he wouldn't slide against the metal. He unlaced his boots, took off his socks, then released them on top of the tube. He only heard a thud three seconds after they had been thrown. "That's high." He looked. "Like some ten floors." He then paused. "I'm not sure the smoke will reach it here."

Mauro looked at the tube, then back. "We could close the door and wait. They won't be coming anytime soon."

Maybe. Then maybe not. "Let's go down. One can never know."

"I'll go first," Mauro offered.

He pushed his feet against the sides, then his hands, and didn't fall. Larzen exhaled, then did the same. It wasn't that hard to keep himself from falling, except that he was already exhausted from bending the bars. "We'd better hurry. They could kill us quite easily if they reach the top of the tube and we're still here."

"No kidding."

It was a tricky balance, to climb down without falling and not doing it too slowly. So far, they've managed, but he still had a long way to go. Distant bells rang. Great. Now they were warning the entire temple about their escape.

RIADNE HAD to find another magician to lead her outside this ballroom. Unfortunately, she wasn't sure what to do after that, having no sword to behead them if things got ugly. Still, she entertained one of them who was asking her about the Solanas.

They had talked to her before, wanting to get a sense of their powers, where they lived, and their secrets, and she had given very little away. Now it was similar, and she kept talking about unimportant, minor details, like how Dada, who she claimed was now dead, prepared crows. The magician was getting bored, and this was a horrible strategy. She'd need to bury down her horror and get fun and flirty. Soon.

Then she felt something. It was like getting rid of a piece of meat stuck in her teeth, but it wasn't in her mouth, but in her entire body. The stone on the roof. Zora had done it. The question now was what Riadne was going to do with it. She took a deep breath. This wasn't the moment. She needed to get out of that ballroom and then use her power against small groups of people. And she had to figure out how to free Larzen before any of that.

A bell rang, and even if it wasn't close, she could feel it reverberating within her. The doors of the room were closed, and one of the apprentices then spoke in some sort of magnifying cone.

"The festivities are over for now. We hope you had a wonderful time. Wait until you're escorted back to your room."

They were all acting like this was normal, but she knew it wasn't. The bells were some kind of warning, and Zora had probably been caught.

ANNOYED, anxious, afraid—those were poor words to describe Griffin's state of mind. He had scheduled a meeting with all the commanders and counselors, but only for the following morning. Those long hours felt like an eternity to him. He had to make sure that everything was running well in Gravel, then had to come to a decision on what to do with Kentosa. He could go there in person and try to negotiate, he could send part of the army, he could threaten them. It all sounded slow and convoluted, considering the little time he had.

Griffin immersed his head in the bathtub. His hair had gotten all tangled and ugly, but it wasn't something he was too worried about right then. What he wanted was to scrub himself and get rid of any trace of King Saro, any trace that there had been someone else in his body. And yet he had a stomachache as a reminder that he hadn't been the one making nutrition decisions for this body in days. And yet all of this was frivolous. The issue was Zora. Zora and Larzen, and how they were far away from him, in a dangerous place, while he was here.

He wasn't sure if he could still dreamwalk, but then he felt something, like a string pulling him. Zora was in danger. He closed his eyes and felt himself floating over the sea, but then a wall of bright light was raised, blocking his path. The woman, goddess, whatever, appeared in front of him.

"Griffin. Go back. This is not your battle and you can't help her. You'll distract her."

"But I could..." He didn't even know. Advise her? Maybe. He could go to places where she couldn't. "I can help her."

"Don't distract her. Not now. Later, perhaps. Go back."

Griffin was then by a small house by a river. Again. He considered knocking on the door, but then he felt something cold all around him.

He opened his eyes and realized that the water was chilly. He was patient, but everything had a limit. He closed his eyes again, trying to dreamwalk, but nothing happened.

ZORA LOOKED at the four guards. She noticed that one of them had a terrible grip on his sword, horrifying her inner teacher.

In less than a second, a flood of memories came to her from the Dark Valley, from the moment she decided to teach kids. A lot of it was sword fighting, and she spent a long time working on their grip. "There's no point having a sword if you don't grip it right," she used to say. Their students spent hours and hours working on their grips, both for two hands and one hand. Zora knew it was important.

And why was she thinking about it now? Well, that guard with that ridiculous grip. She glanced at the others. While none of them held their swords like a spoon, the way that guard was doing, they weren't holding them that well. Their posture wasn't good either. These were not like the soldiers in Gravel, well trained. They were not like the champions in the

Royal Games, the best in the kingdom. Zora had learned to use a sword since before she could walk. These were four noobs.

She said, "Give up. Let me go. I could help you escape. Why are you protecting those magicians? They're using you."

"Quiet."

"Please. I don't want to hurt you. Truly."

They laughed, and yes, it was dirty, but Zora took the opening to strike. With one movement of her sword, she knocked the weapons from three men, then stabbed the fourth. She couldn't even think about what she was doing, but moved on instinct, as if they were human shadows, or shadow wolves.

Thunder was still heavily enchanted and was light, fast, and precise, but hit with strength and had a sharp blade. The four guards were defeated and fallen before she could even think twice. She took the belt from one of them, which had room for a sword on the hip, and put Thunder there. Fearing more pursuers, she then slid down the protrusion on the wall, falling on the grass by it. The issue now was getting to Riadne—and the others.

RIADNE COULD WAIT until they were all away from these magicians, and then try to use her magic. Or she could take a chance while they were all here.

She felt her magic flooding back to her, felt its power in her body, cursing through her veins. It wasn't something that she had noticed before, but it was like feeling her blood circulating, feeling her heart, and it was her magic. Pulsing as if begging her to release it.

Focusing on control, she sang.

The magician in front of her frowned. "You."

Riadne looked around her and realized the guards, the aspirants, and the apprentices were all looking at her, as if waiting for a command, while the magicians glared at her. Well, at least now she knew that her magic didn't work on them. That counted as progress, right?

"Get the magicians," she said, commanding everyone under her control.

Then she got up, meaning to try to run to the door, hoping that the magicians would be stopped by the others. But two of them moved their hands in front of them in a circle, from where they formed balls. Red energy balls.

Perhaps Riadne didn't know much about other types of magic, but she did know that light and energy could be reflected. Or at least hoped. She grabbed a tray from the floor. As a red ball moved towards her, she used the tray as a shield. It worked! The energy ball was redirected to the window, where it hit a curtain, making a hole in it.

"Get trays or take cover," she ordered the others.

She could perhaps order them to advance on the magicians, but then many of them would be killed. Riadne had to come up with another plan. Quicky. She had miscalculated. But then, how was she supposed to know these magicians actually had some magic? For all she knew, they were perverted charlatans. Immortal perverted charlatans. That should have given her a clue.

She had to escape that room, but there were four magicians blocking her way to the door, and two magicians on either side of her. All of them about to attack her at the same time with those energy balls.

Not good, not good, not good.

But Riadne was an expert at getting out of tight situations. Or at least she thought so.

The door of the room opened again, but none of the masters turned back, so focused they were on Riadne.

Perhaps she would be super fast and block six balls of energy? At the same time?

Then something odd happened, and it was so fast that it took her some time to process it. The magicians in front of her stopped doing the energy balls. Riadne saw from her peripheral vision that the ones on her sides were still about to attack her, and jumped on the floor to dodge their blasts. She looked up and saw the four magicians fallen, their heads rolling in front of them.

Zora had come up from behind them, and had been quite fast. Now they'd need to deal with two very angry magicians on Riadne's sides.

Zora was running in the direction of the one on her right, so she sang again, then ordered, "Get his hands," meaning the one on her left.

Soon Zora beheaded the first one while the remaining master was being attacked by the people in the room. When his hands were held, Zora ran to him and beheaded him as well.

Zora then approached her. The girl's eyes were fire, her face pure focus and fury. She looked terrifying. "Let's get Larzen and Mauro."

Riadne nodded, then sang again. "Cause confusion, set things on fire."

"Except books," Zora said.

"Not the library or archives," Riadne commanded them.

She ran with Zora out of the room and down the stairs. When they found an apprentice in red robes, she sang to him, then asked, "Take me to the prisoners. The ones they examine or get blood."

The young man trembled, as if making a lot of effort to resist her.

Riadne sighed. "Don't be silly, half your masters are dead, there's no need to resist me."

"We... can't. Not... the... cells," he said.

"Explain why," Riadne commanded.

"They're dead. All dead. Death gas. Now the door is sealed. Nobody can go there."

The apprentice was telling the truth. Riadne felt dizzy, the temple turning around while her legs gave way.

Larzen was dead? And it was her fault. Her fault for not stopping him, for not preventing him from coming. By Astrea, she was so stupid. She could have sent him away if she had put in some effort into humiliating him. Her eyes were stinging with tears, her body shaking, and she let out a scream.

THE FLOOR TREMBLED UNDERNEATH ZORA, and it wasn't an impression. It was as if Riadne's scream was so loud that it shook the island. Zora should be crying or screaming as well. Larzen and Mauro were her friends—and she had let them down, had led them to this. But she wasn't going to give up that easily.

Zora crouched by Riadne and yelled, "We don't know. We don't know. They could have escaped. Don't give up on them."

Riadne glared at her. "It's all your fault, you sneaky little peasant."

She was furious, and Zora didn't blame her. "Yes, it is. But we're going to get them out. I don't believe they're dead, we're going to save them."

Riadne covered her face with her hands, then stopped and stared at a ring she was wearing, which had a glowing pink stone. It was that fake magic ring she'd bought in the village.

"You're right." Riadne then looked at the floor. "Why there's a crack..." She looked up. "In the whole building?"

Indeed the walls and the ceiling had a gap. "Your scream, I think."

The apprentice then blinked, as if waking up, then he moved his hand to his belt, where he had a sword, but before he did anything, Riadne sang again, and his eyes went glassy.

She turned to Zora. "Let's find Larzen."

"And Mauro," she added.

DURING THE DESCENT through the tube, Larzen had contemplated several ways they could be killed—and none of them were pleasant.

As much as the cell area had that strange poisonous gas, he didn't doubt that the people in this magic temple could have some kind of mask preventing them from breathing the poison, or maybe even be immune to it.

But Mauro, and then Larzen, got to the bottom unharmed. They were in some kind of natural cave system, on a steep, humid, rocky slope. Of course, if things were thrown down the tube, they likely rolled down the incline. Apart from a faint light coming from the room high above, it was all dark, and he couldn't see anything.

"Let's walk away from the tube. And up. Just in case."

The caves were completely dark, and Larzen moved with difficulty, unable to see anything, but even so he went first, as he thought it was his duty.

"That night vision potion would have come in handy now," Mauro said.

"Or a torch. I should have considered bringing some kind of light. But it obviously would have been hard, with all the climbing down and stuff." He sighed. "This place gives me the creeps."

"And we're probably under sea level."

That made sense. "Likely. And it means this cave doesn't have any opening to the outside, or else it would be flooded by now."

"Exactly."

They got to a part of the cave that wasn't sloped anymore. "We need to find a way up." Larzen sighed. "There could be another tube, another opening like that."

"An opening could bring in some light. We might see it."

"We'd better hurry before they figure out where we are and throw a bunch of these poison bombs down here."

Mauro laughed. "Are you always so cheerful?"

"I'm being realistic. You were the one who suggested we come here."

"Because it was the only way."

"We'll find an exit. We just need to keep looking. I mean, searching. We aren't looking at anything right now."

He kept touching the wall and stepping carefully ahead of him, to prevent falling into a hole or something. They moved slowly, and then finally the tunnel climbed up.

Larzen exhaled. "We might be on the right track."

Then a thunderous sound startled him, and the wall and ground trembled.

"Was..." Mauro sounded unsure. "That an earthquake?"

"No idea."

Larzen kept climbing up, then found a solid rock wall in front of him. There was only rock, rock, and more rock. He swallowed, disbelief taking over him. "It's a dead end."

"It's fine. We can go back and see if we find any bifurcation or something."

Mauro probably knew as well as him that there was a chance that this cave had no exit, but still, they had to keep looking.

Larzen tried to think. "When we came up, I was touching

the left side. I'll go down touching the other side, so that if there's an opening, we'll find it."

And then a sound made him shudder. A sound like a river, and what should be calming and relaxing in any situation was terrifying now.

"Do you hear that?" He was just checking if he was going insane or something.

"Running water."

Right, so it wasn't only him. They turned around and descended that part of the cave, but when they reached a lower part, water was reaching their ankles. The earthquake had likely caused a fissure in the rocks from which seawater was entering the cave. If they didn't find an exit soon, they'd be drowned.

26

LOVE LIGHT

Riadne wasn't feeling that intense surge of power anymore. And it made sense, if she had cracked the island and the building.

She had a hard time believing it had been her, though. Not that it mattered now.

The ring was brilliant, and for the first time, she felt the magic in it, felt as if it was connected to her, and that it would allow her to find Larzen. She knew Zora was worried about her friend, but the only way to find Mauro would be if he was with the prince. King. Whatever. Larzen.

The apprentice was still under her control, and as she looked at the ring, she had a hunch that she had to go down. Down, down, deep down into the island. "Take us to the lowest place we can go. Some..." The image rushed through her mind. "Underground caves."

He led them to a flight of stairs going down somewhere that smelled old and moldy. Hum. This magic temple looked beautiful and imposing, but the reality was that most of it was dark and dank.

They came to a hall from where there were three sets of

doors. In front of it, five guards, two apprentices, and the ginger magician who she thought had the keys to the prison. Right. Riadne should have commanded the apprentice to take them down through the most discreet way, not right into the heat of the action.

To make matters worse, the magician was wearing a chain-mail hood covering him down to his shoulders.

Riadne was going to try to appeal to her charm. "Hey!" She put her hands on her waist and shook her head. "I can't believe you left me there. Talking to myself."

He sneered and looked at her and Zora. "So it's you two. You should have both been imprisoned when you came." He smiled. "A mistake we'll fix now."

Riadne didn't even understand what was happening, but saw something blue moving, and sang to command the others, not the magician. She then saw his head falling off.

Zora turned to her, shrugged, and pointed at her sword. "Enchanted."

Handy. It had cut through his chain-mail. Riadne didn't know how much she could command the guards and masters here, so she just told them to forget they'd seen them. "Keep leading us down," she told the apprentice under her control.

He opened one of the doors, which led to a set of stairs. They came to a large room with long wooden tables, where some ten men worked polishing metal and cutting some pink stones. They were manufacturing magical tools, and didn't raise their eyes or try to stop them. Based on their ragged gray clothes and their tired appearance, they were slaves. Or else "servants", hoping for their chance to become apprentices. A chance that would likely never come. She wanted to sing, tell them to stop what they were doing and run away, but she was losing the grasp on her magic. And it wouldn't be right to do that to them. They could be killed if they tried to escape. Perhaps they had nowhere to escape to.

The apprentice took two torches, carried one, and gave the other to Zora. They descended spiral wooden stairs for a long time until they came to a large cave with some pink parts on the walls. So that was where they got the stones.

Riadne shuddered thinking that her ring had been made here, by those workers who were almost slaves. But the ring was shining. Larzen had given it to her with his love. Fake love. But it worked. Riadne's love... She knew the answer, and it wrecked her. Her love for Larzen was real. At least it would be useful to save his life and find him.

There were three passages leading away from that cave, and while she looked at the ring and tried to decide which one to take, she felt a sharp jolt of pain. Oh, great, it was that time of the month. But no, she should only have her period in some eight, nine days. With horror, she realized how she'd been completely careless with Larzen. Irresponsible.

But no, she was feeling pain on her back. If it were her period, it would be on the lower back, not... Not between her shoulder blades.

Riadne took a deep breath and closed her eyes.

"Are you all right?" Zora asked.

"As all right as I can be." She was dying. If that didn't put everything in perspective, she didn't know what did. But she had to find the right cave now. "There." She pointed to the left one, hoping she was right.

Why didn't these wings wait at least a day, two? Now she would need to find Larzen and help them escape with the equivalent of heavy cramps on her back.

The cave descended until a part where it was flooded. "Is this normal? This water?" she asked the apprentice.

"No."

And yet she felt Larzen was around this area. "Wait here," she told the others, and took Zora's torch.

Riadne then stepped in that water until it was up to her

chest. She could feel it was rising and feared drowning, feared that Larzen had drowned, all because she had lost control of her magic. If that was really what had happened.

She turned right and saw a thin opening to a higher tunnel. Larzen was there, with Mauro.

"Riadne!" So much relief in his voice, so much fire in his eyes.

She could barely believe he was there, alive, well. "Can you pass through?"

"Yes."

Larzen jumped into the water, splashing it around him. He was so beautiful in the light of her torch, and touched her face, looking into her eyes. "You're here. You're alive." He sounded glad to see her.

Riadne wanted to laugh and cry and kiss and hug him. She loved those beautiful eyes.

Mauro jumped after him, and she looked away. "Let's hurry."

"How did you find us?" Larzen asked.

She raised an eyebrow. "Well, I have many talents, you know."

They turned a corner and reached Zora and the apprentice, but he was no longer holding a torch. Or standing.

"He attacked me," Zora said, partly out of breath, her eyes wide.

Riadne felt guilty about it. "I'm sorry. I should have realized my magic wouldn't hold him."

The girl shook her head, then smiled, seeing Larzen and Mauro. "We're all together. That's what matters."

They went up the same way they had come down. Riadne controlled one of the workers to tell them where the boats were, and they were soon on the inner docks, where three rowboats were attached.

"Destroy the other boats," she ordered the man and two soldiers who had caught up with them.

They were leaving the Magic Temple, leaving Rock Island, and she could barely believe it.

Mauro and Larzen rowed the boat as it reached calm night waters. Riadne felt as if she were waking up from a nightmare. Waking up in dreadful pain, but still.

Larzen's clothes were wet and his hair was messy and sweaty, and yet he looked so good. He was good. He had always treated her with honor and respect even when he learned she had been planning on having his family killed.

Perhaps there was an alternate universe where he could love her, and he would love her fully, with all her flaws. In this reality, she was dying. But she'd help him save his kingdom. Even short, her life would be worth it.

They were all silent as they reached the pier. Manee and Lia's boat was still there. It took some effort to get them to wake up, and some effort to convince them to take off at night.

When they were getting ready to depart, Riadne still couldn't take her eyes out of the sea.

Perhaps sensing her worry, Larzen sat by her. "They destroyed the boats. Now it will take some time before they can reach us, unless they can fly."

Zora, who was nearby, then said, "Erm, I have bad news on that."

"They can fly?" Larzen asked in disbelief.

"There was something on the roof," the girl said.

"We'll be away soon," Larzen said. "Then of course there's the issue of getting back to Gravel, where there's a prize on my head and all that. But I guess we'll figure it out."

They were moving away from the shore very slowly, when Zora pointed at something in the sky. It was like a bright red-orange star. "There. They're coming after us."

"What's coming?" Mauro was behind them.

"It's... a strange flying thing," Zora explained.

"Not a problem," he said. He then went back to the cabin and returned with his bow and arrow. After some four or five shots, the thing fell in the water.

"I feel bad for them," Zora said. "For everyone who's on that island."

Riadne felt the same. "I thought about commanding them to run away, but I don't have that much control. I... I also wish I could have done more."

"We can't judge," Mauro said. "We don't know that they weren't happy."

"I got the impression that many of them ended up killed," Zora said.

The huge warrior sighed. "Most of them."

Riadne turned to Zora. "How many magicians did you kill?"

The girl looked down. "I... I'd rather not talk about it. I'll try to rest. Call me if you want me to behead anyone."

LARZEN WAS LEFT ALONE with Riadne, staring at the ocean and the stars. He knew she was exhausted, and yet he had to talk to her.

"You didn't tell me how you found me," he said.

She shrugged and looked away. "It doesn't matter."

He looked at a brilliant pink stone on her finger. "It was the ring, wasn't it?"

She smirked, as if amused. "The fake love ring? Maybe."

"And is it fake?"

She looked at her hand. "No, I think it was manufactured in the Magic Temple, with a pink magic stone whatever." She looked at him and smiled. "So it's real."

She was trying to veer the conversation away, even if she knew he wasn't talking about the magic trinket.

He took a deep breath. "I thought I was going to die there. And it was an important learning experience."

"Hmm, I bet we'll still have lots of learning opportunities in the next few days."

He laughed. "You don't want me to talk to you seriously, do you?"

"Serious is usually boring or scary."

"Or just plain honest. Real. You know what I realized?"

She raised an eyebrow. "That evil magic temples are evil?"

"I missed you. In all the times in that cell, there were many things in my mind. I'm worried about my kingdom, I'm sad about Kiran, worried about Griffin, but all these thoughts were minor. I couldn't stop thinking about you."

Strangely, he didn't feel awkward or scared saying this. And he didn't fear being mocked or rejected. It was as if he had passed beyond the stage of fear.

She looked away. "That's... nice. Or dumb. I don't know."

He put his hand on her cheek and slowly turned her to face him. "Look at me. Look at me in the eyes and tell me you don't feel anything for me. I can take it. I won't be mad. But say it. I'm tired of pretending. I'm tired of playing games."

She shook her head slowly, and her eyes were misty, then she looked down. "I'm dying, Larzen." She sounded as if she choked back tears. "I'm dying."

He held her in his arms, and asked quietly, "It's your wings?"

She nodded.

No, not yet, it was too early. He couldn't lose her. "We'll find a way," he said. "Let's see how your brother is doing. I swear, I'll do everything to save you. I'll save you, Riadne, I promise."

She just shook her head.

"You don't believe me." He took a deep breath. "You don't trust me."

"I'm scared," was all she said, before resting her face on his chest.

Larzen just held her, feeling her warmth, his shirt getting wet with her tears. She was breaking out of her tough shell, and he knew that it took courage to do so. To show her vulnerable side. The fact that she trusted him enough to let him see her in this state told him all he needed to know.

ZORA HAD TROUBLED DREAMS, seeing master Smyr over and over, his severed head laughing at her. She saw herself in the garden of Rock Island, that beautiful garden, surrounded by the masters she had killed, all of them putting their heads back into their bodies, while she had no sword.

"Zora," a voice called her. It was Griffin, and now she wanted to run because he was going to find out she was a murderer. There was blood in her hands, blood in her dress, and she wanted to run.

Then she was down in the caves in the island, and the walls were closing in around her, about to kill her.

"Zora." That voice again. It was Griffin; he was holding her.

"It's you." She exhaled and looked around. She was in the garden, but there were no magicians there.

"Where are you?" he asked.

There was a mix of images and memories in her mind. "I... don't know."

"You're dreaming." He ran his hand through her hair. "Are you still on Rock Island?"

Still that confusion. "I don't know where I am."

"I want you to listen, then. In the Magic Temple, on that

island, their leaders are not human, at least not anymore. They can't be killed. You have to find a way to run."

Blood, beheadings, and master Smyr's face came to her mind. "I killed eight of them. Or nine, ten. I think I killed them." More memories came to her. "We're coming back to Gravel."

"I'm back here too."

"What?" Her heart was leaping with joy. "Back to Gravel?" Her surroundings were now fading.

"Yes," he said. "It's going to make your return easier." This was incredible, almost too good to be true. He then asked, "You're with my brother, right?"

She nodded.

He smiled. That smile could shatter her heart into thousands of pieces and then put them all back. "There won't be a prize on his head anymore. You can travel freely. Come to the castle."

"We're going to the Dark Valley."

It was as if they were in the midst of nothingness now. He nodded and kissed her forehead. "I'll meet you there."

Then there was no more garden or masters, just her bed back home, where she slept peacefully.

RIADNE DIDN'T KNOW how long she remained there, in silence, after her tears had dried. Tears she had no idea had been inside her all this time. Larzen just held her. He didn't try to make her stop crying, didn't try to cheer her up, didn't tell her everything would be fine. He just held her, and it was all she needed.

But they had to talk. They had so much to discuss. Or rather, she had so much to say. "That day on the island," she started. "I lied. I said it was bad. It wasn't."

He had a light chuckle. "I thought we had decided not to talk about it anymore."

"I told you horrible things. None of that was true. It was wonderful. Magical. Perfect."

"Riadne. Let's not start lying, shall we? We both know it was crappy and rushed. I'd rather you forgot it."

"Or intense and passionate," she said. "But thanks for saying it was crappy." She was partly joking, but just partly.

"I meant me. You're always perfect."

Perfect? That was an odd way to describe her. She lowered her head. "Not always."

"I'll have to agree with you on that."

She then said what was on her mind, "You do know there's a chance we won't find a solution and I'll die in a matter of days, right?"

"We'll find a solution, I'm positive we will. But death is always a possibility. We don't know how long we'll live. I could have died on that island. However many days you have to live, and I have to live, I want to spend them with you."

She was still leaning on his chest and could hear his heart beating. "But if you're a king—"

"I do what I want."

"I thought you wanted a princess from a kingdom of gold."

"And you believed it? I wanted you."

It sounded too good to be true. "After all I did?"

"Well, to be fair, that was before... But then, after a while, I got to know you better, the real you. I don't condone everything you did, no. But still, you're a good person. If you made mistakes, it was from your... perhaps misguided desire to help your people. I... I can respect that."

"I..." What was even her problem? "I don't want to get hurt, that's all."

He broke the hug and looked into her eyes. "You think I'd hurt you?"

"I don't know," she blurted. It was all so strange and new.

He nodded. "It's fair. I'll gain your trust."

"No, it's not. I'm the one you can't trust."

"But I trust you. You know why? Because when I don't trust you, when I get angry at you, everything hurts, it all feels wrong. When I trust you, I'm happy."

She looked away, at the ocean. "I'm also happier when I trust you. When I'm with you."

"And yet you won't say it looking in my eyes."

"They're too blue, they're distracting."

"We'll make it work." He put his hand over hers.

"You won't think I want you just because you're a king?"

"Don't be silly, Riadne. You forget I know all about your plans, and marrying a king was *not* part of them. If anything, my irresistible charm made you give up on your poorly thought murderous plans."

Riadne chuckled. "Quite irresistible, Larzen."

She wanted to hope, wanted to love, wanted to believe everything was possible, but she had that fear inside her. So many things could go wrong. "There's another problem," she said. "Let's say I survive. Let's say my wings come out. How am I going to dress? What are people going to say?"

He shrugged. "I don't know. Maybe there's a fashion manual in one of those books? People will get used to it?"

"Would *you* get used to it?"

"We'd need to work it out, like, how it works in terms of... sleeping positions."

"You weren't thinking about sleeping."

He shrugged. "Well, similar. And you got my point."

"But you'll want children. Will you want monstrous children?"

"Wings are not monstrous. I'd love to have wings. Not if

they killed me, of course. But flying sounds amazing. They'll be lucky kids."

"If they survive."

"I'll find a solution. I promise you. Even if it's the last thing I do in my life. Even if we run out of time for you. I promise you I'll do what I can to stop your people from suffering. I'm promising you, Riadne, and it's a big deal. I don't promise in vain."

"I know. I trust you." She rested her face on his chest again, the sound of his heart calming her. "And yes, of course I want to spend the rest of my days with you. That shouldn't even be a question." She looked at him. "When I was on that island, I also couldn't stop thinking about you. You were all I worried about. That's what caused the earthquake. I thought you were dead."

His eyes widened. "You can cause earthquakes?"

"I guess. I didn't know anything about that either. Perhaps the new books will have some answers."

"So you did get them."

She nodded. "Zora did. I'll look at them as soon as I have some time. Perhaps we will find solutions there."

He sighed. "Let's hope we do. We're running out of time."

Indeed. With every ache in her back, she felt her remaining time disappearing. And then there was Lukas. If she found a cure for their wings, she hoped she wasn't too late for him.

GRIFFIN HAD DREAMWALKED—WHILE sleeping. He sat up on the bed and rubbed his eyes, then looked around, thankful to be back in his room, back to himself, even if he wasn't sure how long it would last.

Or had it all been a dream? If Zora and Larzen were safe,

he wouldn't need to worry about getting them back and dealing with Kentosa. Half of his problems would be solved. And then there was the other half.

He had to make sure everything in the kingdom was in order, get guards to instruct people to stay indoors, remove all signs asking for Larzen's head, and make a speech explaining he had been mistaken.

That part would be embarrassing. He felt his face getting hot just imagining himself saying, "Oopsies, I said my brother was a traitor and a threat, but I guess I got confused or something."

He rested his forehead on his hand and took a deep breath. It was better than not being here and not saying any of that.

And then there was his dream. Perhaps it was nothing. Perhaps it was just a dream, but again he saw that little house near a river. That was the King's River. It was as if the dreams were trying to tell him something, but he didn't know what. Didn't know what that house could have. Perhaps it was some kind of answer. Perhaps it was nothing.

27

GOING BACK

The boat had spent part of the night by an island, and they set off in the morning. Zora had been up with the sun, eager to know if any of the books she got would be useful.

When Riadne came out of her cabin, she gave them to her.

"I'll look at them." Riadne nodded, then frowned, as if in pain.

"Are you hurt?"

She paused, as if thinking, then said, "I think my wings are coming out. It hurts."

Already? This was awful. But Zora refrained from showing shock or fear and said, "I'll get you a potion. For the pain. You don't need to look at the books now."

Riadne shook her head. "It will only get worse. I might as well look at them while I can." Meaning while she lived. "Zora." It was as if she had something important to say.

"What?"

"I... it was difficult being in the Magic Temple, wasn't it?"

"We got out. I think back to the ones left behind. I... I couldn't believe there was so much evil in the world."

Riadne sighed. "There is evil, Zora. Here and there. You saw it with Kiran. Not as bad, for sure. But still. I have a story to tell you. One I never told anyone."

Zora was surprised that she would trust her.

The Solana continued, "I was sent to Linaria to be a servant. More like an attendant, serving the queen or other nobles. It's supposed to be a good job. I was thirteen, and I was sent to a small school in the castle to learn to read."

"But..." Zora was almost going to say that she didn't read continental, but perhaps that was the point in the story.

"I was sitting in a class with younger children, and I was fine. But there was this noble, he said I was too old to be there, that he was going to give me private classes."

It sounded good. No, based on Riadne's face, it wasn't good.

"Those magicians on the island reminded me of him. Creepy old men." The redhead sighed. "But like with master Smyr, nothing actually happened. I decided I didn't want to read anymore, and I hid in the kitchens. I convinced the cooks to let me be a helper there. The man, well, he jumped from a high tower." She closed her eyes.

It took a moment for the meaning of the words to sink in, for Zora to understand what Riadne was confessing. If she could convince people to do what she wanted, it wouldn't be hard for her to... "I'm so sorry," Zora said.

Riadne shook her head. "I never told anyone because it was as if I was in the wrong, as if it was my fault somehow. I kept thinking back about it, and thinking I shouldn't feel traumatized. Nothing happened, right? If anything, I was the murderer. But now I understand. Even if nothing happened, it was still traumatizing. It was still hard to be in that position, not knowing who to trust. I'm saying this... So you know why I can't read."

"You *can* read."

"I can't read Continental. But it's not that I'm lazy or stupid."

"Nobody said that."

"I know. I'm the one who thinks that sometimes. And also, so you understand that what you went through in the Magic Temple, it hurts. Even if nothing happened."

It was true. Zora wasn't sure what to say. "Thank you. For trusting me."

"I should have trusted more people. But it's hard, you know, when you are young and don't know who to turn to." She then winced in pain.

"It *is* hard." Zora sighed. "But I'll go get you a potion. At least there's one type of pain we can deal with right now."

"Yes." Riadne grimaced. "That will be a good idea."

Zora went back to the cabin and checked if there was any ingredient left. A lot of it had been in her bag, which remained in that room in the underground of the island. She felt bad thinking about Alma, Sarina, and Lea. She wished she could have done more.

Mauro sat up, perhaps awoken by her noise.

"Hey," she said.

"Are you making potions?" His voice was still sleepy.

"I'm looking for ingredients."

"I need something to heal my wounds."

Zora frowned. "What wounds? Can I see them?"

"Are you sure?"

"My parents are healers. I'm not squeamish."

He raised his shirt to show a series of cuts in his stomach.

"What is that?"

"They were testing if I had advanced healing abilities."

"I assume you don't?"

He shook his head.

"That's horrible."

"It's nothing, Zora, really. I was lucky."

She covered her mouth with her hands, not wanting to imagine what could have happened if he had been unlucky. "I'm so sorry I brought you here."

"I chose to come." He shrugged. "I didn't do much, but I guess I helped you find that island."

"You did. You fought with us, you fixed the cart, you got this boat."

He shrugged. "So don't be sorry I came."

Zora shook her head. "You're right. I'm thankful you're here, and I'll get you something."

She went to the kitchen to try to find some common ingredients and do the best she could, working on the table. Then she gave a poultice to Mauro and brought a potion to Riadne, who was sitting on a bench on the back of the boat, now with Larzen beside her.

"Here," Zora said.

Riadne took it, then smiled at Larzen. "For the pain."

He frowned. "I thought it had stopped hurting."

"It didn't."

Zora didn't want to press her, but she was curious, so she asked, "What did you find so far?"

Riadne sighed. "This is... wonderful. Really. There's so much here. But I'll be honest. These books are older than whatever happened in Gravel. The one I took from the castle, it was as if it had been left there on purpose, almost as if someone knew it would be found. These? They must have been stolen or collected sometime before all that."

Zora's shoulders dropped. She couldn't believe she'd made them do all of that for no answers, but she tried to be cheerful. "Well, at least there's something useful there."

Riadne nodded. "It's about our magic. It's true. It can be

connected to the earth and the wind, too. I guess it explains why I caused a crack on the island. And I'm looking at the books. They're not like your texts, that you can run your eyes over them. They're different; we need to focus to get the meaning, so I'm going slowly."

"If you learn more about your magic, who knows, it might be our solution. And there might be something about your wings."

Riadne ran her hand over a page. "I hope so. There are some things here, some super powerful magic, but it talks about some heart stone."

"What does it look like?"

"It's purple."

Zora ran back to her bag, then took the stone she had retrieved from the roof, went outside, and showed it to Riadne. "This?"

Her jaw dropped. "You took it."

Zora shrugged. "Well, yes, I wasn't going to leave it there."

"That might be it."

"So you'll be able to do some super powerful Solana magic?"

"While I live, probably."

How long she had to live was a huge question hanging on them. Zora also wondered if Lukas was still alive. And now she remembered her dream and wondered if it had been real.

She almost told the others, but knew they would still be cautious when entering Gravel. She wanted to hang onto her hope that Griffin had survived, that he was back, but feared hoping too much.

347

GRIFFIN HAD to hurry if he wanted to reach his destination before sundown. But he had to do this. The morning had been busy with commanders and other crown assistants. He kept the lame story that he had been deceived and was confused, all the while in disbelief that they never suspected that it hadn't been him ordering his brother to be captured and, worst of all, wearing ridiculous clothes. To be fair, that was the part he had trouble forgiving. But he had to move on.

I'll meet you in the Dark Valley, he'd told Zora, and he wasn't sure if it had been dreamwalking or a normal dream, or even if she would remember it. Still, from what he knew about her, she'd likely head back to her beloved home. He wanted to see her so badly, but he was also anxious, as he still didn't know how to find a solution to his problem, a solution to his kingdom, and he regretted having involved Zora in any of that.

He rode Power, his beloved stallion. From the top of a hill, he realized that the vision in his dreams pointed to something real. The little house was exactly like he'd seen it. There were more scattered houses around it, in a simple village.

He dismounted, then tied his horse, approached the house, and knocked. And knocked. A woman carrying a basket with flowers approached him.

"Can I help you?" She was frowning, and likely didn't recognize him.

He pointed at the house. "Do you live here?"

"Why? I don't owe anything. There's nothing for you here."

Griffin raised his hands, showing his palms. "I mean no harm. Truly. I just..."

How was he going to explain it? *Had weird dreams about this place?* "I just wanted to see it."

"Go away, whoever you are. You have no right to enter my house."

"So you do live here."

She glared at him. "Go away."

The woman was definitely hiding something. He took a deep breath. "Listen, whatever you have, just tell me. I might be able to help you."

The woman frowned again. Then he heard a sound coming from the house. And then another sound. It was a grunt of pain.

"Who's inside?" he asked.

"Nobody."

"I'll force the door open and enter if you don't answer me."

She threw the basket on the ground and crossed her arms. "Fine. Use your strength. Some people don't want to be found, so leave them."

A grunt again, and he thought he recognized the voice. He took a deep breath again, trying to calm down. "I think it's my brother who's there."

"Oh, really, and what's his name?"

"Kiran."

"Like the king?" She burst out laughing.

"Who's in there?"

"Nobody. Now if it's your brother you're looking for, go somewhere else."

Two boys came running towards her. One of them asked, "Is he taking the poet away?"

"No, he's not," the woman told the kid, then eyed Griffin.

"Just let me see him. If it's not my brother I'll leave him. I promise." He had a faint hope that it was Kiran in that house, and would never walk away not knowing.

She looked at him up and down. "You're from the castle, aren't you? He doesn't want to come back."

"I won't force him to come back."

The woman sighed. "Fine." She opened the door. It was a

house with a table, a bed, and a sofa in just one room. Griffin couldn't believe who lay on the bed.

"Kiran?" he approached the young man grunting. His older brother.

Kiran shook his head. "Develson Williamson. Develson. I'm a poet."

That was the name his brother used to sign his poems, but Griffin didn't understand why he was saying it was his real name.

The woman was by his side. "He had a lot of fractures and was almost dying, but he's been getting better." She pointed to the sofa. "I was sleeping there. During this time, when he started to get better, some kids came to see him. He told them stories, funny rhymes. He said he didn't want to go back to the castle. Please don't force him to go. I don't know what he did there, but he's bringing us joy here."

"He's in pain. He needs a better healer."

"No. He was doing well. He was getting better. Then something happened, like something in his lungs. I don't know. But he doesn't want to go away."

"Develson," Griffin said. "Do you recognize me?"

"Maybe. What do I care?"

"You don't want to go to the castle?"

"No castle. No castle."

"You need a healer."

"She's a good healer. I was born again. Did you know—" he grunted in pain.

It was odd. Griffin would be lying if the idea of killing Kiran hadn't crossed his mind, but seeing him like that made him sad. He remembered the older brother he used to admire, remembered the times they had played together. Not a lot, really. Their age difference was too big. But still, he was his brother. Seeing him in pain made him pity him.

"Why don't you want to go to the castle?"

"I don't like the king."

"Who's the king?"

"Kiran. I hate him. I hate him."

Griffin wasn't sure if something had affected his head or what, but what worried him most now was his brother's pain. "What if I took you to a healer not in the castle?"

"I like it here. There's peace and joy and nature." He grimaced as if in pain.

"What if I promise to bring you back?"

"No castle." He then grunted again.

Griffin turned to the woman. "You clearly did a wonderful job with him, and you will be rewarded."

She snorted. "What are you going to give me? Gold? I can't eat it."

"Think about something else, then. But he's in pain. I don't doubt your healing abilities, but this is beyond you. I promise you I'll bring him back, at least to say goodbye, if he chooses not to stay."

"What if he dies?"

"You won't feel guilty."

She sighed. "Do it, then."

Griffin nodded. It was all getting more complicated than he had imagined, and now he was really running out of time if he didn't want to get caught on the road at night.

THE SOFT, rocking movements in the carriage reminded Zora of when she went to Gravel city for the first time. There had been so much curiosity and hope, innocence and wonder.

Now she was making her way to the Dark Valley, wearing a peasant's linen dress. At least this carriage was much better than traveling on those carts. Larzen had bought it in the Marshes once he realized that it didn't seem that the soldiers were still looking for him. They even had a coachman.

Mauro had remained back there, glad to be on his way home, perhaps glad to be alive. Zora hoped she could visit him and Sam one day, when there was peace, when they could maybe show her the famous Marshes evening parties, when entire families danced together. Mauro was a good friend, and had helped them a lot, from finding the boat to destroying that floating, flying thing that could have chased them through the seas. Just thinking back about it gave her chills.

Riadne was sleeping, leaning her head on Larzen's shoulder. It seemed that they had found some understanding. For all her faults, Riadne did love him fiercely, and love like that was always a beautiful thing to behold.

She still didn't know how they would fix the issue of the shadow creatures and the Shadow Kingdom, and if her dream had been true. Part of her regretted having dragged Riadne, Larzen, and Mauro to Rock Island, but then, she had found some books. Another part of her still remembered everyone that had been left behind, left in that horrible magic temple.

It was easy to tell herself she couldn't fix everyone's problems. Well, it was true. Perhaps killing some of those masters, especially Smyr, might have made a difference. Perhaps removing that stone was helpful too. Or maybe she was making excuses not to feel guilty. Not that it helped; she still felt guilty and unable to rid herself of the horrible images from that Magic Temple.

She looked out the window. Being outside her valley, outside walls, had been so new for her once, and yet now she yearned for the safety of her home. For her parents, her niece and nephew, her sister, her students. Well, it wasn't the confinement of the walls that she yearned for.

Still, far in the distance, she could see them rising against the horizon. And she also saw a black horse galloping towards them. And on that horse...

She tapped on the side of the carriage. "Stop it."

Without even waiting for the vehicle to be fully stopped, and ignoring whatever question half-asleep Larzen asked, she opened the door and jumped out.

How could he ever have said he didn't look princely?

Griffin on a horse, all dressed in black, was the most amazing sight she'd ever seen. True that he was at least wearing sleeves. And it was real Griffin, she knew it. It was something about his eyes, his stance, or perhaps she felt it was him. He looked like a hero in stories.

Her eyes got misty, and then her entire body convulsed with emotion. All the trapped tears burst out, the tears she hadn't shed from the moment she had lost him in that cave. And then he had his arms around her.

"Zora, love."

She cried even more, knowing he still loved her, knowing that nothing was lost.

He continued, "You're getting worse. I know you always cry when you see me, but now you're bawling."

She punched him lightly on the stomach, but had difficulty getting her words out. After some time, she looked at him. "I feared I had lost you."

He looked at her, but behind his teasing there was some sadness as he ran his hand over her face and looked at her. In fact, he also had tears in his eyes.

She smiled. "Look who's talking. You're also crying."

"I know."

"There's something wrong?"

He tucked a strand of her hair behind her ear. "A few things, yes, but... we'll figure it out."

He kissed her cheek, then the corner of her lips. She

loved the way he invited her to kiss him instead of doing it. It wasn't hesitant as in afraid or insecure, but instead, secure enough that he would accept whatever answer she gave him. She could taste her tears in his lips, in his tongue, and let herself get lost in that sensation, enveloped in that amazing hug.

They broke the kiss, and she was greeted with his amazing smile.

He touched her face with both hands. "I missed you so much."

"But you're back. How?"

His smile faded, and he closed his eyes and took a deep breath. "We'll talk about it."

Zora felt a knot in her stomach. Something wasn't right. "What is it?"

She then heard someone clearing their throat behind her, turned, and saw Larzen standing behind them.

"As delighted as I am to be ignored by my own brother, and as endearing as your meeting is, it's late and the sun will set soon. We need to get indoors."

Griffin got up, approached Larzen, and hugged him.

After a few seconds, Larzen said, "If you keep being that affectionate I'm going to think you're still the impostor."

"Shut up," Griffin said, but he broke the hug. "I'll meet you in the Dark Valley," he told his brother. He then turned to Zora. "Ride with me."

Larzen whistled. "Subtle, brother, quite subtle."

Griffin just laughed and shook his head, then took her hand. Soon they were galloping to the gates of the Dark Valley, and it was better than any dream she had, except for the part where she kept wondering what was wrong.

28

MEETINGS

Riadne had watched the scene from the window of the carriage. She still wasn't sure how awkward it would be to talk to Griffin again, and certainly wasn't going to disturb the meeting of lovers or brothers.

She sighed. Lukas. Was she going to meet him again? Or learn about his passing? Perhaps she should have asked Griffin if he knew anything, but maybe he hadn't even entered the valley yet. A jolt of pain on her back reminded her that she was next. An uncomfortable reminder.

Larzen was smiling when he entered the carriage, but he got serious when he saw her face. "You're worried about your brother."

"Maybe not worried. I should have accepted his death. I should be ready. Maybe I'm just wondering..."

Larzen put a hand over hers. "You hope he's alive. And maybe he is. Whatever happens, I'm here for you."

"Truly? And when your brother disapproves of your choice? And says I'm only interested in you because you're a king?" That was another reason she wasn't looking forward to meeting Griffin.

Larzen frowned, then waved a hand. "Phew. We've had this discussion. I could be a beggar and you'd still fall for me."

He managed to make her laugh. "I'm glad you know the truth."

"I always do. And you'd be surprised by how little crap my brother gives about anything that isn't related to the royal guard. Or his dogs. Or his girl." He raised an eyebrow. "And remember you're the sunbeam of my moonlight."

"That doesn't make any sense."

"It's supposed to make sense? Well, then, you're the acid in my stomach."

"Oh." She meant ew, but it sounded off. "I have no words, Larzen."

"I made you speechless, cocoon of my worm." He grimaced. "Yikes. That came wrong. I was thinking about a butterfly, you know? How you make me happy I want to—" He paused, perhaps remembering her wings. In fact, he just reminded her of that. "Sorry. I'm crappy today. It's all wrong."

"Look at the bright side. You got a brother back."

"I don't know Riadne, I don't know for how long. He was too worried. And hugged me too much." He smiled, but his face was tense.

"You're worried too."

He held her hand, sighed, and looked outside. "Worrying doesn't solve anything."

"But you can't help it."

He looked at her. "I can try to trust that we'll find an answer. We'll find a solution. I have to."

She nodded, then said something else that was in her mind. "You haven't kissed me."

"You do know it takes two, right?"

"It's not like you gave me the opportunity."

"I'm truly ashamed. Truly, Riadne, for our night. I don't

want you to think that it's all I want. I want to hear your dreams and hopes and fears. I want to hold your hand. I want to watch the stars by your side."

"Why are you ashamed? We both did it. I want many nights like that. If I survive."

His smile faded, and it was like a shadow over his beautiful eyes. No, she didn't want him to be sad. She pulled the curtain on her side, then the other curtain, by his window, and sat on his lap.

He smiled. "What are you doing?"

Riadne shrugged, then ran her hand over his chest. "You said it takes two. I'm doing my part. I want to see the stars beside you. And hold your hands. And hear and keep your secrets. But also—"

Words left her as she got lost in the feel of his kiss.

GRIFFIN WAS HOLDING tight on Zora's waist as the gate to the Dark Valley rose. It wasn't that he was afraid she'd fall, but that he wanted to hold her and never let go.

"Weren't they afraid of the horse?" she asked.

He recalled how he entered the valley, this time with authority to speak for the king, and able to have the gates open without difficulty. "I came in trotting slowly. And they know that no creatures spawn in small places anymore." He kissed her neck. "I bet you'll be happy to see your family."

"I will." They were at a slow pace and she asked, "How did you escape?"

"I think we should all sit and talk. I want to know how you escaped too."

He sighed. The main reason he'd come was to tell her all about Grota, the Void, prepare Larzen, make sure they understood what was happening, what happened, but he still didn't know what to do. "We'll all talk together."

"Griffin, there's something you need to know."

There was something about her voice that made him shudder with worry. "What?"

"It's nothing bad. At least I don't think so. You know the false Alegra?"

"She was traveling with you, wasn't she?"

"How..." She paused. "You saw it in your dreams? The dreams, they were real, weren't they?"

"They were, and I saw you on a boat with Larzen, the Marshes champion, and the false Alegra, yes. Not that I knew she wasn't the real Alegra. But you explained some of it to me."

Zora paused. "Anyway, she's been helping us. And she's nice. But what I want you to know is that she loves Larzen."

Griffin rolled his eyes. "You don't say. I wonder why..."

"She does. I don't know how he feels, though. But we'll need her."

Zora imagined the best in people. But at the same time, she had spent time with that false Alegra. "Do you trust her?"

"I do."

Griffin paused. "If you want me to trust her, then I'll trust her." He still thought she was after Larzen because of the crown. Ha! He had some news for her. Still, she wasn't that bad. "Plus, I found out she didn't try to kill you."

"Do you know who did it?" Her tone was surprised.

"Stavos. He tried to scare you with the knife and with the dogs. I threw him in a cell, and I'll see if Larzen can take care of his trial. I can't. I just want him dead." It had taken a lot of self-control to leave him unharmed.

She was silent for a moment, then asked, "Why did he want to kill or scare me?"

"Some people are stupid. He thought you were ruining the games. But you weren't."

"I wasn't?" She laughed. "I thought you hated that I was competing."

"I was just worried about you. Too worried. But I'm glad you participated. It's how I met you."

He kissed the back of her head, and she chuckled. Soon he saw the village and got to their destination. He tied the horse by Zora's house, where they had improvised a stable with a drinking basin. Of course it was lit by two torches, since they hadn't changed their habits much in the valley.

He glanced and saw her hugging her mother and then father. She looked so cute even if she was wearing a dress that was so not Zora. This was a moment of happiness. A moment that wasn't going to last.

He almost felt nauseous trying to imagine her face when he told her about the deal he'd made and was starting to wonder if he had made a great mistake. He wondered if it had been selfishness, if it had been all because he wanted to see her one last time. And now he had to find a solution for his kingdom.

RIADNE RAN to the village in the valley holding Larzen's hand. The coachman had been given shelter in the outpost. They were running because they didn't want to be out in the open at night, even if technically they were in the safest area in the kingdom.

As the sky darkened, many lamps, torches, and bonfires were visible in the hill and the forest, and the valley looked as if it was involved in brilliant magic. It was magical and unreal because Larzen was holding her hand. Her back still hurt a lot, but she made an effort not to whimper or grimace because seeing worry in Larzen's face also pained her.

They got to the village, but had no idea where to go, until they saw Griffin at a distance, beckoning to them. Larzen didn't let go of her hand as they approached him.

She wasn't looking forward to talking to Griffin, but she had to. "Is my brother... alive?"

Griffin frowned. "Brother? I just got here. I'm sorry. I don't know." To his credit, he did look apologetic, then added, "No. Wait. They had a visitor. What does your brother have?"

It was Larzen who replied, "Ingrown wings."

"Like black marks on his back? Oh." He frowned. "Wings. They were already treating somebody who had that." He glanced at Riadne. "So I think your brother is alive."

She exhaled in relief. "Is he well?"

Griffin shook his head. "I don't know. They just, they knew what those marks were and had someone they were treating already."

"Hang on," Larzen said. "Who else had these marks?"

"You'll see soon."

Riadne didn't think she heard it right. "There's another Solana in the valley?"

"Maybe. Unless you're not the only people who get wings."

"Who is it?" Larzen insisted.

Griffin glanced at Riadne. "You won't like it. I haven't told Zora either."

"So your plan is to kill us with curiosity," Larzen said.

"No. I just need to explain it right." He pointed to a large house. "It's there."

The door opened, and it was like a vision, a miracle. Lukas was there, standing. She ran to him and wanted to hug him, but he pushed her.

"It still hurts." He had a smile, though.

Tris came up beside him. "Good to see you. He's still bleeding a lot, but Zora's father has been keeping it under control."

Riadne felt her eyes stinging. She couldn't believe that Lukas was there. "I was afraid I wouldn't see you again."

He smiled. "I'm tougher than I look, what can I do?"

LARZEN WAS RELIEVED that Griffin didn't say anything mean to Riadne or show any displeasure at the fact he was holding her hand. He knew they had been involved before, but that was in the past. Neither of them had feelings for the other anymore, and it didn't matter.

But then Griffin turned to him. "I have something to show you."

He led him to a different room. There, lying on his stomach, was Kiran.

Larzen had been angry at his brother, but all that dissolved and turned into relief at seeing him.

"Kiran?"

His brother grimaced and said, "No. Why are you all insane like that?"

Griffin approached Larzen and rolled his eyes. "He's Develson Williamson. A poet. That's all."

Larzen frowned. "I know he wrote those poems, but..."

Griffin shrugged. "He says he's no king."

Larzen sighed, then looked at his back. "He's sprouting wings?"

"I guess. I didn't know any of that either."

Larzen patted Kiran's head. "I'm glad to see you, Develson. You're my favorite poet."

"I'm going to be a flying poet. That's amazing, isn't it?"

"It certainly is."

When they got out of the room, he asked Griffin, "Where did you find him?"

"In a little house. Apparently he was thrown in the river but survived. He still has some fractures. And now he has the issue with the wings. And I guess something's not right in his head."

Larzen paused. "Wings. His mother. He's a Solana too."

Griffin shook his head. "Lots of information. If it keeps like that, I'm going to be the next one who doesn't remember my own name."

29

PLANNING

Griffin went with Larzen to the lunch hall of the Dark Valley school, where Zora's sister was heating some leftovers.

"We weren't expecting that many visitors. Or any visitors, for that matter," she said.

"I can help," he offered.

She pointed to a pile of dishes. "Can you help me set the table? Careful with shadows. We know in theory they're no longer spawning in small places, but still."

Griffin took the plates from the pile and was setting them on the table when Zora showed up. She had changed to a leather set. The thing with that outfit was that it accentuated her curves. He almost dropped the plates as he tried to shut down some very inappropriate thoughts and memories.

He'd spent a long time imagining what she would look like under that, and now he knew what she looked like and couldn't shut that image from his mind. But they had to eat. And had to discuss important things.

Zora sat by him, then whispered, "Why are you looking at me like you've never seen me before?"

"Trust me," he whispered back. "I'm looking at you like someone who's seen you."

Color rose to her face, then she ran her hand through his hair, with some difficulty, to be fair, as he hadn't managed to get rid of all the tangles. She smiled. "I still can't believe you're here."

He looked down. "I know. It's all..." He then kissed her cheek, perhaps to refrain from talking, perhaps because he wasn't ready to explain anything yet.

They ate, cleared the plates, then sat down again.

"All right," Larzen said. "It's time for the dreaded *serious conversation*. Who wants to start?"

"Well," false Alegra, Riadne, said. "Considering I might die soon, I'd rather start."

He didn't know what she was talking about. "What do you mean die soon?"

"Exactly." She had a cold smile.

Griffin hated that smile and wanted to dig a hole and bury himself in shame, thinking that he ever had gotten involved with her.

She continued, "I'll explain all that."

Her explanation was about her people, the issue with their wings, then her plan to have him, Larzen, and Kiran kill each other. At this point Griffin was flabbergasted that Larzen and even Zora considered her an ally, maybe even a friend, and maybe even more, in Larzen's case. He had been thinking that Kiran was the one who'd gone gaga, but perhaps he wasn't the only one.

But Griffin just listened. She continued, explaining that Larzen had found out about her plans. And then the story was very poorly explained because his brother had caught her and yet somehow kept doing her wishes, except that he locked up Lukas and the real Alegra, whose true name was Tris.

It was all very strange. Or maybe not that strange, when he considered the way Larzen looked at Riadne. Great. She had got him in her hook, perhaps even using her magic. She then talked about the old book she found in the secret archives in the Gravel library, saying it had writings in her language, and that it explained that the Blood Cup was a fail-safe, and wasn't meant to undo his curse, but rather to undo the spell blocking the magic from the Shadow Kingdom.

Griffin remembered the memories he'd seen while dreamwalking, and it made sense. He muttered, "Of course."

"Do you know more about it?" Zora asked.

He nodded, but then said, "Go on. I'll explain what I know later."

Riadne shrugged. "This was it. And it all went wrong, and then Zora wanted to go to Rock Island and find more books, and we had no better plan."

Griffin shook his head. "The magic master sent to me... he said that island had strong, immortal magicians controlling it. There was no way anyone could get out. How did you get out?"

"Well..." Zora sighed. "We were all imprisoned. Sort of. But I found that decapitating the magicians worked. I won't say it is a permanent solution, but I think it is. I saw no headless walking bodies. I also took out their big purple stone, and it was blocking Riadne's magic. So it was a mix of Riadne singing, me slashing, and then Mauro and Larzen breaking doors. We got out. And I got the books."

"You..." He didn't even know what to think, and couldn't picture his cute Zora chopping heads off, even if he knew she was a decent fighter. "Decapitated the masters? Stole an important stone and rare books?"

Zora shrugged. "I only decapitated the ones who were in my way. I didn't go after them. I did my best not to hurt anyone else."

He still had a hard time believing it. "But the magicians have magic."

"Yes, they do, but they use their hands." She made a gesture, like making a circle in front of her stomach. "So while they prepared their magic, I went there..." She made a cutting motion. "With your sword. I have to give it back to you."

"You can have it, but..." He shook his head in disbelief. "You sound like it was easy."

"It was horrible. And terrifying. But we're back."

Riadne added, "I am reading the books, and they might have something useful."

Might. "Do they know who you are?"

Larzen paused. "They knew who I was."

"Right." Griffin was trying to access the situation. "So you stole their books, their stone, and now they know who you are and where you live. Am I the only one who's seeing the problem here?"

"They have more important issues," Zora said. "Their building was on fire and cracked in two, and their mines flooded."

"You *cracked* their building?"

"*She* did." Zora pointed at false Alegra.

"It wasn't on purpose, though," Riadne said. "But we could build some wardens against those masters. And they might be weak without their stone. They might not be sure if Larzen's a real king or prince. Those are not our immediate problems. I think we have bigger problems, don't we?"

"Yes." Griffin nodded. He told them about his time in Grota, how he was inhabiting their king's body, and how he prevented them from opening the portal from the other side. "But they could still eventually do it," he added.

He mentioned that he had help from Amina and some guards, and that the kingdom was controlled by the Void. He then told them about his time dreamwalking, and how he figured out what happened in Gravel. He mentioned the ancient king, the ring, and how he communicated with the Void.

"But Kiran has a ring like that," Larzen said.

"I know, but even in the dreams of the past, it stopped working. I think... I think someone replaced it and destroyed or hid the real ring."

"A ring with a black stone?" Zora perked up. "I think I saw a magician wearing something like that."

"Black rings are common, Zora," Larzen said, "It's unlikely to be the same."

Griffin agreed, then told them about the old Gravel king being possessed, then killed by his own son, who then thought it was the Solanas' fault. He turned to Riadne. "I'm sorry." Despite everything, her people had suffered tremendously, and they had been trying to fight the Void. Perhaps it was true that she would be able to help them.

She shook her head. "It's not your fault."

"And how did you come back?" Zora asked.

Griffin closed his eyes. "That's the worst part. I... it was a hunch, a thought that there could be some hope. And I might have made a mistake."

Larzen chuckled. "Right, and you were all scolding us for going to Rock Island, now I see why." He then looked at Griffin and got serious, perhaps realizing he wasn't laughing.

"I'm sorry if it sounded as if I was scolding you. I was just worried. What I did doesn't compare to you going to Rock Island." He shook his head and took a deep breath, trying to find the words to start. He finally said, "I was caught. By the Void itself. He wanted to torture me, but it didn't work, as I wasn't that connected to that body anyway. But then..." Griffin realized he was ashamed of having accepted the deal. "I... I thought it would give us a chance."

Zora put a hand on his shoulder. "Just say it. We know you meant your best."

Griffin held her hand and sighed. "He, the Void, threatened to hurt you. But I could... I could have warned you. But then, there was the Grota King's wife. She was an enemy of the Void. She said, 'the kingdom's yours' as if it was the answer, as if there was an answer. The Void said he'd send me back here and I would have ten days to become king and invite him to Gravel, or else he'd bring the people I love to his kingdom, meaning bringing their souls, making them possess people from Grota. I think he means you," he told Zora, "and maybe you," he told Larzen.

"Maybe." Larzen smiled. "Should I be flattered or offended? I'm assuming you're not going to invite him and not going to be king."

He shook his head. "But then in ten days..."

"I think you're wrong," Riadne told Griffin.

He rolled his eyes. "Of course I am. It wasn't a good deal."

"It's not what I mean. What did you say?" she asked. "What were the words?"

"I... don't recall. He said he'd bring the people I love."

"You're sure about that? The people you love?"

"Yes."

"Well, then, it's obviously not only Zora and Larzen. He wouldn't make a deal for that."

"It's worth it. He'd have another shot at convincing the Gravel king." Griffin was also thinking of Kiran. Two shots, and with Kiran going gaga, he would perhaps agree to do anything. Perhaps none of it was an accident.

"True." False Alegra nodded. "But I think he means the people of Gravel. The people you love. You do love them, don't you?"

Her words sounded right. "So I made the most idiotic lose-lose deal ever? I... And you know what? Amina might be the Void's enemy, but she'd certainly be glad to get it out of Grota. I thought she meant something."

"But you trusted her, didn't you?" Zora asked.

"I did, but..."

She held his hand. "A wise woman told me to trust my heart. That was how I ended up going to Rock Island."

"Bad example, Zora."

"I still think it was right. But if you trusted her, you had a reason to do so. And you said she helped you. So maybe her words meant something." Zora was too good and too trusting.

He sighed. "So what is the solution?"

"Wait," Riadne said. "Give me some time. The Solanas were fighting against the Void and Grota. They were his enemy. It's no wonder he tried to get them all killed. It means... I'll read what I have. Maybe I'll find answers. Maybe you did the right thing."

Griffin nodded.

"Riadne," Larzen said. "Before even touching any book you're going to be examined and start the same treatment as your brother."

"I can read while I do that. The wings aren't sprouting in my eyes."

"Wait," Griffin said. "Your wings are also sprouting? How come you aren't whimpering in pain?"

She rolled her eyes. "I'm a woman. We can deal with constant pain. And to be fair, our wings are higher and smaller. Speaking of which, who's the second Solana here?"

Griffin sighed. "I was going to tell you." He looked at Zora, who she knew was afraid of Kiran. "He doesn't remember who he was, or he wants to pretend he isn't himself. He's like a different person. It's Kiran. He's alive."

Zora's eyes widened.

"He's changed," Griffin assured her. "Very changed. And I guess he's part Solana too."

"So he never had the curse," false Alegra said. "He was.. uh, that way, because he chose to be like that."

"But he's not the same person anymore," Griffin explained. "He's saying his name is Develson Williamson."

"The poet?" Zora asked.

"That was always him, but now he's saying it's his real name and he's not Kiran."

"Oh."

"I suggest we all rest," Larzen said. "We still have a few days to find a solution. We'll need sharp minds, not sharp swords." He glanced at Zora. "Nothing against super sharp enchanted blades, by the way."

She smiled.

He continued, "But we all had a long day. We're under no condition to try to think about all that. Let's let it simmer. And Riadne needs to be treated right away." He got up, pulled her hand, and then they retreated to Zora's house.

The lunchroom was silent. Zora looked at him, then caressed his hair.

Griffin pushed her hand away. "It's all tangled and ugly. That stupid king doesn't know what it's like to have hair."

"It's not ugly." She smiled.

"Say it. You're mad at me, aren't you? I'm putting you in danger. The entire kingdom in danger."

"Of course not. I know why you did what you did. Hope. You hoped that you could find a solution. If you remained there, the Void would still be a threat, the Shadow Kingdom would still be a threat, and they could open the portal."

"Speaking of which, any idea where the portal is on this side?"

"No. I mean, Larzen hasn't heard of any place like that. Perhaps it was destroyed?"

He shook his head. "I don't think it can be destroyed."

"We'll find a solution. I know we will." There was something so calming about her eyes that he believed anything was possible.

She caressed his hair again, and he wrapped his arms around her and pulled her for a kiss. He had missed her taste, her feel, her smell. He could barely believe he was touching her waist, her hips, pulling her closer, feeling his heart accelerate and her breathing get heavier, wanting to kiss all of her, even if he knew he shouldn't.

"Zora!" someone called her.

Griffin let her go.

Her mother was walking in the lunchroom. "Zora, dear, your bed is ready, and we have prepared a bed in the waiting room for Prince Griffin."

He smiled. "You're very kind."

"No, it's not good enough for your highness. But we weren't expecting you."

"Again, I apologize."

Zora eyed him and mouthed, "So polite."

They followed Zora's mother. There was a bed prepared on the floor in the room next to where Kiran was. Zora retreated to her bedroom without even giving him a goodbye kiss, maybe embarrassed by being caught kissing him.

Griffin lay down, having no idea how anyone was supposed to sleep without covers. After some minutes, a door opened, and Zora appeared. She was wearing lighter pants and a shirt, probably meant for sleeping. She crouched by him and whispered, "Come to my room."

"I don't want to disobey your parents, Zora. They'll stop liking me then they'll forbid you to see me, thinking I'm a bad influence."

"They sent us a single hammock," she whispered.

"That was for safety, it's different. I don't want them to catch me in your room, Zora. It's a breach of trust."

"Fine. Move over, then." She pushed him, as if meaning to lie by his side.

"Anyone can walk on us here."

She was already lying beside him and smiled. "Which means we'll behave and my parents won't be mad."

"You mean *I'll* behave."

"You always do. I missed you too much."

"I know." He caressed her face and her hair. "We're back to cuddling. I missed it."

"And kissing, so it's a little better."

"Zora, did you really spend all those nights letting me hug you and thought there was nothing happening between us?"

She looked away quickly, as if embarrassed. "I don't know what I was thinking."

"Come here."

He wrapped his arms around her and kissed her, forgetting all sense of time and place.

He wished this could last forever, knew it couldn't, but that was a worry for tomorrow. He was also glad they weren't in her bedroom, as he'd promised her he was going to go slower, and now, with her in his arms, he kept thinking about their time together, kept wanting to kiss her in all the places he shouldn't, kept wanting so many things, and yet knowing it was a matter of time. If they had it. For now, being together was what mattered.

LARZEN WATCHED as Riadne lay down on a high table, a shirt tied around her neck so as to free her back. Zanel, who was Zora's father, was going to treat her.

"We've found that some cuts around the area help," the man said. "And the potion that Zora sent, too. We just don't understand why the wounds don't stop bleeding, but we've been giving blood to your brother, and he's faring well."

Riadne frowned. "Blood magic?"

"No. We just replace the blood you lose, that's all," the man explained.

Larzen bit his nails as he watched it. It was a good idea that this Void hadn't taken him. If a supernatural creature showed up right then, promising to save Riadne, he didn't know if he would refuse to give it the kingdom.

Those were dark thoughts. Lukas was alive. Perhaps there was an answer in those costly books.

And then there was Griffin's dilemma. If he accepted the deal, the Void would come to Gravel and they'd soon be like the Shadow Kingdom, powering up through suffering. If he refused, everyone would be taken to the other side.

He understood that his brother had made this decision as a desperate attempt to have some time, to try to find an alternate solution, but he wasn't sure if there was any in sight.

THE SOUND of steps woke up Zora.

"Zora's sleeping with the prince!" a high voice said. A child's voice. Little Eneida was coming in the room, Kala after her, carrying little Raphael.

"Sorry," Kala said.

"No." Zora sat up. "I slept in my room. I just came... to say good morning to him. And to see you."

Griffin was sitting up, too. "Hello."

Zora got up and picked up her niece. "I missed you, you know? How are you?"

"No spider anymore. No spider."

Kala sighed. "Things have changed."

"I know. What happened here? After we left?"

"We saved a lot of soldiers from the creatures. And you had escaped. They left us alone. Some people took the chance and escaped the valley. Seth among them."

Zora exhaled, relieved. "Good for him, I guess."

Her sister nodded. "You won't need to worry anymore. Well, I'll wait for you in the kitchen. Come, Eneida."

After Kala left, Zora turned to Griffin. "See? You should have come to my room."

He shook his head. "Then it would be worse."

"Did you dreamwalk?" She was wondering if perhaps he could have found an answer.

"No. I mean, why would I leave my body when it was right where I wanted?" He gave her his amazing smile, then looked down. "But I should try it, I know."

"We'll figure it all out." She then tried to think, now that she had a clear mind after a wonderful night of sleep. "She said that the kingdom's yours, right?"

"Yes, and it seemed important, as if she'd given her life to tell me that."

Zora smiled. "I think I have an idea."

"What is it?"

"I need to talk to Riadne."

He widened his eyes. "You're going to tell her and not me?"

"I need to know if it's possible."

"Just tell me."

"He said you'd need to be a king and invite him to your kingdom, right?"

"Yes."

"He didn't specify the size or location of it."

Griffin tried to recall the conversation. "I believe he meant Gravel."

"Yes, but we could split the kingdom. What if we could create a place like the Dark Valley, make it a kingdom, and name you king? But a place that's empty. You said he gains power from suffering. There wouldn't be anyone to suffer. And anyone for him to influence."

His eyes lit up. "Maybe. But... it sounds too easy. And what if he escapes?"

"That's what I want to check with Riadne. How to make strong walls, how to make a prison."

"But I think I would need to be inside it when I invite him."

"Maybe you can get out. You see how that's the solution? But we'll need to research and do it right."

He nodded. "Let's look into it."

Something else came to her mind. "I know where the portal is. In our world."

"Where?"

"The Bent River. Solanas can move the earth. Or at least they could. It doesn't sound like they know much about it now. That river used to be different. I think the portal is in the wide part, under the lake. That's another possibility, maybe if we destroy it, maybe it would break the connection."

He was thoughtful. "But then why didn't the Solanas destroy the portal?"

"I don't know."

He kissed her cheek. "You woke up full of ideas."

It felt so good to get that kiss, to be near him again. "Because I spent the night with you. I'm happy, and I want to hope that it will all be all right."

"You give me hope too."

RIADNE FELT odd to trust strangers who didn't even know about Solanas' existence until a few days before. To trust them to do what generations of her people had not been able to.

But then, there was a new potion in the mix, and the Dark Valley carried ancient knowledge, from before the time the kingdom hunted the Solanas.

Lukas was on a bed beside her after receiving more cuts in the back and then some blood. She got only the cuts, and so far wasn't bleeding too much. For once, she allowed herself to hope. If she kept at it, she would start to sound like Zora.

Larzen was snoozing on a chair.

Tris came into the room. "How are you?"

"Great. All things considered. And you?"

"The beginning here was difficult, when we were afraid someone would come after me, but after a while, they decided nobody was coming. I started to help with the school." She looked down. "It felt good."

"You sound like feeling good makes you guilty."

The princess chuckled. "I do? Maybe I do. Maybe I latched on to my pain to remember... Remember the person I lost. It was as if finding joy was a betrayal. And it is hard. Some images still haunt me."

Riadne knew that Tris's family had killed a young man she loved and couldn't imagine how much pain it caused her. "It's never easy."

Tris shook her head. "But I think I need purpose. Revenge was my purpose. It kept me alive, kept the fight in me. But I'm not sure it will solve anything."

"So you gave up on killing your family?"

She shook her head. "I don't know. I really don't."

Lukas smiled. "She's been great company."

Tris also smiled. "True. I wanted to learn some of their medicine. Did you know there are different types of human blood? You need to find the right one, then you can replace it."

"Sounds like blood magic to me."

Tris frowned. "Does it even exist?"

Riadne sighed. "A few days ago, I would say no, there's no such thing, that it's a lie invented to persecute people who wield magic, but... After what I've seen..." The image of those heads rolling was also stuck in her mind. "There is evil magic out there, Tris, there sure is."

"You found the Magic Temple in Kentosa, right?"

"We did, and it's the most horrible place I've ever been to, and consider that I've lived with royalty before."

"I'm royalty," Larzen protested. Perhaps he wasn't sleeping.

"And so is Tris," Riadne added. "But so is Kiran."

"He's different now," Larzen said.

"Old Kiran, then. Using his power to have people under his control, coerce people. You give someone like that powerful magic..."

"Boom." Larzen made a gesture with his hands. "That's how we get a cursed kingdom."

Riadne sighed. "I'm not sure it comes with a boom. More like bad weeds growing and taking over."

"Cheerful talk, sister," Lukas said.

"Realistic."

Lukas chuckled. "I don't know about you, but I'm here hurting and I want to hear about beautiful forests, meadows, lovely beaches, children giggling. They're real too."

The door opened, bringing Zora in, all glowing. The girl who had traveled with them and defeated the magicians on Rock Island had been but a shadow of the one who stood there.

It had been her pain and worry and fear. But now she was full of hope, even though she was probably aware that Griffin was about to face a difficult choice that would have disastrous consequences no matter what.

Riadne still didn't understand how come nobody had slapped him. The only reason she hadn't slapped him herself was because it wasn't her place to do so.

"Riadne, I wanted to ask you something."

"Alone?" It was going to be hard to move right then, and she didn't want to send the others away.

"No, no. Listen up," Zora said. "I was thinking, I know there is a lot about Solanas power in these books, and you know some of it too."

"Yes."

"Can we create another Dark Valley? A place with strong, magical walls? Then we could make it a kingdom and name Griffin king of it, and then he can invite that thing there."

Riadne sighed and tried to think. "I see your point. It makes sense. But the walls around here, they're older than even the squabble with that other kingdom. They were made when Solanas were at the height of their power, and many of them worked on it. I can't. I can't make a wall like that, not even if I get Dada's help. I don't think any Solana could in such a short time. Like I said, this one took years. But it was meant as a sort of magical prison."

The girl's face darkened. "You found something about the walls in the valley?"

"I found something about protective walls and plans for making a prison in Gravel. The book I'm reading is old, but by putting the pieces together, I can assume that."

"But the Dark Valley would work?" Larzen asked.

It probably would. "Yes, but... What about all the people here?"

He looked at Zora. "You understand what I'm getting at, don't you?"

Zora frowned. "Get Griffin... to invite that thing... to the Dark Valley?"

"We'd need to get the people out first," Larzen said. "And we'll need to plan it right away."

It made sense. Riadne then said, "If you use the Dark Valley, I can help. Help seal it. It's doable. And it might be our answer."

An answer Zora probably hated.

30

CELEBRATION

*Z*ora looked back at the hill on the valley that was visible from above the wall. The sky was darkening, but only few and far lights were now visible in it. The Dark Valley was no longer scintillating like it used to be. And then her eyes got misty thinking about all the memories, the lives, and the stories left behind.

She felt someone putting a hand on her shoulder, and looked to see her mother. "I'm so sorry," Zora said.

"Don't say that." Her mother had that calming voice that always put her at ease. "We need to give the example. If we're happy and confident, they'll follow."

"But nobody is around us now. Aren't you mad at me?"

"For freeing us from the confinement of walls? No, dear."

"I'll miss the valley. So many memories left there." All her childhood and most of her youth.

"The memories come with us."

Zora glanced at the improvised, quickly built village. It was surrounded by walls, not as high or strong as the Dark Valley, and certainly not magical, but enough to keep most of the shadow creatures away.

Griffin had discovered that the villages that had done that were having no casualties. And yet there were deaths because of shadow creatures all over Gravel. She hoped this would be over soon.

Her parents had called back all the rangers from the Dark Valley and Griffin and Larzen had sent in extra soldiers to speed up construction so that the people from her village could be relocated and have a safe place to spend the nights, even if the real reconstruction would take months. The houses were small and simple for now, with the exception of the school, which had been a priority.

It was for the best, and yet it still hurt to see the place she loved so much being abandoned.

"All change is traumatic, Zora," her mother said. "Even change for good."

"Many will leave."

"They would have left the moment they were allowed to. And it's for the best."

"Thank you for your help." Without her family arguing strongly for the relocation, and working hard to convince reticent villagers, this wouldn't have been possible.

"It wasn't that hard. You don't understand it. You went outside. You saw the rest of the world. It's easy to look back and romanticize the valley. For those of us who grew up here..." Zora realized her mother was one of them. "Leaving has always been our dream, even if we tried to keep a happy face and make the best we could. That place is a prison. It's not meant for people. This is the best thing that can happen."

"Once it's all over, will you help me? With the Village of Knowledge?"

"We will, but we want some time to travel. You can't be the only adventurer in the family."

Zora laughed. Her plan had been to start something similar to the Magic Temple, a place for learning, a place where knowledge from all over the world was preserved and cultivated, but without the creepiness and abuse of power seen in Rock Island.

She thought that they could also teach other people some medicine techniques from the Dark Valley. Griffin and Larzen seemed to like the idea, even if they never had time to discuss it in details.

She eventually wanted to have the Solana books translated, and work on tracing a more precise history of Gravel. It would be New Gravel now. The Dark Valley was going to be Gravel. So many plans for when there would be no more shadow creatures. So many plans for when the Void was defeated. If it was defeated. But it had to be. At least imprisoned. Good enough for now. Hopefully good enough forever.

These last few days had been a lot of work. Zora hadn't participated in the construction itself, but had helped coordinate the move, and dealing with families arguing about the location of their improvised houses wasn't the easiest thing to do. But it was over now. Tomorrow would be the great day.

Kiran, or rather, Develson Williamson, had signed official documents abdicating the throne, even if he thought it was a great joke because he had never been a king. Griffin was appointed king of Gravel, which was now only the Dark Valley. Larzen was appointed king of New Gravel, which was all the rest of the kingdom. They even had a coronation, but the crowns were made from twigs and leaves. There would be a public, formal ceremony in Gravel City, but there was no time for that now.

"Zora!" Griffin was running towards her, and she realized her mother had retreated somewhere. "You'll want to see this," he said, and smiled. "Or maybe hear it."

He took her hand and pulled it towards the outpost. She knew that many soldiers who had come to help with the construction were also crammed in it. But in front of the building, they had a bonfire, and two young men and one woman had string instruments.

"There will be live music," he said. "I know you like it."

"I do."

When the music started, some people started dancing, and she saw many villagers from the Dark Valley coming to watch, and eventually dancing too. Even a couple of her students were there and waved.

Griffin pulled her hand. "I hate dancing, but I'll open an exception tonight."

"Is that a charming way to ask me to dance?"

"It won't get any better than that."

They joined in the celebration. There wasn't any wine and there wasn't much food other than some roasted carrots. But for her, it was the celebration of hope. Hope for a different future for her people. Hope for a solution for the kingdom. Hope for a future with Griffin.

THERE WAS SO much to learn, so much lost knowledge, Riadne could barely believe the trove of treasure in these books. She had found a procedure for the wings, but it was about making cuts years before they sprouted. It gave her hope for Aelle. And then there was so much about the heart stone, so many possibilities.

One of the other healers had applied a salve on her back, as they were trying new ingredients, but for now she was alone with Larzen.

He sat on a chair watching her and said, "You need to rest. You'll have a lot of time to read those books."

That was a very optimistic thought, but she didn't want to contradict him. She still wasn't sure how long she would live, even if more and more she was hoping she wasn't dying. But she didn't want to spend the rest of her life bleeding either. She smiled. "But it's about the Void too. There could be something else here."

"We're planning the final details tonight, Riadne. There won't be time to come up with something different."

"I know. But I really think, you know, there's stuff here about our spirit guide, Astrea, and she was fighting an old entity, but called it Nothingness. I think it's the same."

"Possibly. But you didn't find a way to kill it, did you?"

"You can't kill something if it doesn't have a corporeal form."

He raised an eyebrow. "But you can trap it."

She sighed. "I wish Dada were here."

"I couldn't send messengers to bring her, I mean, I wasn't going to reveal the Sky Abode."

"I know. I'm not complaining. And I wouldn't want you to leave and go there either. It's just a thought." A thought that she could use some more guidance, more support. She had an idea. "Give me that book."

"This here? The one you said was a poem book?"

"It's wise sayings, and supposed to inspire you when you're in doubt."

"I thought you were certain."

"I don't think anybody is ever truly certain of anything, unless they are fools."

"I am certain," he said.

"Of what?"

He stared at her and paused, then looked away and said, "Of many things. That the sun exists for example."

"It could be an illusion, but yes, an existing illusion nonetheless. But I mean decisions. Can you ever be certain that you're making the right choice when it's something that has never been done before?"

"I guess not." He took the book and passed it to her.

She took a deep breath, then opened the book at a random page, then rolled her eyes.

"What is it?" Larzen asked.

"It's..." It was hard to translate it exactly. "Friendship and love are the greatest powers."

"Well, aren't you quite powerful, then?"

"I don't know. I wouldn't call myself a very friendly or loving person."

He snorted. "Of course." But there was a coldness there.

She did love him, though, but wasn't sure if she should say it, or how to say it, or perhaps if she had already shown it through actions. Or perhaps she just wanted him to say it first. Or hoped, at least. She sighed. "But when I love it's... quite powerful. I guess I get the point of the book, I'm just not sure how it relates to tomorrow."

Someone knocked on the door.

"Come in," Larzen said.

Zora and Griffin entered. They both had the bright eyes of a young couple in love, and her cheeks were red.

"There's music by the outpost," she said. "We were dancing."

Larzen frowned. "I thought you hated dancing, Griffin."

"It was live music. Zora likes it. Maybe I never hated dancing, I just hadn't found the right company."

Zora laughed, then looked at Riadne. "Your back?"

"The same." Did she expect a miraculous recovery or something?

"Will you be able to travel tomorrow?"

Riadne shrugged. "We've gone through this. It's an hour from here, I'll have potions, and I'll take extra bandages to be changed."

"We'll take a comfortable carriage," Larzen added.

But even if it wasn't comfortable, Riadne had to do it.

"We need to make sure we do it at the same time," Riadne said. "I'll use the heart stone to undo the magic in the portal."

Griffin turned to Larzen. "You're sure it was a big arch?"

"I am. You should have come with me."

"I was busy!"

"I know," Larzen said. "I dove into the lake and saw a structure just like you described. It has to be the portal, and it makes sense that the Solanas changed the river and maybe even changed the landscape to hide it, even if it's an impressive display of power."

"Well, Riadne alone cracked the Magic Temple. And the Island," Zora said.

Larzen turned to her. "I still don't understand how you did it."

"It wasn't on purpose. I think I got upset or angry, so my magic got wonky."

Larzen nodded. "Well, I hope you don't get angry tomorrow, Riadne. We don't want wonky magic."

"It's quite powerful, though," Zora added.

Riadne sighed. "The heart stone is powerful. The Solanas at the time when there was the whole thing with the Shadow Kingdom didn't have it. If they had it, they could have undone the magic of the portal. I have the heart stone, so I'll be able to annul its magic. And I want it to be at the same time so as to get the Void by surprise. If he's planning to do something, like bring creatures from the Shadow Kingdom or something, he won't be able to do so, and it will be too late for him to come up with anything else."

Larzen sighed. "What I don't like about it is being far from here tomorrow. If something goes wrong..."

"But he'll be trapped, right?" Zora asked. "And won't have a corporeal form or anyone that he can control, so he won't be able to hurt anyone, if there's nobody there."

"Everything I read about this type of entity says that." She turned to Griffin. Weird how it wasn't awkward to talk to him anymore. Not that they had become best buddies or anything. "Your experience in the Shadow Kingdom was like that, wasn't it? The Void never touched you personally, he only affected other people who could hurt you."

"Yes, pretty much it. I'll be alone—"

"I still wish I could come with you," Zora said.

Griffin glared at her. "I'll order my guards to put you in a cell if you insist. But you can stay on the other side of the gates."

Zora crossed her arms and looked away. "Fine."

"He's right," Larzen said. "The whole point is that we don't want to give the Void any fuel."

"But if something happens..." she said.

Griffin turned to her. "You'll be right on the other side, where the Void can't touch you. We've had this conversation. He guaranteed he wouldn't hurt me, and even if he hadn't guaranteed anything, I can only invite him to my kingdom, he can't go where he hasn't been called, so he won't be able to leave those walls, and there isn't anyone in the valley he could command. It's safe and it will be fine."

Zora still didn't look happy. Griffin pulled her close and kissed her forehead. "It will be fine." The kiss did the trick, as she nodded.

Zora then turned to Larzen, perhaps to change the subject. "Everything arranged for your trip tomorrow?"

"It's all good. I will take a pocket watch with me, and you'll have one here. Ten o'clock." His eyes met Riadne's. There was confidence there. More than confidence, trust. That look alone made her feel invincible.

"Perfect," Griffin said.

Zora then turned to Riadne. "Did you find anything else in your book?"

So much. But there was one thing that had caught her

attention. "It talks a lot about Astrea, our spirit guide. I could incorporate her using the heart stone."

"What for?"

"No idea. And there are some things on cure, potions, and everything."

Zora's eyes widened, excitement in her voice. "Something for the wings?" It was nice that she cared.

"Maybe." Riadne didn't want to give anyone false hope. "But let's get those bigger issues dealt with first."

"We will."

"I guess we'll let you rest then," Griffin said, then took Zora's hand. "Goodnight."

Larzen watched as they left, then sat by her and held her hands. "I trust you, you know? And I know you'll destroy the magic in that portal. And if you're saying that the walls around the valley are strong for a magical prison, then they are. I think it will all go well."

There was always a possibility of something going wrong, but on the other hand, they were probably capable of fixing it.

"I'll be with you, so I'll be super powerful Riadne. But you have to kiss me more."

"Hum." He approached her bed. "You demand great effort from me, but I guess I have no choice, since it's for the good of the kingdom."

He laughed, then leaned over and kissed her. And perhaps there was something indeed powerful and magical in that kiss. And perhaps Riadne was getting sappy and senti-mental. Perhaps. And there was nothing wrong with that. It felt good. Amazing, in fact.

TRIS SAT with Lukas by the fire, looking at the joyous celebration. Perhaps these people had lost their real houses, but they no longer were confined by walls. They were celebrating their freedom. Freedom. Meanwhile, was Tris building her own inner walls?

Lukas had just changed his bandages so that he could sit here. Tall and broad shouldered, he had an impressive figure, even sitting down. But what she liked about him was that he never forced, never pressed, never asked for much, and yet she knew that one day he would find someone who loved him back and walk away from her. Unless... But she wasn't sure she could make such a decision.

"I haven't asked your plans," she said.

He raised an eyebrow. "Other than dying a non-painful death?"

She shook her head. "You're still alive and you're stable. Worst case you'll need to be getting blood from time to time. Best case you'll get healed. Then what?"

"If I tell you I want to stay here, you won't think I'm stalking you?"

She paused. "No. Zora said you should call other Solanas, set a place where you can study, translate and preserve your knowledge. Even teach it to others. It would give you a purpose, and you wouldn't need to hide who you are. Makes more sense than me staying here." She smiled. "Are you going to think I'm stalking you?"

He had a half smile. "I'll think you're hiding. But it's fine. Sometimes we have to do that."

She sighed. She owed him the truth. "Did I tell you why my parents killed Krim?"

"Not exactly."

"He wasn't rich or noble. He was just part of our small army, and he taught me knife throwing. They..." She closed her eyes, burying painful memories. "Found us together...

and said he was forcing me, even if I told them I loved him and it had been my choice. And they knew it! They tortured him and made me watch to teach *me* a lesson. *Me*. To make me feel guilty. To ensure I would never choose someone who wasn't to their liking. And I don't want to listen to them, obey them, but I can't put someone else through the same—"

"I get it. You're saying you'll never get involved with me because I'm not a noble." Well, that was straight to the point, but correct. He added, "That's fine. My question is: if you *could* get involved with me, would you want to?"

"I don't know." Her mind was a confused jumble, images of Krim bleeding getting replaced with Lukas.

He smiled and stared at the fire. "That's a maybe. Maybes are always full of wonderful possibilities."

"And horrid possibilities."

"What if we don't worry about the future, and just live in the present? I'm fine with being friends, Tris, and you don't need to be thinking this over. I like your company regardless. I'm not lying when I say you've been a good friend and a wonderful companion. You're the bravest person I know."

She chuckled. "Right. What about Zora? Your sister?"

"Zora is a trained warrior, like all the Dark Valley people. My sister has incredibly powerful magic. Even for a Solana, she is powerful. But you, you were not prepared to fight, yet you improvised weapons, faced shadow creatures on your own, and dragged me to safety when you didn't have to. When you had nothing to gain. That's quite something."

She felt her face getting hot. "I should be braver. I shouldn't be afraid of my family. I'm in Gravel. They're not going to come here to punish me."

"Why would they punish you?"

She made the decision in a split second and kissed his cheek. "For this." She looked into his eyes. "And for whatever comes next. We had a bumpy start, but you're good company too."

He stared at her lips. "And what comes next?"

"Exactly what you're thinking."

Grinning, he said, "You have no idea where my mind is going."

"I'm not afraid. I want to find out."

His lips felt soft on hers, his mouth and tongue moving slowly, exploring, while her body relaxed. She wasn't sure if she loved him; her heart had been hurt too recently. But she was willing to give it a try—and enjoying it so far.

GRIFFIN WAS GOING to sleep in a house with Zora. It was just a square building with an improvised bed by a corner, like most of the improvised houses in the new village, but it was enough for them.

Trying to keep them apart hadn't worked, and when they were still in the Dark Valley, in her parents' house, they had slept together every evening in the waiting room. There was nothing better than sleeping with her in his arms, her scent so comforting and calming.

Tonight, they were alone for the first time, where they wouldn't be disturbed. The first time since the cave.

But he knew that her thoughts were on what he was going to do tomorrow. They trusted that everything would go well, but still.

He sat by her on the mattress, caressing her soft hair. "I'll be right by the gate and you'll be outside it, watching me the whole time." He smiled and pointed to a sword with a purplish glow on the corner. "And I have my new magic enchanted sword."

She smiled, such a lovely shy smile. "It's not magic."

"It is, Zora. Since I came back, everything has been magic."

"I don't know what sorcery you did for my parents to let me be here with you."

"Oh, I have my ways." He laughed. "No, I think they trust me."

"As they should."

He brushed his lips against her cheek. "Hmm, I'm not so sure."

She turned and looked at him. "I trust you. And that's what matters."

Her eyes met his, and then he kissed her, feeling all her warmth and love—and desire too. Soon they were lying on the mattress, her body under his, and he took the moment to cover her with kisses and caresses, barely noticing his fingers unlacing her top, then his lips trailing down her body with kisses, basking in the warmth and softness of her skin. So many places to kiss.

She was the one who unbuttoned and took off his vest, which was good because he was burning, but then the soft feel of her hands caressing his chest brought him shivers. Then even more shivers as she unlaced his pants, but he raised her head to look into her eyes, just to make sure this was something she really wanted. He wasn't in a hurry. But there was trust and determination, and even wonder in those beautiful, calm eyes. So much trust, knowing he wouldn't push her farther than she was comfortable. And no fear.

He had promised himself he was going to go more slowly, but there was so much trust and love between them. There was a line he wasn't supposed to cross yet, and he wasn't going to, but there was a whole field before it. A whole field for them to get to know each other, for her fears to dissolve slowly as they got closer and closer.

31

OVER WALLS

It was so strange to stand outside the gate to the Dark Valley and want to get in. Zora wished she could go with Griffin, but understood that it would be too risky, and she could be a liability. Still, if something happened, she wanted to be near.

He took her face in both his hands and kissed her, then said, "I love you, you know?"

She shook her head and noticed that her eyes were getting misty. "You don't have to say it now. You're getting out. We'll talk after all this is done." She smiled. "And we have unfinished business."

He gave her his amazing smile. "I know." Then he kissed her cheek. "I just felt like saying it."

She ran her hand over his hair. "I love you too. If you need help, I'm here."

"You're in charge and you have reinforcements. In case something happens. I know you'll have my back."

Zora nodded. There were soldiers and rangers by the gates, just in case. And Griffin had asked her to lead them.

She had never led any soldiers, but according to him, it was easier than leading kids.

"I'll keep an eye out."

RIADNE STOOD BY THE LAKE, while Larzen looked at his watch. She wore a dress tied up around her neck, exposing her back, which had a salve but no bandages, as they had found that they made things worse. To cover that up, she had a ridiculous little cape, loose enough not to touch her back.

He looked at her. "Five minutes until ten o'clock. You're sure you don't need to go underwater?"

"I think you want to see me undressed."

Larzen chuckled. "That's not even a question. I always do."

They had some guards at a distance to make sure they weren't disturbed, but they were otherwise alone. Still, the heart stone was in a bag, and she put her hands inside it, so that nobody would see the stone. She felt its energy flowing through her, and then a song, a song of destruction, a song of undoing, taking away the magic from that portal, breaking the connection between this world and the other.

She felt that her magic was working, she felt as if a tunnel was being shut, and yet, there was something else. Something strange. Something wrong. And it wasn't something wrong with the portal.

GRIFFIN KNEW that there was a risk in what he was doing. Knew that there was a chance he would die, and it hurt to look back at Zora and imagine leaving her.

But he also knew that he was surrounded by a magical wall, and that there was no way the Void would leave it to go to the rest of Gravel, or rather, New Gravel, so at least everyone else would be safe.

"It's time!" Zora yelled.

He turned back and smiled at her, standing by the gate. The inner gate. It wasn't what they had agreed, but now there was no time to argue or try to ask her to move back.

He crouched and made a circle on the ground. "Void, this is my kingdom, and I welcome you to give it strength, and use the power of its land."

Those were the words. So simple. Deceivingly simple. He could imagine an unaware king saying them without realizing the consequences. King. King of an empty valley.

A few minutes passed. Nothing happened, and Griffin retreated to the gate, walking backwards, so that he had an eye on the place he had marked on the ground. He heard the sound of metal screeching, but turned to Zora and said, "Don't open it. Not yet."

"Crouch under, come," she said.

Sometimes she had a way of talking to him that made it impossible to say no. He crossed the gate, which was closed right after.

Finally, a voice said, "My dear King Griffin, you've made a lovely arrangement. You know I wasn't going to hurt the people in your kingdom, and if it were big and surrounded by nothing but sea and mountains, it was going to be tricky. Like this, it's perfect. I can have all of New Gravel as my source of power."

It was eerie to hear that voice here. Griffin said, "If you can get out, sure. I'm glad you enjoyed our arrangement."

"Oh, I can't get out, no. But why should I?"

Five brilliant red balls appeared in front of the gate, then, where the balls were, four men and one woman appeared, all dressed in dark red robes.

"They're the magicians!" Zora said. "From Rock Island."

The Void continued, "I have slaves to do the work for me."

"We need to go in and behead them," Zora said.

"That's what the Void wants, Zora. And if we go in, he can use our suffering to power up."

"So we'll just leave them there?" she asked.

"You're so silly, so silly," the Void said. "You think you're the only kingdom with a connection to me. Kingdom, yes, but not the only people. My slaves have been amassing tremendous power. I don't need more power."

There was a strange red glow around the magicians. Something bad was about to happen.

Griffin turned to the soldiers and commanders. "Gregor, go to the village and get everyone to walk away as far as they can. Now. The others, prepare to fight."

"We're going in?" Zora asked.

"Absolutely not. But I fear they'll come out. Let's get away from the gate."

He pulled her hand, and they passed the second gate and were outside the walls. The magicians were throwing magic balls at the bars so that they wouldn't resist much longer. Griffin risked a peek and saw that matters were about to get worse.

"They're growing."

"What?"

"Don't look." He pushed her away. "They're still aiming at the gate."

"And the balls are getting bigger?" she asked.

"Not the balls. The magicians."

She caught a breath, surprised.

He turned to the soldiers. There were so few of them, and they were not the best. Griffin had requested the ones who would be good with construction. What a stupid oversight. "I want archers at a distance. You'll soon see giants across the wall. Aim for the eyes. Arrows anywhere else won't do anything."

"I'm not even sure about the eyes, Griffin," Zora whispered. "They're not human."

"But you killed many of them."

"But they were smaller, and I got them by surprise. And now, I don't even think it's them anymore, it's like they're empty shells."

Griffin recalled King Saro's father, cutting his own son's fingers under the Void's orders. "Probably."

A large thing came flying from the wall. A tree. Great, they were throwing things now.

"Retreat, retreat," he ordered his soldiers.

He ran away from the gate with Zora.

"Perhaps they can't get out," she said.

"They can." Griffin just knew it, based on what he'd seen in Grota. Still, so far they were just throwing trees and some rocks, so it was a matter of running away, but as they got taller, they could throw further and further.

He looked back and could see a head appearing from above the wall.

Zora also looked back. "Aren't you glad I killed nine of them?"

"Extremely. Aren't we lucky? All we'll have to deal with are five giant monsters."

"Better than fourteen." She then whispered in his ear. "The heart stone maybe could do something."

"Pity it's down by the lake, far away."

"But she'll come back. All we need is to gain time."

He covered his face with his hands. No weapons, no catapults, not even towers for archers. What a stupid miscalculation.

And if they had any questions on whether these giants could get out or not, it was answered now, as one of them climbed out of the wall. "I'll climb on him, and I want you to run." She frowned. He continued, "Run and organize the retreat and get our remaining forces to at least delay them. I need you to do that."

He ran towards the magician, who tried to throw balls of energy on him, but he was faster. Perhaps they weren't very well adjusted to their bodies yet, and so they were clumsy.

He jumped on the robes the magician was wearing and climbed his way up to his neck. He hit it with his sword, but it was like having a tiny axe and trying to cut down a gigantic tree. Something caught Griffin. A huge hand, now about to squeeze his body. Perhaps he'd miscalculated again. And then he was still in the hand, but falling, then reached out and slowed down his fall with his sword, cutting through the robe. The hand had been cut off, and Zora was climbing down.

"Aren't you glad I'm here?" she said.

"Always glad to see you, love."

"We'll need bigger swords if we want to stand a chance."

Griffin saw that there was another hand coming towards them and said, "Jump!"

They fell on the ground and took cover under some bushes. He looked at Zora. "I guess you're not commanding our forces."

"I told them to retreat and get reinforcements and bigger weapons from Gravel City."

"That will take a whole day."

"But arrows and swords are like needles to them. They won't even delay them. We'd just be wasting lives. We need to plan a way to find some huge blades and throw at them. Like a catapult with blades or something. That would work."

The magician was now stepping on the houses of the improvised village.

"In a few days, for sure. Meanwhile, they'll lay waste to the kingdom." He closed his eyes. "And the Void will get stronger. And so will they."

"All we can do for now is run and hide."

"Like ants."

"You have a better idea?"

He didn't. Of course he didn't. He could barely think amidst all this chaos, and then there was the regret in knowing it was his fault.

"Let's try to get to Gravel City and try to make some giant blade catapults before they destroy the castle. And the entire kingdom."

THE NERVE. The freaking nerve. Riadne was going to kill Larzen once this was all over. Two of the soldiers were holding her.

He crossed his arms and smiled. "You can't try anything."

"It's Astrea, Larzen. She's the only one who can save us."

"Your idea makes no sense."

She just sang and controlled his guards. "Detain him."

Riadne held the heart stone. She knew that allowing Astrea to possess her could mean her death, but she felt that it was the only right thing to do. She had no clue what was happening, but the earth was trembling. There was rumbling and she could feel the fear coming from the Dark Valley, even at such a distance. She was a Solana, and this was her fight. Even if it was her last fight.

AMONG ALL THE CHAOS, Zora was thankful that Griffin was alive, was here with her, even if the situation was dire and they had no solution in sight. He was trying to find a horse, but they had run away. Two more magicians were climbing out of the walls now.

Zora then saw a bright light in the sky. A light that landed in the Dark Valley.

"Look. Something. I think we have some help."

The magicians started to get smaller again.

He sighed. "Thanks to whatever it is. Now we can behead them."

"But we need to be sneaky, and get them by surprise."

They approached the area where they last had seen one of them, and now found the magician in the normal, human size. Griffin threw a pebble in another direction, and when he looked away, swung his sword and cut his head.

Griffin definitely looked much more elegant and natural doing that than Zora.

He then looked at her and shouted, "Down."

She crouched just in time for him to throw his sword at something, and then saw a head falling in front of her.

Griffin extended a hand to her, concern clear in his eyes, his voice tight. "He almost got you."

Before he got overprotective and told her to go away or something, she said, "There's one more outside."

"By the gate." He ran, and she followed.

This master was sitting on a rock, crouching as if in pain. Zora didn't pity him, though, and cut off his head.

Then they ran to the gate, and Zora peeked through it to see what was happening. "That's Riadne. Or... not really her."

It was Riadne, but she had some wings made of light, and her eyes had brilliant light too. "Astrea," Zora muttered.

Riadne, or rather Astrea, was in front of one of the

masters, or what had been him, as he now seemed to be made of black smoke, and his clothes were charred.

"I think the Void has taken his body," Griffin observed.

The female magician was lying down, perhaps dead

"He can be killed, then," Griffin said.

It was as if the Void was pulling light from Astrea, and she was pulling his darkness. Still, there was smoke coming out of her body, which was turning darker and darker.

It couldn't be. Zora put a hand over her mouth in horror. "But he's killing her."

Griffin was serious, observing the scene, then said, "I'll go in. He can't hurt me. You stay where you are. If you step inside the Dark Valley, the Void can control you. Listen to me. Just open the gate."

Zora didn't want him to go, wanted to protest, but she knew that this was it, this was their chance to defeat the Void, and Griffin would never forgive her if she stopped him.

Astrea didn't seem to be doing too well, as she was now getting so dark that she'd soon look like the magician possessed by the Void. Zora raised the gates, and Griffin walked in. There was no strange booming voice. Of course, the Void was that thing in the male magician, and didn't seem to notice Griffin walking in.

Then Riadne fell to the ground, no more light coming from her. *No.* This was terrible.

The Void turned to Griffin, and as much as in theory he wouldn't harm him, it took Zora all her self-control not to run in and help him. Her heart was tight, and she wanted to scream, but dug her nails into her palms instead, shoving down her panic, as she couldn't distract Griffin, who was now facing that disgusting thing.

Then the female magician got up, now with brilliant eyes like Riadne a minute before. The Void was focused on Griffin and didn't see her coming up from behind and running her sword through his chest. The Void screamed, and then Griffin ran to him and cut his head, which flew far away.

The ground rumbled. Zora lifted the gates and ran to Riadne, who was lying on the ground, pale. Griffin was crouching by her and took her pulse. "She's not breathing."

Zora pressed her hands on Riadne's chest, even if she knew that it would hurt her back. She had never really done it, and wasn't sure it would work, but she pushed her chest, trying to get her heart to beat again, trying to bring her life back. It wouldn't be fair for her to die. Zora pushed, pushed, pushed.

"I'll go get help," Griffin said, then he ran away.

"Riadne, please wake up," Zora pleaded. "Come back. I didn't like you at first, but now I do. And I have a feeling that you have a wonderful gift coming. You have to live." Tears were running down Zora's eyes, but she kept pushing Riadne's chest. "There's hope and there's life and there's love for you. Come back. Please."

She didn't know how long she kept doing it. Anyone else would perhaps have quit, but Zora had learned to hope, and to keep the hope fueling her. And plus, Riadne was a Solana. The same way that it had allowed Kiran, or rather, Develson, to survive, it would perhaps allow her to survive this too. They were tougher than most people.

Then she realized she was in the Dark Valley and there was no voice anymore, and no magicians, as they had all been killed. Perhaps there would be no more shadow creatures, and perhaps her people could return to the valley. The ones who wanted, at least.

A horse and a cart appeared with her sister and father, and they took Riadne to the Dark Valley village, since the improvised village outside had been mostly destroyed. Zora remained there, exhausted, near the gate, waiting for Griffin.

Some minutes later a horse came in with Larzen on it, pale and sweaty.

"What happened?"

So much. "Riadne's not feeling well." Technically, she was almost dead, but that wasn't something Larzen should hear, at least not like that. "But my father and my sister are treating her. In the village there."

Larzen nodded and went in that direction.

32

HOPE

The last Larzen had seen of Riadne, she'd been furious. After she had enchanted his soldiers, it took a long time for them to listen to him again, and when they let him go, he dashed to the Dark Valley. The heart stone was still with him, and he thought Riadne could need it.

He found her at what used to be Zora's house, now without barely any furniture. But the structure of the beds remained, and Riadne was lying in one of them, Zora's father and sister by her. Larzen asked them to go away for two minutes, which they did reluctantly. He then put the heart stone between Riadne's hands and held them.

"Riadne, please. Do what you can do with this power. Astrea, if you exist, give her life back. Please. I'll do anything."

"Careful with what you promise," he heard a woman's voice coming from nowhere. "Don't go making bargains with incorporeal entities, young king. It's a bad decision. She'll survive. But find the ring and destroy it before anyone else has stupid ideas. The Void is my brother. He's not dead, the same way I'm not dead, but he won't bother you anytime soon. Enjoy your respite."

Riadne exhaled and opened her eyes. "Larzen? Did you die too?"

"I'm very much alive. And so are you. I mean, you're a little alive, at least."

"I love you. Love you, love you, love you a thousand times. Love you so much I can't even breathe. But I'm not scared."

He was so surprised at her words. And happy. He didn't want to ever hold back his feelings again. Holding her hand, he said, "Well, try to forget the love and breathe, then. And I love you too. But that's quite obvious. You know I'm a man of taste."

She chuckled. "Amazing taste, Larzen, amazing."

GRIFFIN WOULD NEED a long time to rest. He'd run like crazy to try to find someone who could treat Riadne. Despite the past, she had saved his kingdom, Zora liked her, and Larzen, well, it was pretty obvious that he loved her.

He found Zora in her house, which was still messy and without much furniture. They would need to organize the residents of the Dark Valley again and get them back. He wasn't sure if they'd be happy or annoyed.

"How is she?" he asked.

"Alive and feeling better. She needed the heart stone. Larzen brought it."

"He's here too?"

She nodded. "Let's talk to them. I think she wants to explain what happened."

He took her hand and they walked into a room where Larzen was sitting by Riadne, her back bleeding through a bandage.

"Thank you," Griffin told her.

Riadne shook her head. "It was my duty. And my fight too.

It was the Void's fault that we were hunted and killed, if you think about it. And it was his fault we had our problem with our wings. I think part of it was a consequence of blocking his magic in the kingdom. We blocked some of ours. So I had to do it. I'm glad I helped."

He nodded.

"How did you do it?" Zora asked? "Was it... Astrea?"

Riadne nodded. "Yes. With the heart stone, she was able to possess me, and I guess she can fly and put up a good fight, so I'm assuming she came here and made a difference." She then asked, "Was it Astrea who killed the Void, or someone else?"

Griffin hesitated. "I... beheaded him. And it seems that Astrea took control of a magician for a moment before I did it. Does it make any difference?"

"It might. Magic works in funny ways."

"I heard a voice," Larzen said, and Riadne cast him a worried glance. "A woman's voice, and I didn't make any deals. But she said we have to destroy the ring."

"One of the magicians might have had it," Zora said. "It makes sense, right? The people on Rock Island collect relics. Someone must have stolen the real ring and replaced it with a replica. And then they started talking to the Void and getting instructions on how to gain magical power from him."

"I wonder why he didn't go there instead," Griffin said.

Riadne was thoughtful. "I think he needs the land."

Zora said, "He could have told them to move the Magic Temple out of the island."

"Perhaps he would one day." Riadne shrugged. "Time works differently for entities like him."

Larzen turned to Griffin. "And now you're the king of the Dark Valley. An inhabited place. How do you feel?"

This whole king talk made him uncomfortable. He shook

his head. "I can abdicate my throne. I mean, what am I going to do with it?"

"The village of knowledge," Zora said. "I think it would be nicer if it was in the valley. But you don't have to be king, of course. It would be a great way for former rangers to have something to do, otherwise this place will die." Her eyes were brilliant, full of hope, and she looked magnificent.

But Griffin still had some questions. "But what if there are still shadow creatures?"

"There won't be any," Riadne said. "First, the portal was deactivated. Second, the Void is gone. Without his magic, there won't be any shadow creatures."

"We can build the Village of Knowledge here, then." Zora's eyes were so bright, so beautiful. She turned to Riadne. "We could even bring Aelle, other Solanas."

Riadne nodded. "Yes, I like the idea."

"I also like it," Larzen said. "I think knowledge could eventually outweigh gold. And this is a good place. But we should also look into the Dark Valley model, the way they deal with education. I think it would be something we could implement in the rest of the kingdom. School for all children."

Griffin found it odd that his brother was thinking about all that, but it was true that he'd always wanted to help the kingdom.

Zora grimaced. "What do you mean? There isn't school for all children in Gravel?"

Oh, Zora. She was quite intelligent, but sometimes he had to be reminded that she'd been brought up in a place isolated from the rest of the kingdom.

"There isn't," Larzen said. "But I think it's doable and can be good. Would you help me with that?"

"No, no, excuse me, brother," Griffin interrupted. "But

she's in the Dark Valley, and as the king here, she's *my* subject." It was a joke. Sort of. But he didn't want Larzen thinking he could give her orders or something.

Zora glared at him. "Your *subject*?"

"No. My..." He chuckled. "I'm joking, but not really. It's just... let's coordinate this right." He turned to his brother and wiggled his eyebrows. "Cooperation between two kingdoms."

Larzen shook his head, feigning worry. "This king thing is getting to your head. Speaking of cooperation and other kingdoms, where's our rebel princess, Tris?"

"She was helping us, didn't you see her?" Zora said. "And she wants to help with the Village of Knowledge. She says she's not ready to go back to Linaria."

Larzen covered his face with his hands, and this time it didn't seem that fake. "They're going to think we kidnapped her."

Zora shrugged. "Well, she *was* kidnapped."

"Twice," Riadne added. "But she's giving up on murderous plans. They should be happy. But... let me explain one thing I just realized. Astrea and Void are siblings."

"She told me that," Larzen said. "Talk about a problematic family."

"Yes." Riadne smiled. "You're lucky that you love each other, you even love your crazy poet brother, not that I mind him as a crazy poet. But as I was saying, I heard a prophecy, but I got it wrong. It was the siblings destroying each other. And I had a role in it. So... I would like to apologize for my previous murderous plans. I know I caused problems and did things I shouldn't. I'm sorry."

"I'd rather forget it," Griffin said, and he really wished she hadn't brought that up because he didn't want to remember any of the things she had done.

"Me too," Larzen added. "Let's never mention any of that."

Zora cleared her throat. "So, the Village of Knowledge, we could start planning it, right?"

"And the schools in New Gravel," Larzen added. "We have a bright future ahead of us." He then cast a worried glance at Riadne's back.

"Stop it," she said. "You're looking at me like I'm dying. I told you. It's going to be fine from now on. I'll heal, Lukas will heal, Develson Williamson will heal, even if we won't have wings."

"At least you got to fly once," Zora said.

Riadne shook her head. "It wasn't me. I don't even remember any of that. I mean, you think I'd get into a fight? No way. But hey, Aelle will fly. If she wants to. I'm looking forward to seeing what the future brings."

Zora was smiling. "I can't wait to see this valley changed. And have real hope for it."

Griffin had a lot of hope too. And it was so good to look forward and plan.

"I can't wait for the party," Larzen said.

There would be many celebrations, but it was as if his brother were talking about something specific.

"What party?" Zora asked.

Larzen smiled. "Are you crazy? Wedding party. Or parties. It needs to be in Gravel city." He looked at Zora. "Even yours, since it's royalty and all. We could do it at the same time. It shows unity."

Griffin wanted to strangle his brother.

"I..." Zora was confused. No wonder. "We didn't." She turned to Larzen. "We didn't plan it."

Griffin took her hand. "Zora, how do you think I got your parents to let me sleep in the same house as you? I asked for their permission to marry you. I was going to ask you on a better occasion, but Larzen here ruined it."

"I never ruin anything."

Riadne shook her head. "I wasn't proposed either, if it helps."

"Well, I'm proposing now," Larzen said. "You kneel and ask, and it's boring. You talk about a party, it's exciting and nobody can say no." He turned to Zora. "And you're going to be the queen of the Dark Valley, how's that?

"I..." Zora's eyes were misty.

"Make up your minds, then," Larzen said, apparently quite determined to ruin their moment. "If it's too much of a burden, you can always return Gravel to New Gravel."

"They can't," Riadne said. "Where there's magic of that caliber involved, it's better not to mess with it."

"Sorry, then." Larzen shrugged. "You have no choice."

"Sure." Griffin was getting tired of his brother's interruptions and told him, "We'll be right back."

He pulled Zora outside and they stood behind the house, in the shade of its walls. Her eyes were misty now, and he wrapped his arms around her, feeling her heart beating against his. "Should I be worried or are these tears a yes?"

She nodded softly, and he hugged her even tighter. Sometimes he couldn't believe that this was real, that he was back, that he got to hug and hold her and plan for the future, but perhaps it helped him value all that he had, how lucky he was.

But then something funny came to Griffin's mind. "Remember what I told you when I met you?"

She thought for a moment. "That I have a problem with unprovoked violence?"

He hadn't expected that and burst into laughter. "That, yes." She also chuckled. It felt good to tease her. He then added, "I mean after that, in the Gravel castle."

"I... don't recall." She was looking at him as if expecting something serious, important.

Griffin ran his hand through his hair. "I said I was confident you'd find a great match. I was right. I was right, Zora."

She glared at him. "Congratulations. Absolutely right." But then she smiled. "Worth more than gold."

CHANGE, even good change, was traumatic. Zora's mother was wise.

This was no longer the valley where she had grown up. Many villagers had left, but many people had come. There were young people from Gravel and some even from other kingdoms, all ready to learn. She was happy, even if her horrible memories from Rock Island never went away. Perhaps it was good. It was a reminder for her to make sure there would be no abuse of power.

Lukas was in the village of knowledge with Aelle and two more Solanas that used to live in Linaria. So few of them left. But they could put together their knowledge, help translate their books, make sure their stories were told. Even Dada visited them sometimes. It was nice.

Tris was there too, focused and excited about building something new. She and Lukas were quite close, even if Zora wasn't sure how much.

So much change to the Dark Valley, even if she wasn't living there all the time. At least not yet. As Griffin was still involved in New Gravel, and she was helping set the schools and an education plan for the kingdom, she spent most of her time in Gravel City, in the castle. It was just a half a day's journey to the Dark Valley, so she went back and forth a lot.

So much work, and so much hope. It was as if hope was becoming something tangible. Hope for the future of the kingdom.

Her wedding was tomorrow. At the same time as Larzen

and Riadne. She thought it was a nice way for him to show that Griffin was as important as him. The other brother had disappeared, become a traveling poet. Zora didn't miss him.

Griffin had said that Larzen wanted a double wedding so that the subjects would pay attention to Zora and not notice that the King's bride looked exactly like the one they all thought was princess Alegra. Well, it did split the gossip. And Riadne already was showing a small baby bump. Quite early and unplanned. It had been that potion of truth that had made them careless. But they were happy, so Zora didn't feel too bad. And what a tough baby, having survived so much.

Anyway, splitting the gossip was a good thing. There were some rumors that the king and prince were marrying two witches. Two? She had no idea why her name was on that list. Or maybe she had. Not everyone was comfortable with the idea of change, the idea of science and knowledge, and she was from the Dark Valley. Oh, well.

She was excited for the party, and to see Mauro again. He had become a hero and received prizes for his contribution. And Loretta would be there, too. Zora couldn't wait to see her, especially now that she had a little girl. Griffin had promised he'd apologize for having sent her away. He probably would. He knew how to be soft-spoken and charismatic when he wanted.

A couple months ago, she would have been terrified of a wedding, not because of having to stand in front of hundreds of people or wearing an uncomfortable dress, but because of what would happen at night.

But this would be one night after so many. Many nights when they got to know each other slowly, when she listened to her body, and he always respected her limits. Trust and patience over many nights had done the trick. And what a trick. It was never about what she could do to him, but always about the two of them together, sharing their moments. Expressing their love with their bodies. Together.

All she wanted now was to rush back home. Home. She was thinking about the Gravel Castle as home now. She took another look at the Dark Valley. But this was her home too. One where there was real hope.

THANKS!

Thanks so much for following Zora, Griffin, Larzen, and Riadne on their journey. These characters were a lot of fun to write, but it would be quite sad without the readers.

So thanks so much for picking up this book.

I also want to thank all the reviewers, bloggers, and bookstagrammers, and authors who helped promote this series! You're all so amazing.

If you haven't yet done so, a review helps readers like you find their ideal books and help smaller authors like me! A review is always appreciated.

Hope to see you again soon with new characters and a new series!

If you want to make sure you won't miss anything you can sign up for my newsletter at dayleitao.com.

ABOUT THE AUTHOR

I love to give life to characters and connect with readers. I'm originally from Brazil and I live in Montreal, Canada, with my son.

You can check my ramblings at my blog and also sign up for my newsletter at:

dayleitao.com

Find me on social media:

[O] instagram.com/day_leitao_ya
[BB] bookbub.com/profile/day-leitao
[g] goodreads.com/dayleitao

START A NEW SERIES

Do you want more magic, romance, adventure and fun? *Portals to Whyland* goes from magic shoes to magic kisses, with alternate dimensions, mysterious magic, strange castles, complicated romances, friendships between girls, first kisses, and teen angst.

You can start with Kissing Magic, an action-packed, emotional enemies-to-lovers story.

Check it out at https://dayleitao.com/books/kissing-magic/

Greedy, cunning, and selfish, Sian is not someone to be trusted. But when Karina is called to break his spell with a kiss, she accepts it.

She's smart enough not to fall in love—or at least to tell herself not to.

But when an ancient darkness is awakened, she realizes that risking a broken heart is the smallest of her problems.